FANTASTIC CREATURES

A Fellowship of Fantasy anthology

Dear Reader,

Welcome to The Fellowship of Fantasy's Fantastic Creatures Anthology. Herein, you'll find all manner of mythical creatures, both modern and ancient, from around the world. Some may try to eat you, while others just want to be your friend.

As you read, keep your eyes on those sneaky Kappas, don't pet Fluffy, don't swim in the lake, but do get indoors by midnight. There are many dangers lurking within, but no graphic content. All the stories here fall below a PG-13 rating. If you get into trouble call upon Sir Manly Strongarm, the miracle man, or one of our other numerous adventurers.

The Fellowship of Fantasy is an online group of writers dedicated to presenting the best in clean fantasy stories of any stripe. Some tackle epic quests to save the world, while others prefer more urban settings. Whether you enjoy contemporary tales, romantic re-tellings, or something else entirely, you're sure to find stories that speak to you.

Thank you for joining us. We hope you have a swift and safe journey.

Sincerely,
The Fellowship of Fantasy Authors

CONTENTS

A. R. Silverberry
Stuck in a desolate town and down on his luck, Doc Turner takes on
a mysterious case in order to help a friend. He soon gets more than
he bargained for in this hilarious tall tale that will leave children
smiling and adults in stitches.

Lea Doué
When Ryll loses her necklace down a well, a tiny dragon fishes it up
for her. All he asks in return is to eat from her plate and sleep on her
pillow. Is there more to this little creature than meets the eye?

Julie C. Gilbert
Keio has always wanted to visit the Golden City, but not like this. He
and his friend, Clara, are swept up with the other youths in their
village because the local lord seeks something special, something they
both possess.

Intisar Khanani
Maggie has always loved playing hide-and-seek with her Ma, searching
together for hidden things. But when Maggie finally finds what her
mother has been looking for, their lives will be irrevocably changed.

Caren Rich

Small town, big trouble. Something is killing local fisherman. Faced with another boring summer, the sheriff's twin daughters, Ella and Lena, set out to solve the mystery of Asgina Lake.

Morgan Smith

The prince is getting married.

So, why are the villagers terrified?

One brave young lady enters a battle of wills that will require both luck and wit to survive.

David Millican

A last missive from the man who inadvertently caused the end of the world. (Note: contains some violent scenes unsuitable for young readers.)

L. Palmer

Can giant squids fly? Nadia DeLayne has one chance to preserve her partner's legacy. She has a plan: build dirigible, avoid accidents, and convince the sentient kraken to fly.

No problem.

Nicole Zoltack
A monster killed her parents....
Melinda has one goal: avenge her parents, but to do that, she needs a
magical sword. To her delight, she finds a blacksmith willing to imbue
a sword with gems. But there's a catch. First, she needs to steal the
jewels ... from a dragon.

Frank B. Luke
After witnessing rescuing a warrior and her griffin, a knight and a
miracleman set out with her on a quest to deliver a secret message.

Lelia Rose Foreman
Hanako is a smart little girl, but not very good at listening. When she
disregards her mother's warning not to play by the river, will she end
up a meal for the menacing Kappa?

Arthur Daigle
A good king dies. The whole town mourns. The heirs fight for the
throne. But who will celebrate the life that was?

David Millican

Ancient and powerful weapon—check.

Knowledge, power, and will to hunt down a dangerous demon—

done.

Hot helper with a demon's heart—wait, what?

A professional demon hunter just got more than he bargained for.

(Note: contains some violent scenes unsuitable for young readers.)

Jessica L. Elliott

Talori's father loses everything in a shady business deal, including her

and her sister. What is a plain mermaid to do?

Kandi J. Wyatt

A centaur named Alastriona inherited *Kingdom Defender* from her

father upon his untimely death, but has yet to unlock its fabled

powers. Perhaps the elf she meets can awaken the sword.

D. G. Driver

A girl agrees to cover a mysterious midnight shift so her friend can

attend a concert. The hardest part will be staying awake, right? But

everything changes when the babies all wake up at midnight. And

they're hungry.

(Note: contains violence unsuitable for young readers)

Three Steaks and a Box of Chocolates

The day Burt McCall backfired into Dead End I got my last and most peculiar patient. I'd been standing on the termite-riddled planks of the sidewalk watching dust devils and my sign swinging in the wind. The two customers in the Dry Gulch Saloon hadn't moved in their chairs all day. For all anyone knew, they could've been dead.

Then Burt parked in front of the post office and that got my attention. If he had anyone to write to, no one knew about it. He came out a minute later with a small package. He tossed it into his tow truck and headed across the street to my establishment.

"Why don't you take that rusty can of yours out of town before you hurt someone?" I said, itching to know what was in the package.

"I ain't happy to see you, either," he replied. "But I got something that needs doctorin'."

I looked him over. From his worn boots to his weathered face, he was none too pretty to look at. But a wealth of silver tumbled from beneath his old hat, and his eyes hadn't lost their youthful spark.

"You never paid for last time," I said.

"I'd think you'd want the business." He stared meaningfully at my sign:

DOC TURNER

HEALING ARTIST

Its groaning in the wind seemed to emphasize his point. Fact was, no one had passed beneath it for quite a spell. I admit I'd tightened my belt a notch or three.

"This better be good," I said.

Inside my office, he reached into his pocket, pulled out a lump of gold,

9

and slammed it on my desk. "That oughtta cover what I owe. Consider the rest a down payment. You'll get a whole lot more if you help me."

"Is it real?"

"Test it yourself."

I didn't need to. I'd seen enough nuggets to know the real McCoy from the metal of fools—though, as for fools, Burt might take the cake. He seemed to make a profession of chasing crackpot dreams.

"You didn't pull this from that sand patch of yours. Who'd you steal it from? That way, I'm prepared when they come after me for it."

"Now that plain hurts, Doc. I've been tellin' you all along there's gold there, and there's the proof. Just like I told you there's water."

"The day you find water I eat my boots."

"Then you better put a fire under the pot so you can cook 'em when you get back. You gonna help me or not?"

I rose, put on my hat, and grabbed my medicine bag. Business had dried up since the new doctor set up down in Black Rock. He was young and knew how to charm the ladies. I'm past my prime on that score and maybe behind the times in doctoring. I figured Burt's gold would cover me for six months. Mainly, I wanted something to do besides watching dust devils. If anything else was happening in Dead End, nobody told me about it.

"Well, what do you need me for?" I asked.

"Fluffy ain't feelin' good."

"You want me to drive all the way over to your dump in this heat for a cat? Anyway, you don't like cats."

He gave me a sly smile. "I don't. Fluffy's special."

I let that slide. "What's wrong with her?"

"I think she's got a toothache." He was looking at a photo on my wall, me standing beside a sleeping elephant, a red-and-white big top in the background. "You sure you didn't kill that elephant?"

"Couldn't. He was the circus's prize possession. But he went berserk when they sold his lady friend. Elephants are loyal that way. I used something that would drop a dinosaur and they paid me well for it." I was feeling a little sad thinking about it. It was probably the last good bit of coin I'd seen. If things didn't turn around soon, I'd have to close shop. The thought of moving at my age didn't appeal to my bones, which were about as shaky as Burt's truck.

"You still got that tranquilizer?"

"Probably somewhere."

"Get it. Fluffy doesn't like pain."

I squinted at him like he was a crazy man, which he probably was. That didn't matter. He wouldn't drive clear to Dead End unless he needed to. Something was afoot, and I aimed to find out what. I threw some hypos and elephant tranquilizer into my bag. We piled into his truck and started bouncing down the road, sending up clouds of dirt.

I hung on for fear of falling out. "If you'd brush that cat's teeth, it wouldn't have a toothache."

"I never heard of such a thing." He grinned with those yellow teeth of his.

"Tackling your own once a week might not be a bad idea either."

He came to a sudden stop in front of Newsom's Hardware. "Fine."

He hopped out and a minute later returned with a push broom and a crowbar.

"What's that for?"

"An ounce of prevention."

How many times the engine exploded no one would want to find out, but an hour later his mountain came into view. As the story goes, a bespectacled gent named Norman Fable from one of those big universities back east inspected it for a mining company. He declared it a likely place to find gold or silver. Everyone and their uncle descended on the place. For two decades they punched holes all over it and found zip. Now most people call it Fable Mountain. It seems a respectable way to immortalize the man.

The Indians round here call it Awanyu, after their serpent god. They got it right. From this side, it looked like a snake stretched out on the floor of the desert, the east peak its head, the west peak an eroded cliff that curved up like a tail.

Miles passed with nothing but cactuses, the sweat on the back of your neck, and horse flies the size of buffaloes. Burt was by himself out here. A lonely feeling settled into my bones.

His lean-to came into view, stuck against the base of the mountain. There wasn't a well in sight.

"How do you survive out here without water?"

He gave me that sidelong look again. "I got water."

"You old fibber. The only water is floating around your brain."

"Well, you can add your hat to your boots. Looks like you're losin' weight, anyway."

"I mean it, Burt. How do you get by?" Fact was, I cared about him.

He pointed to a clay disk with painted triangles and spirals hanging from his rearview mirror. "Amulets."

"You can't get by on luck."

"It ain't luck. It's magic. That's what Indian Bob says. He ought to know."

"If that's from Indian Bob you got swindled. He's no more Indian than you are."

"Not so, I'm two-thirds Hopi and two-thirds Chippewa."

"Where do the McCalls fit in?"

"The lost tribe. You can't count 'em."

I didn't want to argue. He was rather sensitive on the subject, and told all kinds of tales about giant bears, birds, and skunks, and rolling heads that gobbled up bad people. He swore he'd seen them hereabouts, but then again, he'd claimed he'd seen a sea serpent in his navy days. Said it would bring him luck one day.

He pulled up to the lean-to and took up his package and the broom and crowbar he'd bought at Newsom's. I followed him inside, hoping it would be cooler. The concept of shade didn't seem to apply there, and sweat was rolling down my face. He offered me a pull from a canteen. I expected the water to be dusty. It was surprisingly cold and sweet.

He watched me drink. "Don't be bashful. There's plenty where that came from."

I didn't need a second invitation and poured half of it down my shirt. When the last drop trickled down my throat, I looked at him guiltily. "Sorry, I should've left you some."

He shrugged. "Take it, we'll refill it."

I looked around, trying to figure this out. No well outside. Not even a water tank. An old wood-burning stove sat in one corner, a narrow cot in the other. An iron skillet, a Dutch oven, and a big spoon hung from the ceiling. A buffalo hide was nailed to one wall, probably to cover gaps in the planks that bands of light streamed through. More amulets were scattered about, long feathers, beads, bits of carved turquoise, dreamcatchers. If he was finding his dreams, I couldn't see it.

The front of the room was as clean as any bachelor's, but toward the rear, a layer of dirt covered the floor. A curtain hung over the back wall. It stirred, though no wind came through the open windows.

He lit a lantern and gave it to me. Smiling to himself, he put the package in a knapsack, slung it over his shoulder, and took up the broom and crowbar.

With my medicine bag in one hand and the lantern in the other, I followed him to the curtain, wondering what all this was leading to. He parted the curtain. More dirt was piled to the left and right but dead ahead the wall had been torn away, revealing an opening large enough to step through.

Inside, the temperature dropped. At first, I thought this was a mineshaft from the Fable days, but the walls were rocky and irregular, suggesting it was a cave. I turned to look back at the dirt piled near the opening. It looked fresh.

"How'd you know to dig here?" I asked.

"I did a sweat with Indian Bob and had a vision. It showed me the spot."

The passage angled down. Cool air wafted from below. As pleasant as it was to get out of the heat, that forlorn feeling settled on me hard.

"Why do you live like this, Burt?"

His eyes were flames in the glow of the lantern. "Like what?"

"Alone. This place makes Dead End seem crowded."

"I'm not alone. I got Fluffy."

That didn't reassure me.

Neither of us spoke for a spell. He probably figured I'd run the other way if he said more. All I could do was see how this played out.

Finally he said, "If you found somethin' valuable, would you share it?"

I considered. If I wanted to be a Rockefeller, I'd have taken a different road. "Sure would. Guess I don't need much."

"That's what I figured. And we're friends, right? I can trust you?"

"I'd have to be to go along with whatever you're brewing here."

"Figured that too. That's why I came to you and not that fake in Black Rock." He wiped his eyes, which had grown misty. "Friendship's a rare thing, Doc." After a pause, he added, "Love, too."

A few steps farther the passage opened into a cavern so vast, the lantern couldn't penetrate the limits of it. What got my heart pounding was the low, rhythmic lapping of waves.

"Well, I'll be," I said. "You found water." And not just a trickle. This was a sea, broad, wide, and gleaming dimly.

Not far away, a deep moan echoed off the walls. I could conjure a lot of things in my mind and nothing to fit that sound. My heart froze.

I swallowed, trying to moisten my throat, which was drier than the Mojave. "Is that what you brought me here for?"

Burt set down the broom and crowbar and walked to the shore. "Yep."

"What is it?"

"You can decide for yourself."

I looked behind me, wondering how long it would take to get back to sunshine, where scorpions and hungry coyotes seemed suddenly friendly. "Maybe I don't want any part of it."

He turned back to me, hands on his hips. "You took a hippocritic oath."

"I'm beginning to feel like I did. Did I ever tell you I dropped out of medical school? Why do think I opened shop in Dead End?"

He came up and put a reassuring hand on my shoulder. "That don't matter," he replied. "You can cure the warts off a hog. I'm livin' proof."

Small splashes drew near. Something was coming, cutting smoothly in and out of the water.

"Look, Doc, you don't have anythin' to worry about. I told you, she's a pussycat."

A groan like a sick cow reverberated through the chamber.

"Is that her meow?"

Burt wrung his hands. "She's in pain. I don't know what to do for her."

I waited, holding my breath, listening with dread and fascination as the splashes came on. Then I saw her, emerging from the darkness, first her eyes, shining like coins for a titan, then her brontosaurus head, which seemed to float above the water. A monstrous neck followed. Trailing thirty feet behind, her body looped through the water like a giant hose.

The water must have been deep almost up to the shore. She left her body submerged and dropped her head on a flat rock as a dog that was feeling pathetic and under the weather might.

Burt patted her head and scratched where her ears would be if she were a cat. "This here's the doctor I told you 'bout."

She moaned again, but not so loud. Her eyes rolled until they locked on me. They were intelligent and hopeful.

Since she hadn't snatched Burt in those jaws of hers and dragged him underwater, I approached.

"Why do you think it's her tooth?" I asked.

"She isn't eatin' normal."

"How do you know?"

"She won't touch anythin' I give her."

"What do you give her, a cow?"

He nodded to the water. "She catches lots of fish there. Three times a week I give her steak and some of these." He pulled the post-office package from his knapsack and unwrapped it. Inside was a box of Dormel's chocolates.

"You give her that?"

He gave me a bashful look. "She loves 'em."

I shook my head, pretty certain what the problem was. "Well, I better have a look. Will she open up and not snap my head off?"

He stroked her nose. "Let Doc have a look and I'll give you some of the toffee ones."

I swear she almost smiled at that and her head went up and down in what might have been a nod. She opened wide and displayed a set of nine-inch teeth the like of which haven't been seen since this planet's infancy.

I handed Burt the lantern. "If I die, I'll kill you."

He held it close while I bent in for a look. Those daggers were pearly white near the top, but a brown deposit had formed on the bottom. One back tooth looked pretty bad. The gum around it was swollen too.

I rose and tapped the chocolate box. "That's your problem. It'll rot her teeth in no time."

"Can you do somethin' for her?"

"A tooth has to come out." I rubbed my chin, studying her, trying to figure how to do it. She looked at me, her eyes innocent and trusting. If I hurt her she'd flail and make hamburger out of me with a whip from her tail, though she didn't mean a lick of harm.

"Thought so. Well, you brought the tranquilizer."

"That's not it, Burt. I can't exactly dig it out."

"You gotta help me, Doc. I'm lost without her."

He wasn't the only one. It dawned on me I'd been lost a long time. Maybe she was the way out. A strange urgency gripped me. I had to do this or

I was a goner; I'd blow away like dust.

I looked around and then back the way we came. "How far is it to your cabin?"

"Maybe a hundred fifty feet."

"How much cable you got on your tow?"

His face lit up. "Two hundred."

"Let's prep her. I want her down deep when we do this."

Burt coaxed her mouth back open. "This is goin' to hurt a little. You just hold on. Doc's goin' to fix you up."

It might seem questionable to a sane person why I would put my faith in such reassurances, but I'd seen enough of her to risk it. I keep a supply of anesthetic in my bag and started with that, giving her a dozen shots around the tooth. For good measure, I added a few injections of penicillin. Next, I loaded four hypos with elephant tranquilizer. I didn't bring a gun and wouldn't have used it if I had. The sound would have scared her. I felt the scales on her throat and found a vein pulsing like a drum. Holding my breath, I stuck one in. She didn't flinch. Probably wasn't much more than a fleabite to her.

"Let's head up," I said, closing my bag. "Tell her to stay put. If she goes unconscious and slips into the water, she could drown."

"No sayin' what she'll do on drugs." He handed me the keys to his truck. "You get the cable. I'll keep an eye on her."

He had a point about the drugs. I thought I'd better stay in case she had a reaction. What I would do for a creature like her was up for question. They didn't cover that in medical school.

I glanced at my watch. "Tell you what, let's see how she does."

We waited fifteen minutes. Those giant eyes never closed. They did sink to half-mast. That great head of hers lolled on the rock.

"Let's go," I said. "We got about forty minutes to do this."

He squatted before her. "Don't go nowhere and I'll give you more of these." He held up the chocolates.

The dreamy expression on her face got dreamier.

We debated what she was on the way to his truck. Burt thought she was like that creature spotted in '33 in northern Scotland. Wherever she came from, I was pretty certain she was Awanyu. Stories come from somewhere. If you came right down to it, the Hopis got things right. Maybe Indian Bob had some of their blood after all.

To tell the truth, I was preoccupied with something else. How in the devil was I going to grab on to that tooth? I kept picturing it from all kinds of angles. The tooth broke in each scenario, leaving the root.

By the time we were topside, I thought of something. "Have you got a hand drill with a big bit?"

He found one in the back. The bit was just under an inch. It would have to do.

Burt backed his truck as close to the front door as he could. Using the hydraulic, he fed out both lines, which had swivel hooks attached to chains. He took one. I took the other. On the way back down, I studied the passage walls. I saw no evidence of prospecting. Where had he gotten that nugget?

When I asked, he gave me that sly smile. "Get that tooth out and you'll see."

Below, the creature still lolled at the water's edge. Her eyes hadn't closed, but the dreamy expression hadn't worn off, which gave me small comfort. I didn't know how she would react to what I had in mind or if it would even work.

Burt got her mouth open again. The tooth was conical. Using the drill at the base, I worked away at it, first on one side, then the other, enlarging both holes a little at a time. In my wildest dreams, I never thought I'd have my head so close to a monster's epiglottis. She was a good girl though and didn't stir once. Pretty soon the holes were large enough to work the hooks in.

Now came the tricky part. One of us had to go topside and retract the cable. She needed Burt to keep her calm, but she might need me for another shot. We flipped for it.

He went. I stayed.

"Stay put," he told her before leaving. "No matter what happens, stay put."

I watched the cable. We'd left some slack, so I'd have some warning. I checked my watch every few minutes. The tranquilizer could wear off anytime. Bless his heart, it didn't take as long as I'd thought. I'm certain he ran all the way—he cared that much about her.

The cable pulled taut. Her eyes flared. With a cry she yanked her head back and out popped the tooth, as neat as a cork. I'm here to tell you it's hard to gauge a monster's expression, but this one seemed relieved.

I thought she might sink back to the rock. Instead, she reared back and dove, her long body flowing into the water.

Burt ran up, panting.

"Sorry," I said. "She's gone."

"She dove?"

I nodded.

He picked up the tooth and turned it in both hands. "She ain't gone. She's gettin' your reward."

Sure enough, she resurfaced and swam toward us with something gleaming in her mouth. When she reached the shore, she deposited a nugget the size of Kansas. Nearly a foot long, to be more precise.

Since then, I've debated with myself about what she was and whether others like her roam the rivers and byways underground. Sometimes I question if the whole thing happened, but the gold fetched a pretty penny, and I'm set up well now. I sold my practice in Dead End to a traveling snake oil salesman and moved to San Francisco, where the fog and ladies are more to my liking. Whatever happens from here on out, I won't end up beside those two hombres in the Dry Gulch Saloon.

Burt probably has more gold tucked away than me, but he stayed at the knees of Awanyu. I thought with all that water down there he'd license the rights or put in a golf course or something. He steadfastly refuses. To the world, he's a hermit. I know better. He found his life companion, and that's all there is to it.

Every now and then I get a letter from him. He tells me he brushes Fluffy's teeth regularly with the push broom and scores around her gumline with the crowbar. He doesn't live extravagantly, but pays for weekly deliveries.

I have it on high authority they consist of three steaks and a box of chocolates.

A. R. Silverberry writes fantasy adventures for children and adults. His novel, Wyndano's Cloak, won multiple awards, including the Benjamin Franklin Awards gold medal for Juvenile/Young Adult Fiction. The Stream, his second novel, was honored as a Shelf Unbound Notable Book, and was shortlisted in ForeWord Review's Book of the Year Awards. His love for fantasy fiction was sparked by a babysitter, who, with a seemingly endless supply of Oz books, read him to sleep. Fairy tales, Tolkien, and the spine-tingling tales of Robert E. Howard sealed the deal. He's lived most of his life in Northern California. As a child, it was an easy hike from his house to a forest path, where pixies or fairies surely lurked beyond the next bend. Find him at www.arsilverberry.com or on Facebook at http://www.bit.ly/2fb2RSL.

Snapdragon

Ryll's heart beat an unfamiliar rhythm—happy and exultant—as she raced down the narrow garden path. The edges were overgrown with peonies and thyme all the way to her sanctuary near the healer's crumbling cottage.

This new feeling would either tear her to pieces or send her flying into the sky like a dragon.

When she reached the old well behind the abandoned cottage, she sank to her knees in the evening shadows. The healer had left before she and her sister had been born, dismissed along with the other men on the manor. Now only Ryll and her twin sister, Chrys, remained, along with three servants who had nowhere else to go. No one would bother her here. No one cared.

She leaned over the few remaining stones that ringed the well and looked into the still water. Five feet across and deeper than anyone could guess, the well had stayed full to the top through all Ryll's seventeen years. She stared now at the necklace swinging gently around her neck: a tiny rose in solid gold on a delicate silver chain. It was the most exquisite gift she'd ever received.

It was also the only gift. And the cooper's son Andolph had given it to her.

But why her?

She let her gaze wander over her reflection, knowing exactly what she would see. Sleek black hair swung down past her chin, inches away from tickling the surface of the water. Wary eyes, narrowed even more than usual. The water didn't reflect their color, but she knew. The servants knew. And Andolph knew.

Most of the villagers tolerated her and her sister, but as daughters of a sorceress, they would always be looked upon with distrust. Especially because of what their mother had done to them.

Rustling on the other side of the well distracted her. A tiny white dragon adjusted its perch on a crimson snapdragon. It watched, curious, tilting its head from side to side as if listening. He'd been watching her quite often the past few weeks.

She smiled. "You don't mind the color, do you?" The little dragon had chosen a flower the same shade as her eyes.

She'd given up trying to convince herself her eyes were amber or some outlandish shade of purplish-brown. And they were nothing compared to her skin. She might be able to lower her eyes in the village to hide their unnatural color, but she could do nothing to hide the black rose-like thorns protruding from almost every inch of her face, her hands, and her arms. Everywhere.

Thankfully, where her own skin rubbed together, the thorns were more like nettles, and she was immune to their sting. Her mother had experimented with clothing in their early years, and Ryll had learned to fashion long-sleeved dresses from weaver dragon silk, which was almost impenetrable to her thorns when woven tightly and more comfortable than chain mail.

Chrys could wear anything. Her beauty was unmarred. Her skin was smooth and brown, her small eyes clear and black. But her touch was death—their mother had infused her skin with poison. They were both cursed to be untouchable for as long as they stayed together, safe from the dangers of men.

Until now.

Andolph, the boy with the strong hands and large black eyes, had seen Ryll's imperfections and didn't care.

"Every thorn needs a rose," she whispered, repeating his words. They might not be the most poetic, but they were the most beautiful that had ever been said to her.

The little dragon sneezed, or snorted, and the snapdragon swayed under the sudden movement.

She removed the necklace from around her neck and ran the chain across her fingers. The ends snagged on the back of her hand, and she shook her wrist to loosen it. She let her mind wander into traitorous territory for a moment, imagining the healer's cottage restored, dark-haired children playing in the garden, and a tall young man who smiled when she entered the room.

She stretched out onto her stomach in the grass, elbows propped on the flat stones of the well, pouring the golden rose and silver chain from one hand to the other.

Chrys would scold her. She would order her to lose the necklace, or worse, return it. Their mother would have done the same. Ryll couldn't betray her sister, even if abandoning her would end the curse, but she longed for . . . something more. A family. A normal life. Andolph was proof that was possible. His interest had grown little by little the past few weeks. It didn't

19

matter that he'd never shown her any attention before then. She understood his reluctance to approach her.

The dragon sneezed again. Ryll startled and glanced up at it. A stone shifted under her elbow, and the necklace slipped from her fingers into the dark water with a hiss and a *blurp*.

She plunged her arm in, but it was too late. The golden rose disappeared into the depths, trailing the silver chain behind it like a shooting star. She sat up quickly, the green sleeve of her dress plastered to her arm. Her skin burned hot and cold at the same time as shock and dismay coursed through her. Chrys would rejoice at the accident, but Ryll refused to lose what might be her only chance to have a future with someone.

She took a deep breath and dove into the well head first. The thin dress immediately clung to her legs, hindering her ability to swim deeper, and for the first time ever, she regretted its strength. She floated back to the surface and dragged herself out. The necklace must be on the bottom by now. She pulled the front hem of her skirt through to the back and tied it in a knot around her waist, revealing more of her legs than she ever had before, but she didn't care. There was no one around to see, anyway.

She dove again, kicking deep into the blackness and cold. If only her unnatural red eyes held the power to see in the dark—her skin crawled to think of sticking her hand into unseen muck and old bones at the bottom of the well.

But she didn't reach the bottom. She tried a second time and a third, but the water was too deep. She couldn't hold her breath long enough. The well was too narrow for proper swimming, and it was dark. So dark.

She floated at the edge, blinking water out of her eyes, and sniffed loudly. The tiny dragon fluttered over to a nearby stone and settled beside her hand, placing a paw the size of her pinkie nail on her wrist. She'd never seen such a small dragon up close, and she didn't recognize his species. White scales, iridescent like mother-of-pearl, overlapped smoothly along his body from his nose to the tip of his tail, reflecting the pinks and oranges of the sunset. He folded soft-furred wings tightly against his sides and looked at her with large blue eyes.

"I'm not giving up." She nudged the dragon's paw off her hand, took a deep breath, and sank down into the water. Down and down, stretching her small frame as far as she could, waiting for her toes to hit stone or sand. Mud. Bones. Anything.

How deep was the well? Did it even have a bottom?

She surfaced again, panted, took another breath and dove. Three more times. Or four. She lost count. The little dragon waited for her on the stone each time. Her limbs grew watery. Her chest burned. She took another breath, ready to try again, but her arm slipped on the wet stones, and she dropped down into the water too soon. Spluttering, she surfaced and grasped handfuls of grass and dirt in her effort to reach dry ground. The dragon tugged on her dress, trying uselessly to help her out. She made it halfway and flopped onto her back, legs dangling in the water. The dragon perched on her shoulder and peered into her eyes.

"Just catching my breath." She coughed and closed her eyes. If she kept them closed, she wouldn't notice the approaching darkness. Garden and well would be the same inky black.

She sat up, and the dragon fluttered to the ground. Her shoulders drooped, and a tear slipped from her eye, threading its way between the thorns on her cheek. Who was she kidding? She had no energy left to dive again. The necklace was lost.

"Don't cry, please," said a voice, too soft and deep and distinctly masculine to be Chrys or any of the servants.

Unless someone was hiding in the bushes, she and the dragon were the only ones around, and dragons didn't talk.

"Let me help you," the voice said.

She studied the dragon where he sat on a stone by her knee with a hopeful gleam in his eyes. "Did you say something?"

"Yes. I said I can help you." His lips stretched and moved carefully around his sharp teeth to form the words. It shouldn't have been possible, but she was used to seeing impossible in the mirror every day. Being on the receiving end of a curse, no matter how well-intentioned, she recognized one when she saw it.

"Why would you help me?" And how? He was so small.

"You need me." He stood. Paced from one end of the stone to the other. Sat. "And I would ask for something in return."

Of course he would.

"You can keep trying yourself," he said, "but it's almost dark. I just thought—"

"Okay." Barely half an hour of light remained, and the moon would rise late tonight. It wouldn't hurt to let the dragon try, if he thought he could do it; although even if he were able to reach it, the rose itself would be a handful for him, not to mention the chain.

"What do you want?" she said.

"Nothing much." His soft voice lowered, and she bent her ear close to hear him. "I want a friend. I want to sit with you at your table and eat from your plate, to be your companion during the day, and sleep on your pillow at night."

She'd never had a friend, but his request, odd as it was, seemed easy enough to grant. "I'll do what you ask and be your friend if you get the necklace for me."

The dragon nodded, extended his wings, and slipped soundlessly into the water, his shiny white scales disappearing quickly into the murky depths.

21

She pulled her knees up and wrapped her arms around them carefully so as not to press the thorns on her legs into the softer nettled skin under her arms. Waiting, she rocked back and forth, listening to the night creatures wake and rustle among the bushes and trees. How long would it take him to swim to the bottom, as small as he was, when she hadn't been able to reach it herself? Brave little dragon. He'd taken on an impossible task to win her friendship. He deserved that and more whether he succeeded or not.

His white snout broke the surface, and he scrambled to the edge of the well, sopping wings flopping uselessly behind him. He pulled himself onto a stone and shook himself dry.

"You didn't find it."

"I think I almost reached the bottom, but these wings got in the way." He extended them to their full length, which was barely wider than her hand span. "No good for swimming."

Another tear slipped down her cheek.

He folded his wings tightly against his sides. "I'll try again." He darted into the well before she had a chance to reply.

Once again he surfaced without the necklace. He paced, his blue eyes narrowed in a frown. "I can do this," he muttered. "I have to do this." Without warning, he flew off straight overhead, circled, and then dove into the well like an arrow, wings firmly tucked to his sides.

She stood and untied her dress from around her waist, shook out the wet folds, and squeezed water from her hair. She waited, shivering in the night air. When had it grown so dark? She had to get home while she could still see the way, but she wouldn't leave the dragon alone.

Finally, his white scales appeared beneath the surface as he struggled to swim with a silver chain grasped in his fingers. He'd found it!

A tingling excitement spread throughout her body, and she scooped them both out of the water. She laid him gently in the grass, untangled the necklace from his talons, and slipped the chain around her neck.

Chrys would be angry at her for being late to supper, but she didn't care. She had the necklace. She had Andolph.

She turned and ran as quickly as she dared back through the garden towards the manor.

"Don't forget your promise." The dragon's voice followed her like the whisper of leaves.

He would catch up with her once he'd rested. He could fly, after all, while she had to rely on shaky legs and human eyes.

Candles burned in the windows when she arrived at the manor. She straightened her shoulders and entered through the back door. Only when she'd reached the safety of her room did she realize she'd forgotten to thank her new friend.

She changed quickly for supper, tying her damp hair back with a ribbon and pulling on a faded blue dress. She adjusted the rose at her collarbone and entered the dining room with her head high.

Chrys sat at the head of the table. Her black eyes flashed when she saw the necklace, and her jaw tightened.

Ryll sat across from her, sinking gratefully onto her cushion. She filled her plate and ate in silence as her sister glared at her.

"You went shopping today, I see." Chrys's graceful hands lifted her water glass to her lips.

"You know I didn't."

"Who gave it to you?"

She swallowed twice before she could answer. "Andolph."

"Men don't give gifts like that lightly—it's a promise of more. What makes you so special that he would give you such a thing? You've never spoken to him in your life."

"How do you know? You hardly ever go into the village." Chrys was right, though. Ryll had never spoken to Andolph until a few weeks ago when he'd approached her outside the flower shop.

"It's gaudy and inappropriate. Take it off."

Ryll wrapped her fingers around the rose protectively, but before she could respond, something banged against the window from the outside.

The dragon.

"What is that?" Chrys asked.

Ryll opened the window.

"Don't let it in!"

The dragon flew into the room and landed on the back of an empty chair. He glanced from one girl to the other a few times before his gaze settled on Ryll. She took her seat and patted the table next to her plate.

He landed neatly and sat with his tail curled around his feet. "You remembered your promise."

Chrys gasped.

"Of course I did." Not sure what he ate, she pushed a sliver of beef and a stalk of asparagus towards his side of the plate.

"What . . . who . . . what are you doing, Ryll? Have you gone mad?"

"I have not. I've made a friend. He helped me this evening, and I intend to repay him for his kindness."

Her sister's breathing grew louder, and her fingers clenched into fists on the table. "*He* has to leave. Do you know what you've invited into our home?"

She looked her sister in the eyes. "I'm not stupid." She paused and then said the next words carefully. "And I don't care."

"He's a *man*. You've brought a man into our house, and you will get rid of him immediately."

"I will not!" Ryll lowered her voice. "He's my guest, and he may stay as long as he likes."

Had Chrys been the one with red eyes, they would have suited her well as she glared at the dragon. "Well. Does your guest have a name?"

A name. She'd never asked if he had a name. Surely he had one.

The dragon cleared his throat. "My name is Jorey. Pleased to meet you."

Chrys sneered. "He's no different than the one who gave you that necklace, that Randolph."

"Andolph."

"Whatever. He couldn't possibly like you. He's lying. Men can't be trusted, and that dragon can't be trusted. He's not helping you to be nice."

The dragon had already told her what he wanted: friendship. An easy enough thing to give when you got it in return. But what did Andolph want? Ryll touched the rose on its silver chain. To give her such a gift, surely he saw their future together.

But how did he know a future was possible? Neither she nor her sister had told anyone how to break their curse, although everyone knew all curses could be broken.

"See," Chrys said. "You can't tell me he didn't ask for something in return for helping you."

"He did ask for something."

Her expression turned smug, a silent *I-told-you-so*. She turned to Jorey. "Just don't expect her to break your curse for you, lizard."

"I expect no such thing." He speared the sliver of beef with his talon and bit into it.

They ate quietly for a few moments.

Chrys couldn't stay silent. "What did he do to deserve being turned into a puny white dragon?"

Jorey answered as if she'd spoken to him. "I'm a farmer's son. I did nothing except fall into the path of a sorceress testing her powers. Not everything that happens to people is deserved." He sliced off a ring of asparagus. "What did you do to deserve your … condition?"

Ryll put a hand to her mouth. No one ever asked them about their curse. No one. Ever.

Chrys stood abruptly, silky hair swishing around her face as she leaned forward. "I don't have to answer to a runt dragon-man. Keep out of my sight." She slammed the door on her way out.

Ryll sighed. "My sister is harmless." Except for her touch, of course. "Still, I'd stay out of her way, if I were you."

"I have no interest in your sister." He fluttered onto her shoulder and grasped a thorn on her neck to steady himself. "But I think there's more poison in her than what's on the surface."

Standing, Ryll made her way to her bedroom. "You don't know her. She's looking out for me like she's always done."

"She's looking out for herself. If you find someone to be with, where does that leave her? Alone and defenseless, and that's not somewhere she wants to be."

"What do you know about it?"

"I haven't just watched you the past few weeks. I've listened, too. I pick up on things."

Nosy dragon. What was he doing watching her, anyway? She reached her room and closed the door, locking it behind her out of habit. At least she wouldn't have to explain things to him. Not that she owed him an explanation, but they were friends now, and she found an unexpected comfort in having someone to talk to.

One of the servants had lit a candle. Ryll lit five more and placed them around the room.

The dragon jumped from her shoulder and glided to the dressing table. "Why does the dark frighten you so much?"

She froze. No one had ever asked her to explain. She'd never spoken about it, not even to Chrys. Images crowded into her mind as if seeking release. "I...."

"It's okay. You don't have to tell me, but I'm here if you want to talk." He crouched on the scored wood, pearly scales shimmering in the candlelight, and looked at her with concern. "Friend, remember?"

She nodded, and the words spilled unbidden from her tongue. "They took our mother away in the middle of the night. They tried to take us, too...." She could still feel the rough gloves on her arms—how they snagged on the thorns. Her sister's screams. Chrys had managed to touch someone's skin, and their captors had dropped both of them immediately. The man was sick for months after, and the entire village was ordered to leave them be. They had the one they wanted.

She and Chrys never saw their mother again.

"It was ten years ago. I can still hear their boots in the dark."

The dragon nestled his head on her hand where it rested on the desk, his tiny face fitting perfectly between the thorns. In less than a day, he'd touched her more than anyone had in years. Maybe ever. Even Andolph had kept his fingers clear when he placed the necklace around her throat.

"I'm sorry," he said.

"It's not your fault."

"I should have helped you sooner. You had to run home in the dark because of my own fear."

"I don't understand."

"I've never reached out to anyone before. People mistrust sorcery, but I knew you would understand. That you wouldn't hate me. I should have spoken to you sooner."

"I'm glad you spoke when you did."

His blue eyes blinked rapidly, and he bared his teeth in an attempt at a smile.

She nudged him off her hand and grinned. "Now, I need to get ready for bed, but people keep asking questions."

He clamped a paw around his snout and gestured in a human-like way for her to proceed.

"Would you mind?" She opened the desk drawer. "I don't have a privacy screen."

He hopped in, and she closed it gently.

Quickly, she slipped into a dark green weaver silk nightgown, held up by thin straps at the shoulders, shook her hair loose, and draped the necklace over a bouquet of dried lavender. She opened the drawer, but there was no movement. A knot formed in her throat. Had something squashed him when the drawer closed?

"Jorey?"

He crawled out and balanced on the edge.

She let out a relieved breath. "I thought you'd been hurt."

"I'm tougher than I look." He extended his wings to their fullest, bared his teeth, and crouched in a menacing pose.

"That's cute. I'll guard my toes."

He snorted and folded his wings. "No respect for dragons around here," he mumbled.

"Maybe." She paused. "But I do respect what you did for me today. Thank you."

His scales took on a pale pink color, and he dipped his head.

Could dragons blush?

He growled, or cleared his throat. "You still owe me a place on your pillow."

"Oh, right." She climbed into the narrow bed, covered in snagged and torn weaver silk, snuggled in, and patted the spot next to her head. "Will this do?"

Jorey flew over and curled up next to her ear. "You don't snore, do you?"

She chuckled. "I don't think so, but I'd worry more about being impaled if I were you." She turned her head to look at him, careful to stay flat on her back. She'd learned the hard way that it was the safest position to sleep in.

"You don't scare me." He studied her, his bright blue eyes following the lines of her shoulder and neck, her face. "You don't have any thorns on your ears."

She brought a hand up self-consciously.

He touched a spot near her wrist. "Where do the scars come from? This one looks like a burn mark."

"It's nothing." She pulled the sheet up to her neck and slid her arms underneath. "I've tried to get rid of the thorns a few times. Burning them, clipping, digging them out. I used to file them down on my hands, but it takes too much effort, and I could still see the black crescents on my skin where they were lying in wait, ready to grow again."

"Sounds painful."

You have no idea. If he were anyone else, she would have said it aloud, but he might be the only one who could understand what she'd been through. "It would have been worth it if I could have felt normal in the end."

He didn't respond but curled into a ball and wrapped his tail around himself. He looked like a giant pearl resting on her pillow. "There's no such thing as normal. We all have thorns, but most of us carry them inside where no one can see how they hurt us."

"I thought you were a farmer's son, not a philosopher."

He flashed his dragon smile. "Goodnight, Ryll."

She couldn't remember the last time someone had bid her goodnight. "Sleep well, Jorey."

Before the first edge of dawn appeared, Ryll woke to a thump outside her window. She sat bolt upright, heartbeat loud in her ears.

Jorey was gone.

The door was closed, still locked from the inside.

The curtains fluttered.

She ran to the window and looked outside. Silver moonlight shone on a short, hooded figure retreating towards the front of the manor. She clamored over the windowsill, landing hard on her feet, and took off after the thief. No, the kidnapper.

Resisting the urge to scream, she barreled into the cloaked figure from behind, knocking them both to the ground. She rolled off quickly, hoping she hadn't harmed Jorey.

"Let him go," she said, panting.

"Mercy, miss." The woman held her arms in front of her face. "You can have it, just don't hurt me." She pulled out a burlap pouch from a fold of her cloak and held it at arm's length, refusing to look at Ryll's face.

She snatched the pouch. No need to see the woman's features to know who it was. "Tell your mistress to leave my friend alone." How dare Chrys send her own maid to kidnap Jorey. Did she think Ryll wouldn't guess? No one else knew he was here. No one else cared.

"Yes, miss. Thank you, miss." She stumbled backwards on her hands and feet and then righted herself and ran off into the woods.

"Jorey?" She untied the string and stretched out the opening of the pouch.

He emerged up to his shoulders, panting, and drooped over her finger.

27

Wild blue eyes looked up into hers. "You came after me. In the dark."

She glanced at the curtained windows of the manor, the shadowed bushes and black sky, and pressed her arms tightly against her sides. "Yeah, I guess I did."

He climbed onto her hand and made his way up her bare arm, using the thorns as handholds and twitching his wings free when they snagged. When he reached her shoulder, he sat down with a small sigh. "Thank you."

She crushed the pouch in her hand and returned to her room.

Jorey would travel with her to the village in the morning. She spent the last hour before dawn curled up on the bed with the dragon cupped in her hand. He'd fallen asleep within minutes, clearly exhausted, and his snore filled the air like the soft buzzing of a bee.

She kept watch until the acrid smoke of the burnt-out candles woke him.

His nose twitched and he stretched each limb while his eyes remained closed, his wings flopping over the sides of her hand. One eye opened. "Good morning."

Her lips curled up in response. She would have to get used to smiling if he stayed around, although, he hadn't said how long that would be. Her smile faded. They were friends now, so even if he left, he would surely return. Wouldn't he?

"What's wrong?"

"Oh, nothing." She carried him to the desk, and he obligingly hopped into the drawer. "I'm just thinking of the best way to take you into the village with me." She closed the drawer.

"You want me with you?" he said, his voice muffled through the wood.

"Of course, I do, especially after last night." She would give Chrys a personal warning when she saw her at supper. "I can't lose you like that."

The golden rose went around her neck first. Her skin tingled at the thought of seeing Andolph again. Goosebumps raced up her arms, and the thorns shivered in response. She pulled on a sleeveless dress in deep plum and cinched it with a wide leather belt, looping the pouch string through the buckle. She'd decided it was the best way for Jorey to travel. He was too small to fly the whole way, and he couldn't travel far on her shoulder. If he lost his balance, he could stab himself on a thorn.

She opened the drawer as she ran a comb through her hair. "Ready?"

He blinked up at her. "Wow. You look amazing."

The comb clattered to the floor.

"That color is good on you."

She had no words.

"Ryll? You'll let the flies in."

Her mouth snapped shut, and she cleared her throat. She tried to imagine Andolph saying those words to her after the curse was broken, but it would never feel the same as hearing it right now for the first time, with her red eyes and her skin covered in black thorns and scars.

"We should go." She held the pouch open. "I'll leave the strings loose."

"Right." He fluttered over and settled himself inside. "You do know I have wings."

"Use them whenever you want, but it's a fair distance. I thought you might like to ride."

"I'm not complaining."

Jorey bounced around in the pouch most of the walk, and they chatted about the scenery and how it differed from his home in the north. They passed a few farmhouses and a few fellow travelers on the road. No one spoke to them.

"We're going to see your ... friend, aren't we?"

"You're my friend. I'm still not sure what Andolph is. More, I hope."

"With a gift like that around your neck, I would say so." He paused. "Is he a good man?"

"He's well-liked and a hard worker. The girls can't keep their eyes off him."

"Including you."

Including her, but she was the one he'd noticed back. "He's never been unkind to me." He'd also never stood up for her, but few had. Jorey didn't need to know that. It didn't matter now.

Jorey snorted and took to the air, his white scales disappearing against the clouds.

Her hands shook, and she clenched them into fists. How would Andolph greet her today? If nothing else, he would be surprised—she never came to the village more than once a week. She walked the last few miles alone.

Jorey landed on her shoulder.

"How was the view?"

"Same as usual. Sheep in the fields, a young couple glued together in back of a shop."

She curled a hand around the rose. Andolph would be busy at work this time of day.

"Oh, and a gray cat trying to steal a pheasant hanging in the butcher's window. Hilarious. I don't think he'll get it down before he's caught."

She smiled absently.

Jorey climbed wordlessly down the thorns on her arm and into the pouch.

She entered the village, head high, eyes forward. Although many people glanced her way, they quickly averted their eyes. She ignored them and marched straight to the cooper's shop, bypassed the front door, and circled around to the back alley, which was filled with barrels and wooden casks.

"Andolph?" He wouldn't answer, of course, because he wasn't there.

"Ryll?" He was there. Something bumped into a barrel and quick footsteps retreated on the gravel. Andolph appeared, straightening his tunic over his broad shoulders.

Her heart beat an unfamiliar rhythm.

Betrayal.

She refused to listen.

"Just running off some silly kids. What are you doing here? I wasn't expecting you until next week."

Kids. It was just kids. She swallowed hard, conscious of the way it made the thorns on her throat wave. "I wanted to see you again. I … thought you would be pleased to see me."

"Ah." He glanced over his shoulder. "Yes, I'm pleased to see you, of course."

Jorey fidgeted in the pouch.

Andolph made no move towards her. Yesterday, he'd run his fingers through her hair and told her how silky it felt against his skin.

"I can come back another time. I'm sure you're busy." She turned to leave.

"Wait."

She stopped and faced him again.

He stepped closer and looked into her eyes. "I wish…." Another step, and he glanced away. "There has to be some way to break your curse." He studied her hair. "You know, so we can be together."

She said nothing, barely daring to breath. She could tell him right now how simple it would be, and yet how difficult for her.

"Maybe a kiss?" he said. His gaze fell to her lips, one of the few spots completely free of thorns. "A true love's kiss. It works in the storybooks."

Jorey snorted, but Andolph didn't seem to hear.

Ryll knew it wouldn't work, but her stomach fluttered at the thought of Andolph being so close. "I guess it wouldn't hurt to try."

A triumphant smile flashed in his eyes.

Maybe she would get a happily-ever-after just like in the storybooks.

Closing the gap between them, Andolph clasped his hands behind his back, and leaned forward. Ryll closed her eyes and felt his lips tickle against hers for one short moment. That was all.

He huffed.

She opened her eyes.

He took a step back and folded his arms. "Nothing happened."

Jorey exploded from the pouch and flew straight up into the air, just like he'd done when he'd retrieved the necklace. Ryll ignored him, concentrating on Andolph's frown. Had he not even enjoyed the kiss?

Andolph shook his head slowly. "This isn't going to work. Do you even know how to break your own curse?"

She felt as if he'd throw ice water in her face. The chill dripped its way down her spine and into her hands, her chest, her heart. "What if I said no? Are you willing to take the chance that it can't be broken?"

Jorey reappeared, gliding low over the shop roof. He landed on the corner behind Andolph.

"No. I'm done." Andolph shifted back and forth. He looked over his shoulder again and spoke louder. "I said I'm done with this."

A young man, a friend of Andolph, appeared from behind a different row of barrels. A smile lit his face.

She'd never seen a less welcoming sight.

"You lost the bet, Andy. You said you'd break the curse, but she looks as disgusting as ever."

Her jaw clenched.

"I can't believe she fell for it." The young man approached her, and Ryll backed up until she bumped into a stack of wood. He looked her up and down. "I'm not afraid of you, you know."

"I'm not afraid of you, either," she whispered.

"I can tell," he sneered.

Andolph watched nervously, but he said nothing.

"I think I might like one of those kisses. You—"

A white blur whizzed by, and the young man's head whipped to the side. He swore and put a hand to his temple.

Jorey had taken a chunk of hair with him, and he rained it down on top of the man.

"What is that thing?" He swatted at the air, jumping in circles as Jorey darted to and fro, leading him away from her. After several tries, his hand connected with the dragon and knocked him to the ground.

Jorey didn't move.

The man lifted his foot, but she wouldn't let him stomp on her friend. Her defender. For the first time in her life, she used her thorns for the defense her mother had intended. She lashed out at the man's arms, swiping with the backs of her hands. He howled and toppled into Andolph, and they both stumbled before righting themselves.

Eyes wide, Andolph pulled his friend towards the front of the shop.

Ryll wrapped her fingers around the golden rose and yanked hard, snapping the silver chain. She threw it at Andolph's feet. "Every thorn needs a rose."

She didn't wait to see if he picked it up.

Using the thorns on her fingers, she ripped a strip off the end of her dress and tied the ends together in sling fashion over her shoulder. She scooped Jorey off the ground and settled him inside to keep him safe from the nettles on her palms. He looked almost grey against the plum fabric.

Over the years, she'd learned to keep her tears inside. Her sister detested weakness. That, and blotting her face had shredded more handkerchiefs than

31

they could spare. Now, she let the tears flow. Andolph's betrayal had cut her deeply, as if every thorn on her body had been turned inward at the same time. But he was nothing to her, in the end, except a hope for something more. She cried now for her friend, the only person who'd ever come to her aid—and he'd done it more than once.

She wouldn't let her sister, or anyone else, take that away from her.

She made it to her sanctuary after the sun started its evening descent. Jorey's breaths came evenly, but he didn't stir otherwise. She lifted him gently out of the sling and placed him on a bed of moss near the well, arranging his wings as comfortably as she could manage. Covering her hand with the scrap of dress, she dipped her finger in the water and wiped down his face and shoulders, then she lay down beside him, shielding him from the sun, and fell asleep.

The sun had disappeared behind the trees when she woke, and orange fingers spread across the sky. Jorey was gone from his mossy bed. She sat up too quickly, and her head spun.

"I'm here." He perched on a crimson snapdragon, just as he'd done the evening before. "Are you okay?"

"I was going to ask you the same question."

"I have a headache. Nothing new. I've had one ever since being squeezed into this too-small body. What happened after I got knocked down?"

"Nothing. I ran them off." She put a hand to her head, hardly able to believe she'd stood up for herself.

"There's blood on your hands."

There was—on the backs where she'd slashed Andolph's friend. She dipped them in the well and swirled them around until they came clean. She explained what had happened.

"Wish I could've seen that." Jorey flew over and landed on her knee.

"You saw too much as it is. I have to get home." She stood, and he swooped onto her shoulder.

"Will you let me eat with you again?" he said hesitantly.

"Yes. You may eat with me whenever you want and sleep on my pillow. I'll be your companion for as long as you like. I'm your friend."

He sighed, and a puff of air tickled her ear.

"Jorey?"

"Yes?"

"Thank you for what you did for me in the village."

"If I'd been myself, I would have done a lot more."

His words warmed her on the walk back to the manor.

Until she saw her sister's face. Chrys stood just inside the back door, blocking the entrance, eyes narrowed. Anger oozed from her, a poison more potent than any their mother had left her.

Ryll strode up and pushed past her, heedless of her sister's touch but careful to keep Jorey on her far side. Chrys backed away to avoid the thorns on Ryll's arm, just as Ryll knew she would.

"Where are you going?"

"I'm leaving."

Chrys gasped.

Ryll turned to face her. She hadn't thought about leaving, not really, until just then. She had no idea where she would go or what she would do.

"You can't."

"You kidnapped my friend."

"What?" Confusion clouded Chrys's face, and then understanding. "You can't mean that talking lizard."

Ryll refused to argue. "I'm sorry. I won't live like this anymore."

"You can't leave me." A note of panic entered her voice. "We're only safe when we're together."

"Safe from what, Chrys? From living? I'm not clinging to my defenses anymore just because I'm afraid of getting hurt. I won't win any battles if I don't come out and fight, and there are battles worth winning." She glanced at Jorey.

"You're joking, right? This dragon has put you up to this. He's a man, Ryll. You can't trust anything he says."

She stood her ground, fists clenched at her sides.

Tears filled her sister's eyes. "What will I do?"

"No one will know the curse is broken."

"They will, especially without you around as a visual warning."

Jorey growled softly.

Ryll's nails bit into her palms. "So, I'm just here for your own benefit?" Like a guard dog.

"You're leaving for yours." Chrys wrapped her arms around herself. "I would come with you, but I think you've already left me."

Her sister would never leave the manor. "You left me a long time ago."

Chrys's face hardened as the last rays of the sun disappeared below the horizon. She glared at Jorey. "This is all *his* fault. You've been acting strange ever since you brought him home."

Jorey shook. No, his whole body hummed against her shoulder, the sensation echoing into her jaw.

Her sister's hand darted forward and snatched him. Before Ryll could draw breath to gasp, Chrys threw the little dragon up against the far wall. Sparks and embers exploded around his body, and sulfurous smoke filled the air.

Ryll turned away, coughing and fanning the air in front of her face.

Chrys shrieked and ran from the room.

"Jorey?" Ryll blinked tears from her eyes. She tiptoed through the smoke, scanning the floor carefully for the mother-of-pearl scales.

Instead, she saw toes. Hairy, manly toes attached to hairy, muscular legs. She squeezed her eyes shut.

Soft footsteps padded across the room, and then a *thunk* on the side table by the door, followed by a swishing sound.

She opened her eyes. A man stood across from her, his lower half wrapped in a crimson tablecloth. He was taller than most men in the village, with skin and hair as white as moonlight. Blue eyes stared at her intently.

"Jorey?"

He smiled.

She laughed and took a step forward. "What...."

"You treated me like a man for one full day." His voice was the same, only louder and deeper. He shrugged. "That's all it took, but I couldn't ask outright."

"Of course." Even being on the receiving end of a curse, Ryll didn't understand sorcery or those who practiced it. But, who did?

"If you still plan on leaving, will you come with me?" He paused. "I'm just a farmer's son, but if you've nowhere else to go...."

Chrys would be fine without her. Better, even, once she let go of the barriers she'd created to keep people away.

Jorey spoke again, as if trying to convince her to join him. "Friends, remember?"

He needn't have bothered. "Friends is a good start."

While she packed a few belongings, Jorey changed into some old clothes he found in the healer's cottage. They met again at the well.

As they walked on the moonlit path away from Ryll's sister, the curse unraveled, and her thorns fell away one by one, leaving behind small crescent-shaped scars. She glanced at Jorey with his mother-of-pearl skin, confident that her future would hold more happily-ever-afters than her past. If not, she would make her own.

Jorey took her hand, and Ryll's heart soared like a dragon.

Lea Doué is the author of *The Firethorn Crown*, a re-imagining of Grimm's "The Twelve Dancing Princesses," and the first in The Firethorn Chronicles, a series inspired by fairytales and other stories. Lea currently lives in Nova Scotia, Canada with her husband and their two boys, a rescue greyhound, and three cats. But sadly, no dragons.

www.leadoue.com
www.facebook.com/leadoueauthor

The Golden City Captives

I. The Mountain Flames

The fireflies swept down the hill in a gorgeous, undulating wave, until the whole forest above the village of Stillwater appeared to be on fire. Up and down the dirt-covered street, people stuck their heads out of doors and windows, transfixed by the sight. The golden stream flowed closer by the second, heightening the anticipation.

Legends, promises, and prophecies filled every mind in a jumble of excitement. Keio wondered what the gods had in store this time. The People of Light—the Gantari—had finally decided to choose their champions.

Every youth secretly hoped he or she might be one of the lucky few to experience the wonders of the Golden City, where people didn't go hungry and the streets shimmered with gemstones. Keio tried to picture his mother in the soft silks city women supposedly wore. He imagined working for a wealthy prince, maybe tending his horses or feeding his sheep. If he was good, the prince might sponsor him, so he could earn a commission in the king's army or apprentice to a blacksmith or pick up some other respectable trade.

The strongest, bravest, and most beautiful of the youths raced into the street, puffed out their chests, and waited for the fireflies to inspect them. Keio longed to go with them, but a glance back at Mother doused his daydreams. Her expression made no sense. It mixed terror and heartbreak. He'd only seen an expression like that one other time in his life: the day the village watchmen brought back his father's body and left it across the doorway of their one-room home.

Keio didn't want to think about that time. He turned back to the commotion on the streets.

The lights zipped around Carmichael and Bree before moving on to

Jorash and Kaim. Some of the lights stayed near them but most moved on. His friend, Clara Mills, waved from next door before a large hand pulled her back through the window. Keio saw a large section of lights break off from the rest and approach his house, but he never suspected they'd show any interest in him. At twelve, he figured he didn't have much chance of being chosen.

A single firefly separated from the new pack and flew in close, practically touching Keio's nose. He waved it away. This close, he could see its face. The features were human only in miniature.

Fire Fairies!

He'd always wanted to see one up close. The delicate creature wore shiny green armor with a spiked breastplate and matching helmet. He bore no weapons, but Keio's skin tingled, indicating a strong magical presence. The fairy's lovely, translucent wings beat the air furiously.

The fairy held his hands in front of his body then clapped twice. He emitted a single, high-pitched noise that had Keio clamping his hands over his ears and leaping away from the thing. Suddenly, thousands of fairies surrounded him, encasing him in a cocoon formed by their bodies. Keio thrashed at the sides, but though he could see through the capsule, he might as well have been fighting the wind. Mother gasped and rushed forward, but a new wave of fairies held her back.

She screamed and reached for him, but the case surrounding him muffled the noise.

The case drew tight across Keio's shoulders and pressed down on his head. He shuddered and tried not to breathe. Realization seeped through his numb mind as a ring of fairies banded together and encircled his wrists and ankles, pulling painfully tight. Keio looked desperately at his mother as horror and truth slammed into him. These fairies had come only to capture and enslave people.

Keio saw his mother fall to her knees and pray for deliverance. Then, the fairies reached out and touched the capsule.

His vision clouded and his lungs felt like they would burst. He clenched his eyes shut but little starbursts of light flashed behind his eyelids. Pain mounted in his head, along with a steadily growing ringing in his ears. When he thought his head might shatter, suddenly the capsule burst, dumping him onto cold, wet grass.

The rich, damp smell calmed him some. Muffled pops followed quickly by thuds announced the arrival of more captives. Keio forced himself to roll onto his back so he could sit up and cast his gaze about frantically, trying to locate his mother. His wrists and ankles still wore bands of interlocked Fire Fairies. Testing the strength of those bonds only resulted in sore wrists and ankles. The only people he saw were other children from his village.

He couldn't see much beyond this small clearing. Here, the light from the Fire Fairies showed him the grass and a few of his neighbors. But beyond lay absolute darkness. Water seeped through his pants, leaving him chilled. As he took in his surroundings, Keio noted that even the stars couldn't penetrate the intense light from the Fire Fairies.

A dozen children screamed, cried, or called out questions, but nobody answered.

"What are you doing?" demanded a male voice. The harshly delivered question caused most captives to fall silent. Keio had never heard such an accent before. The words came out clipped and short, like the speaker feared he'd run out of time to speak. The man stepped out of the darkness into the circle of light, almost treading on one of the children. "This wasn't the agreed upon meeting place."

A Fire Fairy dropped down from the circle above, growing in size and stature until she was about the size of his mother's water kettle. Movement from her delicate wings caused a gentle breeze to touch Keio's face and allowed this new Fire Fairy to hover above the crowd a few feet from the man. Flowing white robes encased her body. Long brown hair hung to her waist. A flower crown perched on her head, giving her a regal air. Her chin inclined upward.

"We want answers first," said the fairy. Her voice rang out, reaching every ear. "Why is the demand for captives suddenly so high?"

The man glared at the Fire Fairy and shook his fist at her. The movement caused his cloak to fall back, revealing a small patch high on the right side of his chest. The symbol woven into the fabric featured a golden, winged creature.

"Do not forget your place, forest witch." His voice was pitched low, carrying extra threat. "You know whom we hold. Do your job, take your payment, and don't ask questions."

The Fire Fairy froze with her gaze fixed on the man. Keio could tell a struggle happened inside of her, but only flickers of it showed up in her expression. Finally, she nodded stiffly and let her eyes fall shut.

"That threat is getting old," said the fairy.

"But it's still effective," the man reminded her. He grinned, reached into his cloak, and pulled out a small pouch. He shook it gently then tossed it onto the ground. "Here is a gesture of good will from my master. I'm told it's fresh."

The bag hit the ground, and a small puff of bright yellow dust shot upward.

The fairy eyed the package, looking stricken. Keio thought she might cry. Slowly, she raised her hands and made a waving gesture.

"Take them then, but tell your master he has them all now. There are no more Children of Promise to be found in these lands. He must release the queen."

"He'll do what he likes, and you'll follow orders if you value her life."

"It has been fourteen years!" cried the Fire Fairy. "One more and she will die without us, as we will without her. We have done everything asked of us!"

"I don't make those decisions," replied the man. His haughty attitude drained away, and he suddenly looked worried. Shaking himself, the man drew his shoulders back. "The rest of the payment's at the rendezvous. I'll have some men deliver it as soon as the prisoners are secure." He opened his mouth to say more but then shut it firmly, spun on his heel, and strode out of the light.

Keio didn't have a lot of time to consider the strange exchange.

More men stepped into the circle of light and picked up the children. The Fire Fairy bonds were replaced with rough rope cords. Those who fought back were knocked out with swift strikes. Keio kept himself still as they hauled him up and loaded him into the back of a large wagon waiting just outside the light.

Keio's breath left in a hurry when something small slammed into him.

"Where have you been?" hissed Clara Mills. She tightened her grip around him, pinning his arms to his chest. Her neck craned back to look at him. "We have to get out of here!"

A sword clanged off the side of the cage, followed by a grumpy order for quiet.

Clara let go and drew Keio into the center of the crowd where they could talk. Small conversations buzzed around them. Keio stumbled, hampered by the ropes around his legs. Unlike the fairy bonds, which had kept his ankles locked together, the rope bonds allowed about six inches of movement at a time.

"How did you get free?" Keio demanded.

"They weren't that tight," Clara said with a shrug. Her voice, though quieter than before, still zipped out with her usual frantic pace. "I just slipped them off. Don't worry. I'll put them back on if we're still here later. But we shouldn't be here later. We need to get out. Now." Clara reinforced the sense of urgency by squeezing Keio's right hand painfully.

"Calm down," Keio ordered. He leaned toward her and resisted the urge to pull his hand free. "We're in trouble, but at least we're together."

Clara swatted his hand.

"Do something!" Her expression flickered between worry and hope.

Keio regarded his friend curiously.

"Why are you looking at me like that? I'm in the same cage you're in."

Clara clung to his hand but avoided his gaze.

"You know those weird dreams I get sometimes?"

Keio nodded.

"Well, last night I had one and it featured you," said Clara.

"Me? What about me?"

"You were in a large arena, and so was I. We were bound to large stakes." Her voice shook slightly as she delivered her report. "I was there, but I wasn't the focus. You were. If that's the future, Keio, we need to change it."

"Why? You want to be the center of attention?"

"Keio! Please. This is serious. I don't often get much of a sense for a dream, but I know this: if we enter that arena, everything will change forever." Finishing the report seemed to exhaust Clara. She shut her eyes to rest.

Keio pulled her close and let her fall asleep. Adjusting his position, he cradled his friend as best he could despite bound hands. She confused him. Although the same age as Keio, Clara often spoke with wisdom far beyond her years. Her Dream Gift had always fascinated him, even if the foresight often changed little about the future.

II. The Selection

Shortly after dawn, an increase in the murmurs told Keio their journey would soon end. A quick check confirmed the feeling that they neared their destination. He hadn't slept a wink, preferring to spend the time thinking. He nudged Clara awake.

"Put the ropes back on," he instructed. "We're almost ... wherever they're taking us."

Clara's eyes snapped wide. Quickly, she worked her feet back into the loops meant to restrain her and slipped her hands back into the bonds that would attach them to her waist. Whomever had tied her up had wanted to be thorough. The man hadn't counted on Clara being able to work her hands free.

Keio was glad his captor had gotten lazy or run out of rope. His wrists were raw from the coarse cords, but at least he could move them away from his body.

When they entered the city, Keio immediately felt the change as the wagon wheels left the rough dirt roads and slid onto a smooth path paved with bright red bricks. Chatter from a busy market reached him, along with the scent of freshly baked bread. Keio's stomach rumbled, reminding him he hadn't eaten in hours.

The city was alive, but the streets along their path remained strangely deserted, save for the stoic soldiers watching from the walls that separated the city sections. Occasionally, Keio would spot furtive movement near a window or catch a glimpse of a shade being pulled shut. Once a small child leaned out a window and stared down at them solemnly, waving a sad farewell to them. A woman wearing bright red silks pulled the child back.

Keio and Clara exchanged questioning glances. They worked their way to the edge to get a better look, but the move only gained them a closer look at the heavy brick walls they passed. They'd maneuvered to the back as well, and Keio caught sight of another horse-drawn wagon lumbering up behind them. Two men dressed like the man who'd spoken with the Fire Fairy rode horses in between the two prisoner transports.

Both wagons pulled into a large, beautiful courtyard that boasted a huge fountain in the center. The children pressed themselves against the cage bars and gaped at the watery spray bubbling up out of the fountain. Keio had never seen anything like it. His parched throat ached to taste the water. He couldn't take his eyes off the fountain, until the wagon finally turned around the right side of the massive dwelling, leaving it behind. Even then, it filled his mind's eye until an urgent tap from Clara refocused him.

He hadn't realized the wagon had come to rest before a dark, foreboding building. The prisoners were hustled out of the wagons and into the building. They went quietly, having spent their anger and tears somewhere on the long ride. Keio couldn't hold Clara's hand, but he made sure she walked in front of him so he could keep an eye on her. His head felt light from lack of food, but since that feeling was familiar to him, he paid it no mind.

Soldiers herded them inside and positioned them in two straight lines. Keio and Clara found themselves in the middle of the front row. As such, they had a perfect view as the prisoners from the other wagon marched in at sword point. Keio's heart sank when he saw his mother among the last to step through the doorway.

Where is Clara's father?

Keio wasn't sure whether to be glad to know Mr. Mills had avoided the roundup or worried about him.

The man who had spoken with the Fire Fairy stepped through the doorway and tugged on a rope next to the door. Large, heavy drapes drew back from massive banks of windows, flooding the room with light. The man then addressed the adults huddled in small groups near the door.

"Find your children," he ordered. When nobody moved, he added, "Any unclaimed child will be killed."

That got them moving.

Keio's mother practically smothered him. The same thing happened to every other child, except Clara. She stood next to Keio trembling but trying to remain brave.

Everybody held their breath.

Before the men could pull Clara out of line, Keio felt his friend slam into his side as his mother drew her close.

"She's mine," declared his mother. "They're both mine."

"Is this true?" the lead captor addressed the entire crowd.

Keio heard nothing and sensed no movement.

Finally, a man cleared his throat.

"Aye," said the man.

"How did the girl come to have such fair hair?" asked the lead soldier.

Keio grew very conscious of the dark color of his hair, which matched his mother's perfectly.

"She favors her father," Keio's mother answered. "My first husband died of a fever, and my second husband died by the sword."

He was suddenly grateful Clara looked a few years younger than him.

While the man considered whether or not she spoke truth, the door opened and every soldier stiffened.

The two men who would have killed Clara scrambled to the left side, saluted by bringing their right fists up to their left shoulders, and studied the ground.

The lead soldier stood taller.

The new man had a commanding presence, magnified by ornate, deep red robes. They looked heavy. Gold bands lined the collars and wove back and forth across the front, making the robe look like cracked glass.

"Captain Dominick, what is this rabble doing standing here?" The man's voice snapped the rebuke.

"Forgive me, Lord Ewald. There was some confusion over the lineage of one of the youths," Captain Dominick explained.

Lord Ewald waved the explanation away.

"Never mind. Summon more men. We'll do this here. Just be quick about it. My daughter will arrive soon, and I want nothing to disturb her. Do you understand?"

"Yes, my lord," Captain Dominick said. He turned to the man standing on his left and issued an order that echoed what Lord Ewald had just dictated.

"When Sarah enters, have them kneel, Captain. She will make her choices. Those can be properly stored. Take the rest to the market and fetch me the best price possible."

"As you say, so shall it be," the captain said, accepting the order.

Keio felt his mother's whole arm tremble as she drew him closer still.

"And move the adults off to the side and keep them quiet. I don't want Sarah distracted," said Lord Ewald.

The soldiers hurried to complete the order. Several cries rang out as parents were forced to release their grips upon their children. Keio's mother let go, but not before squeezing his hand reassuringly. She walked after the others before the soldiers could lay hands upon her.

Lord Ewald started pacing in front of the lines of children. "What could be taking so long? How long does it take to get dressed and answer a simple summons?"

As the questions weren't addressed to anyone, nobody answered.

Keio and the other children tried to stand still, but the tension made them fidgety. Every slight movement drew baleful glares from the guards.

At last, the door swung inward. A young soldier entered and held the door for a small figure. Keio hadn't known what to expect, but the delicate girl who swept gracefully in took him by surprise. He couldn't judge her age very well, but he guessed she might be a year or two older than him. The light blue gown hugged her body close, and the sheer cloak that accompanied it draped like fairy wings.

"You're late," groused Lord Ewald.

"I apologize, Father. My hair took longer than expected to fix. Please, forgive me." The girl glided up to Lord Ewald and placed a hand affectionately on his arm. Her light, lively voice fit her very well. The hair she spoke of indeed appeared to have taken some time to arrange. The long blonde tresses had been swept up, braided, and artfully pinned up around her head, leaving only select strands to hang down next to her face.

Keio liked her for no good reason. Not enjoying the reaction, he scowled.

Lord Ewald's features softened, but he cleared his throat and spoke gruffly. "Very well, but don't let it happen again." Lord Ewald turned to the captain and barked an order. "Get them kneeling!"

"That's not necessary, Father," said the girl.

Nevertheless, the soldiers scurried to do as bid. Somebody kicked Keio's right calf, causing his legs to buckle. Strong hands guided him down. He landed hard upon his knees with his bound hands resting in front of him. Frightened squeaks and muffled cries of pain rang out up and down the line.

Lord Ewald rubbed his hands together in anticipation. Then, he stepped behind the girl and placed large, ring-covered hands upon her shoulders.

"This is the moment. Choose wisely, my child."

Dipping her shoulders, the girl slipped free of her father's grasp and walked to the right side of the prisoners, off to Keio's left. She circled the whole group before starting around again, this time pausing in front of each captive. When she reached Keio, she stopped and knelt, looking him deep in the eyes.

He tried to look away, but her right hand reached out and briefly touched his chin. A spark of power from her hand set his teeth tingling. Her eyes widened, but otherwise, she didn't react. Standing, she moved on, stopping at several others. Finally, she completed one more circuit and returned to where she'd started.

"Have you made your choices about which ones might have magic in them?" Lord Ewald demanded impatiently.

"I have." Gesturing to Keio and Clara, she added, "That boy and girl have the Divine Touch upon them, but I do not know whether that means what you hope it means, Father."

"Excellent. Thank you, my dear. You may go now." Lord Ewald's tone made the suggestion an order.

"May I return and see them in private later?" asked the girl. "I might be able to gain more insight when we're alone."

Keio knew Lord Ewald wanted to deny the request, but her last statement convinced him.

"Keep your visit short," Lord Ewald said. "I'll have Captain Dominick arrange something for you." He looked pointedly at the captain. "Secure the ones she selected and find their parents. Clear the rest of this rabble out." He hesitated. "See if Lady Arvista wants any of them for the household staff before you take them to market."

Once again, Keio felt strong hands fall upon him. The children around him shrank away. He didn't know whether to be grateful the girl had chosen him or envious of those headed for the slave market. He watched helplessly as his mother was culled from the group of adults and whisked away. The terrified expression on Clara's face broke his heart too.

III. A Terrible Choice

Keio was locked in a small cage, with Clara in a similar situation on his right. He couldn't even stand up straight without hitting his head on the top, so he remained seated, leaning against the back bars in a doomed effort to find a comfortable position.

Clara spent a few minutes pushing and pulling at the bars before lying down on the cold, hard ground. She couldn't quite lie flat, but if she bent her knees, she fit quite nicely within the tiny space.

Keio took in the large room they'd been brought to. A row of ten cages lined both walls with a wide path between them. On the way here, Keio had been guided past a half-dozen doors spaced well away from each other. He assumed they too held twenty cages. He'd been disappointed to find that the other cages were empty. It would have been helpful to be able to question somebody more familiar with the place.

"Keio, I'm scared," said Clara. "Why did she pick us? What is the Divine Touch?"

One of the two guards standing outside their cages turned around and kicked the front of Clara's prison, causing both of them to flinch.

"No talking to each other!"

"Then, you tell us," Keio demanded. With considerable effort, he maneuvered so that his face came close to the front bars. "Who was that girl? What was she looking for?"

"I'm not tellin' you—"

"Don't torment them, Desmond," said the other guard. He spoke slowly but his quiet voice carried a ring of command. "If you upset them, Lady Sarah's going to know about it."

"I'm not afraid of that half-breed witch!" snapped Desmond. "She can—
"

The other guard's hand shot out and slammed into the first guard's throat, cutting off further words and sending the man straight to the ground.

"For your own sake, stop talking," suggested the calm guard.

Red-faced, the guard named Desmond slowly picked himself up and glared at the other man.

"Gentlemen, that will be enough," said Lady Sarah. She stood in the threshold with her hands neatly folded in front of her. A stony expression said she'd probably heard the entire exchange. "My father has granted me a short audience with the children bearing the Divine Touch. Kindly leave us and return in half an hour."

Mumbling acknowledgments, the guards quickly marched out.

As Lady Sarah stepped through, a servant girl came in on her heels carrying a tray holding bread, fruit, and cheese as well as two large mugs. Keio guessed the mugs held water, but at this point, he'd have drunk anything. Clara scrambled around until she sat in a position much like Keio's, nose pressed to the bars.

"Set the tray near the cages and leave us," instructed Lady Sarah.

The servant girl dipped in a curtsy and obeyed.

"Will there be anything else, mi'lady?" asked the girl.

Lady Sarah checked to see that the guards were out of hearing range before replying.

"No, thank you, Lexi. Please go watch the door. I do not trust them not to return early. After you've signaled their approach, you may have your midday meal. I apologize for making you wait so long."

"It's happy to help, I am." The girl's lilting accent lightened Keio's mood almost as much as the gentle exchange with Lady Sarah. Lexi curtsied again, deeper this time, then nodded at Keio and Clara before turning to leave the room. She shut the door behind her.

Lexi had placed the tray halfway between their cages but just out of reach.

Lady Sarah bent down and moved the tray close enough for them to touch.

Clara eyed the tray then looked to Keio for a decision. He tried to think, but the hunger was making that difficult.

"I am aware you do not trust me," said Lady Sarah. "Not that I blame you for that, but we haven't much time. If I prove the food is sound, will you listen to what I must say?"

Keio nodded, and Clara did the same, though with a bit more enthusiasm.

Picking up the loaf of bread, Lady Sarah broke it in half, ate a small piece from the middle, then handed a large chunk to each of them. Likewise, she proved that neither mug contained a poison before handing them over. Convinced, they tucked into the food eagerly. Despite her impatience, Lady

Sarah let them enjoy the food for several minutes before speaking. She passed these intervening moments by gazing out the room's single window. A skylight let in enough light to see by.

When the last of the food had been consumed, Keio and Clara thanked the lady for her kindness. Keio knew the food was meant to buy goodwill and it definitely worked.

"Why are you sad, Lady Sarah?"

Clara's question surprised Keio, but he hid it well, eager to hear the lady's answer. She'd been facing away from them for quite a while. The only sign of sadness was a dip in her shoulders. When she turned to face them, Keio saw the shine of unshed tears in her eyes. The lady attempted a smile, but the effort was dim at best.

"Because I have a terrible choice to make." Lady Sarah dashed away some tears and drew a deep breath to gain some composure. Blowing out the breath in one long whoosh, she continued, "And I need your help."

"With what?" Keio asked. He didn't bother hiding the suspicion flavoring his tone.

Lady Sarah gestured for patience.

"First, let me answer the question Clara voiced earlier," said the lady. She drew close, pulled back the empty tray, and sat in the cleared space. "I chose you because you have the Divine Touch. That means there's a good chance you're a shapeshifter. My father and I hope this is so, though for vastly different reasons."

"Why?" asked Clara.

"How do you know her name?" Keio inquired at the same time.

"I know both of your names, Keio," replied the lady. Her smile brightened for a moment. "It's part of the legacy of being a 'half-breed witch.'"

They gasped, but she waved away their shock.

"Of course, I heard the guard. Do not concern yourselves with my feelings. What he said was true in a way." Lady Sarah leaned closer and met both their eyes for a long second. "My mother is of the fair folk."

"The queen," Keio murmured, recalling the confrontation between Captain Dominick and the Fire Fairy.

"Yes, my mother is queen of the Serafin. The people of these lands call them Fire Fairies," Lady Sarah explained. "To her people, 'queen' is more than a title. It's a position of power. Until her death and the rise of a new queen, she's the only one who can make the skoni, which is simply called 'fairy dust.' It enhances a Serafin's powers."

Keio's mind made the appropriate connections. "That's how your father controls them."

Lady Sarah's expression turned troubled. "I do not know everything that transpired, but in the years before my birth, there was a war between the

Serafin and the Gantari. One of my mother's advisors betrayed her, allowing the Gantari king to capture her. That effectively ended the war because the traitor could not become the true queen while my mother yet lived. Instead, the Serafin as a whole were enslaved, but before this was truly known, my mother was gifted to my father for his service during the war."

"Why are you telling us this?" Clara asked, brushing away a tear.

"You need to understand why I'm asking you for help, and what I'm asking you to do," said Lady Sarah. "And the terrible choice I've made."

"How can we help?" Keio wondered.

"I believe the power I sense in both of you means you are shapeshifters, but I could be wrong. If so, then my plan is doomed."

"Why would it matter?" Clara inquired, narrowly beating Keio to the question.

"What's so important about shapeshifters?" Keio asked.

"My father hopes you're shapeshifters so he can gift you to the king and improve his status among the nobles, but I want you to escape with my mother." Lady Sarah forged on with her proposal, speaking faster by the second. "Freeing her will release the Fire Fairies from their obligations to my father and give the resistance a chance to grow."

"Why would you help the rebels?" Keio queried. He, of course, knew about the rebellion against King Agenor. It had been going on for his whole life. His father always claimed it was nothing more than malcontents making noise.

"Because I must!" Lady Sarah declared. She tugged at the sleeves of her ornate gown. "You may think this finery exempts me from suffering, but my mother's legacy ensures that I feel more than most. The slave markets are daily filled with a misery that's hard to define, and that is but one example of the wrongs that exist under this king. If I do nothing to counter my father's actions, my soul bears the stain of their blood."

Her passionate speech resonated with Keio.

"How can we help?" he asked.

"No chains can hold shapeshifters for long," said Lady Sarah. "In two days' time, King Agenor is due to visit. My father will want to impress him, so he'll likely bring you two to the arena and force your first change."

"How can he do that?" Clara wondered.

Lady Sarah winced and her expression turned troubled.

"Triggers for a first change differ for every person, but generally it involves either pain or distress," she explained. "Father will likely threaten Keio's mother. If I had more time, I might be able to teach you how to change early. After the first change, you should have the ability to shift at will, but I'm afraid we'll have to wait for my father's method to work. I'm sorry about that. If the power I sense in you speaks true, chances are good at least one of you will be able to fly. You must carry my mother back to her people.

She can show you the way."

"If she is of the fair folk, why hasn't she flown away already?" Keio asked.

Tears pooled in Sarah's eyes, but she held them back.

"She can't or won't. The first thing my father did before making her his wife was to clip her wings. Without her people, they've never healed properly. And even if she does manage such a healing, there's still me. She won't leave while I'm here. I'm only half fae. I may not ever grow wings."

"That's awful," said Clara.

"What will you do if we cannot shift or change into a form incapable of flight?" asked Keio.

This time the tears did fall.

"I don't want to think about that." Lady Sarah drew a shuddering breath and just barely kept from sobbing, though tears flowed freely now. "My mother has requested I still free her people, but I don't know if I can."

Keio followed the logic instantly.

Only two things could free the Fire Fairies from Lord Ewald's control: restoring their queen or destroying her.

IV. The Arena

Over the next two days, Keio and Clara spent many long hours in the cramped, uncomfortable cages, but they looked forward to each brief visit with Lady Sarah. During the half-hour sessions, she would let them out to stretch and eat. The guards were responsible for making sure they had regular reprieves, but Lady Sarah rightly didn't trust them.

When the three of them were alone, they spent most of the time talking through the plan details, trading stories, and discussing various prophecies. They found Lady Sarah intelligent and devoutly religious. She had many personal theories about the One's plans for delivering the kingdom from oppression. Planning was difficult without knowing what manner of creature—if any—they would shift into. The lady's Gift could only predict that their affinity for transformation magic would be strong, nothing more.

Mid-afternoon on the second day, their visit got cut short by a loud trumpet blast. Lady Sarah stiffened and hurried to the window.

Keio followed with Clara right by his side.

As they reached her, Lady Sarah whirled and caught both of their shoulders. Her normally pale features looked extra ghostly in the cheerful light streaming down from the skylight.

"Quickly. Into the cages," said Lady Sarah. "The guards will be back any moment."

Footsteps could already be heard in the hallway. Keio and Clara barely made it back inside before the door slammed open and an entire squad of soldiers rushed in. Lady Sarah stood with her back pressed against the cages to prevent the soldiers from seeing Keio and Clara's movements as they fumbled to snap the locks back into place.

"What is the meaning of this?" demanded Lady Sarah. Her voice sailed high with the question. "You frightened me half to death!"

"The king has arrived," announced Captain Dominick.

Keio couldn't see him through the fabric of Lady Sarah's maroon dress, but he recognized the voice.

"Lord Ewald sent me to fetch his prizes," continued the captain. "He also said you should return to your chambers to prepare for the reception."

Lady Sarah suddenly jerked forward.

"Let go of me!" she commanded. She sailed into a wall of five waiting soldiers.

Two grasped her elbows in a manner that both supported and restrained her.

"My men will escort you to your chambers now. It's for your safety, of course, Lady Sarah." The captain's voice dripped with false courtesy. "Appearances must be maintained for the king."

Now that Lady Sarah wasn't obstructing his view, Keio saw that Captain Dominick wore a fancy uniform with bright red pants and a shiny silver breastplate. His well-polished helmet had a long red-and-white-feather sticking out of it. The rest of the men wore dark blue uniforms. Only two others had silver breastplates. Keio figured they must be officers.

Struggling to free her arms, Lady Sarah tried to move forward.

The captain's next words stilled her.

"You may also wish to have a word with your mother. Lady Arvista's health has been unpredictable of late. She could take an ill turn at any moment."

Anger brought some color back into Lady Sarah's cheeks. Her chest heaved with suppressed rage and her hands formed fists. She gave the captain a tight, icy smile. Slipping free, she walked right up to the captain.

"Thank you for your concern, captain. It seems I have much to do today. I'd best hurry. Please, step aside."

Keio wanted to cheer.

Captain Dominick looked like he'd swallowed something foul, but he stepped out of her way and watched her exit. His orders to his men were short and gruff but unnecessary. They were already moving to unlock the cages and pull Keio and Clara free.

The first precious second where nothing hindered Keio caused his heart to leap with the sheer joy of being outside the hated cage. A group of soldiers whisked him away to a room three floors down where he was ordered into a large basin filled with warm water.

A large, kind woman barked orders from behind a privacy screen, making sure he cleaned behind his ears and scrubbed his hair until it gleamed. It was the longest, most thorough washing Keio had ever experienced. Once he was finished, the woman rubbed a cool salve on the remains of the rope burns.

Now clean and dry, Keio let the woman dress him in soft, brightly colored silks. The loose pants billowed around his legs. Likewise, the long golden sleeves hung loosely on his thin frame. A bright red belt was cinched tight at his waist. She showed him his image in a large mirror, confirming his suspicion that he must look like a kite.

Clara had been taken elsewhere, but Keio assumed she was receiving similar treatment. He could almost believe everything would be all right. Thoughts of Lady Sarah's plan seemed distant and unnecessary until the soldiers returned to escort him down to the reception hall. Keio listened as Captain Dominick delivered strict orders not to speak or do anything except endure inspection with a pleasant smile. Keio didn't feel much like smiling until he saw Clara. His friend looked like a princess. She wore a bright yellow dress, and her hair had been braided and pinned up around her head much as Lady Sarah's had been the first time they met her.

Together, Keio and Clara bore an hour's worth of being on display. They stood on a raised platform and nervously eyed the crowd. King Agenor and his advisors circled like birds of prey. They poked and prodded the children, discussing the finer points of their appearances. The women in the crowd held hushed discussions behind fancy handheld fans. At first, the attention was intriguing, but it quickly grew tedious. By the end, Keio wanted to rip off the fine silks and run screaming through the crowd.

Finally, at the end of forever, the king changed everything with a simple statement.

"I'll admit they're fine specimens, Lord Ewald. Let us see what, if anything, lies inside these creatures. If it's truly remarkable, I'll grant you three more towns and one city of your choice."

"That is most generous, my king," said Lord Ewald. "If they disappoint you, I will grant you use of my Fire Fairy army for a full year."

The men shook on the wager, setting off a few frantic minutes of bets being placed.

Keio's disgust grew every second he spent in these people's presence.

When each man seemed satisfied with his wager, soldiers took Keio and Clara away to separate destinations again. This time, no warm bath awaited Keio. Instead, the soldiers quickly stripped away the silks and replaced them with simple brown trousers and a white shirt. They fitted his wrists and ankles with metal cuffs that linked them together with a sturdy chain.

They brought him down to the back of the massive house where well-dressed people gathered in droves. Clara and her escorts were already waiting for them. She too wore simple clothes, though her shirt was a pale blue color that matched her eyes. Keio wished they hadn't bound her.

Both children were lifted up into yet another cage. This time, solid gold rods formed the bars. The soldiers secured their chains to two wooden poles with rusty metal rings coming out the top. The first bump as the wagon started moving almost knocked Keio and Clara off their feet. Clara sent Keio a nervous look. He wanted to reassure her, but he could barely maintain his balance as the wagon continued down the streets. Standing gave them an excellent view of the city as they wound through various sections, both rich and poor.

Grim-faced people lined the paths. From time to time, Keio saw someone reach up and place two fingers on their foreheads between their eyes. It took him a while to identify the gesture as a sad salute and a tribute to the doomed. He wondered why they showed up at all until he noticed the soldiers interspersed at regular intervals. Most of the population was captive in one form or another. The realization shattered the last of the good feelings left from the kind treatment they'd received in the afternoon. The kindness had almost convinced him this place could be the Golden City of his dreams. He still had little confidence in Lady Sarah's plan, but he admired her for the conviction to stand against her father.

They left the walls of the city behind and traveled the short distance to the arena, which sat next to the city like a large decorative egg. The arena looked big from the outside, but its imposing atmosphere was magnified once inside. The lack of a roof allowed the sun to bath everything in the center in broad beams. The spectator stands rose up the same to every side except the far right which held a magnificent viewing platform obviously meant for the important people.

A thick layer of fine, yellow sand covered everything in the middle, preventing the horse-drawn wagon from getting far. Keio and Clara were unloaded near two tall pillars and led inside by a proud escort of officers wearing shiny breastplates. Keio couldn't look into them without squinting, so he shut his eyes and allowed his legs to follow the soldiers' directions. His heart fluttered when he finally opened his eyes and noticed that his mother was already present. She had been tied to a pole threaded through large holes in a wooden platform positioned on the left side beneath the grandstand. A rope wrapped around her waist and a metal chain bound her hands above her head.

Keio wanted to transform right now, but he didn't know how. Lady Sarah had tried to prepare him for what might come, but the sight hit him hard anyway. He was led up the right side of a second wooden platform, facing his mother, and forced to kneel before a metal stake with a ring fixed on top. Soldiers secured the wrist chains to the metal stake then added a single, jeweled collar, which they fitted around Keio's neck. The spark of hatred blossomed into a raging flame when he heard a whimper from Clara.

Spear-toting soldiers surrounded them on three sides.

Keio tried to ignore his mother's plight but could think of little else. Straining against the collar, he looked at the grandstand holding the royal entourage.

"What's wrong with them?" Lord Ewald grumbled the question to Lady Sarah.

"The protective instincts have not yet asserted themselves, Father."

Her words pierced Keio's chest. Despite her warning, they still sounded like a betrayal. His gaze flew to the other platform where three soldiers lifted his mother's chin with the tips of their spears. The sharp blades opened shallow cuts at her throat. A fractional amount of pressure would kill her.

Desperation consumed Keio. A strange energy filled him, making him feel like his blood had suddenly caught fire. It wasn't exactly painful, though he wouldn't call it pleasant either. He spread his arms as wide as they would go and yanked back on the chain linking him to the metal stake. It rattled but stayed in place. Heat and pressure mounted inside him until he thought his skin would burst. He clenched his eyes shut and drew his fists in toward his chest in an effort to contain the sensation as it turned painful.

He screamed—at least he tried to. What came out was a powerful screech.

Keio didn't realize he was flying until he hovered six meters above the wooden platforms. The shock almost knocked him out of the air. He twisted his head this way and that, trying to see what he'd become. He couldn't see much, but his hands looked like an eagle's claws, his feet had the appearance of a lion's paws, and he caught flashes of a long, sleek tail with a tuft of fur at the very tip.

A collective gasp drew his attention downward. His vision had improved a hundredfold. He could see individual beads of sweat and tears that trickled down his mother's face. Enraged, he screeched again and dove at the soldiers still menacing his mother with their spears. At the last moment, they tried to turn the weapons on him, but Keio slammed into them with crushing force, flinging them off the platform in different directions.

"Griffin!"

The awed whisper reached Keio's ears as he caught his reflection in the armored breastplates of the soldiers. He felt lightheaded as a half-dozen eagle heads blinked back at him.

V. Breaking Free

The sight of his new form frightened Keio. Instinctively, he dug his claws into the wooden platform. The strong talons ripped into the soft wood. He wanted to free his mother, but he had no hands. He dared not touch her for fear of harming her. His body was too new to be trusted. Every time he tried to shout at the men to let her go, another screech split the dusty air. He fluttered his wings in frustration and scratched at the platform floor.

Shock kept everybody rooted in place for a while, but as it wore away, the soldiers picked up their spears and pointed them Keio's way.

"Fly, Keio!" Mother whispered. "Get away."

His vigorous head shake needed no interpretation.

Many people started speaking at once, but one voice rang out above the others.

"Submit or she dies!" roared Captain Dominick.

Keio's head whipped toward the platform he'd come from.

The captain stood behind Clara with one arm wrapped around her waist. The other held a sword across her neck.

"No, Keio!" Lady Sarah shouted. She leaned over the railing, gripping it hard. "Fly!"

Lord Ewald backhanded her, sending her crashing into two soldiers. They caught her arms and held tight.

"Hold her!" Lord Ewald snapped, even though they were already doing so.

"No, please!" begged Lady Ewald. She addressed her husband directly. "Leave her alone!"

Lord Ewald glared down at his wife.

"I don't know what she did, but I know she's responsible." Anger spiked inside Keio. He rose up four meters to get a better perspective.

Do you trust me? Lady Sarah's voice appeared within Keio's mind like one of his own thoughts.

He jerked his head negative.

Stick to the plan. He cannot kill her. I promise.

A small, frightened cry from Clara contradicted the thoughts.

"Capture that griffin!" ordered the king. "But do not kill him!"

The royal guards snapped to attention then moved to obey their king.

Forget me. Save my mother and escape. That's all that matters. Your friend will be fine.

Keio tilted his head and pierced Lady Sarah with a sharp look.

I cannot guarantee your mother's safety, but I will die protecting her.

"What will it be, griffin?" challenged Captain Dominick. "Who should die first?" The second question held a lot of mocking as well as scorn. He gestured with his sword.

Twisting his head around, Keio saw that the king's soldiers had made it to his mother. Their swords and spears leveled at the captive.

Every eye went to Keio, awaiting his decision.

If he surrendered, he might save some of them, but he would be condemning them to permanent captivity. In the span of a second, his eagle eyes took in each person. His mother's eyes were shut and her lips moved in silent prayers. She would tell him to escape. Clara looked frightened beyond words but resigned to her fate either way. He knew where Lady Sarah stood.

Reaching a decision, Keio released a primal war cry and dove for the grandstand. Soldiers and nobles alike scrambled backward as fast as they could. The wind from Keio's powerful wings flattened everybody in a short radius of his target, except Lady Ewald. She stood alone in the center with her arms held wide in welcome. As Keio landed next to her she delicately climbed up to a position just behind his head, tucking her knees between his shoulder blades.

"Do not fear. We will not abandon them," promised Lady Ewald. She spoke low so only Keio's keen ears could hear. "My people are coming."

With a cry of rage, Captain Dominick threw Clara against the wooden piece to which she was chained. Raising his sword high, he plunged it downward at her back. Keio screeched in helpless rage, expecting to see his friend pinned to the pole.

Instead, the sword rang as if the captain had struck solid stone.

Clara held tight to the pole. Tears streamed down her face. She blinked rapidly, and Keio saw the change in her eyes. The normally gentle blue orbs flipped to a brilliant gold color and the pupils lengthened into vertical slits. Next, her pale skin darkened and hardened. She screamed as the mass of her body increased a thousand fold instantly. The wooden platform creaked and cracked under the sudden weight. Clara's scream changed pitch, deepening into a roar that shook the entire arena.

The chains holding Clara snapped into multiple pieces and flew in random directions. One piece struck a soldier in the forehead, knocking him out. The wooden platform trembled then collapsed. Clara stood up, causing Captain Dominick to slide down off her back with a terrified scream. She stalked toward the soldiers on the other platform, but they scattered like ants from a kicked hill.

"Dragon!" The cry rose up from everywhere.

Men shouted and hurried to form battle lines, but without proper coordination, their efforts were paltry. The king and Lord Ewald each shouted directions, often contradicting each other.

A stream of fire sent the shaky lines scattering in disarray.

Keio trotted over to Lady Sarah who also climbed onto his back. The soldiers with her made no move to stop her. The sight of Clara's transformation into a blue-green dragon had stolen their bravado.

The sky darkened as the arena filled with small flying forms.

The crowd murmured restlessly, hunkered down to stay out of the confrontation.

"Let us go set your mother free," said Lady Sarah.

Keio flew to the platform holding his mother and knelt so Lady Sarah could dismount. As she had done with the locks to their cages, Lady Sarah conquered the latches with a simple touch. Once free of the ropes and chains, Keio's mother threw her arms around his feathered neck.

"We must hurry," said Lady Ewald. "The king's forces will regroup soon."

Keio suddenly realized they had a problem. He could carry Lady Sarah and Lady Ewald, but beyond that, he wouldn't be able to fly. He looked to Clara, thinking perhaps she might be able to help. She could certainly bear more weight than Keio. However, she appeared less confident about flying. There was no way for an inexperienced person to safely ride her.

Lady Sarah must have performed the same mental calculations, for she reached up and placed a hand on Keio's face.

"You must leave me," she whispered.

"No!" The protest came from Lady Sarah's mother, but Keio's heart echoed it.

"I alone stand the best chance of surviving what comes," said Lady Sarah. "Keio, carry our mothers on your back."

"My people can save you," declared Lady Ewald.

"They cannot save us both, mother," said Lady Sarah. "Now, go."

She spun around and ran toward the soldiers still harrying Clara. Some soldiers finally started shooting arrows.

Clara knocked an entire row of soldiers over with a sweep of her spiked tail. She then joined the battle in the sky, trading blows with the twin black dragons that had formed from the royal guards. Together, she and the Fire Fairies fought them to a draw.

Keio wanted to join the fight, but he couldn't do so and keep his mother and Lady Ewald safe. He did the next best thing and flew high above the arena. He adjusted his altitude when he saw that the battle for the sky moved quickly in his direction.

"All who seek freedom should flee now!" shouted Lady Sarah. "Follow the Fire Fairies!"

Many people fled as she suggested. Several others in the crowd jumped over the walls into the sandpit and grabbed weapons, forming a makeshift defensive line in front of Lady Sarah.

A twin line of Fire Fairies formed and blinked in quick succession, one right after the other, literally lighting the road to freedom. Lady Sarah kept busy directing the stream of refugees into that flow.

Keio saw movement behind Lady Sarah. He screeched a warning, but it got lost in all the activity.

"Save my daughter," ordered Lady Ewald.

Keio prepared to dive, but a stream of Fire Fairies fell from the sky.

"Kill the rebel!" cried the king.

The figure of a royal guard appeared behind Lady Sarah and paused, before plunging a small dagger into the girl's side. She cried out and fell forward into a surprised Captain Dominick's arms. The crowd of refugees closed ranks around them, sweeping Lady Sarah up and carrying her on their shoulders. A blazing wall of Fire Fairies formed behind the refugees.

"Stand down!" ordered Lord Ewald. "Let them leave!" The man had fallen to his knees when he saw his daughter fall, but now he struggled to stand.

"Kill them!" King Agenor shouted.

"Defend them!" countered Lord Ewald. "You will not further harm my daughter, sir!"

"This is treason, Ewald!"

The men glared at each other. The two factions of soldiers formed uneasy battle lines, eyeing their commanders nervously.

"So be it," hissed Lord Ewald. "The City of Oswald officially secedes. We can finish this now or later. The choice is yours."

"You will regret this!" cried the king. With that, his two black dragons dove from the sky to retrieve him.

"We must go. There's still too much danger here, and Sarah's time is short. Only the full efforts of my people's healers can help my daughter now. I will show you the way," said Lady Ewald. Her voice was heavy with grief.

Somehow Keio knew the battle would go ill for Lord Ewald's forces if he fled. For a moment, he hovered, caught in currents of indecision. Everybody would tell him to follow the plan and go, but if he left, King Agenor would escape and return with a larger force. More people would suffer. Then again, if they didn't leave soon, Lady Sarah could die.

She could perish either way.

Screeching frantically to Clara, Keio dove for the ground aiming for the area behind Lord Ewald's forces. Thankfully, their long friendship superseded words. Clara positioned herself above Keio protectively, while he gently dropped off his charges.

"You be careful," his mother warned as she slid off his back and drew Lady Ewald with her.

A single, powerful bound brought Keio into the exact center of the arena. He sent out a screeching challenge that brought sudden silence to the remaining crowd. Those looking to flee paused. The men holding Lady Sarah stopped moving and arranged themselves into a tighter protective ring around her.

Seeing Keio return, the king ordered his dragons to dive into the arena.

"Do you mean to challenge me, boy?" demanded the king.

Calming his heart, Keio willed his body to transform back into his human body. The crowd gasped. Clara bellowed in frustration. He wasn't sure he could turn back into a griffin at will, but he trusted Lady Sarah's word that he would.

"I do," he answered formally. Keio knew the legend on every heart and mind as well as anybody. A captive from the Golden City would set the kingdom free. Confidence surged through him. It was like Lady Sarah's spirit joined with his, willing him to speak. "Reveal your true nature!"

The king leapt down a few feet from Keio, flanked by his two black dragons who transformed into hulking men simultaneously. He laughed and leapt forward suddenly, knocking Keio back with a firm push.

Keio just barely kept his feet.

A dagger appeared in the king's hand.

"I owe you nothing, boy, but your insolence has earned you death," said the king.

As King Agenor swung with the dagger, Keio ducked and initiated the change. The blade swished over head as his sharp beak tore into the king's ankle. The man's pained scream quickly changed pitch as he transformed into a large, powerful snake and wrapped tightly around Keio's feathered neck.

The snake's bulk and sudden movement nearly snapped Keio's neck, but he tucked his powerful legs beneath himself and tore into the snake with his talons. For a wild minute, they tumbled, kicking up a cloud of dust. His talons kept it at bay, but it had a firm grip around his neck. At last, Keio shook himself loose from the snake.

Suddenly, the snake went limp, slid to the ground, and transformed back into a man. He lay on his back as if asleep.

Keio had no idea what had just happened.

One of the large black men stepped forward, knelt, and laid a bloody dagger at Keio's feet.

"You have shown him for what he is and given us courage to seize our freedom. If you will allow it, I am at your service."

"I too will serve you, griffin," said the other soldier.

Keio started to shake his head, but Lady Sarah's voice once again appeared in his mind, though not as strong as before.

Clara's dream foretold this, Keio. If you do not accept this burden, a civil war will consume this land. Right the wrongs. Preserve the future. Become king and they will follow you. Go to my father. He can help.

Heart pounding, Keio flew into the sky, completed a quick lap around the arena, and gently touched down in front of Lord Ewald who had climbed onto the remaining platform.

The man looked ashen.

"I never thought I'd see this day." His voice started out hesitant and got stronger as he continued. Since everybody else hardly dared to breathe, they heard every word. "King Agenor died without an heir. As First Lord, I must take up his banner or choose a successor. Far be it for me to argue with prophecy, but you have my service as an advisor should you wish it. I'm sure my daughter will say the same."

As one, the huge crowd around the arena dropped to their knees.

Terrified, Keio looked to Clara.

Still in dragon form, she blew a blast of fire in salute to the new king.

When not teaching high school chemistry, Julie C. Gilbert writes Young Adult scifi stories about genetically altered children, Christian mysteries featuring FBI agents, and mystery/thrillers that typically fall in the Lei Crime Kindle World. In other news, she builds Legos, waits for the next Star Wars movie, and drinks crazy amounts of tea.

http://www.juliecgilbert.com/
https://www.facebook.com/JulieCGilbert2013

Seekers

Ever since I can remember, Ma and I used to play hide-and-seek while Da was out fishing. It wasn't the sort of hide-and-seek I learned to play in school later on, where everyone hides and one person seeks. No, with Ma, we were both seekers, and what we sought had already been hidden.

"Let's seek for gloves today," she would say after breakfast. "If I were a little glove that a brownie had hidden away, where would I be?" And we would be off, searching every nook and cranny, every dusty corner, the places behind drawers where papers are lost, even lifting off the grates from the heating ducts. And the trick, of course, was never to leave a clue for the brownie to know you had been searching. Every wrinkle in your sheet had to be returned just so, every side table had to be put back exactly where it had been, and every curling piece of wall paper had to be glued back down.

At first, we just sought for things at home, little things that we might really have lost. Then, as I got older, we would go to Da's workshop, just up from the dock where he kept his boat, and while we waited for him to come home, we would seek in his workshop.

"You've got good sharp eyes, Maggie," Ma would say, "but even if you close your eyes, you can seek. Try it." And I would. I would close my eyes and take a deep breath, smelling the myriad scents of the workshop with its greasy machine parts and corners of dry bread, its salt-stiff nets and bits of leather rubbed dark with use. I could feel a faint draft on my cheeks, the damp kiss of sea air. I could even taste the salt and fish on my lips and on the tip of my tongue.

"Maybe by the door," I would say when I as small. And then, as I got older, "Maybe in the corner behind the workbench." And Ma and I would go and look, studying the wall beside the door, tracing our hands over the wood as if we might find a secret compartment, or pulling back the workbench to study the corner, the cabinets bolted to the floor—was there too much space there? Space that hadn't been accounted for? We were always done seeking by the time Da arrived, sitting together on the bench and chatting, or standing outside on the dock, waving to him as he directed his boat in.

When I was five, we found what we were seeking. I didn't know it, of course. We had found so many other things along the way. In the public gardens we had found lost dog collars and a red scarf and glass bottles of all different colors and sizes and once a wedding ring that Ma took in to the police and that they returned after two months. Ma gave it to me and I kept it in the little wooden box on my dresser with my favorite seashell and a blue glass bead we found at the zoo. We found shiny coins and broken dolls, shredded blankets and old library books, which Ma always took back to the library as well. And so it wasn't all that strange to me that, when we found the old, moth-eaten cloak smooth as skin, Ma called off our seeking for the day.

We found it, of all places, in the little alley behind Da's friend Alec's house. Uncle Alec kept a workshop in the alley, as he was a carpenter and not a fisherman, and in the course of our seeking, we slipped into his workshop. We had seen him walking to the pub, so we knew we were in the clear for an hour. Ma and I giggled as we slipped inside.

"Now, Maggie, close your eyes and feel for it. If you were a hidden treasure, where would you be?"

I closed my eyes and let the workshop seep into me, and when I opened my eyes I was already pointing to the far wall with its cabinets and racks of tools. "I'd be in the center cabinet," I said. "Maybe hidden in a false bottom."

Once we lifted the tools out, taking careful note of how we would have to set each one back, Ma let me run my hands over the bottom of the cabinet until I found the edge with my fingers. We lifted it up carefully, and there it was: the moth-eaten ragged old cloak that made me think of water-creatures, otters and seals and the like. It was neither fur nor cloth, soft and pliant as my mother's skin, if much darker. And it wasn't a cloak really, so much as a half-cloak, for it wasn't that big at all.

"Oh," Ma said softly. And then, with a little edge to her voice, "It looks like Alec's been stealing. Someone must be missing this." She stood up and began to fold it. "Perhaps we should leave it with the police."

Ma was always right about taking things to the police. Together, we put everything else back as we'd found it, but by the time we left the workshop it was very nearly nap time, so we went home instead of to the police and Ma tucked me in bed. Then she went and put on her little pink-and-white polka dot kerchief to keep her dark hair from flying about, and she wrapped her old green shawl around her shoulders. She came back to my room with her market basket over her arm. I could see the basket was heavy, but Ma explained that directly.

"I've got to take some food over to Aunt Kate's house," she said. "I should have thought of it earlier when we were there."

"What for?" I asked sleepily.

"It's very sad," she said gently, coming in to sit beside me. "Someone Aunt Kate loves has died."

"Oh," I said, turning on my back to look at Ma. In the half-light, with her polka dot kerchief and her bottle-green shawl, with her face slim and pretty and her eyes wide and sad, she was the most beautiful person I had ever seen. "Will she be okay?"

"Yes," Ma said at once. "She hasn't lost a part of herself. That's much harder."

I nodded.

"I'm going to let Mrs. O'Malley know you're asleep, so when you wake up you can just go see her."

"Okay," I said.

She squeezed my hand, then bent over to kiss me on the cheek. She whispered something in my ear which I didn't quite hear, not until the apartment door clicked shut and my mother was already gone, walking smartly down the street toward Aunt Kate and Uncle Alec's house and the little workshop in the alley out back. *Come and visit me one day.* And then, because it was nap time, I closed my eyes, rolled over, and drifted off to a sleep.

I dreamed that Ma and I sought for shells on the rocky beaches, but when I found one and held it to my ear I could not hear the sea, though its waves washed at my feet.

Da came home late that night, his face white and his clothes sweaty and smelling of smoke.

"Where's your Ma?" he asked as I came out of my room. I had not gone up to Mrs. O'Malley's flat, even though I knew she would have cookies and lemonade for me, and a little white dog to play with. Instead I waited in my room after I woke up and played with my seashell from the wooden box on my dresser, though I was afraid to hold it to my ear.

"She went out," I said, inexplicably certain that I did not want to tell him anymore than that.

"Where?"

I shrugged.

He collapsed into a chair, staring blankly at the wall. "She's gone?"

"What happened, Da?" I asked, because I did not know how to answer him.

"Alec's dead." Da rubbed his face, smearing his cheeks with black stuff. "There was a fire in his workshop while he was in there. He couldn't get out." He took a gasping breath and then looked at me. "I shouldn't have told you that."

"Aunt Kate," I said, thinking of Ma.

"She's okay—well, as okay as a woman can be with a little one on the way and her husband dead. It was the strangest thing. Someone had just left some food on their doorstep when the fire broke out. She kept going on about it as if it had been an omen. Just some bloody bread and jam and fruits. Probably some friend of hers stopped by and she didn't hear their knock." Da shook his head. "Get me a beer, would you, Maggie?"

I came back in with the bottle and perched on a chair to watch him. He flicked off the cap using the edge of the side table and we both watched as it spun a small arc to the floor. "Where'd you say your Ma was?"

I shake my head. "She was going out somewhere. She told Mrs. O'Malley."

Da relaxed at that, took a swig from the bottle. "Why are you up so late?"

"I was waiting for you."

"Good girl," he said, reaching over to muss my hair. "Get to sleep, now. I'm going to finish this beer and then go check with Mrs. O'Malley, just make sure your Ma's okay."

And so I went to bed, even though I knew that when I woke up in the morning, Ma would not be back, would never be back, just as Aunt Kate would never get her husband back. Da cried for a week after that, stayed home and drank and wept like a child, except that I was a child and I didn't cry at all. I brought him water and hid when he threw things or yelled for more beer, and made myself sandwiches, and visited Mrs. O'Malley for cookies and lemonade and food as well.

Mrs. O'Malley told me about how the police and the Coast Guard were searching for Ma, and how she was sure that they would find her and bring her back, but I'd seen the news when Da was too slow or drunk to change the channel when I came into the room. I knew what the reporters said: that they'd found her basket with all her clothes out on the north shore, and her footprints leading down to the water, and that was all.

A year later, when I was in school and learning how other children played hide-and-seek, Da married Aunt Kate and she came to live in our flat with my new little brother. Aunt Kate, I found, didn't understand about seeking, and after asking her once in a round-about side-of-your-eye sort of way, I didn't ask again. But I didn't forget, and sometimes when I went out to play I would slip away from the other children and seek. Mostly, I wanted to remember how seeking worked, and I wanted to open my eyes and find Ma watching me, her brown eyes bright and sparkling as she waited for me to direct our search. But she was never there when I opened my eyes, and it wasn't quite so fun then to find the lost watches, lonely earrings, and forgotten pens.

At the end of the year, my class went to the beach for a picnic. We had buddies, and mine was Gracie, who was thin and pretty and absolutely wretched. She wore dresses and bows in her hair and the teachers cooed over her, and I suspected that they gave her sweets when the other children weren't around. Soon enough, she decided she didn't want to be my buddy and went off to play with her two other friends who had been buddied up together.

I found a seashell and lifted it up to my ear, a little worried, and for a moment, I heard nothing at all, not even the laughter of the children getting their feet wet in the puddles left by the tide as it pulled it out, and then, sure as my heartbeat, I heard my mother's voice. *Come and visit me.*

I followed the pull of her voice the way I found hidden things, closing my eyes and listening deep down inside, tasting the sea salt air and listening to the shouting of the gulls. Then I walked the length of the shore, threaded my way over the far dunes, and followed the rocky path down past the cliffs to the little grotto, sliding down the loose shale to the wide stones where the seals sun themselves.

Ma waited for me in the water beside the rocks, her bare shoulders pale in the afternoon. I'd never seen her shoulders before. They seemed much lighter than I thought they would be, but then even her face was paler. She smiled, and called my name quietly, her voice the sound of the waves washing against the rocks. I hurried across the rocks to her. When I reached her, I realized she held the old skin cloak against her front. It was no longer the shabby thing I remembered but soft and shining and pearled with water.

"Hallo, Maggie," Ma said again.

"Hallo, Ma."

"I missed you."

"I missed you, too." We looked at each other a long while, then Ma looked out across the water.

"How's your Da?"

"He married Aunt Kate."

She nodded thoughtfully. "You doing okay?"

I shrugged. She watched me, her eyes sad. "Did you ever want to meet your other Grammy?"

"Your ma?" I asked. She nodded. "I'd like that."

"Come swim with me," she said, reaching a hand out to me. Her fingers were as long and slender and lovely as I recalled. If I reached out my hand I could just touch her fingertips. She took a step closer, so that her cloak brushed the gray stone, and her fingers closed gently around mine, steadying me.

"Will we be gone long?"

"As long as you like."

"Okay."

She smiled and then let go of my hand to lift something out of the water: a little tiny cloak much like hers. "Change into this first."

I left my clothes in a pile on the rocks, though Ma made me fold them up nice and put a small stone on them so they wouldn't fly away. Then she helped me put the cloak on, which actually fit quite well, wrapping me up cozy and warm so I hardly got wet when I slid into the water next to her. And then we swam, Ma wearing her cloak, dark as a sea creature and swift as the wind, and me in mine just beside her. We raced through the shallows, darting between the fish, and arcing up for breaths of air, and then headed out together into the deeper waters, leaving behind Gracie and the kindergarten class, and the old dock with my father's fishing boat he hardly used any more, and the seashell and the wedding ring and the blue glass bead all in the little wooden box on my dresser, and my new little brother and my new mother and my old Da with his beer-sad eyes and his new job in a factory, and my little pile of clothes folded just so for the coast guard to find.

Intisar Khanani grew up a nomad and world traveler. Born in Wisconsin, she has lived in five different states as well as on the coast of the Red Sea. She first remembers seeing snow on a wintry street in Zurich, Switzerland, and vaguely recollects having breakfast with the orangutans at the Singapore Zoo when she was five.

Intisar currently resides in Cincinnati, Ohio, with her husband and two young daughters. Until recently, she wrote grants and developed projects to address community health and infant mortality with the Cincinnati Health Department—which was as close as she could get to saving the world. Now she focuses her time on her two passions: raising her family and writing fantasy.

Intisar's latest projects include a companion trilogy to her debut novel *Thorn*, featuring Rae, the heroine introduced in her free short story, "The Bone Knife," and *The Sunbolt Chronicles*, featuring a young thief with a propensity to play hero when people need saving, and her nemesis, the dark mage intent on taking over The Eleven Kingdoms.

http://booksbyintisar.com

http://facebook.com/booksbyintisar

Mystery of Asgina Lake

Officer Randell stood next to the covered body, puzzled by the red marks that twisted around the exposed wrist. Unlike rope burns, this wound had small circular marks as well as a smooth red line that ran up the arm to the elbow. Like something had latched on, refusing to let go. The burning Alabama sun scorched him. Randell scratched his temple while reviewing the case notes from the first responder.

"Hi, Dad. Is this one of the missing fishermen?"

Randell glanced over his shoulder and grimaced. His teenage daughter Ella strode to his side. He sighed. If Ella was here, her twin sister Lena wouldn't be far behind. He searched the scene. There she was, talking to the medical examiner. "Yes, this is Tony Rivers." He pointed at the victim with his ball point pen. "What are you two doing here?"

"We were bored at Aunt Ellen's. We heard a body washed up, thought you might want some company." Ella handed a fresh cup of hot coffee to her father, and then she canvassed the area surrounding the body.

Lena drifted over and bent over the body for a better view. Both fraternal twins had inherited their mother's tall frame and cream-colored skin with a smattering of bronze freckles across the bridge of their button noses and icy blue eyes. The hair was the kicker. Ella was blessed with his thick chestnut-brown hair which she kept braided down her back. Lena wasn't that lucky. She kept her hair hidden beneath a black knitted beanie that bulged from the mass it contained. One blond wisp gave the color away.

"The M.E. says he probably drowned." Lena used a stick to point to the red marks. "Do you think he was held underwater? These marks are unusual."

Randell pressed his lips together. His eyes narrowed at the twins. When his wife died two years after they were born, his strange work hours, mixed with the unusual demands of a small town cop, made raising the girls alone problematic. At the moment, he regretted allowing them so much time on the job with him. "Go home."

"Come on, Dad. We're bored. There's nothing to do at Aunt Ellen's. She had us washing her mama's china," Ella said standing with her hands on her narrow hips. "At this rate, *this* summer will be as boring as the past three."

"She won't trust us to eat off her china, but she made us wash it. Our summer essay is going to reek of binge watching *S.H.I.E.L.D.* and reading comics. Again." Lena paused before adding, "Do you think he was murdered?"

"No. Now, go home." They were starting to circle, like fire ants. If he didn't contain them soon, the twins would make this their summer project. He grabbed each of the girls by the shoulder and pulled them away from the body, only releasing them when they reached the yellow crime scene tape at the edge of the parking lot. He dug into his pocket, retrieved several small bills, and thrust them into Lena's hand. "Here, go to the diner. Eat some ice cream."

"Ice cream? What are we, five?" Lena asked.

"I wish. Then I could put you over my knee and spank you." He turned to another officer. "Joe," he yelled, "do not let these two back into the crime scene. They're not allowed any information. Do you understand?"

Lena rolled her eyes and Ella huffed while shaking her head in frustration before saying, "We're not kids, Dad. We can help."

"Don't." He pointed a finger at each of them. "You *are* children. Fifteen-year-old kids. And I plan on you staying young. You don't need to know about these things. This isn't one of your *Nancy Drew* books. This is a real dead body. Now, I have to go to Mr. Tony's house to tell his family that he's never coming home." He took a calming breath while looking into the tender faces of his offspring. "Go home. Stay out of it. Be kids."

Ella narrowed her eyes and grumbled, "David Baldacci books! I haven't read *Nancy Drew* since third grade."

Randell's eyes swelled to the size of cathead biscuits, and his faced reddened as he took a step closer.

Lena took Ella's hand. "We're sorry, Dad. We promise not to bother the crime scene again."

The pair walked the half-mile to The Silver Car Diner. The gleaming stainless steel car shone in the sunlight. Passersby squinted from the reflection. The car was bought at auction and then brought back to Asgina Lake. It was a silver Easter egg in a field of boring rocks.

A bell jingled when Ella opened the door. "Rats! All the barstools are taken." She wrinkled her nose. "I guess we'll have to take a booth."

Mabel, an older woman with short gray hair and an apron to match, approached them. "Good afternoon. Now, Lena, I know your daddy tried to teach you good manners. Take that hat off inside."

Lena's eyes bulged.

"Go on now. It's bad manners to wear a hat inside."

The girls exchanged wide-eyed looks. Lena never took her knitted beanie off in public. They tried to eat at the diner when Lula worked. She was kind and gave the twins extra scoops of ice cream.

"Yes, ma'am." She reached her hand up, tugging the beanie from her head. As it inched off, kinky blond curls escaped and encircled her head like a manic halo.

"Wow. That's unfortunate," Mabel said. "You know you might want to put a little oil on that mess to calm it down." She turned to Ella. "Follow me." She led them to a booth in the center of the car, handed them menus, then disappeared.

"I am so sorry, Lena. She's way out of line," Ella said. "Don't listen to Mad Mabel. She's bald as a pig under that wig."

Lena inhaled deeply and swished a stray curl out of her eyes. "Let's just order." She poured water from her glass into the palm of her hand, using it to smooth out her hair enough to pull it back into a ponytail with a holder she kept on her wrist.

They ordered two bowls of ice cream before scanning the other patrons. Most were retirees with nothing better to do than drink coffee and gossip.

A raisin-like elderly man sat on a bar stool nursing a cup of coffee. The newspaper spread out before him read, *Another Fisherman Missing, Total Now 10.*

The young man next to him said, "I'm telling you there is something in the lake. I went fishing yesterday and saw this huge shadow in the water." He held his arms far apart for emphasis.

"It's just a school of fish," the old man said.

"It wasn't a school of fish," retorted the young one.

The diner grew silent as they listened to his tale. He described the cloud swimming toward him, bumping his boat, then swimming off, only to return and erupt in a furious swirl of rocking waves.

"I had to crank up the motor and leave before I capsized," the young man finished.

Grumbles of doubt spread like melted butter as questions from patrons were tossed about.

A sharp voice rose above the ruckus. "Stay out of the lake or die."

Heads snapped to the back corner where an old lady sat in a booth. Lena squinted at her but didn't recognize the figure. The lady's long, straight, silver hair sat in contrast to her wrinkly, dark skin. She wore silver bangles up to her elbows, and large silver earrings hung from her drooping earlobes. She lit a corn cob pipe, inhaled, and ignored the stunned silence that swept through the diner.

"Ma'am, this is a non-smoking diner," Mabel said sternly, placing hands on her ample hips.

The lady blew a curly ribbon of silver-blue smoke. Eyes darted from the woman to Mabel and back again. No one moved. Tension swelled as the two stared at each other.

Mabel cleared her throat. "I said, *No. Smoking.*"

The stranger blew another ribbon of smoke. "Humph. Tell the police to close the lake permanently."

Mabel muttered, "Crazy woman," and stomped off to refill the coffee cups of patrons pretending not to watch the standoff.

The twins exchanged looks. Beneath the heavy scent of tobacco, they could smell a secret. They dropped their fudge covered spoons to the table, slid out of the booth, and walked over to the old woman.

Lena pushed Ella forward.

"Ma'am?" Ella's voice quivered. She grabbed her sister's hand. "We were wondering what you meant about the lake." She took a step backward. No one ever defied Mabel. Yet, this woman did. They felt a sense of awe wrapped in a layer of fear.

The lady's sharp black eyes surveyed the twins. "How old are you?" She took a puff on her pipe.

"Old enough." Lena straightened her shoulders in false courage. "What's your name?"

The old woman grinned, revealing several missing front teeth. "Eudora. What do you care about the lake?"

Lena edged closer jutting out her jaw. "It's summer. We like to swim in the lake."

Eudora leaned forward to examine the pair closely. "Y'all don't look like swimmers to me. More like indoor girls." She chewed the end of her pipe. "Fine, I'll tell you. The police won't find anything because they don't know where to look. Do you know what Asgina means?"

They shook their heads.

"It means ghost. Ghost Lake. Years ago, before the whites moved in, this area was home to a large Chickasaw settlement. A great center of trade. The hunting and fishing were abundant." She paused for a smoke. "Until the ghost fish came and killed many strong warriors."

One corner of Lena's mouth cocked in doubt. "Hold on a minute. If a creature like that was in the lake, we would have known about it by now."

Eudora shook her head and wagged a bony finger at Lena. "What, you only believe what's on TV?" She rolled her eyes before continuing. "Legend says the ghost fish only emerge when the lake god is angry."

"Lake god!" The twins exchanged a look of disbelief.

"Just wait. They will kill again. Stay out of the lake."

The girls returned to their booth and settled in, periodically glancing back at Eudora. Ella removed a crumpled map from her pocket. She smoothed it flat with the palms of her hands. "Dad has the beach blocked off here. The western edge is too muddy. We'd never make it past the bog." She drew her finger to the northern edge of the lake. "I think we should try crossing here."

"What are you talking about?" Lena asked.

A wide grin spread across Ella's face. "Ghost fish. It's brilliant. If we hike to where the fishermen disappeared, we can find them ... the ghost fish not the fishermen. That'd be gross."

Lena rolled her eyes. "It would be helpful if we knew where the fishermen disappeared." She took a bite of melted chocolate fudge ripple with bacon before continuing, "What do you hope to find?"

"Think about it." Ella's pale blue eyes sparkled. "If we can find these ghost fish and take a picture of them, maybe we can get on one of those cable shows. That would be so cool."

Lena sighed, "Or we could just sound like idiots. We don't even know if it's one fish or a slew. Besides, no one can prove Nessy is real. *Annnnnd* people are still fighting about that hairy guy up north. What makes you think we can prove there's a monster in Asgina Lake?"

"Have a little faith, sis. Something's out there. You heard that guy at the counter." She pointed toward the fisherman still talking. "Why else would all those men drown?"

"Beer," Lena said flatly. She crossed her thin arms over her Doctor Who T-shirt.

Ella screwed up her face before responding, "Granted, beer may have something to do with the situation, but it doesn't explain the red marks on Mr. Tony's wrist."

"It does if he was murdered."

Ella slapped her hands together. "Exactly. If that's the case, Dad will solve the murder. If not the case, it's up to us. The added bonus is that the adventure will give you something to write about for the summer essay you're so worried about."

Lena scratched her head. An errant curl broke free and gave the illusion of a golden question mark above her head. "Fine. I'll give you one night. If we don't find the monster by dawn, that's it. Let's be clear, I'm only going to keep you out of trouble and for the possibility of having a good story for school."

"Deal."

At home, Lena grabbed her backpack then added her hiking essentials: extra socks, binoculars, and bug spray. Along with firecrackers. Lena loved the thumb-sized M-90 firecrackers and never went camping without them. They were perfect noise makers to keep bears away.

"I borrowed Aunt Ellen's phone," Ella said as she walked in, dropping her pack onto the bed.

"You're diggin' us in deeper, sis. When Dad finds out you stole Aunt Ellen's phone, we'll be grounded forever."

"Borrowed," Ella repeated. She wiggled the phone in the air for emphasis. "If Dad would get with the times and buy us phones I wouldn't have to *borrow* Aunt Ellen's. I packed a lighter, water, and food. You ready?"

Lena zipped her bag closed before slipping it on to her back. "Let's go."

They cut across the high school practice field and into the woods. The sun still sat high in the sky; nightfall would be hours away. Lena listened to music from her iPod, bobbing her head in time. Ella tracked their progress on her map, making little tick marks for every mile they passed. When they reached the small gas station on the edge of town, the thick woods beyond were unknown territory.

Ella looked at the dense pine woods then back at her map. "According to this, if we head south we should hit the lake. There's a cabin with a pier along the northern edge."

"Cabin?" Lena took the map and scanned it. "You mean we have to walk past the Indian mounds? You didn't tell me that." Her voice rose to a shrill pitch.

"I was afraid you'd chicken out."

Lena dropped her gaze, kicked some rocks, and grumbled, "Hand me Auntie's phone."

Ella dug the phone from her pocket before handing it over to her sister.

Lena tapped on the screen then held it for Ella to see. "Now, we have a compass. I've also downloaded a GPS app that should tell us when we get off track. Hopefully, it's smart enough to direct us to the lake. Let's go before I change my mind."

"Wait." Ella took a moment to spray them both down with bug repellent. "I don't want Zika Virus."

Lena coughed as the chemical mist attacked her senses. She waved a hand in front of her face to clear the air. "That smell will keep your monster away."

They followed a winding path through the thick pine forest. The deeper they went, the darker it got. The ground morphed from lush green grass to prickly weeds in sand. Tiny sand spurs clung to their socks like pom-poms.

Small saw palmettos fanned the space between the pines.

The deer trail opened into a small clearing with a squat mound. It looked like a giant had slapped a pyramid's point and squashed it flat. A small path ran along the bottom edge. Tall moss-covered oaks hung over the area. Sunlight fought to reach the ground. Deep shadows clung to the mound, adding a haunted feeling. The retreating sun bathed the area in a gentle golden light. Ella and Lena slowed and watched from the corner of their eyes. The mound stood three tiers tall and finished with a small, fat square at the top. Kudzu vines worked hard to cover the area, but enough space let them see the stairs leading to the top.

The twins skirted the edge of the clearing, giving the structure a wide berth.

Most people believed the mound was haunted and stayed away. Ella stopped, gazing at the looming mass of grass-covered clay in front of her. A large crow landed on the lower ledge. He pecked at the surface and squawked as he stretched his black-satin wings. Ella turned, inching toward the mound.

"Ella," Lena's voice squeaked as she whispered. "Ella, what are you doing? We need to stay on the trail." Her gaze darted around the shadows. A toad croaked. She jumped and ran to her sister, grabbing her arm.

"Just wait a second. I want to get a better look." Ella bent down, picked up a pebble, and tossed it at the bird.

Cawwwwa! He squawked before flying away.

"What's to see? It's a pile of dirt." Lena's eyes pleaded to leave.

"Then why are you scared?"

Lena straightened her back. "I'm. Not. Scared."

Ella wiggled away from Lena's grip. She ran her hand along the lowest wall of the mound and followed it several feet away from Lena. "I just thought maybe there would be carvings or something on it."

"They weren't Mayan. They didn't do carvings. This was probably just a trash pile." Lena scuttled up to Ella, close enough to feel her body heat. Swallowing her fear, she helped Ella pull away leaves and vines from a section of the base, exposing the hard rock beneath.

Ella tapped it with her knuckles. "It sounds solid."

"Of course, it is. How else would it have survived all this time against floods and hurricanes? Are you ready to go now? We have a monster to catch."

"I just expected it to be packed dirt." Shrugging her shoulders, Ella continued to follow the perimeter of the base. "Do you think that's the same crow?" She pointed at the black bird resting on another section of the mound.

"No. It's a different bird. Has to be. Nothing to see." Lena threw a rock at the bird but missed.

Cawwa! He hollered in contempt.

"Look, Lena, there's an opening." Ella jerked back the cover of kudzu, revealing a tiny opening, no larger than a small bathroom window. She dropped her backpack to the ground and took out the lighter.

"What are you doing?" demanded Lena.

"I remember Dad telling us about this once. He came out here with his scout troop. He said the walls are painted inside. Come on."

Lena dropped her bag next to Ella's and scanned the shadows for any sign of movement. They scrunched down and crawled through the door. The small entryway was pitch-black compared to the outside world. Ella flicked the lighter on and ran her hands across the walls. Each wall was covered with drawings depicting life of the local indigenous people. A few still had remains of paint. They followed the wall until it came to a dead-end.

Ella used Auntie's phone to snap a few pictures. "I bet we could use this in history class next year." Her voice rang with a hint of laughter.

Lena wasn't listening. She stared at a series of etchings in the corner. The edges were rough like they were made in a hurry. She ran her fingers over the pictographs of men with spears on the edge of the water. "Look at this." She didn't wait for her sister to respond, but grabbed her by the neck and tugged.

"Ouch!" Ella pulled away, rubbing her neck.

"What does this look like?"

"Fishing."

"With spears? Look closer. I bet this is our lake. Look at the water." Lena pointed to a section of the wall.

Ella held the phone closer for extra light. "Um, it could be the lake." She squinted at the picture. "I don't know what that is." The etching showed something below the water. It was big, undefined, and surrounded by men with spears holding torches.

"That's your lake monster," Lena said.

"First off, he's not mine. Second, it looks like a kid scratched it into the wall."

"Maybe," Lena admitted with a shrug. "I thought you wanted to find this thing."

"I do. I just don't know that this helps. Come on, let's go. The dust is making it hard to breathe."

Once back outside in the fresh air, Ella checked the app to make sure the dot still followed the blue line. "There should be a campsite just past this ridge. I say we eat a snack when we get there."

Lena mumbled agreement. They walked up the ridge before descending into a small pasture. A large tree trunk rested near the center where a rock ring marked the camp's fire pit. "A camp circle." Ella unzipped her backpack, fished out snacks before sitting on the trunk. She held out a stick of alligator jerky. "Want some?"

"In a minute, I want to look around." A cool breeze blew through the camp. Lena shivered. "Something feels off." She walked past the stone circle.

On the clearing's edge, she found the remains of a camp—sleeping bag, utensils, and an ice chest—all set up, waiting for the camper to return with a string of fresh caught fish. Lena ran a finger across the ice chest leaving a trail through a thick layer of dirt. She walked back to Ella and the tree trunk. "I think someone is already at this campsite. I found supplies on the other side of that live oak." She shivered again.

Ella held up the bag of jerky.

Lena took a piece and chewed on it.

"Really? I don't think they'd mind if we stayed for a minute," Ella said.

"The camp looks freshly made, but old at the same time. There's a layer of dirt on everything."

Ella kicked the debris in the fire circle before placing her hand over it. "It doesn't look like they made a fire recently. The coals are cold."

"Maybe they just got here."

"Maybe they never left." Ella grinned, winking at Lena.

"Knock it off. Come on, let's keep going. I want this over with."

Ella read the map. "It's less than a quarter-mile to the lake."

They walked down a well-worn path from the campsite to the lake. The trees opened to jagged blades of grass and a darkening sky. A muggy breeze blew off the lake, carrying the scent of decay. "I'm suffocating in this heat. I could use a swim."

"No! We can't go swimming," Lena said panicked.

"I know. It's just hot." Ella looked up and down the empty lake. Not a single swimmer or boater could be seen.

"Now, what do we do?"

Ella wrinkled her face as she chewed the corner of her lip. After a few moments, she pointed at the pier. "Maybe we can see something from there."

It took them a few minutes to pick their way over to the pier. There, they waited for what seemed like hours. Impatient to see something. Anything. Ella started throwing pebbles in the water while Lena read comic books.

Finally, Lena broke the silence, "Your plan has a flaw."

"What's that?"

"We don't have a boat. No one has drowned except fishermen in boats."

Ella frowned. "I didn't think of that. Maybe we do have to get in the water."

"Yeah—no. It'll be dark soon. I'm going to go make a fire on the beach." Lena walked down the pier and collected driftwood to build a fire. Camping was their dad's favorite weekend activity. Tonight, Lena was thankful for his insistence on learning basic survival skills. She leaned over and blew on the dry pine straw, fanning the small flame. A large splash broke her concentration.

Her twin was doing the backstroke toward the center of Asgina Lake.

"Ella! Alligators live in the lake." Lena jumped up and ran to the pier.

"Get out of the water!"

Ella paused mid-stroke to say, "It's the only way to be sure."

"Daddy'll kill me if you get eaten by a gator. Get out!" Lena stomped her foot for emphasis. A pile of clothes sat discarded nearby. Ella had planned this all along. She was wearing her swimsuit.

Ella stopped swimming. "Do you see anything?"

Lena grumbled, pulled her binoculars from her pack, and scanned the lake. "Nothing." She moved her head as she looked through the lenses. "Wait. I do see something." She focused the apparatus. A large cloud floating beneath the surface was headed in their direction. "What is that?" In the setting sun, the cloud became difficult to see. "Get out! Something's headed toward us."

Ella freestyle swam as fast as she could. She grabbed hold of the wooden ladder and wiped the water from her eyes before taking hold of Lena's offered hand. Lena hoisted her sister onto the wooden planks. Ella hopped up and grabbed the binoculars. "Where is it?"

Lena pointed toward the horizon. "Do you see it?"

Ella adjusted the lenses. "Maybe, it looks like a black cloud." She set the binoculars down. "I don't see anything above the water," she said squinting.

Without warning, the cloud melted away.

"What happened?"

"It vanished." Lena sprinted the length of the pier back to their supplies.

Ella yanked open her pack, withdrew a raw hot dog, and tossed it twenty feet in the air. It arched and plopped into the water, not far from the pier. She threw another one closer to them. The twins bent over the water, watching intently.

"There!" Lena yelled, pointing mid-way to the horizon.

A black snake, almost three feet long, swam on the surface toward the hot dog. Another, followed by a dozen more, went after the sacrifice. Scales on the snakes' backs glowed a silvery white. The gentle glide became a whirlpool of churning water white with froth.

"That can't be it. Those are snakes not fish," Lena said.

"What kind of snake? I've never seen them before. They have fish scales."

Lena leaned on a light pole over the water for a better look. The lake's surface stilled to glass once again. The sun retreated, leaving only twilight and the golden glow of the fire on the beach.

"Ghost fish," Lena mumbled.

"What?"

"That's what Eudora called them. Ghost fish."

"But they're snakes not fish. Snakes can't drown a man. They're no bigger than a water moccasin," Ella said, pointing toward the lake.

The water beneath the pier churned. White foam erupted in great plumes, covering the surface. The pier shook. Lena wobbled, unable to keep her feet, she fell to the planks. Ella clung to the light pole for balance. A black snake curled around the pole, its silver scales glistened as it lashed out at Ella. The snake grabbed her by the foot, yanking her hard.

"Ahhh!" Ella screamed. "Lena!" The snake tightened its grip. Her piercing scream echoed across the lake.

Lena jumped up and ran to Ella. She grabbed her arm, fighting to keep her sister on the pier. The snake fought back. The water churned more, and a loud hum like an engine came from the water. Ella's body inched toward the water as the creature pulled. Lena braced her feet against the light pole. "Ella, you're slipping!"

"Fire!" Ella gasped. "The mound showed fire."

Lena's eyes widened in understanding. She glanced at the fire just on shore. *Was there time? Firecrackers!* "Ella, hold on." She wrapped Ella's hands around the pole, then took the few steps to her bag. Ella screamed. She was barely holding on now. She would be in the water in seconds.

Lena grabbed the firecrackers and returned to the water's edge, ready to sprint when she had the chance. She took out three M-90 firecrackers, twisted the fuses together, and lit them all at once. She held the flaming tubes of black powder over the water. The illumination gave the girls a clear view of the snakes slithering beneath the surface. Their silver scales gleamed. Lena dropped the firecrackers. A deafening crack ripped across the lake. The snakes nearest the flame scattered, and their grip loosened around Ella's ankle just enough for her to tighten her hold on the light pole. "When I drop the next firecracker, Ella, wrap as much of your body around the pole as you can. If more snakes get a hold of you—"

"I know," Ella cried.

Lena lit three more tubes then dropped them directly beneath Ella. As soon as she released the firecrackers she ran. *Bang.* It only took seconds to clear the pier. She slid in the sand as she halted near the fire. She yanked a flaming branch from the edge of the fire and bolted back to her sister slowing only a little to keep the flames from extinguishing.

Standing on the pier's edge, Lena held the torch over the water. The snakes swam together, morphing into a single entity. A large head rose from the water, connected to a long neck. Each snake was visible, wiggling in unison until it loomed over the twins as one monster. The watermelon-sized head leaned toward them. A hundred eyes stared at Lena as a tentacle of snakes reached for them. The grip on Ella's leg tightened, and one solid jerk pulled her free from the pier. One strained hand held tight to the pole, she shrieked in terror.

Lena swallowed hard before tossing the torch at the beast's center where it gripped Ella's leg.

Ella unleashed a yell worthy of a B-movie scream queen as the flame hit her ankle. The monster bellowed before separating into individual snakes and letting go. Lena grabbed her twin's hand and hoisted her onto the pier where they collapsed. The water erupted in a swell. An angry rumble shook the platform as snakes threw themselves onto the pier, attempting to grab their escaping prey. Lena pulled Ella up, and they ran for the safety of the campfire.

Upon reaching the fire, Lena whirled and held her twin tight as her eyes scanned Asgina Lake for any sign of the ghost fish. There were none. The lake was dead calm.

"Dad'll never believe this." Ella whimpered, holding a shirt to her burned ankle. Above the burn was a series of circular marks matching those on Mr. Tony's corpse.

"True. But now I have an awesome story for the summer vacation essay when school starts."

"Yeah, but do you know anything about appeasing vengeful lake gods?"

Ella's body relaxed as she laughed. Lena took the phone and sent a quick text to her father. There was nothing to do now but wait.

Officer Randell grimaced at the phone in his hand. His instincts told him his girls were up to something, but he didn't have the time to follow through. Now, he had no choice. Lena's text was short: *Dad-Ella injured. At pier on Lake. Stay out of water.* It took him only a few minutes to grab Joe and head out on ATVs. He didn't know what happened, but his emotions went from worry to angry and back to worry.

Within thirty minutes he cleared the tree line. He slowed to a halt and searched the horizon. A bright orange glow grabbed his attention. "There they are," he said pointing at the campfire. He kicked the ATV into gear, following the edge of the lake toward the camp. As they approached, Lena jumped up and down and waved her arms. Officer Randell pulled to a stop between his daughters and the lake. He tossed his helmet down, grabbed the first aid kit, and hurried to his daughters.

"Dad, I am so glad to see you," Lena said, grabbing him in a hug. She released him as he moved toward Ella.

"What happened?" he asked, kissing her on the head.

Fat tears rolled from Ella's eyes as she pulled the shirt from her ankle. An angry red burn covered a section of her lower leg, mingled with circular marks. "I'm sorry Dad. We just wanted to find the monster."

His brow wrinkled. "Joe, call the station. Have the doctor meet us there. Ella has a burn."

"Yes, sir."

Officer Randell smiled at Ella. "It'll be okay. It doesn't look that bad. How did you get burned?"

Lena stepped from the shadows and explained about Eudora's story and their trip to the lake. "We just wanted to find the monster. The marks on her leg match those of Mr. Tony."

Randell turned the flashlight beam on her ankle. He sighed. "There are no such things as monsters or lake gods. What did this?" his voice was sharp.

"I told you. A snake wrapped around her ankle and tried to pull her into the water," said Lena.

"Snakes don't do that," he said.

Ella grabbed her father by the arm. "Dad, you have to close the lake. We're telling the truth. The snakes are afraid of fire, but that's it." Great tears slid down her face.

"Joe, take Lena back. I'll take Ella."

"Yes, sir. Dispatch said the doctor will be at the department waiting on us."

"Thanks. I'm going to take a quick look around." He picked Ella up and placed her on the ATV, strapping her in, before walking to the pier. He scanned his flashlight up and down the lake. He wanted to believe his daughters but the idea was insane. Still. The marks on Ella's leg matched those found on Mr. Tony. His feet fell heavily on the pier, echoing off the water beneath. As much trouble as the twins got into, lying wasn't something they normally did. He bent to pick up the backpack and comic books that were strewn across the pier. *Swamp Thing #1* was on top. He stuffed it all in the bag. His forehead wrinkled as he pulled out a pack of open hot dogs. Clearly the girls had planned on a campout. He walked to the edge of the pier and dumped out the remaining hot dogs.

A jumble of screams erupted from the shore. Ella and Lena waved their arms frantically. Randell couldn't make out what they said, but he could tell from their agitation, something was wrong. He slung the backpack on his shoulder, took a last look around, and started walking toward the shore. Pale yellow circles of light from the lampposts guided his feet. The hair on the back of his neck stood on end.

"Randell, get off the pier!" Joe's voice broke through the radio attached to Randell's shoulder.

He looked up to see Joe waving his arms at the end of the pier. His cop senses were going crazy. He could feel something behind him. A strange humming noise mixed with splashing water filled the lake. Instinct took over. He ran as fast as he could, refusing to give in to the urge to look behind him. The pier shook from vibrations of something heavy hitting the wooden planks.

Joe took out his service pistol and fired. Randell dove for the sand and rolled over on impact before sitting up. He stared at the pier. All he saw was churning white water.

"Did you hit it?"

"No. I don't know," said Joe. "What was that?"

"I didn't see it. What did it look like?" Randell asked.

Joe swallowed hard, looking from Randell to the twins who now knelt next to their father, and the lake. "I don't know. It was like a giant snake or something. I don't know."

Randell grabbed the radio from his shoulder. "I want Lake Asgina closed until further notice. Nothing and no one is allowed in or on the water."

He had no idea what was in the lake or even how to get rid of it. The one thing he knew was no one else would be attacked. He would keep it closed for as long as it took. He hugged his daughters tightly, thankful they were safe. His mind raced with what could have happened.

Randell kissed each girl on the head. "I'm sorry I didn't believe you. I never thought something like that could be out there. I...." Unable to finish the sentence he pulled them closer as his eyes, scanned the calm surface of the lake.

Caren Rich grew up in a small town in Alabama. The swamps and bayous have fueled her imagination and inspired her writing. Her short stories may cross genres but they are rooted in the history and culture of the South. Caren's favorite holiday is Christmas, which has greatly influenced her writing. She enjoys reading mysteries, fantasy, and always makes time for a good fairy tale. She lives on the coast with her husband and two daughters. All three are a constant source of inspiration. She also has an imaginary pet gator named Roux.

Website: http://www.ckrich.com
Newsletter: http://eepurl.com/bwV6x1

Skin Deep

based on a Scandinavian folktale

In the village of Anhof, the alehouse was filled to bursting, and not one man in five could hear himself think.

The problem of the king's eldest son was well-known, of course. The curse was held to be a famous one, although, since not a single villager here had ever ventured farther than to the yearly market held at Liffing, only five miles east, it is unclear what their definition of "famous" might have been.

This characterization, moreover, did not deter them from recounting to each other the sad tale of the king's feckless queen, who had not seemed to be able to bear any children for some years after the marriage was solemnized and had, in the end, resorted to seeking out a certain wise woman who lived high up in the mountains, and who was known to have strange, arcane powers in such matters.

The charm's instructions had seemed quite clear. The queen was to eat two onions, while standing in a sacred grove in the full light of the turning moon, and then walk backwards three times around the carved, hogbacked stone in the grove's centre. After which, she was under strict instruction to make her way back to the castle, speaking to no one, and to join her husband in their bed.

In due course, the queen had given birth to twins, and that was when the stories split apart. Had she eaten the onions peeled or unpeeled, and had the witch withheld this vital detail? Had she inadvertently uttered a word, sometime between the carefully enacted ritual and her bedchamber door?

The more charitable held to the view that the witch had purposefully not said whether the onions had to be peeled or not, and that if a woman stubbed her toe and swore under her breath as she walked past the guard at the door, it would be unfair of anyone to be cursed, since she had not spoken those words *to* any being but herself.

The mean-minded said that it was just like the woman to have not managed a simple task without error.

It did not, in the end, matter too terribly much to anyone what exactly had gone wrong. The point was, something had.

One of the boys was pronounced as everything a king's son should be. He was utterly unblemished, had the requisite number of fingers and toes, and he looked out upon the world, from the very first, with a clear and untroubled gaze of lambent blue.

The other, the elder—well, for a long time, the adage "least said, soonest mended" was held to be the wisest course, especially if one wanted to avoid arrest and consignment to a dungeon.

But people will talk. Late at night, in the alehouses, a traveling tinker might mutter a word or three. A couple of shepherd boys might murmur to each other what that tinker had said. And down by the river, when they went to do the washing in the spring, the women might relay what little they knew.

A monstrosity. Scaled and serpentine; fanged and taloned; and dangerous, most of all. It demanded raw flesh at every mealtime—no, not merely raw: living flesh. A Great Wyrm, some whispered, but wingless, and with legs, able to walk and to speak.

And to kill: his strength was almost immediately legendary.

Not a man, and yet with a man's clear intelligence, and, as the years went by, with a man's desires, apparently.

At first, it had been sorrowfully hoped that the aberration would not long survive. After all, babes with deformities did not frequently live much past the first months, even when they were not an utter abomination. Later on, it was merely an existence to be carefully ignored, both out of kindness and self-preservation.

And then, just as the king had concluded a very worthy betrothal for his younger son, the problem had reared its scaly head and demanded that the rule of law be respected. It was not to be born, said the elder royal offspring, that the ancient statute requiring the younger son remain single until the elder had been safely married off be set aside. He would not countenance this. He could not.

He demanded his bride.

And so, where once the tale had been a slightly pleasurable if somewhat terrifying matter for discreet gossip, it now formed a material and immediate problem for every merchant, farmer, or craftsman in the country.

In a well-appointed throne room, decorated with embroidered hangings depicting various hunting scenes, and laid with a floor of alternating black and grey slate flagging, the king was harassing his counselors for an answer to this most pressing dilemma.

Strewn about the floor was a veritable snowfall of parchment sheets. All of them had been copied out in perfect, ornate hands, and all of them bore impressive seals and ribbons.

And all of them, in the most polite and courteous of words and impressive phrases, couched amid expressions of sincere but heartfelt regret, contained at their hub, a simple word.

No.

No, they would not, for any amount of gold plate or trade concessions, send their royal daughters to be wedded to the eldest son of King Ranwulf. Nor would they allow the child of any prince, duke or earl to be sacrificed in this endeavor. Indeed, or so the king saw, reading between the lines, they would not attempt to suborn any lesser or especially impoverished member of their nobility or gentry to immolate their daughters in this cause.

Just, no.

"Well," said one counselor, clearing his throat, "Well, we shall have to think of something else."

There was a moment of uncomfortable silence, while everyone tried to think of what "something else" might consist of.

"Perhaps," said the queen, diffidently, "someone might be found among our own people? Oh, I know," she said, catching her husband's impatient glare, "We can't expect any of the nobility to reconsider. But it might be that some of the—er—less well-to-do might attempt it? For a price?"

Ranwulf opened his mouth to object, and then snapped it closed again.

She was right, really, and he knew it. What place had family pride in this? Prince Lind certainly did not care. He had never placed even the slightest value on his family's honour or ancestors.

From the start, Ranwulf had known that his son's demand for a wife had been born of bitterness, resentment and malice, and the outrage that was his eldest son had, moreover, made it plain to all of them that his enormous strength and stamina, not to mention his poisonous fangs, would be put to terrible use should he be thwarted. He had said a great many things, some of which had been naked threats, but the one thing he had not said was that he expected a royal bride.

Just a bride.

Two days later, the proclamation went out.

In Anhof, as elsewhere, the king's words were greeted with disbelief.

The queen's original suggestion had, as was to be expected, been modified by unanimous consent to form more than a request.

It was, in fact, more of a decree than a proclamation. Having come to the sticking point, the wise counselors had transformed her idea into an edict requiring each and every community to forward, with haste, one eligible, unmarried female to the capital, there to be presented to His Royal Highness for inspection as a prospective bride.

The wording was careful, but not a single villager in Anhof, at least, was in any doubt. Theirs was not to reason why. Theirs was to sacrifice some girl—any girl—on the altar of the kingdom's future.

And there wasn't a cursed thing they could do about it.

The proclamation did not spell out any details of the retribution in store, should they fail in this endeavor. It was unnecessary to do so, since the villagers' imaginations could supply prospects far more terrifying than any open words could have done.

It had induced consternation, of course, and fury, and no little anguish.

How could they send a child of theirs into certain and horrific death?

How could they not?

And, in a scene repeated in every corner of the realm, names were slyly, or diffidently, or ruthlessly offered up.

All of which, in Anhof, had the natural effect of causing more discord and heartache than any other local dispute ever had. The tanner was accused of trying to settle old scores. The blacksmith claimed that Weaver Elspeth was merely trying to clear the field for her own daughter to marry the reeve's son, by suggesting that the smith's eldest was admirably suited for a life at court.

It was a set of quarrels that went long into the night.

The trouble was, though, as the alewife eventually pointed out, name who they might, there was no guarantee that the woman selected would be a willing participant.

"You can put a mule to harness," she said, sagely, "but even with the whip, there's no saying they'll pull your wagon, is there?"

This had the unlooked-for effect of silencing everyone. In their minds, they suddenly, separately, tried to imagine telling some girl—not their own daughter, of course, but some girl, any girl—that she had been singled out to save their village's skin by being sent off to an unspecified but obviously bloody fate.

"Perhaps," said the reeve, "Perhaps one of them would consent ... willingly?"

On the following morning, when every unmarried woman, flanked by her family, had assembled themselves on the village green, and when they had listened to a rather pompous speech begging them to consider the future of those families if not the entire village, the reeve was met, not unexpectedly, by a nervous silence.

No girl in Anhof had come unprepared.

All of them had known beforehand what would be asked.

All of them, in their suddenly virtuous hearts, had resolved that this was the one time where their parents' impassioned plea or stern order must be respected.

All, perhaps, except one.

Katya was not the sort of girl that anyone ever took much notice of.

She was neither pretty nor plain. Her hair was unremarkably brown, as were her eyes, and her height was neither so tall as to occasion questions about "the weather up there" nor so small as to be referred to as "the little one." She wasn't outspoken or quarrelsome, and no one, if they thought of her at all, which was seldom, had ever said she was bold or courageous.

She was simply a nonentity, even in her own family, where the only time she was noticed was in the event of an omission of some chore or task being performed, and even then, her mother frequently had to think hard to recall her name.

It was no wonder, then, that when her daughter stepped calmly forward and said, in confident, untroubled tones, "I'll do it," Katya's mother, for several seconds, did not react at all.

Moments later, as a sort of relieved and grateful sigh flowed out from the gathered folk, her mother's brow wrinkled slightly in an effort to collect her thoughts and said, rather disjointedly, "No—no. You mustn't."

It was too late. The reeve had grabbed the girl's hand and pulled her forward, and the blacksmith's wife was patting her on her shoulder with approval. Several of the people present made shift to comfort the grieving mother, but this was a short-lived effort. Katya's mother watched as the carter helped the girl into his wagon, in great haste to be off before the chit thought better of her offer, and merely asked fretfully if anyone knew if Katya had fed the chickens that morning.

The deed was done. Anhof's future was saved.

Katya, if she had thought about it at all, had thought merely that at least she would get to see a real city before she died. The reeve, as an inducement, had mentioned a sum of actual coin for the courageous sacrifice, in order that she might buy some new, fashionable clothes and present herself nicely before her doom. This alone might not have been enough to sway her, but with the mention of an additional payment to the girl's family, and the hint of future considerations, coupled with the fact that she was well aware that not only were her marital prospects in Anhof virtually nil but that her continued existence formed a bit of a block to her three younger siblings' chances as well, had induced her to step forward.

But in addition, Katya had noticed that even quite ordinary happenings that Anhof was witness to had the habit of becoming massively exaggerated, sometimes to mythic proportions, and that consequently, it was more than probable that the tale of the first-born prince's deformities had been embellished and added upon so much that the reality was very likely quite benign.

This belief stood her in good stead through the four-day journey to the capital, where she was installed at a hostelry known to the carter, although she had had to jog his elbow twice to remind him of why they were there, and a third time for him to belatedly recall her name during the introductions.

In the morning, after several repeated questions and a recounting or three of why she was here, she was directed to a good seamstress and various other merchants and began to array herself for the upcoming ordeal.

If she had had dreams of elegant finery, these had by then been put to rest.

The city was cold—much, much colder than Anhof. Damp winds rattled her bedchamber windows, and chill fog dogged her steps as she went down the crowded streets to consult with the recommended dressmaker. She couldn't stop shivering, her nose was permanently red, and by the end of her first evening in the city, the tips of her fingers had started to turn blue.

Instead of the shining silks and gossamer skirts of her imagination, she had chosen heavy linen and serviceable woolens: layer upon layer of them, from unfrilled drawers and a number of scratchy petticoats to two high-necked gowns, a close-buttoned jacket, an oversized shawl and a demi-cloak with a fur-lined hood. She bought thick wool stockings at a stall at the end of the road, sighed over a pair of thin kidskin gloves and paid a quarter of their price for roughly-knitted mittens instead.

In fact, so consuming was the need to somehow, finally, get warm again, that it was not until the appointed morning arrived that Katya really gave her future very much thought.

By dint of three requests the night before and another in the morning, they had brought her some hot water to wash with, and she gritted her teeth and slipped out of her nightdress, trying to not to notice the gooseflesh her skin had become.

She began to dress: first her old shift, then the new underthings. All the petticoats, and the thick socks over top of her old, much-darned ones. Both gowns and the jacket came next, and, after slipping her feet into her new boots, she wrapped the shawl, muffler-like, around her shoulders.

She didn't bother to look in the mirror. Her vague dream of beautiful clothes lifting her finally out of the limbo she had always occupied had lost out to her desperate need to not feel as though icicles were stabbing her all day long. If she had been offered a funeral pyre, she would have jumped in without a thought.

She arrived at the castle gates on foot, since she hadn't been able to catch anyone's attention long enough to bespeak a carriage, a cart or even a tinker's wagon. The wind had reddened her cheeks and she had acquired a case of the sniffles.

Even then, the enormity of her choice failed to sink in.

There were plenty of other girls here, and not all of them were weeping or looking frightened. Not all of them had the look of potential spinsters, resigned to their sacrificial fate. Some of them had apparently weighed the fireside whispers against the possibility of becoming a princess and decided the risk might be worth it. These girls looked well-to-do. They looked excited and confident.

They looked warm.

Katya shivered and drew her cloak more closely around her, huddling into the fur of the hood. Inside, hopefully, there would be fires lit, or charcoal braziers, and the windows shuttered against the chill. She wished they'd get on with this.

The King and Queen came out onto a balcony, and waved graciously. After that, an old man in a dark blue cloak came out and made a speech of thanks, which Katya heard very little of. The wind had picked up again and was blowing the words away.

Finally, the first hopeful bride-to-be was led inside, while the rest of them, commoners all and therefore not worthy of civilized comforts, waited in the courtyard.

Katya's toes turned icy.

There was a sudden scream of anguish, and then a fearful silence.

A guard appeared and motioned to the next girl in line.

The mood in the courtyard had changed. A few of the more confident ones had tried to leave, but the gates were locked and guarded. Several girls had fainted. Many were weeping in terror, and even the ones who, like Katya, had maintained their composure, looked more than apprehensive.

But despite her outward calm, Katya was fighting a rising wave of fear. It seemed the rumours had not lied, not this time, and she had, in a moment of vanity and recklessness, doomed herself.

The line moved her slowly, methodically, inexorably, to her fate. She had lost whatever false courage that had propped her up through the last few days, and she was now not even slightly different than any of the other frightened, despairing girls who had thrown caution to the winds here.

And she was still very, very cold.

And then, suddenly, as if by magic, there was no one in front of her, and a stony-faced guard had grabbed her wrist and was pulling her up the shallow steps and pushing her through the great oaken doors.

Her first thought was that for royalty, they were certainly stingy with even minor comforts.

Her second thought was that rumour had, in this instance, actually been kind.

There was only one small brazier in the room, and beyond that lay the most horrific of sights.

He was coiled up, an enormous snake of a man-thing, iridescent scales shimmering in the pale light from the two lamps set on a table beside him. He was watching her with those cold, unblinking eyes, as black as coal, and she could hear her own breath rasping in her throat as she fought down a scream.

He opened his mouth to reveal long, yellowed fangs, dripping with ichor, and then she really would have screamed, just like the others before her, but she had no breath for it. All that came out of her was a sort of kittenish meow of grief and panic. She shut her mouth and swallowed very hard.

For a moment, they looked across at each other, silently, and as that moment lengthened, Katya became aware of something rather astonishing.

He saw her.

He was looking directly at her, which was a somewhat unusual occurrence for her. Most of the time, people's eyes tended to take her in as a peripheral afterthought, immediately discounted as being of no interest or use to them, but Prince Lind's eyes were most assuredly and unwaveringly on her.

He saw her.

Not as simply the next offering in this deadly performance of tragedy, but as a single, unique being.

He *saw* her.

It wasn't that she found her courage, real or false, at that point. It wasn't as if she felt any relief—quite the reverse, because she could read in his eyes that she was not, even so, precisely a person to him. She was prey, she was a toy, she was a weapon in some battle she did not even begin to understand, and this frightened her far more than his actual appearance.

It was just that being noticed was so new and alien a concept that her fear took a small step backwards to make room for a new sensation: that of curiosity.

"Er," she said, licking her lips. "Er, how'd'ye do, Your Highness?"

The man-thing uncoiled and slid away from the stone chair it had been resting on.

"How do I do?" it asked, and its voice was just what she expected, a sibilant hiss, replete with menace. "How do I do? I do what I like and I do it very well."

"Oh," said Katya, faintly. She had just barely managed not to take a giant leap backward when the serpent-thing slid forward, but it had taken every ounce of willpower not to, and now, as he came just a little closer, she could not think why she had not run screaming from it.

Except that it seemed that that was what he was waiting for.

She was a country girl. She knew what snakes were like. They waited till you moved, before they struck.

She held her ground.

"Tell me," it said, "tell me why you aren't hammering on the door, begging to be let out? Why aren't you screaming? All the others did so."

"It's colder out there," said Katya, after a moment. "It ain't warm in here, but at least I'm out of the wind."

The noise it made then was unnerving, the hiss intertwined with a rattling, clacking sound that echoed around the empty stone walls. It was a second or two before Katya realized that the man-thing was laughing.

She grinned back and stepped up to the brazier.

The mirth was short-lived. Prince Lind looked her over once more. The snake's tongue flicked out between the fangs.

"A pity," it hissed. "A pity, since this is not the way the game is played, my dear."

Game? She thought. What game? But she knew, instinctively, what it was he sought.

Hadn't she played that same game, all her life long, with her mother, her father, her siblings, her entire village? That moment of victory, when through her persistence they finally, wholly and completely, acknowledged her existence, and were, however briefly, ashamed.

But then, no one's life had been at stake.

She reached out her hands toward the warmth of the brazier, trying to think of some way to delay. If no scream came, mayhap someone would come to see what was happening? It was just barely possible that they might, and that they might then try to save her.

A frail hope, but this was now all she had.

She leaned closer to the only source of heat and said, as evenly as she could, "Surely, there's no hurry about it, though? I mean, you could let me warm up, at least."

It made that revolting laughing sound again.

"Just as you like," it said, with mocking courtesy. "Shall I get you some wine?"

She watched in fascination as it slithered to the table and filled a silver cup from a crystal flagon, watched as the thing slid back toward her and held it out.

She took the cup, repressing a shudder as her fingers came into contact with those dry, hardened talons and papery skin, and managed a bleak smile of thanks. The thing drew back its lips, revealing those terrible fangs once more.

She was aware that he knew precisely what she was doing. She was aware, moreover, that her weak little stratagem had amused him. Her heart sank. All her gambit would do was buy her a few more minutes of life.

"You must tell me, of course, when you are comfortable," the Prince said. "Meanwhile, what shall we do to pass the time?"

"Well, you seem to like games, Your Highness. Mayhap we could play one?"

The black, unwinking eyes narrowed.

"A game...." it mused. "Indeed, a game should be played. But for what stakes? Ah, no, my dear, not that. I fear I must disappoint you, there. But you say you wish to be warm? Let us play for your clothing, then. I will dice you for every stitch you stand up in."

Katya blushed. It was an outrageous suggestion, even for a peasant girl, but even while she registered the humiliation, her mind was racing.

"But what will you forfeit, my lord? It hardly seems fair, if you will not spare me, that you should not lose something, even so."

"I never lose," said the Prince.

"So you say," Katya said. "But still, if I must shed my clothes, then you should shed something as well. Your precious skin, perhaps?"

For a moment, she thought she'd gone too far. Her heart thumped loud inside her chest; she thought for certain he must hear it.

But then came that rattling laughter, once more.

"Touché, my dear. I do salute you. Very well. I wager my skin against yours. Shall we begin?"

It was extremely fortunate for Katya that two years before, a mania for playing Hazard had swept her village. It was not clear who had introduced them to this game of the high-born, and even yesterday, Katya would not have counted knowledge of the game in any sense an advantage, since her father had lost three fat geese and a bushel of barley to its lures before her mother had put a stop to his participation.

But at least, when the Prince announced his preference, with another hideous smile and a flick of that impossibly disgusting tongue, she felt reasonably confident that she could manage to play without having to ask too many questions. She understood the rules.

The Prince's assertion that he never lost held some truth. She was forced to give up her cloak and her shawl and then her jacket, in very short order.

But on the fourth cast, she called a main of eight and nicked with a twelve, to the surprise of them both.

There was a moment when it occurred to her that he might not honour the stakes. Indeed, why should she have thought that he would play fair at all? She shrank under his infuriated gaze, but then, he hissed out what seemed to be a sigh, and stepped a little away from the table.

There was a sort of trembling in the air, a vibration that rocked, ever so slightly, the stone floor beneath her feet, and then an odd, tearing sound as the shining scales at his throat seemed to part and fall away. The Prince straightened up and shook himself, and the snakeskin slipped to the floor with a clanking sound.

He won the next two throws, and Katya took off her first gown, and her shoes.

But then she won again, impossibly, because he threw the main he'd called on a chance, and then there were two piles of scaly skins lying in heaps beside her carefully folded things.

He had, even after the first loss, played with an indifferent, careless air, and she could feel his amusement hanging about her. Now, though, he was playing in earnest. He barely looked at her, concentrating his eyes wholly upon the game, but she didn't mind that. He might be watching the dice, but his attention was utterly on her. It was a most novel thing, and despite knowing that no matter what happened, she was still doomed, she was actually enjoying herself.

After she lost her second gown, she was shivering visibly, although she was trying very hard to control it.

Prince Lind muttered a curse, and got up to slide the brazier closer to her side.

"Th-thank you," she managed, between chattering teeth.

"Don't imagine I do it for your benefit," he hissed. "It's monstrous distracting, all that shaking. You want to keep your mind on the game."

A red flannel petticoat joined the clothing on the floor before she won again. This time, when Lind sat down again, it occurred to her that he seemed different.

Smaller.

He called a main of five. The cubes flipped up and through the air and tumbled down.

Eleven. Another skin lost.

She kept her eyes down. The last thing she wanted now was to anger him. At any moment, he might tire of this, and then … she swallowed, and pushed the thought away.

They'd been at this for ages. Why didn't someone come to see what was happening? Why wasn't the guard bringing another victim in here?

She lost another petticoat and her new woolen socks.

The Prince refilled their cups, and clinked his against hers in a sort of half-exasperated salute.

And then she won again.

He got up again, this time very slowly. The snake-tongue flicked out again, and the dark eyes seemed almost to devour her in a fury, but he stepped past her and this time the trembling was real, she could feel the stones rumbling and the walls were shaking and he cried out so loud, she thought he was dying.

It was somehow more terrifying than anything else about this terrifying day. She could hear the roar of an unholy wind whistling past her ears and there was a red mist rising, like a spray of blood, and a high, keening whine, as if there was some small animal caught in a trap.

Katya fell to the floor, her hands over her eyes, and wept in terror.

Somewhere, from very far away, there was a voice, asking her in desperate tones, if she was all right. Begging her to say she was, to say anything, to please be all right.

From even farther off, there was a frantic thumping of fists on wood.

And then a strong arm was around her shoulders, and a man's voice was whispering "Hush, now, love. It's all right. I swear it."

Katya pulled her hands away from her face and looked up into deep brown eyes.

Eyes that saw her, and only her.

Below those eye was a straight, aquiline nose and a tender mouth, and his arms tightened around her shoulders.

The pounding on the door grew more agitated and frantic.

She looked at the man holding her. Behind him lay five snake-like skins and half of her own wardrobe. One of the wine-cups had fallen from the table and lay on the floor beside them.

"Wha- what happened?" she whispered.

"I don't know," he said, bewildered. "In truth I don't, but—oh, my love, whatever it was is down to you!"

She sat up, suddenly very aware of his arms and her half-dressed condition, and blushed a deep red.

The pounding was now joined by some shouting.

Prince Lind—well, she assumed it was still Prince Lind, although how he could have become so transformed was not something she could grasp, not in her present state—Prince Lind seemed disposed to ignore the rising clamor outside the room.

"You have a name, I imagine?" he said, smiling down at her. "I don't mind telling you it's going to be deuced awkward introducing my bride if I don't know her name."

"I—oh, you cannot be serious," she said.

"Why not, my love? Why should the Prince not marry the loveliest, bravest, smartest woman in the realm? What else could be more fitting?"

"But I'm just—I mean, I'm only...." Her voice trailed away, in awe and disbelief.

Because Lind still saw her, all of her, and only her.

Because not all beauty is only skin deep.

Morgan Smith has been a goatherd, a landscaper, a weaver, a bookstore owner, a travel writer, and an archaeologist, and she will drop everything to travel anywhere, on the flimsiest of pretexts. Writing is something she has been doing all her life, though, one way or another, and now she thinks she might actually have something to say.

https://morgansmithauthor.wordpress.com/
https://www.facebook.com/morgansmithauthor

The Last Chronicle of Pete Mersill

Insert witty, engaging opening line here. I don't know who these people are that have time to sit around thinking up great opening lines, but I ain't one of them. There's a Fetch waiting to kill me. They've tried to before, but I know this one won't go so well for me. My defiance has finally caught up with me.

The Fetches mostly did away with humanity's will to resist in the first month of their rule. I missed that month. Most of it I spent blackout-drunk behind the Liquors & Country Ham Store off of I-65 in Bowling Green, Kentucky. I'd run out of gas about a mile up the interstate and was called home by the twin beacons of Waffle Houses to either side of the exit. But it was the Liquors & Country Ham Store that told me I had found my final resting place.

Six days and nineteen hours before that I had blown brain matter all over the face of my twelve year-old daughter as I shot the wrong man. On live television no less. Yeah, I'm that kind of screw-up.

Oh, get off your high horses you hoity-toity, poor excuses for cattle. You sat there and did nothing while our world was being taken over. You have no room to judge me. Yeah, so I blew the brains out of an innocent man but at least I took action. At least I'm still taking action. What are you doing? Letting them tighten your leashes and suck your life energy from you? Just be glad I didn't kill your Fetch.

For those of you who are uninitiated, which is who this journal is for, to kill a Fetch you must first kill the human it feeds from. Fetches gain their power and sustain their existence by leeching power from their humans. That means when I slit a Fetch's throat, it just takes life energy from its human to sustain it. In return the human suffers the pain of the wound without the actual cut. Eventually with enough cuts, the human expires and the Fetch dies.

Die isn't quite the right word. They move on to their next plane of existence, the next world, or whatever they call it. Though they don't move on so much anymore. At least not since Nicole gave magic to hers. Nicole is such an ordinary name to bring down the reign of humanity on Earth, but then again, so is Pete. I'm Pete, if you didn't bother to read the cover page. And if you didn't, then give the journal to the person sitting next to you because the job of saving the earth isn't for idiots.

I'm sorry, that was harsh. Maybe the cover page got torn off and you have no idea what I'm talking about. My name is Pete Mersill and I am fifty-five … ish. Time has less meaning in this new world. Twenty years ago, on live TV, as I said before, I shot the President of the United States through the temple as he shook hands with my daughter. I liked the guy, had no beef with him. I voted for him. But I thought he was the human behind the Fetch trying to take over the world.

I'm getting ahead of myself some. Most of you, by you I mean the uninitiated, don't even know what a Fetch is beyond some Irish mythical creature. You don't know that it's the name of the things you see creeping around your bedroom at night. Or that they're the things you catch a glimpse of out of the corner of your eye but disappear when you turn to look at them. There are those that are visible to everyone, you just didn't know they were Fetches. Those who've chosen to stay rather than move on to their next world. You call them Overlords.

The world has no idea what the Overlords are, but the prevailing theory at the moment is that they're aliens. Which, by the loosest definition of the word, is true. They're not from here. Fetches, and other creatures like them, are from a different … plane, dimension, existence? I don't know the right word. It is a place laid on top of our world. No, that's not right. They exist in the same place and at the same time just in slightly different, frequencies? That doesn't explain it either but you can ask a mystic or a physicist about that. I'm neither. I'm a brute from Wyoming that smashes things first and asks questions later. See the above assassination of the President for further clarification.

And while we're on the point of clarification, as to the events and conversations recorded in this journal, they are accurate to the best of my ability. Though my abilities are pretty accurate. A side effect of killing my Fetch, and other Fetches to a lesser degree, is the ability to see parts of my history like YouTube videos. I don't know if I'm looking at my memories or the actual events in time, but I can recall almost everything that has ever happened to me with perfect clarity. Just a piece of advice for when it happens to you: don't watch your birth.

Twenty years ago I had a horrible job as the night manager for a grocery chain. I had the laziest crew, a manager that didn't care, and a job that sucked the joy out of my life and marriage. My daughter, Marissa, was the only good thing in my life, so I worked hard to provide for her.

Every night I straightened, faced, cleaned, and organized that giant store almost by myself. As time went by I got better at the job. They had said the job was impossible, but I was finishing with one or even two hours left to go. Yet, something ate at me, didn't sit right in my stomach. My crew would thank me for doing jobs I hadn't done, ask me about tasks I hadn't assigned them, and my food would disappear even though I was the only one with a key to the office where it was kept.

I began review tapes from the nights under the guise of trying to catch a late night shoplifter. The Loss Prevention people thought I was crazy, but at the time so did I. For three nights I saw nothing on the tapes. On the fourth, I saw *myself* walk into the freezer at the same time I was wiping down the check stands. I was literally in two places at once.

"Are these tapes synced up?"

"Yeah, why wouldn't they be?" Jones, the tall LP guy, said.

"Because I'm right there and right there," I pointed at the two different screens, "at the same time."

"No, you're right there." They pointed at the freezer.

"And right there." I tapped the image of myself on the screen, except I knew it wasn't me because I hadn't done that last night. Maybe they had reused old tapes and there was bleed through or something.

But that explanation went out the window. "There's nothing on that screen," Jones said.

I stared in shock as his gaze circled around the screen, never once landing on the image of me wiping down the conveyor belts. It was like a little kid trying to avoid looking at his mom when she was trying to get him to look her in the eyes. If I hadn't been ready to soak my trousers, I would have found it funny. As it was, I could feel the breath of a fourth person on my neck. There were only three people in the small room.

I turned to look but there was no one behind me. Through the open door I saw a flash of red slip around the corner. I elbowed the short LP guy out of the way, I never remember his name, and looked down the long hallway. It was empty. The fluorescent lights glaring off of the cream tiles left no shadows. The door leading back to the floor was fifty yards away. Five seconds at Olympic speeds. Two seconds was all it had taken me to get around the corner. The swinging door hung silent and still.

Back in the room, ignoring the shocked looks, I demanded they pull up the last few minutes of the camera placed just outside this room. And there I was again, running out of the room followed by me chasing *me* hot on my heels. Still to this day it makes my head hurt. Of course the LP guys saw nothing and the few other coworkers I grabbed from the break-room were equally baffled by my behavior and agitation.

James, the manager, stepped in and sent me home, telling me to take the next few nights off and get some good sleep. I told him to stop acting like he cared about the store and go back to his games. Probably shouldn't have done that in front of everyone, but I didn't care at the moment. Someone ... something had breathed on the back of my neck. I still felt the moisture of the hot breath.

I was in a daze as I walked out the doors into the light snow that was supposed to turn heavy by tonight. Our apartment was only a couple of blocks away from the store which is why I had taken the job in the first place. I walked to work and my wife would use the car to take our daughter to school. Which is how Zene, the Russian girl from the deli, was able to catch up to me. Her pink and black hair stood out against the gray sky as I turned to see who was calling my name.

"Pete, I heard you have problems with ghosts last night?"

She wasn't pretty, but she wasn't ugly either. My wife Sara was better looking, but I won't lie, she'd been pretty cold the past few years. When Zene, whose real name was Zenechkacaka or something like that, flirted with me, I'd been interested but hadn't acted on it. When she'd found out I was married she'd backed off. But she was fun to talk to, so I made it a point to go to the deli every morning she worked. I'd grab a hot sausage biscuit and chat with her for a minute or two. When I didn't stop by this morning she must have been worried.

"I don't know what happened. I'm probably just tired and...." I couldn't finish the sentence; I knew it was a lie. I knew what I had seen.

"I know you are smart man. You see something, I believe you see it. My aunt, she is ... she knows about these things. You go see her and she will help you." She punched a number into my phone and pivoted to leave but turned back to give me a quick peck on the cheek.

I stared at her running back to the store, trying to convince myself I was thinking about her statement and not watching her backside. Okay, so I was watching. Back at the apartment I waited for Sara to get back. We'd gotten Marissa into one of the more prestigious charter schools on the other side of town, but it was only a thirty-minute round trip. I knew from experience she wouldn't be back for another two hours. I took my shower, ate breakfast, and stared at the number in my phone.

I should have gone to bed, but I dialed knowing I wouldn't sleep with the feeling of being watched. I'd had it before, but this time I didn't dismiss it as a trick of the mind. This time I knew something stood in the corner of my kitchen eating granola out of the jar from the counter. When I looked at it, there was nothing there. But when I looked at the phone I could see the reflected image of a man with no skin munching away as though this were any normal day.

The woman at the other end of the line, younger sounding than I had expected, gave me an address. I waited at the door for Sara, jogging out to meet her as she opened the door to our ancient Jeep Wagoneer. I grabbed the keys out of her hand, kissed her on the cheek, and pulled the driver's door closed behind me. I didn't look at her as I drove off. It hadn't been the first time I smelled cigar smoke on her, and I found it easier to not think about it than to face the consequences of what it would do to Marissa. But I did think of Zene on the drive over.

Zene's aunt turned out to be about three years younger than her, the result of Zene being an unexpected package of joy for her aging parents. She knew something was wrong the moment I stepped through the door. I won't bore you with the details of the next hour of crushing herbs, burning incense, and shaking odd shaped dice out onto the table. I won't bore you because she couldn't tell me anything about what was going on, only that something was going on. She sent me to another woman who sent me to an old man who sent me to a young woman again who tried to send me to Zene's aunt. When she found out I had already been there she sent me to a "last ditch effort" in her words.

This man, a mystic they called him, was Native American, but not from anywhere around Wyoming. He had deep brown skin with a gaunt face and blue eyes that didn't seem out of place. He had what I needed; he knew what I had been seeing. That was the first time I heard the word Fetch. They go by many names, Fetch is the Irish one. He'd used some native word that I couldn't even begin to pronounce, so I latched onto Fetch.

He explained everyone is born with a Fetch, a creature with no existence in this world so it consumes yours. It steals your life energy away so that it can stay here till it is ready to move on. The longer it is here, the more energy it steals, the stronger it will be in the next world. The legends about the Fetch are like any legend, one part truth, and fifty parts stuff people made up. Doppelgangers, changelings, guardian angels, these are all parts of the Fetch legend, though none of the legends have the full truth.

Even Hyan, the mystic, said most of the stuff he knew wasn't reliable. He did know a few things for sure. He told me what they were, what they wanted, and how they stole your life. The most important thing he told me was how to kill mine. I wasn't sure I wanted to but he assured me I needed to.

This is a big deal so pay attention here, humans are immortal. That's right, we never die from old age. How can that be, Pete? You say, I've seen so many old people die. No, what you've seen is so many old people murdered by their Fetches that couldn't bear to be in this world any longer. They can last here permanently but they have no power, no real substance so they want to leave. At least they did before I screwed that all up, but we're still not there yet. You can patiently wait to hate me as everyone else does.

The point is, if there is no Fetch leeching your life energy you'll never die. After you hit about thirty, your body stops aging and you'll live for eternity. This is where we get our legends of vampires, from people who have killed their Fetches. Now, this immortality only applies to aging, not injury, disease, or plain old self-destruction. As far as I learned in the intervening years, only three or four of those who have freed themselves from these leeches have made it past two hundred years old. Of those, only one still lives today. She is three-hundred and sixty, mad as a hatter, and not long for this world. She just can't bear the sustained assault of death time has thrown at her.

If you don't believe me, I have included a picture of my wife and me, taken last year. To her dismay and my joy, she is drooping as bodies do when they make their way into the fifth decade of life. Her skin is tougher and the years of tanning and beauty products have left their mark on her face. I, on the other hand, still look like my studly thirty-six year-old self with all the strength and vigor that youth provides. It can be awkward though as my daughter just turned thirty-two and won't be growing any older. An eternity at the same age as your daughter would be weird. But as I said earlier, I won't live that long. The Fetch waiting for me will make sure of that.

Back to the story, I went home with a knife blessed by Hyan and killed my Fetch two seconds after walking through my front door. I hadn't expected there to be so much blood. I don't know why; it was alive and it was a creature but for some reason I thought it would just die and disappear. It took me days to get the stains out of the carpet. Sara lost her mind. About the dead Fetch, not the carpet. She was cold and horrible to me, but she wasn't completely devoid of humanity.

She'd seen me walk in the door, thrust the knife into empty air, and a translucent-skinned creature fall dead on her coffee table. It didn't break though, which was impressive for a Goodwill purchase. I sat her down and explained what had happened while her Fetch looked on with interest. I kept an eye on it, waiting for it to attack, but it never did. I've learned that while Fetches are still attached to their humans they aren't quite aware of other Fetches. Or even this plane of reality beyond their humans. Some are more aware than others, like my Fetch had been. It has to do with the amount of death you have seen in your life.

I've seen a lot of death in my life, though most of it was before I could remember. My parents, stellar examples of love that they were, joined a cult while I was still in my mother's womb. It didn't take very long for them to lose themselves in the drugs and sex of the culture and I was left to be attended by the other young children in the cult as they got their worship on.

But on the night that they intended to sacrifice me to their prophet, one of the kids, I never did find out who, called in the FBI. With bullets flying, fires burning out of control, and pieces of the cheap metal structures collapsing all around me, I lay on the altar having a good ol' time with my guardian angel. Yep, you guessed it, my Fetch. Fetches appear to you when you're about to die. That is one of the most well-known facts about them.

Except, think about it, how do we know about it if the people they appear to are dying? Because Fetches ain't prophets, they can't tell the future.

They have no special ability to know when you're going to die and when not. They look at the situation around you and determine, "Hey, it looks like this kid's been sent up the creek, might as well come and steal what life force I can before he kicks the bucket." But when you don't die, they fade into the background again excited that they get to keep stealing from you, keep growing in power. Sometimes, like in my case I'm sure, they even step in and protect you, which is where the guardian angel thing comes in.

But the point is, the more you face death, the more it happens around you, the more times you see your Fetch. And the more your Fetch is able to affect you. Or maybe, the more real they become in this world. Once again, I'm not sure how it all works. But what I do know is that the more you see them the more they see you. And that bond grows stronger over time.

And before we move on, you're probably wondering why I killed my Fetch, and my daughter's Fetch, but didn't kill my wife's. Do I really hate her that much? I don't know. When the world went to pot and none of her lovers would take her in, she came crawling back to me. I could have left her, but Marissa still loves her, so I let her stay with me. I treat her as my wife, but when her Fetch finally takes her, it will be the best day of a horrible life. But I didn't kill hers because she was worried it might be nice. I'm not kidding; she was worried about hurting its feelings.

Anyway, once I killed my Fetch, I could see the other Fetches. And I began seeing them in my dreams. And the more Fetches I killed, the clearer my dreams became.

Wait, I realized I missed something. I know this is all over the place but I'm trying to get everything you need to save the world down, but I'm not a writer, you know. I don't even really read that much so you'll have to excuse my weak attempts.

Anyway, you want to know how I killed the Fetches without killing the people. It was the knife that Hyan had given to me. It had some ancient juju on it that destroyed the Fetches' connection to this world, meaning with humans, without letting them move on to the next world. During the craziness of the assassination, I lost the knife. I've learned how to keep them from moving on by myself, the separating from feeding on humans ... that still eludes me.

Anyway, the dreams got clearer with each new Fetch I killed. I didn't go on a rampage or anything, just those whose people I liked or who had helped me. And any Fetch that took too great an interest in me.

The dreams showed this world that we live in now, where technology has been capped and Fetches control humanity's hearts and mind. Humans are slaves to a ruling class of creatures that have no capacity for sympathy, let alone empathy. And people are kept in check by an invisible force of monsters that exactly equal their population. Well, invisible to most. And this new world was created by a single Fetch of such power that it warped reality around it.

This Fetch's human had been brought to the brink of death so many times they and their Fetch shared a single mind and body. Fully aware of each other they began to plot the overthrow of humanity. The human because of the wrongs it had suffered, the Fetch because it wanted more power. And in my dreams this Fetch looked, acted like, and sounded like our President.

So, I began plotting the death of the President, as all sane people would. I was willing to die to keep my baby girl safe from that world. Ten long months I studied his movements, his security details, his habits, anything really that would give me greater insight into him. Ten long months, I prepared for my death shortly after his. Then, in a surprise move, he changed destinations and landed at F.E. Warren Air Force base just three miles south of me.

Marissa's teacher called and said that out of all the students in Cheyenne, she had been chosen to shake his hand on stage and read her story about America. My plans went out the window as I grabbed my uncle's rifle and ran out the door. Of course, Sara had the car, she never stayed home during the day anymore, but I had saved up enough to buy a scooter. I drove faster than was safe, if safe on an interstate on a scooter was a thing to begin with.

There was a ton of security but I found it easy enough to slip through the back when they weren't looking. Fetches tended to look where their humans were about to look, a precognition so to speak, so finding a place where no one was looking was easier than it would seem. I slid around to the side where there was a press booth set up. I climbed the stairs until I was covered by the black cloth. Scrambling up the scaffolding, I peeked out the top, the press below me screened off by another cloth. Laying down I pulled back a flap to give an unhindered view of the stage.

I'd brought the gun because I knew I wouldn't be able to get close enough to stab the Fetch. But with the Fetch and human being one it would die. My little girl and this world of course, would be safe. I was late and Marissa was striding across the stage towards him, confidence that could've only come from her mother clear in her walk. I aimed, heard a scream, and pulled the trigger.

It didn't take me long to figure out I had shot the wrong man. His Fetch stepped out from behind one of the Secret Service agents where it had been hiding. It, being joined with the President, had felt like it needed protection too. The crowd was in chaos and Marissa was screaming, trying to wipe off the gore and mess. Secret Service and Security were swarming towards me as I lay, too stunned to move.

They ripped me out of the scaffolding and I fell twenty feet to the hard clay soil below. With a whoosh I heard the air escape my lungs and a knee dug into my back while hands yanked on my arms. I'd dropped the gun but it was useless now. The crowd had been pushed back and a black Lincoln town car pulled up on the opposite end of the stage. All action came to a halt as the President jumped out of the backseat in his undershirt, boxer-briefs, and black socks. All eyes were on the newcomer as he hustled towards me.

Even the fast-fading Fetch of the real President stared in shocked disbelief. But I saw what none of them did. The new President was a Fetch, fully formed and physically manifested Fetch. Its human, a plain looking slightly overweight girl of about twenty, was inside of it. They moved as one, the Fetch overlaid on the girl, and knelt in front of me. That's when I learned that Fetches can shapeshift.

"Thank you for stopping him. I don't know what he was planning to do." He said in the deep voice of the President.

She winked at me. The Fetch didn't wink, the girl inside winked. She knew I could see.

She stood to address the agent who had hustled up, gun not pointed at the newcomer but not put away either. The agent asked the false President a lot of questions and he gave the woman his answers which she seemed satisfied with and holstered her weapon. We were all whisked away to the Air Force base then, even Marissa who I wasn't allowed to see yet.

Safe inside a hangar the false President told his/her made up story about being switched out for a look alike. About my fake anonymous call to the FBI to rescue her, I apparently had seen something, and my determination to not let the impostor hurt my daughter. I didn't know how much of this had been set up by the false President ahead of time and how much it was chance but I had just handed over the Presidency of the United States to a Fetch. A cold, merciless, life-leeching Fetch.

They cleared out the hangar because the President wanted to *thank* me in person.

"So you know to keep your mouth shut, right? First, who's going to believe you? Second, if they do, you assassinated the President of the United States." It spoke with the girl's voice.

"Who are you?"

"It shouldn't matter, but seeing how much you've helped me today, I think I'll give you a little something. Nicole. My name is Nicole."

"Nicole what?"

"Wells."

"Why are you doing this?"

She waved over a Secret Service agent. It was the one who had driven her to the scene of the shooting. The one that I could now see was also a fully-manifested Fetch. A Fetch that had no human. There wasn't another human close enough to belong to this Fetch and there was something about his look, his feel, which told me he was in this world permanently.

"I was raised by a coven of witches. Most people don't believe in magic, but I assure you it is real. I guess I don't need to assure you of that." She ran her hand along my jawline but it was the President's hand as well. "And they took me to the edge of death so many times it seemed I just lived there."

"One time," the President Fetch said, "I was with her night and day for two weeks. Every time she improved they came to nudge her back to the edge."

"Why?" It was all I could think to ask.

"Because they had no talent for magic so they stole it from me," Nicole said with a dead voice. "And, because they had no talent, they couldn't steal it magically. They had to bleed it and beat it out of me. Though my aunt had … other methods." I didn't want to know about them so I let that statement lie. "But I began to talk to my Fetch, his name is Ghanka by the way, and the more I talked the more we became united."

Ghanka stood and paced away while Nicole remained in front of me. The split was instantaneous and without show.

"One day, something happened to the witches, and they went into hiding. They left me alone for three weeks. Three weeks that resulted in their undoing. Ghanka was solid enough by then to move in this world by himself. He brought me food and bandaged my wounds. And he was waiting for the witches when they returned.

"I didn't know how to use my magic. I had been nothing more than a well to be drunk from before. But he did. He'd been watching them use my magic for ten years. And thanks to the witches, I knew how to give my magic away." She had been looking off into the distance but now she returned her gaze to mine. "Have you ever made love with something that can touch your soul?" She laughed at my discomfort.

The Fetches laughed, too, but it was delayed like the joke had to travel a long distance first.

"I was twelve years old when Ghanka took the magic from my body and killed the witches who had tortured me all of my life." She paused as though a thought had just occurred to her, "Isn't your little girl twelve?"

"Leave her out of this." My voice had more growl in it than I had ever heard.

She held up her hands, "I meant no offense. I only wanted you to see where I'm coming from. Could you imagine what happened to me happening to your daughter?" She looked deep into my eyes and must have seen the pain there. "Yes, I see that you can. Then maybe you'll understand why I can't stand by and let people like them continue to exist."

"But what does taking over the Presidency have to do with any of that?"

"Not much really. It's the taking over of the world that I'm after. I would advise you to go home, buy several years' worth of supplies and head into the mountains. This world is going to get very…." she pulled back the long sleeve of her shirt to reveal a thousand little scars, "painful."

"How is that Fetch still here?" was all I could think to ask as she walked away.

"Who?" She looked over her shoulder at the guard. "Oh, Alric? I've given Fetches the ability to choose whether to stay or go. And those who stay are able to draw their energy from all of humanity rather than just one human. All of humanity except me, of course." She giggled. "Even Ghanka no longer feeds from me."

She became one with Ghanka and walked out the door towards the tarmac where Air Force One was waiting. Marissa came running in with a thousand questions, but I held my finger up to my lips. She was a good girl; she had seen me kill her Fetch and obeyed without hesitation. I went to my store, checked that James wasn't there, and set Marissa to getting every canned good she could into the carts.

Zene was just getting off work, and I told her things were going to get bad. She, like everyone in the world, had heard about the assassination of the impostor President. She put her hand on my cheek and I reveled in the touch. But I pulled away before Marissa could come upon us. She believed me, thinking I had been given some insight for my service to the President, and joined Marissa in stocking up.

I headed to the cash room, which was empty of the day managers who had already gone home, and I took all the cash. The LP guys wouldn't be coming because the camera in the cash room had been out for a week. I was the only one outside of LP that knew about the outage as I had been in the room when the camera broke.

Thirteen hundred dollars' worth of groceries were put on my employee tab. I authorized the transaction, a fire-able offense, and we loaded everything up in Zene's car. At the apartment we transferred our stuff to the Wagoneer. I invited her to go with us, but she said she wanted to be with family. I understood and waved goodbye as we went inside to pack. I'd known Sara wouldn't come from the moment I was told to run. The surprise was that she didn't fight me over custody of Marissa.

"Sweetie, the men I'm going to stay with, they don't really do kids."

Marissa shrugged and went to her room. Sara gave me some snarky comment about not being uppity and bounced her hips out the door. Two seconds later she was back demanding keys to the Wagoneer.

"Sorry, honey, it's in my name. As is the scooter. There's a bus station down the road," I said as I slipped her phone and wallet out of her purse.

"What do you think you're doing?"

"I'm taking back my phone, my credit cards, and my debit card. That's money I made, not you. So, I'll leave you ... seven dollars in cash. That will get you all the way across town." I tucked all of it into my pockets and handed the purse back. She stormed out the door, and I went back to work.

We filled the back of the Wagoneer and part of the back seat as well. I grabbed the six thousand dollars I'd been hiding in a safe bolted to the floor in the closet. It was covered with Star Wars stickers and held boring tax documents in it. But I'd made a false back wall to keep Sara from stealing it. That combined with the 10 K I had taken from the store gave me enough to buy some essentials.

We stopped by the new uber outdoor store on the way out of town. I grabbed a device for satellite TV, internet, and phone, which maxed out my credit cards. I bought a .270, a 30-06, and two twelve gauges with enough ammo to last us a while but not enough to call the authorities about. As well as fishing rods, a two-thousand dollar tent with a shower, heater, and four rooms built in, along with clothes, survival gear, more food, and five thousand dollars on a couple of ATV's and a trailer to pull them on. The sales girl must have thought she was winning the lottery. Apparently they worked on commission, and I dropped over twenty-two thousand in less than an hour and a half. Most of that was the paperwork.

I almost fainted at the amount of money I threw around, but I knew it wouldn't matter when Nicole made her move. The dreams told me this world was about to become a pit of misery and people would work for and be fed by the Fetches. Economy was a word of the past, not the future. I spent what I had left on a motorcycle off of Craigslist. It would be faster to get in and out of town on and, sue me, I bought it because I wanted it.

We were up in the Snowy Ranges for five days before the news broke. We'd found an old campsite at an abandoned mine and set up shop. Three days after we had set up another family joined us. Zene's family. They said it had been unintentional, but her aunt had guided them here so I didn't believe it for a second. Things had already begun to change. Bills were passed by senators and representatives who shouldn't be working together. World leaders changed policies and generals moved troops around.

On the morning of the fifth day, the news was filled with revelations that those in power weren't human. Nicole, on live TV, stepped out of her Fetch and declared Earth under her power. What followed couldn't accurately be called a rebellion. They tried to fight back, but camera crews filmed as mobs took to the streets only to fall asleep as they marched. One man, a retired Gunnery Sergeant, didn't let the lack of energy dissuade him. He pushed on towards the White House, rifle in hand ready to reclaim America. He withered to a frail old man as we watched. As he blew out his last breath, his Fetch appeared before him, straightened, and took its place in the ruling class of Overlords.

By the time the sun was sinking towards the horizon, the overthrow was complete and all signs of rebellion were gone. Early reports said millions dead, possibly hundreds of millions, their bodies turned to dust in the street. All those with a spark of resistance had been culled, their Fetches forced to move on to the next world.

The greater Fetches, as I now call them, gained control over the lesser Fetches through Nicole's magic. The next three weeks were called the purge as the Overlords killed millions of the lesser Fetches while leaving their humans as cattle to be fed from. They also stopped new Fetches from entering this world without their permission. They couldn't risk the world being over populated by Fetches and destroying the crops through overuse.

Zene, her two aunts, and her sister put up a ward around our camp. It kept Fetches out of the camp and with the separation I was able to kill theirs with minimal pain. I went out on several missions to bring back many of the other mystics I had visited months before. They were wandering the mountains looking for me as well, though they said they didn't know that's what they were doing. As the morning of the sixth day arrived our numbers had risen to around sixty people. There was enough food for about seven months and plenty of shelter to go around.

That morning as one of Zene's cousins, a slip of a boy about the same age as Marissa, was out scouting for strays from the town, he saw two men coming up the mountain. He couldn't explain how but he said they just looked wrong. I followed him and found two fully manifested Fetches. Most humans had trouble telling a greater Fetch and human apart if the Fetch wore a human disguise. For me though, it was clear as day. And these two were powerful. I didn't know the redheaded one, but the other was Alric, Nicole's personal bodyguard. Though his features were beginning to change, become more angular.

We headed back and I made the decision to leave. With the others' Fetches dead and the camp not having a road to it, it was beyond unlikely that the attackers would be looking for random stragglers on such a direct path. And as far as Hyan knew, Fetches couldn't find humans through any magical means. I confirmed that I was the target when I left the camp and headed further up the mountain. Their path bent to follow me.

But they didn't know the mountain and I lost them in a rock field. With a hasty goodbye to Marissa, I was off down the mountain on the bike. I didn't go too fast, I wanted them to follow; I wanted to lead them away from Marissa and the others. They were on foot for most of the way; their car was at the bottom of the mountain. I stopped and filled up with gas from their tank while I waited for them to catch up.

The chase across America was far more orderly than I had expected, they didn't break the speed limit. I don't know why they cared about it, must be deep-seated conditioning to not draw attention to themselves. Once we were past Kansas City, I took off like a bullet. The roads were empty, people confined to their homes or work and I held the speedometer as near to the hundred mile an hour mark as my nerves could handle. After a couple of hours and most of my gas, I pulled over forty miles before St. Louis.

I filled up, nobody asked for money anymore, and took a hotel room. When I say took, I programmed my own keys and went up and locked the door. I moved the furniture against the door, propped the mattress in front of the window and used the box springs and frame to hold it in place.

I'd been asleep for about an hour when I felt the presence of the Fetches outside the room. I looked between the front door and the back balcony doors. I hadn't blocked them off because it was my first escape route. If the back had been blocked I would have gone through the adjoining room's front door. But they were out front so I slipped out back and over the railing. Dropping to the ground I ran under them, hoping they wouldn't fall on me from above, and on to my motorcycle without incident.

Alric was there again. There was a darkness about him as I watched him fade in my rear view mirror. He had become something more than a Fetch. He'd joined with something evil and it was corrupting his already corrupted essence.

In my fear and lack of sleep I forgot to keep an eye on the speedometer and you already know about the running out of gas. I took all the scotch I could carry from the Liquors & Country Hams store and waited for them to kill me. I deserved to die so I didn't run anymore, but I wasn't brave enough to face it sober.

But as you can see by this journal, they didn't come for me. Not then, not till now. The greater Fetches rose up and killed Nicole and Ghanka. They liked being able to control the lesser Fetches but didn't like someone having the ability to control them. They had learned how to feed off the entire population of Earth as well as how to keep themselves from moving on. That was all they thought they needed. Turns out Nicole was the one tracking me and without her, I was just another human in a sea of humans. I sat there for two days, three sheets to the wind, maybe four. I don't really know what that phrase means; I was drunk is my point.

My reprieve from the death sentence, my new lease on life didn't have much of an effect on me. I sat and I drank and I ate country ham. It was going to be a race to see who killed me first, alcohol, dehydration, or heart attack. None of these got to the finish line because Sara, yes Sara of all people, found me and cleaned me up.

There was no love in the action. She had been rejected by her now almost neutered men who had no need for their shiny toy. She thought I was the best chance at keeping her alive and free from the influence of her Fetch. Clever girl traced me through my phone and took me back to the mountain camp. To her dismay the wards didn't include her, I don't understand the magic so don't ask me why, and I couldn't kill her Fetch without killing her.

That's when I decided to become a Fetch hunter. The world was heating up, the forests and rivers receding, and everything was turning to refuse in a hot minute. The mystics explained that before the Fetches made their move, there were hundreds, maybe even thousands, of different magical creatures out there. They didn't fight each other. They didn't bother each other because they were evenly balanced. Each creature maintained its territory and they kept the Earth from dying. Now the Fetches had unbalanced everything by pushing the others out. Well, I do have to own up to my part in the destruction.

So, the only way I could see to save humanity and the planet was to kill Fetches. But I couldn't bring myself to kill lesser Fetches by killing their humans first. So the mystics, led by Hyan, made me a map. A magical map no less but I wasn't up to mischief. I was up to murder. It would show the humans who had become aware of their Fetches and joined with them. Greater Fetches had no humans and so no presence that the mystics could track. But where the Greaters gathered, humans became aware of their Fetches. Most chose to join rather than be drained of their life. Those humans I didn't have a problem killing.

Maybe I should have a problem. Maybe I should be sympathetic to their dilemma but I'm not. I never claimed to be a saint. I had only have one goal. One. Give my little girl a better life. And if you stand in the way of that, if you choose them over us, I'll put a bullet in your brain and then rinse and repeat with your Fetch. And I still sleep at night. Yeah, I'm that kind of screwed-up.

Anyway, I finally ended up in Phoenix. I spent the last twenty years traveling the world, righting my wrong one Fetch at a time. Except there is no righting my wrong. No matter how many I kill, millions upon millions of people died for my mistake. And now billions suffer because of it. There is no redemption for me, there is no happy ending. There is no love for Pete. Sorry, had to lighten the tone a little.

And now, after all these years, I have finally drawn the attention of the Greater Fetches. In total, I've killed maybe a hundred of them over that time, out of a couple thousand. But something changed, something made them sit up and take notice of me. Don't know what it was. Their minds are as alien to us as ours are to them. So we moved to the most sun-baked patch of ground that still has a city on it. Fetches don't like the heat; it affects their power somehow. Well, that's not exactly true. They don't like extremes of temperatures, hot or cold.

It's one of the reasons that most of the legends about them come from temperate places like Ireland and Scotland. They were strongest there. But now the world is brown, water has moved north, and much of the planet is uninhabited. And it's in those places that the other hunters gather. The rebels make their stand. There aren't any others like me; they're just normal folks doing their best to fight back. They can't leave the deserts though, or the Greaters will suck their life from them. So, they gather in back alleys of abandoned cities hoping for a miracle.

Suckers, they thought it was me.

"Nope," I told them. "I'm just a mirage." They didn't think that was funny, but I didn't care. Sara, who's tagged along with me all these years because she has nowhere else to go, laughed. She does have her bright spots every now and again. I was only in Phoenix to lay low. I was sure that if I didn't make a move for a couple of months the heat would die down and I could get back to work. Pun most definitely intended.

There were plenty of abandoned houses and I even found some solar panels and a window unit air conditioner. We slept in the walk-in closet off the master bedroom. It was the only place that didn't have an external wall or window and could be closed up. I punched a hole through the dry wall and used a rusted saw I found in the living room as decoration to cut back the two-by-fours. I slid the air conditioner in and hooked the solar panels up to the fancy battery system.

Three months passed like that, us sleeping in a tiny cool room, foraging in the wilds and trashcans for food. Unfortunately killing Fetches didn't pay too well. Especially since the people I freed from the Fetches were usually dead, too. When I got a Greater, people would share stuff with us, but I had trouble with rationing. So, we lived like hunter/gatherers, but what I hunted you couldn't eat.

I found a few more a/c units that were fixable. I wasn't great at mechanical stuff but several of my jobs had required me to be a jack-of-all-trades, so I got the job done. We took them down to the bazaar to trade for food and water. I only had one set of solar panels though so three of the a/c's wouldn't bring in much. But the moment we rode my old motorcycle into the square I knew there was a problem.

Everyone was looking at us, at me. Phoenix was a lawless, transitional town and it wasn't unusual for people to come and go without warning. I shouldn't have stood out in a crowd of strangers but every eye was on me. I left Sara with the bike and threaded my way to a church at the south end of the bazaar. Inside was a local rebel group and they were waiting for me.

"You have a bounty on your head."

"How much?"

"A spot in one of the Overlords' resorts." The wiry, dirty speaker leaned in. "For life."

"And do any of you intend to collect on this bounty?"

"No, sir," the speaker said. "That sounds like about the worst thing I can imagine. Living next to them day after day being able to do nothing about it."

"Why not? Why couldn't you kill them?"

"You know why."

"I wasn't sure if you did. So what's going to happen?"

"Get out of here. They said someone's coming to collect but from what I hear, it's something rather than someone."

"How long?"

"Three days ago. We would've told you sooner, but we didn't know where you were squatting." He sat down on his chair.

"No problem. Thanks for the heads-up. Can I get an escort back through the crowd?"

"No need. They know if they try to collect, we'll make sure they never make it out alive."

"I got good stuff. You'll want it. Plus, what I've got out at the house." I gave them the address, and they sent someone with me to protect the a/c systems.

I didn't run back but I didn't slow down for anyone either. The bike had just under a full tank and I headed out on I-10 for Los Angeles. There was a large grouping of targets there, probably several Greaters. They wouldn't expect me to go on the attack. We came across a band of shippers headed north, and I sent Sara with them. Marissa still lived in the mountains, and I sent a note saying she should help her mother. Sara protested, which shocked me to no end, but when I told her I was on my way to die, she relented.

Following the map, I found myself at the old Capital Records building. How cliché. I pulled out the charm Hyan had made for me, trapping all the Fetches in a half mile radius on this plane and went to work. There were ten Greaters in the building, I could feel them upstairs, which made the Lessers more lively. But as lively as they were, an M4 on semi-automatic was more than they could handle.

I didn't take the time to determine whether they were working with the Fetches or not, I didn't have that luxury. On the top floor I broke into the conference room, or office, it was hard to tell, and found all ten Fetches waiting for me. They were relaxed, sipping amber liquid out of crystal glasses. There were eleven chairs, one of them clearly waiting for me. The nearest Fetch, from an actor I didn't remember the name of, indicated the chair.

I shot him between the eyes. I swung the barrel around the room shooting with a precision only twenty years of killing brings. They dove out of the way screaming for me to stop. I did, when there was one left.

"You didn't need ten of you to talk to me. That was your mistake." I said, rifle pointed at his chest.

He was plain, someone I was sure I had never seen before.

"We wanted to offer you a chance to join us, to rule ove—" I shot him in the heart.

I had heard the pitch before, and I had tortured the truth out as well. They would set me up, lull me, and then kill me. Problem for them was there is no amount of comfort or wealth that could convince me to side with them. That wouldn't make a better world for Marissa.

Pushing through the glass doors out on to Vine St. I realized my mistake. They, the Greaters upstairs, had been the bait. Alric was the trap. He stood outside, the aura of evil causing the air around him to shimmer. I didn't know what he'd joined with, or how he had changed so much but he didn't even look human anymore. Well, he looked human but no one who saw what I saw would say he was human or even a Fetch.

I emptied my magazine into his chest. Thirty rounds of anti-personnel ammo turned his chest into ground hamburger. He smiled at me and advanced. I took off running to the left. My bike was to the right, but he would have too much of an angle in that direction and could cut me off. He was fast. Fast as me, if not a little faster.

I crossed the street in front of a speeding truck and gained a few steps on him. I didn't know the area and didn't know how I was going to escape. I only had one trick up my sleeve and, with the demon Fetch on my tail, it would at most buy me half a minute. We ran for several long blocks, with him pacing me rather than trying to catch me. Like a cat toying with a mouse.

In front of me, across Sunset Blvd. there was a bank. I didn't know what kind. The signage had fallen long ago but the dual ATMs set into the wall were clear markers. The glass doors were broken and I hurdled through looking for the vault. I took another ten steps, pulled the pin on my grenade and threw it at the entryway. It exploded as the Fetch appeared, throwing him back out onto the street.

I found the vault, pushed the emergency lock button, and threw myself inside. L.A. was one of the few places to still have a power plant. It was solar and didn't provide much power but most places weren't using it anymore. I hoped they hadn't thought to turn off the emergency power to the vault. It slid closed behind me and the heavy metal posts sunk home into the walls. It would be at least twenty-four hours before it opened again, maybe up to seventy-two.

It was the safety deposit vault. Everything of perceived value had been looted long ago, all the drawers were open. None of them looked like they had been forced so it had probably been by the bank president. But there were piles of discarded items they hadn't seen the value in.

An electric candle that had the picture of a dead loved one on it. One box was filled with dehydrated astronaut food and pictures of the team that had developed them. In a bigger box was a tuxedo worn by Sean Connery as James Bond. It made a great blanket. And there was this empty notebook that you're reading out of now. And as I write this, the counter on the vault door is falling below twenty minutes.

This is the end for me. Don't get upset, I told you in the beginning there was no hope. I couldn't succeed; I couldn't win. And rightly so. No amount of suffering can help me pay for the mistakes I have made, the misery I have brought into this world. But you're a different matter. Nobody hates you; nobody is looking to collect a bounty on your head. Unless they do, unless they are, and if that is the case, if this journal happens to end up in a jerk's hand, realize you're a jerk and walk away. But if you're not, if you're just a normal person, then you have a chance to make it better.

I've left the charm in the back of the journal. It will help you kill Fetches. I've also left a map to the camp where Marissa is. She's been studying magic and hopefully she'll be able to help you kill Fetches without killing their humans. Take as many people as you can, recruit as many as you can; you need soldiers. I couldn't lead anyone, but you need to. You are the greatest and last chance humanity has to survive. I messed up my chance, don't follow my lead.

Pete Mersill
Destroyer of humanity, killer of innocents, bringer of doom, undeserving father to the greatest daughter in the world....

The door is opening now....

Sorry.

Born deep in the Ozarks, David Millican read and dreamt of the world outside. Traveling the country wherever work was found, like the hobo's of old he rode the rails, sleeping under the starry sky. After quenching his wanderlust the need for home returned. Now you can find him back in the forests of his birth shelling peas, shucking corn, and writing of worlds beyond this one.

Cave focuses primarily on Fantasy and Science Fiction but has been known to dabble in the realms of Mystery. He enjoys the exploration of moral quandaries through the lens of alternate realities. He also enjoys exploring other cultures and customs in his writing which leads to some interesting situations in his stories. Even more interesting search histories on his computer.

Priscilla, The Magnificent, Flying Giant Squid

Nadia DeLayne scanned through Hans Van Clout's pinched writing, hoping everything he'd told her before his death was true. If he was right, in moments she and her small steamship would reach a tower of broken ships visible only at low tide. She'd read the tidal forecasts a hundred times while on the *Exundo*, the ocean liner she'd ridden most of the way out here. Before transferring to her individual vessel this morning, she'd checked her calculations to verify the exact hour she needed to arrive. Hopefully, the creature she was supposed to meet would keep the appointment.

Shutting Van Clout's journal, she gazed out at the placid surface of the ocean. The coordinates had to be correct. If not, she was as much a fool as Van Clout appeared to be when he'd returned from his solo dirigible journey across the ocean.

"I found the world's final wonder," he'd said once they were alone in his office, the reporters and gawkers gone for the day. "The key to proving my masterpiece."

The masterpiece was the *Portentum*, a behemoth of the sky, a dirigible stronger and more powerful than any built before. Nadia knew the machine well. During the weeks of his absence, she had spent sleepless nights in the workshop, designing and testing until the inventor's promises became real, actionable blueprints.

For the past ten years, their roles had been clear: Van Clout was the front man, dazzling the press and financiers with his smile, drawing them all into believing the impossible. Nadia stayed far from all the noise of publicity. She preferred the daily work behind the scenes, leading their crew of engineers, machinists, and chemists into achieving the discoveries and advances needed to fulfill Van Clout's promises.

Even Van Clout, with all his charm and flare, had difficulty selling his last promise: "The *Portentum* will carry a kraken through the sky."

When he told her his plans in private, Nadia's jaw had dropped so far it nearly popped off.

"It's not just any kraken," Van Clout said, leaning close in the dim lamplight. "You'd think it'd be a beast, but no. I had the finest tea time with the creature when I stopped on her island by accident."

"Her?" Nadia had been sure traveling alone had taken his wits.

"Yes. She calls herself Priscilla." He raised his hands as if framing a marquee. "I'll call her Priscilla, The Magnificent, Flying Giant Squid." He dropped his hands. "Giant squid flows better than kraken."

"How did you even have a conversation with a giant squid?"

"A kraken, my dear." He knocked a rhythm on the table. "She learned Morse code from mermaids."

They'd argued long into the night, but Van Clout ended with: "We've long built the impossible with machines. Why can't nature have her own surprises?"

The statement didn't do much to end Nadia's skepticism. Yet, she trusted Van Clout enough to stretch her imagination to include a sentient giant squid.

When Van Clout made the public announcement, the reporters broke into snickers and most financiers kept their distance. Their most loyal backers remained, and Nadia was able to continue building Van Clout's vision.

Then the *Nimbus*, the first passenger-class dirigible Van Clout had built, exploded.

In one second, several hundred lives were lost and Van Clout's design was blamed. Further investigation revealed the explosion's cause was the wrong mix of gasses had been pumped into the aft ballonet, but the damage to Van Clout's reputation was done. Their last backers abandoned the project and the public forgot the automatons, steam cars, and other wonders Van Clout and Nadia had built.

Van Clout grew pale over the next few weeks, hardly eating, and sitting in his office for hours staring at nothing. One morning, nearly a month after the *Nimbus'* explosion, Nadia walked into his office and found him dead.

She half-listened as the coroner said, "He showed signs of extreme stress, which caused his heart attack."

There'd been a week of grieving, of shouting at his empty chair and accusing him of abandoning her, of curling up in a ball in the corner, unable to think or move. However, as she stood over the casket of her closest friend and looked at the room full of mourners who'd abandoned Van Clout, she knew what she needed to do.

As heir to his estate, she liquidated his mansion, his art collection, and every other valuable to finance the dirigible. Now, nearly a year later, The *Portentum* was ready. Within the hour, she would reach the tower of broken ships. All she could do was hope Van Clout hadn't been mad, hope the kraken was real, and hope she could restore Van Clout's legacy.

Priscilla watched the water's surface as she settled on the sand inside a ship's hull, her tentacles hanging over the side. Sunlight shimmered through the water, its warmth gone long before illuminating her tower of broken ships. Most were wood, but a few of the newer steam-powered vessels lay along the edges. The steel hulls made an excellent support, keeping the older ships from tipping over.

Humans were fascinating creatures. When she had been a smaller, daintier kraken, she'd used the suckers on her tentacles to climb up the side of boats and peek inside. Most boats were rather dreary, but some had male and female humans laughing and twirling together in a room full of glittering things. She'd watch, enjoying the wind, listening to the tinkling of what mermaids called "music." Once her scales became too dry, or the first shouts of alarm came, she'd drop back into the ocean.

As she'd grown, the ships tilted as she climbed. Long ago, she'd pulled herself on top of a final ship. Her tentacles were long enough to wrap around the hull, suckers holding fast to the sides. The wood cracked beneath her weight, and the small, finless humans screamed and stabbed at her with pointed sticks. Projectiles pelted at her from long rods spitting out puffs of smoke. Just as the sun's warmth started to reach her, the ship cracked and she tumbled into the deep.

The humans fell with her into the water, their legs kicking helplessly. She shook them once they stopped moving. They never woke as they sank to the ocean floor.

She hadn't climbed on a ship since, unwilling to hurt these land-bound creatures. The rest of her ships were from wrecks she'd found over the years and dragged across the ocean with nets made of kelp.

Priscilla's contemplations broke as a white line stirred on the water's surface, leading her eyes to a tiny vessel approaching her tower. It had to be the human she'd met before. From a pile of shiny objects collected from the ships, she pulled a glass bauble the humans hung from their ceilings and set it on her head.

The decoration was similar to what human females wore, and should make the approaching human feel more comfortable. He seemed a pleasant human when they had first met so many months before. The mermaids said not to trust humans, but Priscilla had to. If he spoke the truth, she'd be able to live the dream she'd never admitted while watching birds soar over the ocean.

Nadia threw a rope around the seaweed-covered mast protruding from the ocean. The rest of the broken ship lay submerged just beneath the surface. She took a deep breath and shook her nervousness out of her hands as she waited.

The past ten months had been spent making sure The *Portentum* was built and wondering if the kraken even existed. She'd never stopped to think about how much her legs would shake as she waited to meet what anyone besides Van Clout would consider a monster of the sea.

A pale dome rose from the water, donned with a perilously-tilting chandelier. The water surged and splashed as several tentacles the width of Nadia's body slammed on top of the broken ship. The creature pulled itself higher and massive black eyes, at least as tall as Nadia, stared at her. Nadia's heart hammered at her chest, warning her to run, but she felt drawn in by those eyes. There was an intelligence in them with a hint of innocence, just as Van Clout had said.

The kraken hit the side of Nadia's boat with her tentacle, knocking Nadia off her feet. She pulled herself onto a bench and grabbed her notebook and pencil. The tentacle moved to the mast and its tip knocked on the wood. Nadia wrote out the dots and dashes.

You not Von Clout.

Nadia grabbed the rubber mallet from her toolbox and tapped it against the side of her own boat.

I am Von Clout's friend Nadia.

The large black eyes seemed to search her.

Where Von Clout?

Nadia blew out her breath. If a sentient kraken existed, then mermaids probably existed. The next question was how large a vocabulary they'd taught the creature. Van Clout's journal suggested short sentences and simple concepts.

Dead, Nadia tapped.

Water slapped against Nadia's vessel as she waited.

Sorry.

I came to finish his promise.

To fly?

Nadia nodded. *Yes. To fly.*

I am Priscilla. How do I fly?

Nadia stretched her neck as she picked up the first waterproof tube carrying her plans. She hoped this kraken could see the diagrams. She'd redrawn maps in basic structures and had drawn the simplest pictures possible. Hopefully, the squid would understand enough to cooperate.

The sun was setting as Nadia sped toward her rendezvous with the *Exundo*. Matters would be easier without explaining Priscilla was beneath the surface, following Nadia back to port. She'd prefer not to ride the passenger ship and dodge questions, but her small ship's fuel reserves would only carry her halfway to the continent.

Right on schedule, the ocean liner appeared on the horizon.

Approaching, Nadia wondered if she was going mad herself. The steel under her feet was real and steady. Yet, she'd spent the past few hours conversing with something which shouldn't exist. Perhaps her next project should involve a unicorn. Priscilla might even know one.

Once she was alongside the *Exundo*, she attached the waiting cables to the hooks on her boat. With a whir, engines pulled her vessel up to the main deck. She handed up her tubes and supplies before climbing up the ladder.

The assigned deckhands made polite conversation with questions like, "How was your trip?" and held back inquiries on the true purpose of her journey.

Nadia gave them monosyllable answers as she stepped onboard. Once she and her gear were in her cabin, she leaned against the wall and shut her eyes.

Before today's meeting, she was sure she'd still think of Priscilla as a beast. Now, she realized Van Clout was right. Priscilla's innocence was charming. Her tentacles were strong enough to snap a ship in half and she could swallow Nadia whole, yet she seemed a child needing to be nurtured.

Someone pounded on her door shouting, "Miss DeLayne! Miss DeLayne!"

Nadia opened the door and raised an eyebrow at a breathless young crewman covered in grease.

"One of the boilers ... they said you helped design it. There's something wrong with—"

The roar of an explosion echoed as the floor buckled and Nadia slammed against the wall. The crewman looked back in panic as alarms blared.

"Something wrong with the pressure?" Nadia said.

The crewman nodded as he held his hand to his head. He opened his mouth to speak when another blast rocked through the ship. He waved vaguely to her before sprinting down the corridor. Nadia sprinted toward the steps as doors clanged open and shouts filled the corridor.

A third blast hit as Nadia stumbled out on the deck. Deckhands were already rushing passengers into lifeboats, including Nadia's small steamship.

Nadia ignored her small vessel being commandeered as she stared back at the smoke billowing from the ship's aft. If any of the engine crew had survived, they'd better escape quickly. Any buildup of heat or cracks from shrapnel and explosions could lead to a chain reaction of boilers blowing.

As Nadia climbed into a wooden lifeboat, she watched the water. Priscilla was out there, watching the ship sink. Nadia knew too little about the kraken to determine what she would do. If she'd judged Priscilla wrong, the creature might try picking up a few of the rowboats as snacks.

The lifeboat slammed into the water as the boat's crewman passed out extra oars and called out orders for paddling. Nadia took an oar and joined in the rowing. As they cleared from where the sinking ship would pull them down, she dared look back.

Nadia held her breath, praying to a deity she wasn't sure she believed in. Everyone should have escaped.

Water lapped along the sides of the lifeboats while the *Exundo* descended into the water. As the light turned into the blue shades of twilight, the ship made its final ripple and was gone. Nadia stood with the other survivors, their hats removed.

The night wore on with small rations, fits of sleep, and flares lighting the sky. Nadia stayed awake, watching each ripple for a sign of Priscilla. At dawn a man began a cheery song to break the morning chill, but Nadia did not join. Instead, she leaned her head on the paddle and shut her eyes.

Shouting erupted and Nadia opened her eyes. Something hard thumped against the lifeboat and several men screamed. She spat out a curse as she stood. The man beside her grabbed her belt and pulled her down.

"Hold still!"

She cringed at the next thump, waiting for the massive tentacles to prove her wrong about Priscilla and wrap around the boat.

The tightness in her chest eased as a large, gray fin rose out of the water. The shark was at least as long as the lifeboat but was no kraken. She began to smile until she noticed the panicked faces around her. Now was not the time to relax.

The crewman picked up his pike and tracked the shark as it slid along. The shark swerved and rammed the boat again. Nadia gripped the side and leaned to help steady the vessel as it tilted up on one side.

The shark circled once more as the crewman tried to aim his spear. Water churned as the shark swam toward them again. Its teeth-filled snout shot from the water, its mouth open and ready to devour. Everyone hunched down. A brave man shot up and thwacked the shark across the nose with an oar, the wood cracking and breaking.

The water frothed as the shark turned away. Nadia let herself breathe as the other men and women held onto the boat, watching for the fin.

The shark rose again, driving for the lifeboat. The crewman tossed the brave man the pike and the man held the weapon high.

The shark approached. Water sprayed as a pair of massive white tentacles sprung from the ocean and wrapped around it. The tentacles pulled down while the shark struggled, its powerful muscles unable to escape from the squid's grasp.

"Row!" yelled the crewman as he grabbed the rudder. A man took the center oars and Nadia joined a few others with the spare oars.

As they rowed, Nadia bit her cheek to keep from grinning. Under her breath, she said, "Come on, Priscilla. Help us out, girl."

She and the other survivors rowed with all their power, pulling the boat away from the roiling battle as the shark and tentacles tossed about in the water.

Water sprayed, followed by a too-quiet stillness. Nadia and her fellow survivors kept rowing even as they pulled further from the other lifeboats. Her arms ached as the crewman called for them to hold.

Wiping her forehead with the back of her hand, she glanced into the ocean. Priscilla moved through the water like a cloud beneath the surface.

Screams broke out as a tentacle rose from the water and knocked on the side of the boat. The crewman wielding the pike started to stand, but Nadia grabbed his arm.

"Put that down. She's trying to help."

"She?" the young man said. "Is this thing your pet?"

Priscilla knocked again.

For lack of a better explanation, Nadia said, "Yes." She reached into her pocket and pulled out her notepad and pencil. "And she's trying to tell us something."

"You can't talk to a giant squid," the crewman said. "Let's go."

"She uses Morse code."

The survivors were silent as they stared at her. Nadia held her face firm even though these were the same incredulous stares Van Clout had faced.

The tentacle thunked against the side once more.

A bearded man's face scrunched and then his eyebrow raised. "That is Morse code. I think it's saying, 'Are you safe?', but I can't quite follow." He looked at Nadia. "Who are you?"

"She's Hans Van Clout's assistant," said another man at the rear of the boat.

"I'm Nadia DeLayne." Mustering Van Clout's confidence, she sat up and said, "And this is Priscilla, who will soon be Van Clout's Magnificent, Flying Giant Squid."

After several rounds of tapping back and forth with Nadia, Priscilla used her tentacles to push the lifeboats together. The usual shouting and screaming echoed through the water, but the humans followed Nadia's orders to tie the tiny ships together. Priscilla put one tentacle through the loop Nadia held out and then propelled herself and her small ships together.

Fish and dolphins scattered as she swam. The journey took a full day and night, with a few hours for Priscilla to rest. As the sun rose, they approached the shore and the long planks of wood and stone the humans had built over the water.

Wait in the bay, Nadia tapped.

Priscilla released the boats and settled herself on a sunken ship lying among the kelp beds. The other marine life kept a wide birth around her while she rested, letting her tentacles float.

Several days passed. Back in her collection of ships, the smaller fish had learned not to fear her and would swim close by. Every now and then mermaids, octopi, and other cephalopods would visit. Sitting here, among strangers, reminded her of the loneliness of being a giant in the sea.

Once Nadia helped her fly, however, everyone would know her.

Nadia half-listened as her chief foreman, Jackson, ran through the list of checks with his crew leaders. Jackson had worked on the last three projects and she trusted the man's sharp eye and firm hand with his workers. The rest of her attention was on the chatter around her. Every day since his death, she'd missed Van Clout for his friendship, mentorship, and vision. Today, she missed him standing as a shield between her and all of this political noise.

"Two-thirds of the ships which should be in port are sitting out there, too afraid to approach your beast. The other third've headed north to other ports. I can't have this, Ms. DeLayne."

"We've three hours till launch, Mayor Graham," she said as she ran her hand over the aluminum hull. "This is Hans Van Clout's final masterpiece. When we succeed, there'll be enough press to take care of the trouble we're causing."

Van Clout would have said something more charming, but Nadia didn't have time for nonsense. The air tank was being filled, the boilers were heating up, and, in a half-hour, the ship would be ready to rise. All she needed was the final check from Jackson and for Priscilla to move into position.

"What do you plan to do with the creature?" one of the few reporters she'd allowed in said. "Professor Bratven says you're going to donate it to the royal aquarium. Is this true?"

She walked away from the reporters and photographers as the mayor grumbled. Wealthy patrons seeking to buy a ride on the first voyage begged for her time. She ignored them as she made final checks. She wasn't going to risk any more lives than she had to. Everything had been measured with precision, but something could still go wrong.

Jackson, the captain, and various crew leaders checked in, giving their approval to launch after a third check. Nadia wished she could examine every rivet and bolt but there was no time. The launch had been announced for today. If she failed, she had nothing. Few investors would risk funding her projects and Van Clout's name would be further thrashed.

She feigned confidence as she came to the bridge and took her seat beside the controls connected to the glass tank waiting in the water. Lifting this tank with Priscilla inside would prove, without a doubt, the strength of the *Portentum* and Van Clout's legacy.

Priscilla pushed from her throne among the kelp and followed the pounding through the water, just as Nadia had said.

She jetted toward the sound until the point of her head hit something clear but solid. Pressing her tentacles to the surface, she tried to understand why she couldn't move forward. Nadia's pictures had shown a box Priscilla would ride in. Priscilla's tentacles sought for all four sides as she swam inside.

She thumped against the side: *Ready*

A clanking echoed as the clear cage rose. The water sloshed around her and Priscilla's body smashed against the glass. Panic spread along her tentacles as the cage swayed and she was raised above the water. She pressed her tentacles to the walls, trying to hold steady.

The swaying became a violent jerk, shoving Priscilla against a wall. Something cold and metal thwacked her tentacle and she tried to pull her appendage back. A chain tangled around her tentacle, digging in and sending sharp pain. She thrashed to try to break free as the cage wobbled and jerked about, threatening to drop her.

The mermaids said not to listen to humans. Kraken weren't meant to fly. She'd been safe back in the ocean instead of in this trap. She should have listened to the mermaids. She shouldn't have come.

The dirigible shook as Nadia leaned over the control panel and punched letters into the machine connected to the rubber mallet hitting a wall of the tank. A sensor attached to the tank would read any vibrations, allowing Priscilla to respond. Right now the sensor was waving wildly as the kraken bashed at the walls of the tank.

"I have to rebalance the engines every time it thrashes," the pilot said as she pulled on the lever to raise the *Portentum*. "The whole ship's going to crash if we don't drop the weight."

"Hold on," Nadia said while changing the message to Priscilla to only the word "calm."

She couldn't drop the tank. There had to be a way to soothe Priscilla. She'd looked the beast in the eye out in the middle of the ocean. There was intelligence there. She didn't know if a kraken was capable of friendship, but she had to hope the beast would trust her.

Over the speaking tube, Jackson shouted, "A chain's broken. There's so many tentacles flying, I can't send anyone down to fix it."

Nadia's fingers clamped on her armrest. The chains should have been strong enough to hold the weight of the creature and water. She'd made the calculations a dozen times and doubled her estimates.

Even with the powerful engines and gas strong enough to balance the weight, they weren't going anywhere with a broken chain. Sitting here on the bridge wasn't going to do any good.

"I'm coming," Nadia said into the speaking horn by her station. She turned her chair and faced the pilot. "Lower the ship till the tank's on the water." She pointed to one of the bridge crew. "You, watch the panel."

As the crew followed her orders, she sprinted toward the maintenance hatch at the aft of the ship. She grabbed a handhold as she stopped beside Jackson and looked out.

Five of the six chains hooked to the open-topped glass tank were taut and creaking, but holding. The remainder of the sixth chain was whipping about, while the end still attached to the tank was wrapped around one of Priscilla's tentacles. The kraken's other tentacles thrashed against the tank and sturdy chains.

"If the beast can hold still, my crew and I can fix it," Jackson said.

The tank rested against the ocean's surface, waves cresting out as Priscilla continued to fight.

Nadia grabbed a maintenance harness and pulled it on.

"What are you doing?"

"I'm heading down to calm her." She tugged on an aviator cap, goggles, and gloves. "Once she's calm, your crew needs to work fast."

"You can't—"

Nadia glared at Jackson as she snapped the last buckle on the harness. He groaned as he hooked her to a maintenance cable tethered to the ship.

"Be careful," he said. "I don't like working for the other inventors."

Nadia's breakfast threatened to visit again as Jackson lowered her toward the tank. One bash of a tentacle and she was looking at a broken neck. She had better be right.

She let out a curse as a tentacle swung toward her. Leaning to the side, she barely dodged. The cable holding her shook, and the engines shuddered. Hovering was rough on any dirigible. Nadia would have to fix that on her next design, if she lived past today.

A tentacle knocked against her cable, sending her into a spin. Nadia held her legs out in a sitting position and kept her arms to her sides. She gasped as she bashed against the side of the tank. As she swung away, her arm stung. It either wasn't broken or was too numb to tell.

Forcing herself to breathe calmly, she waited for her cable to swing back toward the tank. This time, she hit the side of the tank with her feet. Her knees ached from the impact, but she held steady. She stretched her uninjured arm up and grabbed the top of the tank and kicked the side of the tank as hard as she could. She knocked on the glass as hard as she could with her foot.

Priscilla's eyes turned toward the thumping at the side of the cage. Nadia made a silent prayer as she kicked, *Stop.*

The tentacles lowered, except the one caught in the chain and Priscilla tapped against the wall.

Stuck. Hurts.

Nadia looked up. At least three of Jackson's crew were harnessed and ready to fix this mess. She was close, but had to be careful.

To Priscilla, she thumped, *Be still and we will fix.*

The whole tank shook as Priscilla pulled with her chained tentacle. Nadia reached out her injured arm and barely caught hold of the tank's lid. She held tight.

The chain had to be digging in and hurting. With the rest of Priscilla's tentacles still, Nadia pulled herself toward where the chain was snagged. The chain seemed to be just looped around the tentacle. That would be much easier to deal with than if snarled.

Nadia was almost to where the tank tilted down due to the broken chain, when her cable went taut. She tried to pull herself forward again, but the cable pulled her back. Looking up at Jackson several stories higher, she motioned for him to let out the cable. He waved his arms. There was no more cable.

She only needed a little more length. Nadia moved back to the closest steady chain and pulled herself up so she was straddling the eight-inch wide lip of the tank, one leg in the water. She unhooked the cable from her harness and attached it to the chain. Keeping an eye on Priscilla's tentacles, she scooted back to the corner.

She stretched out her arm and was barely able to reach the chain on Priscilla's appendage. Each time she unlooped the chain, her chest eased a little. She allowed herself to smile as she tossed the chain over one more time, freeing Priscilla. As she began to scoot back, Priscilla's tentacle swung, hitting Nadia in the head.

While white blobs filled Nadia's vision, she splashed into the tank.

Priscilla moved her eyes closer to Nadia, watching her float in the water. She waited for the human to kick and struggle as others had done before. There was no movement.

She had only meant to stretch her tentacle. Even when trying not to harm humans, she failed.

With only a little hope, Priscilla wrapped her tentacle around Nadia and shook her. The human's arms flopped and her head shook back and forth. Just as Priscilla let go, Nadia's eyes opened and her legs kicked. Priscilla pushed Nadia onto the cage's edge and into the air humans seemed to need.

Several humans dangled from cables and grabbed Nadia. Priscilla held still as the humans carried Nadia into the flying machine.

Humans moved between the chains above, carrying sticks with fire as they reattached the broken chain. Priscilla laid in the bottom of the tank. She could try to escape, but she had come so far for a chance to fly.

Something thumped against the cage.

This is Nadia. I am safe. Be still and we will fly.

Priscilla's tentacles relaxed, and she let herself float in the water as she looked toward the open ocean. Just as Hans Van Clout and Nadia had promised, the flying machine inched into the air, rising over the bay and shore. Humans were packed along the wooden planks and square ships built on land, their eyes fixed on Priscilla. She thought through the human interactions she'd observed and chose the rising and falling of an appendage. No one returned the gesture but she'd done her best.

The machine carried her along the shore, over cliffs and marshes, over above-land mountains and fields of dark green. She looked up at the sun, the brightness stinging her eyes as its warmth settled into her skin. Birds flew past and the machine flew higher until they were near the clouds.

She rode through the sky for hours, pulling herself up now and then to feel the wind rush over her. The world was so different this high, far from the view within the sea.

The machine turned and soared over the ocean, soon leaving the land a distant speck on the horizon. As the machine lowered, she saw her tower of ships protruding from the water. Her tentacle pressed against the glass as they moved closer. Flying had been more than she dreamed of, but home beckoned.

A thump pounded: *Are you ready for the ocean again?*

She thudded a tentacle against the wall.

Am ready. Thank you, Nadia.

The reply came: *You're welcome, Priscilla, and thank you.*

The tank crashed against the water's surface and lowered into the sea.

Once it was submerged, Priscilla used her tentacles to pull herself out. She swam to her tower of ships and climbed on top. Looking up at the humans, she made one last attempt at waving her appendage before submerging herself in the water and returning home.

Nadia's chest eased as she leaned against the viewport, holding a cool rag to her aching head. Everything had worked as it should. Waking in the tank had been terrifying until Priscilla had pulled her out of the water so gently. There was far more to this kraken than most could see. She belonged in the ocean, free from human control.

Priscilla raised herself to the top of the ships and seemed to wave a tentacle. Nadia smiled and waved back.

"You can't let it go," Mayor Graham said. "Think of everything we'd learn from it. Think of—"

Nadia leaned on the half-wall beside the viewport and glared at the man.

"She fulfilled more than her bargain," she said. "And saved my life. I think she's done enough."

As Priscilla sank back beneath the water, the *Portentum* turned back toward shore. Once they landed, everything would be a whirlwind of reporters and well-wishers. She'd have to hire someone to bother with such distractions. Based on the wide-eyed wonder she'd seen in the crowds below, Van Clout's legacy was secure.

She pressed her hand to the window as she looked toward the horizon. A tear fell along her cheek, and she smiled.

"We did it, Hans."

In between exploring the hidden lives and magic of fictional worlds, L. Palmer lives along the shores of California and works to save the world. She developed her imagination and adventure skills growing up in Girl Scouts, working for ten years at resident summer camps, teaching high school English, attending and working at the University of California Santa Barbara, and reading great books of fantasy and magic.

http://tinyurl.com/truebride

https://twitter.com/L_palmer_1

An Adventurer's Heart

Sweat dripped down Melinda's back, but she ignored it, holding still, breathing slowly, waiting for the right moment to loose her arrow. Just a little farther to the left....

"Get out of the way." A gruff man moved in front of her. With gaps in his yellow-toothed grimace, he knocked her bow and arrow to the side. "You're liable to hurt someone."

Melinda grimaced. The soft thumping of furry paws from the hare running away meant she'd have no dinner that night. Again.

The man kept heckling her, but she ignored him, stomping away and leaving the forest behind. Every copper she found or earned she was stockpiling to purchase a sword. Once upon a time, she had more money than she could ever need, the inheritance she gained when her parents passed.

But their departing to the next plane had not been a peaceful experience. A sea-horse called Helga the Horrific attacked their ship while they had been on a voyage. Melinda had stayed behind to tend to the house, a girl all of nine.

They never returned home.

Too young to tackle such a creature by herself, Melinda squandered most of her parents' wealth to hire supposed heroes and adventurers to avenge her parents for her. None succeeded. Some never bothered to even try, just took her coins and ran. One lost his life. Two at least injured the hippocampus.

But Helga the Horrific still lived, and Melinda, during the past many years, had taken to training herself in the sword and the bow. Her father's blade she lost while engaging a kelpie. Who knew the creature could freeze metal as well as a person?

So now she spent her hours working hard at odd jobs to fetch whatever coins she could, and during her spare time, she trained her body. A terrible, thankless life, but she would not rest. Not yet.

Her stomach grumbled, but she ignored her hunger. Once she was certain no other wanderer was near her, the shadows lengthening from the edge of the forest, she removed her coin pouch from her belt. Actually, she *might* already have enough saved for a dinged and dented sword. Not a finely crafted one like her father's, but as long as the edge was sharp, what did it matter if the hilt was fashioned from gold or another metal?

She pressed onward to town and entered the local tavern. Even if she couldn't spare a copper for some hot soup or a bed, at least she would not be alone.

From her perch in the back corner, she watched a man enter. He ordered himself an ale and another and another, and soon he seemed ready to fall off his stool.

If she were a less honorable person, she would consider relieving him of the rest of his coin pouch, but she wasn't the only person to think that. A small, sniveling man was making his way over, trying to be inconspicuous.

Melinda wandered over, making sure to keep one hand on her own coin pouch to protect it, and bumped into the would-be thief. His glower gave way to a shrug, and he slunk away.

She glared at him until he left the inn and then sat next to the drunk.

"All alone," he muttered. "I have nothing...."

Her snort was loud. He had enough coin to waste on drinking away his sorrows. That was more than she had.

"I might be able to fashion weapons, but I can't wield one...." He buried his face in his hands.

"Wait. You're a blacksmith?"

He said nothing.

"What happened?" she demanded.

Still, he did not reply.

"If you need someone to wield a weapon..." she started.

But he placed his head down on the table and snored.

The bar wench walked over. "I'll make sure he gets home." She smiled sadly at him but before Melinda could ask for details, the bar wench returned to work.

Intrigued, Melinda began to have a germ of an idea....

Once the rising sun woke her, Melinda found herself some berries and nuts for a quick meal to break her fast. Onward she went to the blacksmith's. The wall of heat nearly forced her back outside.

Yes, the man working was the drunk from last night, and he worked hard, showing no signs of being hung over. Bare-chested, his body gleamed with sweat, and, despite the gray in his hair, he did not seem old.

He stepped away from the open flame and stood before her. "What do you want?"

"I—"

"Not interested."

Melinda scowled and crossed her arms. The dismissal annoyed her. She stomped over to a table and dumped out the contents of her purse. "I want a sword, and you will give me one."

He glanced over and shook his head. "Not—"

"I could be the one you need," she said quietly.

A flicker of emotion flashed in his eyes, too quickly for her recognize it. "What are you talking about?"

She flushed and said nothing. After all, she did not know why he needed a warrior. Could she risk her life for someone else's quest when she hadn't fulfilled her own yet?

He gave her a long onceover. "Decent shot, I suppose?"

"The quiver give that away?" She tucked a wisp of red hair behind her ear.

"Your arms look strong. Strong legs, too. Bet you can run and ride. Do you have Amazon blood coursing through your veins?"

Women with amazing strength, endurance, and power. A legendary race although more and more accounts of real Amazons had been whispered lately. A rare compliment, and a sense of pleasure coursed through her. "I wouldn't know. My parents died long ago."

"And obviously an adventurer's heart," he continued.

A reckless smile settled on her lips. "I guess you can say that. Give me a sword and I can prove it."

If she could live to see the day Helga the Horrific was defeated, she would be free to do whatever she wished instead of trying to escape the guilt consuming her. If she had been with her parents, she would have perished, too, yes, but living without them for so many hard and lonely years was eating away at her.

"I'm Drake."

She was tempted to say that she didn't care, but he was taking an interest in her finally, and perhaps that would mean he was warming up to selling her a weapon. "A decent sword," she demanded, pushing the coins toward him.

"That's not enough for a sword." He slapped a dagger onto the table.

"A dagger won't do me any good." Her stomach churned as she gathered her coins. She would rather work harder and earn more coppers than be given such a trifle for her efforts.

"Wait." Drake stared at her in a way she found unnerving. "I…. Yes. Yes, you'll do." He seemed to be talking more to himself than to her.

She stilled. He would use her for his quest after all. "I'll do for what?"

"I used to live in the next town over, Hilfalls, but all of the villagers have fled. Many were killed. I want you to avenge their deaths and kill the beast that destroyed that fair place."

"Your wife," she guessed.

"Nay, my fiancée." He swallowed hard, his grief evident.

"And you—"

"I tried. As did many of the other villagers. But we were a small town and had no knights, no warriors. I make weapons. I don't wield them. Rosamarie had been my whole life. Now I have nothing but my work." His knuckles whitened as he secured the dagger's hilt within his grasp.

"Tell me about the beast."

"Glatisant. A large, dangerous creature with the head of a serpent, the body of a lion. Makes a strange sound, almost like a dog." He spat out the words with disgust and hatred, his eyes full of rage. "They call him Frostclaw."

"Is Frostclaw poisonous?"

"Extremely. One bite, and you have, at most, an hour to live. Rosamarie lasted just ten minutes." Tears ran down Drake's face, and Melinda felt his sorrow. She knew all about being alone in the world.

While she felt deeply moved by his story, she could not help recalling the adventurers who had died trying to avenge her parents. "How can I go up against such a creature without a sword?"

"I will lend you one." He walked over toward the far wall, where a wide assortment of weapons was displayed. Drake selected a beautiful weapon but kept it in his hands as he returned to her. "If you are to succeed, an ordinary blade like this will not be enough."

"Can you enchant the blade?"

"Not without gems. And I know where you can find them." He glanced toward the west.

She followed his gaze. Mount Gavel, home of a large dragon, one that Melinda had already been studying, as the thought of stealing gems to finance her quest for revenge had crossed her mind on more than one occasion.

"You want me to steal from a dragon's hoard of treasures?" Just saying it aloud screamed how insane, foolhardy, and reckless embarking on such a quest would be.

Fortune hunters often failed to survive to tell the tale, prompting the old saying that a dragon and its treasure were never parted, not even by the dragon's death. Then again, Melinda had patience whereas others rushed in without a plan. She did know the layout of the caves within the mountain. Maybe she would have a chance.

"Yes," Drake said without blinking. "You would need an amethyst, the largest one you can find. They protect against poison. Many healers have amethysts tucked in their pockets because they also help with meditation."

She nodded. "Anything else?"

"A pyrite might be a good idea. The shield stone. It increases stamina. Something an adventurer would need, in great quantities."

"An amethyst and a pyrite. Very well. I'll need the sword now." She held out her hand.

Drake held it out of reach. "How can I be sure you won't run off with it?"

"I am doing you a bloody favor," she said through gritted teeth. "I should be the one asking you what you will give me once I give you that blasted creature's head."

"Fine. You may borrow the sword to gain the gemstones. I'll enchant the blade, and you kill Frostclaw. Then the enchanted blade will be yours. I'm not a warrior. I'm not a knight. I can't kill it myself. I'll just die too, but you ... you might be able to avenge the town for me. Will that suffice?"

A ripple of excitement ran down her spine. Not only a sword but one with an enchanted blade! Surely she would be able to avenge her parents with it one day!

She only considered for a moment before announcing, "I promise."

The sun winked, casting hues of orange and red into the darkening sky. Twilight descended as she hurried to the mountain, and soon she began to scale Mount Gavel, passing several diminutive caves, all too small to house a fully grown dragon. Finally, as darkness settled over the land, Melinda located the correct cave, her fingers finding the grooves in a stone archway. Three horizontal claw marks with a much deeper perpendicular one.

A blast of hot air overwhelmed Melinda the moment she stepped foot into the dragon's cave. Heat pressed against her body like an oppressive cloak. As she neared the heart of the cave, the stones glowed with white light. The ground, burned by the dragon's fire, even produced some heat as well. The warmth seeped through her calf-skin boots.

Melinda moved swiftly, but not at a run so as to conserve energy, and she took great pains to listen. A few steps later, she heard a low deep growl and the sound of flapping wings. Melinda halted and held her breath, careful to shield her thoughts as she had all along. Dragons were supremely intelligent creatures, rumored to be able to hear the thoughts of lesser beings, humans included.

Was the dragon merely re-positioning herself, or was she readying to take flight?

Fortunately, the sound of flapping wings intensified then faded, letting Melinda hear the nervous flutters of her heart.

At long last, the cave widened into an enormous room, large enough to fit an entire castle. In the center lay gems of all sizes, shapes, and colors, as well as coins and gold, even a crown.

From behind the treasure, a shadow emerged. Melinda sharply inhaled and crept back to avoid being detected as the dragon moved in front of the treasure horde and used its tail to lift some gems to the top of the pile. With garnet eyes and midnight blue teeth, the dragon stretched out its wings, which nearly spanned the entire room. Although lean, the creature appeared to be a solid mass of muscle. The dragon's scales glittered blue in spots, black in others. Melinda tightened her grip on the sword.

The dragon used an ivory claw to pick a tooth.

Just one slash would ripe me to shreds.

The height of the cave reached sky high, a cathedral-like ceiling with a tiny speck of an opening at the top. A few stars twinkled above the exit. Could that dragon, skinny as it was, really fit through that small crevice?

As if the dragon heard her thoughts even though she concealed them by keeping them behind a mental wall, the dragon took flight, swooping around its treasure pile. Its wings weren't spread completely but folded back upon themselves. Soaring higher and higher, the dragon spiraled its way through the opening and out of the mountain.

Melinda waited several minutes in case the dragon returned, in case the dragon *had* heard her thoughts, but when the winged beast did not return, she rushed to the treasure and tucked an oval pyrite into her coin purse. A small heart-shaped amethyst caught her eye, but she ignored it for an amethyst larger than her hands though rough and unpolished. A jagged sapphire and a huge rock of an opal quickly disappeared, clanking as it jostled the other gems.

A loud thump behind Melinda caused her to whirl around, a citrine dropping to the floor and rolling to the dragon's feet.

'Foolish human,' the dragon said telepathically. 'Did you really think that I did not know you were there?'

The harsh thoughts flooded Melinda's mind, and she grabbed her pounding head. "Get out of my mind, dragon!"

Damn! Why had she been so greedy? She should have only grabbed the stones the blacksmith had mentioned and gotten out of there immediately.

'You are in no position to negotiate.'

Why isn't it attacking me? It's stalling. Melinda carefully kept her thoughts secluded from the dragon.

A sound echoed throughout the cavern. Plip. Plop. Dark drops dripped down its wing and landed on the cave floor, a small puddle forming. Blood. The dragon had been wounded during its venture from the mountain.

'Aye, I'm wounded. And I'm not an *it* either. I'm Doomia.'

So much for her being able to block her thoughts. 'Do you care to know who I am?'

'You call yourself Melinda. You crave adventure. Now, tell me one reason, Melinda the Adventurer, why I shouldn't kill you.'

Melinda stared at the powerful, imposing creature before her, yet she felt no fear. She doubted the dragon would care about her desire to become strong enough to go after the hippocampus or about her deal with the blacksmith.

So she merely mindspoke, 'I don't need a reason. You already have one.' *Otherwise, I would have been dead as soon as you returned.*

Doomia's eyes narrowed to almost nothing, and a huff of steam expelled from her nostrils. The dragon tapped a glistening, white razor sharp claw against the ground. 'A stupid harpy attacked me. She surprised me. She's too small and fast for me to rip her head off. If you bring me the head, you can leave, unharmed.'

'And if I just leave and not kill the harpy?'

'I will hunt you down and kill you.' The dragon almost smiled. 'I won't die from this.'

'You'll let me leave unharmed and with the treasure in my coin purse,' Melinda bargained.

A thin stream of fire left Doomia's mouth, dying out nowhere near Melinda. She held her ground. The light from the fire allowed Melinda to see the dragon's color, more blue than black. Paler than before its flight. *It ... she is more injured than she is letting on.*

'Fine. Go now. The nest is a meter up the mountain.'

Melinda sprinted before the dragon could change her mind. A harpy— foul-smelling death mongers—would be a much easier foe to face than a dragon, even a wounded one. Although this harpy somehow managed to wound a dragon....

At least Melinda had experience fighting against harpies. She had battled one to a draw two years ago.

Once removed from the dragon's line of sight, Melinda slowed her pace, not wishing to expend too much energy before the coming battle. The harpy would have the advantage of its wings, but she had a longer reach with her blade. At least the harpy's resemblance to an eagle stopped short of keen night vision. The darkness would hinder them both equally.

As soon as Melinda reached the exit, she gripped the hilt of the sword with both hands, her gaze darting all around. The night hung high in the sky, without a cloud in sight.

A loud screech sounded, and Melinda was careful not to tighten her muscles as she left the cave behind and turned behind her.

The harpy was perched on a large boulder a short distance away. A female head with overly long black feathers in lieu of hair, the harpy eyed Melinda with huge unblinking pupil-less eyes. Brown and black striped wings were folded by her side, and shorter smaller feathers covered her torso. Her face looked grotesque and ugly, as was common with the creatures, more monsters than hybrids. Black blood covered her eagle claws, and when she smiled, she revealed horrifically overcrowded fangs for teeth, all coated with that same black blood.

Melinda scanned the horizon quickly. No other harpies were in sight, but the dragon had mentioned a nest, so it was possible others lurked nearby.

"You smell of her," the harpy said.

"You attacked her," Melinda returned.

"A friend of yours?"

"No more than yours."

The harpy's laugh was more a grating, terrible wail than a sound of joy. "Yet you're here on her behalf."

"No offense."

"Went after her treasure, didn't you." The harpy cocked her head to the side. "We could join forces. Kill her off. Split the treasure."

Considering the damage the harpy did, it was a tempting offer, and Melinda considered it. Harpies, in general, could not be trusted, though. Dragons, well, they were fierce, yes, and if you crossed them, they would hunt you down and take their time killing you, but a dragon ally would be supremely beneficial.

"Are there other harpies near here?" Melinda asked.

The harpy let out a low hiss. "That blasted dragon hunted down and killed my family while they slept."

So revenge had been the harpy's motivation.

"And why did the dragon kill them?"

Another hiss sounded, and the harpy gnashed her teeth. They glistened and glittered like tiny daggers. "We might've gone after her treasure. She spotted us trying to grab some jewels. We gave them all back, but she just—"

"Fought to protect her treasure."

The harpy narrowed her eyes and let out a screeching cry. She flew faster than Melinda would've thought possible, but the sword forced the harpy back. The winged beast had the advantage of higher ground, but the harpy's fierce and frantic attack required too much energy. Melinda almost lazily moved the sword to block each would be blow until the harpy's human face twisted with exhaustion.

Melinda's arm muscles screamed, but she held her ground, waiting, biding her time, and when the harpy took a wild swipe at her, Melinda finally switched from defense to offense, and with a strong hack, she brought the sword down on the harpy's neck.

It wasn't a fierce enough blow to kill the harpy, but it sent her spiraling to the mountainside. At once, Melinda darted forward and stomped on the harpy's wing to prevent her from flying away.

"I wear your face!" the harpy said. "I'm part human. That dragon—"

Melinda's sword cut off the harpy's speech as it severed the head from its body. Her stomach lurched as she picked it up to give the dragon proof of the kill, and she returned to the dragon's treasure room.

Already the dragon was healing herself, transforming before Melinda's eyes from a weak, feeble, dying creature to her darker, stronger form.

Melinda walked over, dragging the sword beside her. "Here," she said, opting to talk out loud instead of with her mind.

The dragon peeked open an eye. 'You did it. Good.' She closed her eyes.

Melinda lingered.

Without opening her eyes, the dragon added, 'Why are you still here? You got what you wanted. Now go.'

"Did you kill that harpy's family?"

'Is that what she said? Damn harpy. Probably also said she went after my treasure, too.'

"What did she go after?"

Doomia puffed smoke once, twice, three times. Melinda figured the dragon wouldn't answer when she finally mindspoke, 'She ate my eggs.'

Melinda gasped. "I'm—"

'I don't want your apologies. Just go.'

Melinda glanced at the treasure mound on last time. "Goodbye."

'If you come back, I won't hesitate to kill you.'

"Mayhap I could earn more jewels."

The dragon roared, a loud and booming sound that filled the cave, almost like a laugh. 'Like I would willingly give an undeserving human my treasure. I told you to leave.'

'I'm going. I'm going.'

Melinda exited the cave, the moon a swollen silver orb high in the sky. She quickly killed three wild fowl. One she cooked and ate. Although she had no coin, she was able to sweet talk a bartender for a room at the tavern. In exchange, she gave him the other two fowl.

She had done it. She had lived through the greatest thrill of her life.

Already she was thinking that she just might be getting strong enough to take on Helga the Horrific herself.

Bright light poured into the room. Melinda stretched, causing the jewels in her coin purse to jingle. The first leg of her promise complete, she hurried to the blacksmith and dumped the jewels onto the table.

Drake eyed the gems, carefully inspecting each piece before placing them back down. He loving caressed the opal. "You not only survived, you got more than you needed."

"I did. Will you imbue the sword with all of them?" Melinda held up the sapphire, the fire in the background causing the dark blue gem to sparkle and shine.

"The protection stone. Said to increase intelligence, but I can't say I've actually seen any proof to that claim." He spun the opal in his hands. "But this gem, this gem. I'm surprised you picked it...."

"The name's Melinda, and I only grabbed the first ones I saw, after getting the pyrite and sapphire that is."

"That's what you think. Regardless, the opal is a powerful stone."

"In what way?"

"The opal causes the wearer to grow. People aren't the same after they use an opal for long periods of time." Drake stared at her. "You want me to adhere them all to your sword's hilt? Even the opal? Not just the amethyst and pyrite?"

Melinda bit her lip. "Yes. Go ahead."

"As you desire. Come back in a fortnight. Your sword will be ready then." He carried the stones next to his anvil.

Melinda turned to the door, but a nagging memory tugged at her. *What stone had I grabbed when Doomia startled me?* She cleared her throat, and Drake glanced at her, an eyebrow rising. "Tell me about a citrine."

"Ah, the citrine. A true jewel. They help to realize all your dreams, makes all your desires come true. Wealth, happiness, success. A rare gem in this world. Powerful. Did you manage to get one?"

"No." A wave of disappointment settled around her. Everything she could have wanted. But Melinda just nodded. "I'll be back in a fortnight. Be certain the sword is ready."

Drake set about his work, and Melinda watched for a moment. The flames danced and licked higher as he adjusted the temperature. The stones glowed in the small room, bright shapes of blue and purple lighting up the entire room.

When he grabbed the sword, ready to meddle with the hilt, Melinda left. By helping Drake with his revenge, she was increasing the chances she'd one day avenge her parents, too.

The fortnight passed quickly, and Melinda found herself anxious to retrieve her newly-enchanted blade. As soon as the sun's rays peeked over the horizon, Melinda strolled through the smithy's open door.

Drake stood beside the anvil, the sword in his hand, pointing downward. He lifted it up and held it across his hands. Melinda admired his handiwork. The jewels clustered near the blade, below the lion head and wings. A soft whisper resonated from the sword, humming with magical properties, enchanted beyond measure. Even the blade of the sword appeared different, a slight blue shine replaced its earlier dullness.

"It looks wonderful." Melinda reached out to reclaim the prized sword, but Drake grasped the hilt firmly. "Don't worry. I won't fail."

He handed over the sword and held up his hands in frustration. Pain and despair warred in his eyes as they again began to cloud. "Please, I beg of you, succeed where I have failed."

"I so swear."

Hilfalls carried a sense of wretchedness. The entire town seemed dead. Desolation and loneliness drifted on the wind. Dirt and dust covered everything. An eerie silence echoed the isolation as she crept forward. Dead bodies littered the streets, their faces contorted with pain, their bodies covered with blood long since dried. Her stomach churned at the sight.

Many of the windows were broken, the houses ransacked, furniture overturned, possessions of the dead long gone. *Thieves preying on the dead. Rodents of convenience, stealers of heart, sucking the soul from those no longer living. Damn vultures.*

The sound of rushing water drew Melinda to a cracked fountain. Water still dripped, mixing with the dirt, and muddied up her feet. *Must be recent destruction. Frostclaw is close by.*

Behind the fountain, Melinda discovered another body. This one still had a knife in one hand, the other clutching his swollen coin purse. *One of the thieves. Glad he got what he deserved.* Deep purple bruises had formed on his skin in the shape of a small broken "v."

Stones littered the ground, pieces of the houses. *This Glatisant has certainly done damage to the entire town, not just its people. Must be one fearsome creature.*

A low rumbling whispered on the breeze, but as Melinda turned in a circle, she couldn't distinguish the source. A sudden rush of wind from above her head, and the clattering on the roofs startled her. She nearly lost her balance as Frostclaw landed in front of her.

A hideous creature, part snake, lion, leopard, and deer. The serpent head and neck glanced around, long and sleek, even turning its head completely around. The small beady eyes on either side of its head forced the creature to constantly move its head to resume focus on Melinda.

Frostclaw continually barked, sounding like a wild pack of hounds set loose on a hunt. It had yellow eyes with the darkest black orbs, small nose slits and, despite the scales on its neck, a sleek almost smooth appearance. Its small tongue continually flickered in and out of its pink mouth, dripping with venom.

Its body was yellow-orange, speckled with rosettes, like a leopard, and turned to a lighter buff color toward its haunches. Swatting the black tuft of its tail at swirling bugs from the rotting corpses, the Glatisant continued to eye Melinda, and she shivered. *This is not a monster. This creature has intelligence.*

It pawed the ground. Its short legs ended with the hooves of a hart. The two separate cleats had made the broken "v" impressions on the bodies.

Without warning, the creature darted forward, its body barreling toward her. She sidestepped and brought up the sword, but Frostclaw continued forward, running away.

It had killed so many innocents already, was it teasing her, testing her? It turned back around, as if waiting for her, and when she raised the sword, the creature reared before jumping over some stones and behind a building, out of sight.

Now there was no question. The creature wanted her to give chase. So she did. The barking never ceased. She passed many more bodies, her anger at the creature mounting. Although no one she knew had died, the idea that an intelligent creature could knowingly seek out and destroy an entire village caused Melinda's stomach to clench and her teeth to grind. A fleeting thought of her parents made her throat swell up, and Melinda burst forward.

Judging from the barking, the mutant hybrid hid behind the next building. Melinda passed it and hurried down the next alley. The creature's barking became louder, and it lowered its reptilian head just before Melinda slashed. The sword felt lighter than ever, and the tingle up her arm reminded her of the magic now dwelling within it. The Glatisant backed up several steps as Melinda brought the sword back up, but the creature turned and ran before she could follow through with the arc. She barely missed, chopping off the hairy tuft.

Round and round the ruined village they ran. Frostclaw seemed to enjoy the chase, constantly turning its head around to see if she still followed and never showing any signs of wearing down nor making any attempt to fight back. *It's almost like this is some kind of game. Well, I'm not laughing. And I'm done playing.*

Melinda spied a ladder. She shoved the sword back into its sheath and climbed. When she reached the roof, she quickly aimed and fired. The arrow narrowly missed the animal. It stopped and glared at her, its tongue flicking upward. Backtracking, the creature rammed its shoulder into the ladder with such force the entire wooden building shuddered. Melinda leaped to the next rooftop and fired again. The creature ran forward, and Melinda pursued from above, trying to find a decent shot. *But I don't want to waste all my arrows. Wouldn't it be wonderful if a word could command them to return? Boomerang arrows.*

She leaped to another building, this one higher. Her fingers gripped the stone roof, and she clawed her way to the top. Precious seconds passed, and the creature continued its course. Melinda pulled herself up and glanced around. Frostclaw neared the edge of the village and zoomed toward the nearby forest. Melinda fired one more shot, but the creature's tail knocked it away before it hid behind some trees.

Damnable monster!

She raced to the edge of the roof, tossed down her weapons and quiver, grabbed onto the ledge, and dropped down to the ground, ducking into a roll as she landed to prevent injury. Coughing on the dust, she was forced to pause a moment to catch her breath, and then she retrieved the sword and quiver and grabbed the last discarded arrow. All in all, her endurance seemed stronger than ever, and she could only assume that the pyrite was doing its job.

She thundered through the forest, slashing through the underbrush. The barking sounded all around her. A sudden movement on the forest floor caught her eye, and she stabbed. A small garden variety snake dangled from the sword. Her foot removed the dead animal. The barking became louder, and a sharp pain pinched Melinda's right arm. She howled and dropped the sword. The venom quickly spread, and her right arm refused to move. *The poison must be paralytic.* She whirled around and shoved the arrow into Frostclaw's neck. The creature yelped and ran away, the arrow still lodged.

Melinda grabbed the sword and gave chase. Years ago, she had learned how to use both hands with a regular sword, but it had been years since she had practiced, and this sword was much heavier than an ordinary one. Her one arm hung like a dead weight at her side, causing her balance to shift, slowing her down.

Why isn't the amethyst working? Or is it preventing the venom from spreading to the rest of my body?

Melinda tripped over a tree root, landing on her stomach, and the remaining arrows in her quiver tumbled over her head. A heavy weight pressed onto her back, and a snake slithered through her hair and onto her shoulder. The forked tongue licked her ear before it reached forward, trying to grab an arrow in its mouth. Stretching so far allowed Melinda to see another arrow protruding from its neck. Melinda attempted to lift herself up and to shove the creature from her back, but her right arm refused to cooperate, and the creature weighed too much for her to roll it off. She jabbed wildly with the sword. Yelps again replaced the barking, music to Melinda's ears. Frostclaw retreated half a step, enough for Melinda to roll herself beneath the creature as she brought the sword in a sweeping arc and sliced off its head.

The yelps turned to a loud shriek, coming from the monster's belly, and the deer hooves danced before buckling, dark liquid spraying from its neck wound. Blood covered Melinda as she climbed to her feet and thrust the sword into the creature's belly and again into its heart. Finally, the Glatisant stopped moving, the shrieks ceasing.

Melinda put the sword away and wiped some blood from her face. Her fingers began to tingle, and she tried to form a fist. Her fingers hardly moved. *The blood is poisonous, too.*

Slowly she reached for the hilt and touched the amethyst. Strange warmth pulsated from the gem, and the heat spread throughout her body, through her fingers to her chest, even to her numb right arm. Gripping the hilt with fingers that now moved surer, Melinda rubbed the amethyst where the snake had bitten her. A sharp electric shock caused her to cry out. The scent of burning flesh wafted to her nose, and she gagged. Black liquid bubbled from the wound. It dripped onto the ground, causing a sizzling sound when it hit some grass, burning it to ash. Finally, Melinda could feel her arm again.

Melinda tore a large portion of her shirt. In case all of Frostclaw's body was poisonous, she dared not risk touching the head directly. She wrapped it in the cloth and carried it. On the way back through the forest, she picked up her arrows. She deposited them back into her quiver, but they fell through, and she had to collect them again. *Wonderful. Perhaps I can convince Drake to make me one for free.*

Melinda hurried back to the blacksmith's shop. His eyes brightened when he saw her. She handed him the wrapped head. Drake uncovered it, brought it to his face, and whispered words of hatred that weren't quite audible. Glancing up, he started, surprised. "Why are you still here? I already gave you your reward."

"I need a new quiver. The Glatisant destroyed it."

Drake's brows furrowed, and he nodded toward the wall with the blades. Along the floor were some bows, arrows, and quivers.

She secured the largest one and walked outside. The powerful sun's rays blinded her. When her vision cleared, her gaze fell upon Mount Gravel in the nearby distance.

What had the dragon called her?

Ah, yes. Melinda the Adventurer.

Yes, indeed.

And her next adventure would be to avenge her parents.

She was ready.

Nicole Zoltack loves to write fantasy and paranormal stories. Her works include the Magic Incarnate series about a devout girl who learns she is magic itself and the Heroes of Falledge trilogy. She's also a freelance editor and a ghostwriter. When she's not writing about knights, superheroes, or witches, she enjoys spending time with her loving husband, three energetic young boys, and precious baby girl. She enjoys riding horses (pretending they're unicorns, of course!) and going to the PA Renaissance Faire, dressed in garb. She'll also read anything she can get her hands on. Her current favorite TV shows are *The Walking Dead* and *Gotham*.

Website - www.NicoleZoltack.com Newsletter http://www.subscribepage.com/m0k3l8

Destiny's Flight

The loud pounding on my cottage door drove the pleasant dreams from my mind and forced me awake. I wrenched myself away from my place against my wife's back. Pulling on my tunic and leggings, I wondered what the early visitor wanted. Since I served the Father as a miracle man, my first thought was that someone was injured or sick. Was it Byron's mother? The young boy spent so much time sick that Kelestria had joked we should move into the cottage next to theirs. The rays slanting through the window announced the dawn had barely broken. Perhaps Kathryn had been kicked when milking her cow. She might have forgotten to warm her hands first. The news was probably bad; those who wanted me to bless their fields waited until after breakfast.

"Derke! Cousin! Open the door!" The banging continued.

Ah, it was neither of those. My cousin, Sir Manegold Osias, had stopped while passing through the area. Though entitled to stay at the nearby castle of our liege lord, he preferred to stay at the rectory of our village priest. He and I were very close; our mothers were sisters. He, my wife, and I had talked long into the night.

Once I had a shirt and pants on, I tried to smooth my dark brown hair. Then I opened the door and slipped out. I wondered if Manegold ever took off his mail hauberk. Had he even slept? He already had his surcoat on, proudly displaying his family escutcheon—black on the right and blue on the left, a seated golden lion, and two small silver crosses in the top third. I looked up just a bit at him.

"What's wrong, Manegold? Is someone ill?" Slightly my senior and recently knighted, his blue eyes peered at me from under his short-cropped, red-gold hair.

"No, look!"

Following his finger to the sky, I saw two birds silhouetted against the morning sun, one clearly chasing the other.

"You awakened me for ... birds?"

"Look again."

As I squinted, the pursuing bird spat a stream of fire at its prey.

"A wyvern! A rare sight indeed!" I was fully awake now, staring at the wyvern and prey. "What is it chasing?" One did not see wyverns as often as a decade before. Even rarer were the large dragons.

"I don't know," he said, shading his eyes with one hand, "but both have riders."

My back snapped erect. "Riders? Knights Adumbrar ride wyverns!" My cousin was a Knight Luminar, sworn enemies of the Adumbrar.

"So do some practitioners of black magic." That was why he had awakened me!

As a Knight Luminar, he fought the Father's enemies on earth. As a miracle man, I fought them spiritually. He and I rode together whenever we could. "Either way, we have a job to do. I'll tell Kelestria."

I slipped back inside as my wife awakened. Tall and broad shouldered, she came from a long line of farmers on her mother's side. She yawned and stretched as she sat up, fluffing her dark hair. I thought her the most beautiful sight in the world. Smiling and fluttering her eyelashes, she motioned for me to come back to our bed. Sadly, I shook my head.

Her smile faded, her small mouth turning to a frown. "Dear, is something wrong?"

"Manegold spotted a wyvern chasing something in the sky. The wyvern and its prey both have riders." I pulled on my white miracle man's robe over my tunic and leggings.

She shivered even though the morning was unusually warm for the early fall. "You have to go. Do I have time to fix you a lunch?" In our year of marriage, she had quickly come to understand a miracle man's duties. Wherever He called, we went, often at a moment's notice. She rose from the bed, standing almost as tall as me. She grabbed her green dress from the floor and pulled it on over her nightclothes.

I shook my head. "No. We ride as soon as we can."

"You must take something."

"If you have it ready by the time we leave, I will."

"Agreed." We kissed goodbye.

The sun was much higher in the sky as our horses trotted along the road. My cousin and I watched the wyvern and its prey overhead. They were still too high in the sky for us to determine what the prey was. Manegold was attempting to figure out where it was going and race it there.

Kelestria's travel rations jostled against the side of my horse. She had prepared enough for two days. Manegold always traveled with rations. My black mare traveled easily and lightly, nudging my cousin's horse as it moved. Manegold's war horse snorted indignantly and kept ahead.

The wyvern and prey were almost directly overhead; soon they would be ahead of us and we would never reach them. We pressed onward.

"The wyvern is catching up!" Manegold shouted.

I looked. The prey must be tiring. "It won't miss next time it flames."

Sure enough, the wyvern spit fire and flamed the prey. In just a few heartbeats, the falling prey and rider were close enough for me to make out that the flying creature was a griffin.

Those magnificent creatures with the head, forelegs, and wings of an eagle and the body of a lion had not been seen in this part of the world in over a century. The rider hung tightly as they plummeted toward the ground. They crashed through the trees not far from us.

I kept my eyes on the wyvern. "He's descending also."

"He probably wants to make sure they're dead! Come on!" He spurred on his horse.

I dug my heels into my mare's flanks and followed.

We galloped through the forest to the crash.

"They should be just ahead!" shouted Manegold.

We heard the griffin scream in defiance and a sword being drawn. Manegold spurred his horse again. No matter how hard I tried to keep up, they pulled further away.

The Father had smiled on us, because within moments we saw the four combatants. The wounded griffin had spread both wings and hissed and spat at the wyvern and black-mailed knight. The griffin's saddle did not interfere with her fighting at all. (Tradition held that griffins, like dragons, were female until determined to be male.) Her rider, a slight, brown-robed and hooded figure, fought with a long-handled spear. Whoever he was, he showed skill with the spear, but the knight was better with the sword. The black knight pushed an advantage and opened up a wound in the rider's side.

The Adumbrar wore a black mail hauberk with a black surcoat. I could only see his eyes between his coif and helmet. Unlike the Luminar showing their family escutcheons, all Adumbrar knights had a sable shield with a blue band across the middle and a red dragon's head. They cared nothing for individuals only the glory of the group. No one knew who they were underneath the helmet and mail.

"Protect the woman, cousin," Manegold said as he pulled a mail coif across his face. "I'll take care of the knight." He raised his sword in the knights' customary manner.

"Woman?" I saw a curved waist as she pulled her robe tight trying to hold her side.

The Knight Adumbrar raised his sword before his covered face, accepting the challenge. The two knights stepped into combat range, each standing to present their shield to the other.

Drawing my sword, I ran to the woman and griffin. The griffin's claws and beak slashed at the wyvern. Her wings were singed, but the griffin kept the fight so intense and close that the wyvern had no opportunity to breathe fire again. As the two animals rolled in another deadly embrace, I stepped back. It was foolish to get too close to them.

However, I was not limited to my sword in this fight. I crossed myself, invoking the Father, Son, and Spirit to my aid. "Father!" I cried. "Bless the griffin in her strikes."

The griffin's next slash caught the wyvern on the wing. The griffin flapped her wings in the wyvern's face. I could see she was wounded in one wing, but she still held the advantage. I knew I couldn't help in either fight. Manegold would want to fight one-on-one. I took a stance guarding the woman.

In the few seconds I had spent watching the beasts fight, Manegold and the black knight had tested one another. They struck and moved apart quickly, each trying to determine the extent of the other's skill.

Manegold was talented and getting better but was often impatient. I prayed he would be patient today.

Off to the side, the wyvern screamed as the griffin sank her sharp beak into its neck. Blood flowing freely from the wound, the wyvern slumped, dying if not already dead.

Seeing his mount defeated, the black knight spoke for the first time. "The two of us will finish this." The mail coif covering his mouth muffled his deep voice.

"Agreed," Manegold said, striking again with his sword.

The black knight easily parried. "Every day I pray to our Father below that he send me an opponent worthy of my skill. Perhaps tomorrow he will grant that request."

Even from here, I could see Manegold stiffen. The insult struck home. Angry now, he sprang forward as he slashed. The black knight easily stepped to the side and brought his sword handle down on Manegold's neck. My cousin collapsed into the dirt.

The black knight reversed the grip on his sword and tried to stab downward. Manegold rolled quickly to the side, the blade burying itself into the soil for a hand's breadth.

Manegold scurried away and sprang to his feet. Winded from the impact, he needed a moment.

The knight wrenched his sword free and advanced again. He would not give Manegold that moment.

Manegold parried the strike. He would make the Adumbrar earn the victory.

From behind me and low to the ground, a spear flashed past. Tangling in the legs of the black knight, it tripped him. Manegold's opponent dropped his sword.

Moving like lightning, Manegold jumped forward and stood between the knight and his sword. The Adumbrar rolled away, came back to his feet, and ran into the trees.

As the knight fled, Manegold turned to the woman. His voice quivered with rage. "Why did you do that?"

"I saw a way to bring victory and took it."

"You cheated. He and I were in a fair duel. It was not a battlefield melee."

She continued, "When you fight for yourself, I'll leave you alone. When you fight for me, I refuse to leave my *goral* completely in your hands."

"Your what?" I asked, placing my hands on the wound and praying. Her jagged breathing grew stronger and the wound closed.

"The course of events *HaShem* has decreed I will follow even as I choose them myself."

"Your destiny," I said, helping her to her feet. The name she used for the Father marked her as one of the *Ha'am Ha'eretz*. "I am Derke, a miracle man. This is my cousin, Sir Manegold Osias, a Knight Luminar."

"I see that armor frequently back home. But what does 'miracle man' mean?"

"I serve the Father, riding to battle with the knights to pray over them, and at other times I plea for the Father to do mighty deeds on the behalf of those who believe."

"A *navi*! A prophet! Like Elijah and Isaiah."

"Yes, a prophet. Though I would not place myself in their category."

"If *HaShem* has called you like He called them, then you are in their category." She dusted off her robes and pushed the hood back off her head. Brown hair and brown eyes sparkled amidst her dusky skin. "My name is Deborah, daughter of Mordechai." She walked over to the griffin. "This is Chione." She knelt to inspect the singed wing.

Manegold spoke, "Deborah is a very lovely name."

Quizzically, I looked at my cousin. The tone of his voice had changed. He was no longer angry at her. In fact, a goofy smile spread across his face.

The blood drained from my cheeks. Manegold was smitten.

Most of the time, I would be glad for Manegold. He was slightly older than me and deserved the happiness of a good marriage. It was one of the Father's greatest gifts.

However, he had told me last night that his father Frederick had selected a bride for him and arrangements were being made. Breaking the negotiations would be troublesome and could lead to a feud between the houses. The continent's kingdoms had enough trouble already.

Well, this flirtation would go nowhere. I would pray for the griffin's wing to be healed, Deborah and Chione would depart, Manegold would forget about her in short order, and all would be well. "Let me heal your griffin," I said.

I took gentle hold of the wing where the flames had seared it and whispered a prayer of healing. The charred flesh turned healthy and pink. New feathers sprouted and grew to maturity in seconds.

From the other side, Manegold stroked the griffin's wing. "Isn't that better, Chione?"

"*Ki!*" the griffin squawked.

"That means 'yes,'" Deborah said. "She does not speak your language."

"Then how did she know what I asked?"

"She guessed from your tone. All griffins are smart, but Chione is the greatest of all." She stroked her eagle head between the eyes. Chione chirped with pleasure. "Careful with her, though. Her wits are as sharp as her talons. She likes riddles."

"Why was that Adumbrar chasing you?" Manegold asked, never one for idle chatter.

"We carry an urgent message that must go to one of your clerists. The message will be a great help to your war, or they would not want it so badly."

The clerists were knights who had also been called to the priesthood. Besides fighting, they served as chaplains for the rest of the knights and led them in prayers, services, and vigils. The Grand Clerist sat on the high council of the Knights Luminar alongside the Grand Marshall and Grand Jurist. Manegold's father, a jurist, specialized in law and lore.

"There are always clerists at our castles," he said. "The closest one is two days from here by horse. In fact, the master and commander of that castle is a clerist."

"It will be quicker when I ride Chione." She adjusted the straps on Chione's saddle. The saddle was unlike a horse's. Deborah would hold the posts on the collar and place her feet in stirrups that ran along the back instead of down the mount's sides. There was also a rider's belt chained to the rest of the saddle.

Manegold shook his head. "You'll have to stay with us. That Adumbrar almost killed you. He might bring reinforcements."

She started to protest, but I interrupted. "The griffin is tired. We'll have to stay here with you that long anyway." I hated to take Manegold's side right now because I wanted this woman on her way. "Or you could give the message to Manegold."

The woman shook her head. "The message is encrypted. The clerist will know how break the encryption, but it must be delivered in person—*yadh* to *yadh* as we say." She dug into her robes and produced a scroll.

Taking it from her, I tried to read it. "These letters make no sense."

"No one can read it without the key."

"Let's get started, then," Manegold said. "We can prepare at Derke's village."

I mounted my mare, Manegold got on his horse, and Deborah climbed into Chione's saddle. Manegold signaled for me to lead the way. Behind me, I heard him chatting with Deborah as the great beast walked along with us.

Back in my village, I left the horse with Manegold and rushed to the cottage. "Kelestria!" I called. "Manegold and I have to escort a young woman named Deborah and her griffin to the clerists." I rummaged for a pack in which to carry food.

Kelestria stopped weaving. "Tell me more."

"She carries an urgent message, and Manegold is smitten!"

Her eyes widened. "Does she have a chaperon?"

Seeing an escape, I breathed a sigh of relief. "No. She came alone." Propriety forbade a single woman from traveling alone with a single man. Traveling with two men was more scandalous, even though I was a married miracle man. Had I been a priest or monk, my vows of celibacy would allow me to count as a chaperon.

Kelestria rose from the loom and began helping me pack. "I'll come with you." More bread and dried meat went into the basket. She got the water skins from a trunk. "Do you expect more trouble?"

"The griffin killed the wyvern, but the Adumbrar escaped."

"Griffins are rare. She'll be spotted for sure."

I nodded. "I haven't come up with a solution for that problem. Manegold isn't thinking clearly."

"We could borrow a wagon and cover the griffin in the back. Then Deborah can ride with me on the wagon."

I hugged my wife and kissed her. "Perfect." We quickly finished packing. I collected my short bow and a quiver of arrows. We would hunt for food to make the packed rations stretch.

Outside, I introduced my wife to Deborah. Wanting to keep Chione secret, Deborah had left the magnificent beast hidden in the trees. Manegold went to ask Father Phaeus if we could borrow the church's wagon and team of horses.

Father Phaeus suggested we pack the wagon around Chione with goods in case anyone lifted the covers.

We soon had everything ready to go. Outside the village, Deborah removed Chione's saddle but left the collar. Chione settled into the wagon with her head near the front and chirped at Deborah.

Manegold and I rode on either side of the wagon. I took up the side next to Deborah, and he rode near Kelestria. When we stopped to water the horses, the women went upstream to refill the water skins. He spoke while the first two horses drank. The other two grazed.

"I know what you are doing, cousin."

"What am I doing?" I tried to look innocent as I pulled the blankets from Chione so she could drink from the river.

"You mean to keep me from Deborah." Chione's head twitched a bit at her rider's name as she stretched near the river.

"You are going to be engaged."

"Not by choice."

I shook my head. "What does choice matter? Discuss that with Uncle Frederick. Until he says otherwise, I count you as engaged."

He turned his back on me. "Do you know why I envy you?"

"Envy me? We always wanted to be knights, and you are one."

"It was your choice to end your training so soon," he said dismissively.

"So soon! We spent seven years as pages before I withdrew!"

"And in one more month you would have been chosen as a knight's squire."

I shook my head. "That is why I withdrew when I did! I could not conscience the expense my master would undertake for a failed endeavor!"

The first horses finished their drinking, and we took the others.

Continuing, I said, "But you know that, Cousin. What really troubles you? It is not our different callings."

"You were able to marry for love! By giving up your lands and title, you were able to choose your bride!"

I raised my hand to stop him. "That is not why I later renounced my inheritance." I held out my arms covered in their white robes. "The Father called me to minister as a miracle man. He called you to be a Knight Luminar. Rejoice that He called us in accordance with our natural proclivities."

Chione finished drinking and stretched out on the ground, her black eyes locked on us. Riding in the cramped wagon could not be very comfortable.

My next words were soft. "You would not enjoy being a monk or priest."

He laughed without humor. "No, I like the thought of being married too much." Still wearing his spurs, he carefully squatted next to Chione. He rubbed his hands through her furry flanks. The griffin chirped twice and stretched out further. "I think she likes that. But, cousin, would our Lord give us talents and inclinations one way and then call us to something else? It seems like such a waste."

"We are like clay which He molds or metal He shapes. He knows which metal will serve best as a plowshare, which will serve as a stirrup, and which will serve as a sword. We have no right to say 'Why did you make me so?' Your destiny is to be a sword in His hand among the Luminar. Do not fight that nature."

"He calls each of us to holiness, yet our nature is to sin."

I stood agape for a moment. He had surprised me. My cousin did not speak of theology often, yet here he exhibited a quick insight. "We can break anything. Our nature was first to be holy and yearn for holiness. Our first parents chose to mar that." After a breath, I continued, "The women will be back soon."

He nodded. "Please don't tell Deborah I am almost engaged. I fear that I will not love the woman my father selects."

My heart broke for my cousin. The women's approach removed any need for me to speak.

We traveled on. Kelestria asked me to ride next to her. That allowed Deborah and Manegold to speak.

"How did you come to bring the message?" he asked her.

I listened intently.

"An assassin wounded my eldest brother just before he mounted Chione. I grabbed the message, mounted, and we flew."

"So an accident brought you here?"

Deborah shook her head, vigorously. "No accident. *HaShem's* will is why I am here." She smiled. "I imagine my father was livid, though. He is very protective."

"As he should be," Manegold said.

"Yes," I said, "fathers always want what is best for their children, both sons and daughters."

If looks were arrows, Manegold's glare would have killed me. Kelestria punched me on the leg. I remained quiet after that. Chione's chirping from the wagon sounded almost like laughter.

Deborah asked Manegold, "Did I cost you honor today?"

"Some. Out of ignorance. Had you known what interfering would mean, you would have cost me much more."

"Honor is important to you? I've never heard the knights back home speak of it."

"Honor is not something you speak of unless you have need. You live honor." He sat straighter on his horse. "I have always been glad our Lord called me to serve as a Luminar."

I saw Deborah nod. She looked at Manegold admiringly.

The sun was sinking when Deborah asked about a place to camp for the night.

"There is a monastery just over the next hill," I said. "We can request shelter there."

Minutes later we were welcomed in and given cells for the night. The black-robed Abbot Francis, a thin elderly man with only a wisp of hair for his tonsure, told us dinner would be served once the *Lecto Divina* concluded.

"Tell me, Abbot," Manegold began, "an Adumbrar chased her. Will we be safe sleeping with no watch here?"

Francis nodded. "The monastery is blessed against violent harm. Even if a whole patrol of Adumbrar stormed in, they could not kill a single person within a mile of these walls." He then handed us over to a lay brother for the time being. Brother Hector, who appeared to be about my age, told us we were welcome to wash from the road before dinner. We took our animals to the stable before doing anything else.

Inside the stable, Chione lifted her head and started thrashing her wings. She squawked loudly. "*Hatsachanah gadol!*"

"Hush, Chione, the smell isn't any worse than a horse stable back home," Deborah said. Then she whispered, "We don't want to let everyone in the monastery know we have a griffin. I hear monks gossip like washer women."

Chione shook her head. "*Shema li!*"

"She wants me to listen. *Mah-na?*"

"*Lo 'eyeda,*" Chione continued to stare at Deborah.

"She says she doesn't know. *Kiyada't, qera'at-li!*" The woman turned to us. "I told her to call for me when she knows."

She walked away from Chione, and we followed Brother Hector to the dining hall. This monastery was large with several hundred men, gardens, barns, kilns, chapels, a library, and a hospital for the nearby town. At dinner, they served dark bread, herbed cheese, and spiced sausage. The poor monks used herbs to increase the flavors.

As we ate, Kelestria nudged me. "You should say my breads are better." A twinkle in her eye let me know she was joking.

I replied in kind. "Lying is a sin."

Laughing, Kelestria elbowed me. Deborah and Manegold sat across from us, laughing with us.

"Do you eat bread like this back home?" Manegold asked her.

"We usually eat barley bread. Wheat and rye are for special occasions. During one of our feasts, we have a dry bread we call 'the bread of suffering.' It reminds us of how our people suffered in the past."

"That sounds terrible."

"The bitter herbs are worse." As I watched, she would lean in close to Manegold but never too close. She laughed at all the right times and made eye contact with him often. She knew how to tug at a man's heart!

Manegold and Deborah chatted throughout the meal. I ate, uneasily. She was a lovely woman and seemed interested in Manegold. If only Sir Frederick had chosen her! That was next to impossible. She was not from the continent or a knightly family. Frederick's choice—whoever she was—would be wealthy and well-connected politically.

I decided to remind Manegold of his place. "Manegold, when did you say your father expects you?"

"In a week," he said, staring at me, "unless an urgent mission arises."

"Isn't there important news for you when you get back?"

"Oh," said Deborah. "I hope it is good news."

With a simmering look, Manegold rose from the table and left in the direction of our cell. Kelestria poked her knife handle hard into my side.

Manegold and I sat in our guest cell, a small room with two straw mattresses on the dirt floor. He had said nothing to me since dinner.

"I'm sorry, Manegold," I said. "I have intruded where I need not go."

He looked up at me, still silent as a tree.

"I will say nothing more about Deborah. May the Lord bless you, if He wills you to be together." In my heart, I still believed Manegold should do as his father bid, but I had made my case. Manegold would choose his path now.

My cousin relaxed. "Thank you. I know you were thinking of me. I have never met a woman like her."

"She is letting you know she is willing to be pursued. Kelestria explained part of how women work. The layers of intrigue and hints they work within are enough to drive a man mad."

"I prefer the man's way of simply and openly pursuing."

"As do I, but women are not men and never will be. Praise the Father for that! Remember also, you cannot pursue unless she wants to be pursued. Let us retire. Monks always rise early in the morning." My bow and quiver stood in the corner where I left them before dinner.

He shook his head. "I intend to spend the night at vigil in the prayer chapel for our mission."

"Is that why you haven't taken off your sword?"

He paced. "No. Every time I try to take it off, I feel as though I should not."

I raised an eyebrow, but a sudden knock at our door prevented me from saying anything else. I opened it to see Kelestria fretting in the hallway.

"Deborah has not returned from checking on Chione after dinner."

Grabbing his helmet, Manegold hurried down the hall. We followed.

In the stable, we found Chione asleep with no sign of Deborah. The griffin did not rouse easily.

"Where is Deborah?" Manegold asked once he awakened the beast.

Squawking loudly, she clawed at the door to her stable. *"Laqach et-Deborah!"* She repeated her screams.

"None of us speak Hedaic," I said, exasperated.

"But I do," said the abbot huffing and puffing as he came up behind us. Brother Hector stood behind him. "I followed when I saw you running."

"We are grateful. Can you speak to Chione?"

"Certainly. One moment." He turned to the lay brother. "Get the relic from the chapel; you know which one."

The young man nodded and hurried away.

The abbot demonstrated great courage by reaching over the stall door and stroking an agitated griffin's head. *"Mah-zeh tir'iy?"* I guessed he was asking her what she saw.

Chione calmed slightly, hearing words in her own language. *"Habasar hunamani! Wallaqach nazir et-Deborah!"*

"The meat made her sleep, and a monk took Deborah." Looking confused, he repeated part of what Chione had said, *"Nazir?"*

"Wayyarach k'tzel."

The abbot shook his head. "She says that the monk smelled like a shadow. That's nonsense."

Manegold grabbed the old man's shoulders. "Adumbrar means shadow! One of your monks is an Adumbrar Knight."

The abbot's eyes widened. "Not possible! The Father would surely tell us. All the monks were blessed and prayed over. The Spirit would tell us of a traitor."

I added, "I do not know why the Father allows many of the things He does. I know we do His work wherever we are and even those who oppose Him serve Him."

The abbot nodded, clearly still upset. "I will have to inspect all the monks immediately. To think! I heard this monk's confession!"

"Perhaps the knight snuck in tonight disguised," Kelestria added.

The abbot relaxed. "Yes, that is more likely."

Just then, Brother Hector returned with a wooden box that would fit within both hands. The abbot crossed himself and took it. "St. Jerome is the patron saint of translators. Inside this box is his finger bone which will allow us to communicate with Chione."

I reverently took the box and asked, "Can you understand me, Chione?"

"Yes. Now let us hurry. The trail grows colder as we speak!"

Manegold put on his helmet. "This Adumbrar will not survive to see the morning, so I swear."

Kelestria grabbed my sleeve. "I will stay here. You'll travel faster without me."

"No horses," Chione said. "The men will ride me."

I picked up her saddle.

"No time. Just use the collar. It is later than you think."

We hurried outside. Manegold stretched out on Chione's back, holding onto one post with both hands. I kissed Kelestria quickly before climbing onto the other side. I closed my eyes and prayed. The relic box hung about my neck by a thin rope.

"They went this way! He has a horse!" Chione shrieked and leaped into the night air. The ground fell away underneath us, and air rushed past our faces. She flew just above the tree tops. Thankful that I had eaten lightly at dinner, I clenched my jaws.

"Have you ever been in the air before, cousin?" he asked.

"No. Have you?" I answered as my stomach flopped.

"Only by dragon back. Required as part of the training."

"Yet another reason I'm glad I was called differently." I gripped tighter as Chione turned. "Oh, dear!" I didn't ask her to slow down. We needed to find Deborah even if I lost my supper.

As I choked, Chione said, "I see them!" A final burst of speed placed us in front of the knight on horseback. I released the riding post and rolled to the ground. I heard Manegold's mail clinking as he did the same.

Chione stretched to her full height, wings expanded. She screamed at the black-armored knight who had taken her friend.

His horse pawing the ground, the knight flung Deborah to the forest floor. She looked bruised and battered; obviously, she had not been taken easily. Hands tied behind her back, she scurried away from the knight and horse.

The knight drew his sword and charged at us.

We scattered. I ran to the left, thinking we could close on him in a pincer. Manegold ran to the right. Having fought together often, Manegold and I needed no words to form a battle plan.

I clutched the wooden cross around my neck and prayed for all of us to have valor and protection. Then I prayed offensively. The skies clouded and lightning jumped from cloud to cloud, giving us more light. A clap of thunder rocked the forest, but the knight remained seated on his horse. Lightning from the cloudless sky struck a tree on the edge of the combat circle, causing the tree to catch fire.

The Adumbrar shouted out prayers of his own in some infernal tongue. Flames played along his sword, and he swung at Chione. He missed, but Chione's clawed strike was thrown off by her dodge.

I saw Manegold edging around to defend Deborah. Chivalrous to a fault, he would protect her, but if she were not here, he would press against the black knight harder.

Regretting leaving my bow at the monastery, I ran to Deborah and cut the ropes around her wrist with the small knife I wore. She wore no weapon. "Get away!"

Wordlessly, she retreated towards the trees.

The Adumbrar spoke, his voice deep, "Three against one. So much for the Luminar's vaunted fairness."

"You had a chance to fight just me, but you ran. If you wanted a rematch, you should not have kidnapped Deborah."

"The monastery is blessed against violence on its grounds!" He spoke again in that same infernal language and threw something to the ground.

The item twisted and grew until it was four feet high at the shoulder. It stood on four legs that were the same coal black as its body. Bright red eyes glowed in front of horns and ears. Flames came a short way from its mouth when it barked. A devil dog!

The devil dog bounded toward Chione and growled. The knight said, "My hound shall face your griffin and miracle man while you and I finish our duel." He challenged Manegold with his flaming weapon. "But first, I must dismount. We shall fight blade-to-blade, lest any claim my horse gave advantage after I slay you." The black knight dismounted from his horse and repeated the challenge gesture.

Manegold raised his sword in acceptance. The combatants circled one another.

The devil dog spit fire at Chione. She jumped into the air and landed on the other side of the dog. He bounded at me and knocked me to the ground. I rolled where I landed and came up still holding my knife. He came at me again, and I dodged to the side, stabbing into his thick skin as he passed by.

I looked quickly for Chione and saw her making short work of the knight's stallion.

The devil dog made no sound after I stabbed him. He kept running and took my knife with him! Now weaponless, I expected him to press his attack. I was not disappointed. He spun and jumped. I shouted at the top of my lungs for the Father to grant me victory.

He did. In the form of Chione. The griffin descended on the devil dog from the sky and sank all four sets of claws into the hound. It yelped.

Seeing Chione had matters well in hand and knowing better than to jump into a fight like that, I looked back to Manegold.

The two knights had paused for a quick breath from their fight. Blood ran down Manegold's shield arm, but the black knight now limped.

Behind me, I heard Chione squawk in victory. Deborah came out of the forest carrying a lit branch. She stood next to me, and we watched the knights.

"Aren't you going to interfere?" I asked.

She shook her head. "He must win on his own."

The knights struck and parried for another minute.

"Did you follow us and sneak in?" Manegold asked the knight when they paused for breath.

"No. Divination showed me you would be at the monastery. Join us, and you can try it."

"Never! I care not what chicken bones say I will do!"

"Fear them, though. They said I would win this combat!"

With a lunge, the combat resumed. For a brief moment, the Adumbrar had the upper hand, then Manegold dipped his sword low and cut heavily into his opponent's thigh. The Adumbrar fell to his knees.

"Do you yield?" Manegold asked, his sword leveled at the knight's eyes.

"Never," the Adumbrar answered, trying one last time to swing his sword.

Manegold thrust his sword forward, ending the black knight's life. The enemy's body fell to the ground with the clink of chain mail and a thud.

I relaxed as the battle rush drained away. Then I hurried to Manegold's side and eased him to the ground as his strength faded. My prayers for his healing began immediately. His lips moved in quiet praise to the Father for granting victory.

Deborah knelt on his other side and took his hand. "I saw you fight, Manegold. You were magnificent!"

"For you," he said. His wounds closed as I prayed. Soon, he rose from the ground and removed the coif from his face. "Thank you for not interfering in our duel."

She ducked her head. "Doing so again would cost you honor, and a life without honor is worse than an honorable death for you."

I gaped at her. "You would have let the knight kill us all so Manegold could keep his honor?"

She laughed. "Oh, no. If he had killed Manegold, I would have let Chione have the knight. She's hungry, and horse flesh disagrees with her."

157

Chione ripped a chunk of flesh from the devil dog. "This needs salt."

We all laughed. Chione chirped and rubbed against my leg. I reached down and stroked the feathers between her eyes.

We returned to the monastery. Deborah and Manegold talked the whole way. I tried not to listen but still overheard some of their talk.

"I feared when the knight took you."

She laughed. "Not as much as I feared for myself and my mission."

"What would I have told your father? The letter would be my responsibility."

"That I died for the mission. He would understand that *HaShem* willed it."

I retreated into my prayers. Holding Chione's riding post, I didn't worry about wandering off the road. Less than an hour later, we were back at the monastery. Kelestria came running out and threw her arms around me. The abbot followed.

"I was so worried," Kelestria said. "I'll never get used to you being gone."

"Now that I have you, I worry more for myself, too," I whispered. "But I'm happy."

"I wish we could stay in the same cell tonight," she said. "I want you within reach."

I smiled. "The monastery wouldn't allow it. Besides, I have something to tell Manegold."

My wife raised an eyebrow. "Oh?"

Nodding, I said, "I want him to have the same happiness we do. Deborah might be his best chance. At the very least, he is not fighting against her."

She hugged me tighter.

Abbot Francis fretted. "I have asked all the monks. No one came in after you did. How did the Adumbrar get in?"

Manegold replied, "He walked in disguised before we arrived. He told me that he used a divination to know where we were going."

The abbot crossed himself. "Fortune telling! The work of the Devil!"

Abbot Francis and Brother Hector saw us off the next morning. Carved above the monastery gate were the words *"Crux Sacra Sit Mihi Lux. Non Draco Sit Mihi Dux."*

Manegold stared at the words. "What does that mean?" he asked.

"Something about the holy cross and a dragon."

"Let the holy cross be my light. Never let the dragon be my guide," Abbot Francis said. "Our founder, St. Benedict, used to pray that repeatedly. We pray it as well. He also taught, 'Walk in God's ways with the Gospel as our guide.'"

I held out the relic box to Brother Hector.

Brother Hector said, "Take the relic with you and return it when you come back."

After leaving the monastery, Manegold and Deborah talked all day. The two certainly enjoyed one another's company. The Father would bring His will without my interference.

We reached the knights' castle in the late afternoon. As we came over a hill, two mailed knights rode out to greet us.

"Sir Manegold Osias," the lead one said. "Welcome. We did not expect you." Every knight alive knew the symbols on Manegold's shield and surcoat. He was, after all, a direct descendant of one of the Luminars' founders and still used the same arms.

"The visit was not planned," he replied. "This woman bears an urgent message for a clerist."

The second knight saluted, turned, and spurred his horse back to the castle.

Once inside the courtyard, we were escorted to the large receiving room. Chione could walk comfortably through the spacious corridors. An old knight stood in front of a desk with younger knights standing guard. Deborah handed the message to the master and commander. The large cross beneath the escutcheon on his surcoat showed him to be a clerist.

"Sir Thurgood," Manegold said, identifying him by the coat of arms—a silver field with a red cross and three golden eagles.

Sir Thurgood examined the scroll. "This code requires a key phrase to be decrypted. Were you given the key?"

"I have it," Chione said before Deborah could answer. Looking at the master and commander, she said:

Two princes are key
The first of water and stone
Head of 70, giver of 10
The second of fire and air
Stood against 400, fled before 1
On their mountain, see the kingdom

"What!" Manegold exclaimed. "The key can't be that long."

"No," Deborah said. "It's another of Chione's riddles." She turned to the beast. "Can't you just tell us?"

Chione preened. "One cannot deny their nature or their destiny. Riddles are my nature; this one was my destiny." She dipped her head like a bow.

Muttering, we began debating the possibilities. We were fairly certain that the answer would be religious in nature, perhaps two names. Though in a riddle, the princes might not be people. Almost certainly they would not be royalty. After an hour of thinking and arguing, Deborah said, "Moses and Elijah, one the giver of the law, the other the prince of prophets."

As soon as she said it, I slapped my forehead. "Elijah stood firm against the 400 prophets of Ba'al yet ran from Jezebel."

"Moses had 70 elders and gave us the 10 Commandments," Deborah said.

"Moses is water and stone. That must be the Red Sea and the rock he struck," Kelestria said.

"And Elijah called down fire and ascended in a chariot."

Sir Thurgood called for pen and paper. He began working on the code. After a quarter hour, he shook his head. "This can't be correct, Chione. Are you sure we solved the riddle correctly?" He showed the parchment to her.

Chione nodded and sat down. Her shoulders moved like a shrug. "They'd have no trouble reading it in Sheshak and Lev-Qamay."

Thurgood stared at Chione. "Sheshak and Lev-Qamay? There's an Atbash ciphering as well!" He set to work again, feverishly.

"Twice encrypted?" I asked Chione.

"Even if I was captured and tortured to give the riddle, they still wouldn't be able to read the message. Once they had solved the first, they would likely kill me, thinking I had lied to them," she said without emotion.

"Where are Sheshak and Lev-Qamay?" Manegold asked Deborah.

"There is a famous cipher in our land called the Atbash—apparently Sir Thurgood knows it as well. Sheshak and Lev-Qamay are Babel and Chashdim ciphered."

"Praise Heaven!" Sir Thurgood shouted. He looked at Deborah, shock registering on his face as he read it. "This can't be! Do you know what this says?"

"No," Deborah and Chione replied together.

"It is a list of traitors and spies within the nobility! These men have been seeking to undermine the war effort."

Still blinking rapidly, he turned to Deborah. "Young woman," he said, "how did your brother get this list?"

"My father and brother are *Ish Sicarioth*." She said this unflinchingly. It must have been a proper name as the relic did not translate the term for us.

The clerist nodded. "I thought only the dagger-men would obtain such a list."

I turned to Manegold. "Do you know what she means?"

"Her brother and father are accomplished spies and assassins. They are part of an unsanctioned army called the *Qa'ana* that protects her kingdom from any perceived threats."

Deborah simply said, "They are right about the threats more often than not."

"Are you sure the list is accurate?" I asked the clerist, trying to move the topic back to the urgent business.

Sir Thurgood nodded. "I have long suspected several of these men of having divided loyalties. We will investigate carefully but swiftly. Carefully that only the guilty are punished. Swiftly that they cannot get away. They may already be moving into hiding if the Black Star and Adumbrar suspected what you carried." He said the last to Deborah. "You should stay here at the castle for a while at least."

"Happily," she said, smiling and glancing at Manegold.

Deborah stayed a month while the knights investigated and captured the traitors. Only when the Luminar announced they had all of them from the list did she prepare to return home.

She and Manegold were often together, but the day of her departure, I saw she was distraught as the four of us walked together towards Chione who was already saddled. The mighty griffin herself looked sad.

"Manegold," she said, "I have to tell you something." She came to a halt and turned to face him.

"Of course," he replied.

"When I go back, I am to be betrothed."

Manegold staggered. "Betrothed?" Kelestria grabbed my hand in shock.

"Yes. It has been planned for months but will become official then. In a few months, he and I will stand beneath the marriage canopy woven from the branches of trees our parents planted at our births."

"Who…."

"His name is Reuben."

"Is he worthy of you?" I detected anger in Manegold's voice.

"He is from the northern part of my kingdom. I have never met him. We have exchanged a few letters, nothing more. He strikes me as one who follows *HaShem* with all his heart."

"Can you refuse the engagement?"

She shook her head vigorously. "No. I thought I could. I have wanted to ever since I met you, but I cannot." She looked at my cousin, a tear from each eye on her brown cheeks. "You are a good man, Sir Manegold Osias, better than most. Yet you are not part of my *goral*. I prayed for the other answer every time I raised my eyes to Heaven, but *HaShem* has repeatedly told me otherwise. I cannot choose against Him."

Kelestria and I stood in silent horror. Manegold remained standing tall and strong.

"But you do not love … Reuben."

She shook her head sadly this time. "Not yet. Remember this: the will is stronger than the heart. If I determine to love him, I will love him."

Kelestria wrapped my hand tightly in hers as we listened. She sank her head into my shoulder.

Manegold squeezed Deborah's hand. "Do you love me?"

Tears running down her face, Deborah refused to look away. "Do not press for an answer. No matter what I say, you will be hurt. Let me go to my family and people. Stay here and find happiness in a bride. Surely your father searches for one even now."

Manegold winced. "He has found one."

Deborah tried to smile. "Then it will all work out. What is her name?"

"I have never seen her or even been told her name."

"But I know your father would only arrange marriage with a righteous woman. Just as mine would not engage me to a hardhearted man. Fathers want the best for their children."

Manegold's voice took on a hint of desperation. "At least give me a token."

She shook her head vigorously. "The only token you need is from your bride-to-be. *HaShem* tells us that marriage joins two houses. Ours would destroy at least twice that many. Embrace His will. Do not try to leave your destiny."

Manegold released her hands and stepped back. "Then go." His steely face showed no more emotion than the sword at his side.

Deborah mounted Chione and waved good-bye to me and Kelestria. Chione looked down at Manegold and said, "You will find *HaShem's* will by doing what the monks do."

Manegold stiffened. "I was called to be a married knight not a celibate monk!" He turned and strode away.

Kelestria and I said our goodbyes to Deborah and her mount. "I hope you find happiness, Deborah," Kelestria said.

"I will. It's like love. If you determine to find it, you will."

The three of us walked back to the castle slowly in silence. Finally, he broke the silence as we walked through the portcullis.

"And that's the end," my cousin simply said.

"When will your father tell you her name?" Kelestria asked.

"I received a message from him just before Deborah and Chione left." He held out a letter, folded and sealed with his father's signet in hardened wax. He sighed and popped open the paper. "Her name is Suzanna, daughter of Sir Gregory, the Earl of Stisa."

"Stisa lies in the mountains of Fremora. That's a long way from your home," I said.

He nodded and strode away. "Come with me to the library. We can find her family's records of knighthood."

Once inside, he didn't look at the towering shelves of books and scrolls. Instead, he went right for the book he wanted and turned the pages. "Ah, Gregory of Stisa." As he read, he couldn't keep the admiration from his voice. "They have been knights almost as long as my family. Gregory the First, grandfather of my future father-in-law, led one of the successful campaigns to expel invaders from Fremora. For that service, he was awarded the earldom."

I nodded in appreciation. "Uncle Frederick chose well."

Kelestria gasped. "Better than you think! Look here!" She tapped the painting of a shield on the facing page.

Manegold shrugged. "A golden cross on a blue field with three golden suns in splendor on a red stripe in the top."

"And their motto," she continued.

Manegold's read from below the shield. *"Crux Sacra Sit Mihi Lux. Non Draco Sit Mihi Dux.* We read that at the monastery!"

"Don't you see?" Kelestria pressed on. "Chione said you would find the Father's will when you do what the monks do!"

Manegold blinked and caught his breath. He whispered, "Let the Holy Cross be my light; never let the Dragon be my guide."

Frank Luke grew up in Oklahoma, met his future wife at seminary in Missouri, and now resides in Iowa with her and their two boys who keep them very busy. They are associate pastors at a small church outside Knoxville, Iowa. While he earns a living as a web developer, she takes care of the house and boys. Alongside his nonfiction (sermons, church lessons, and answers at hermeneutics.stackexchange.com), he writes fantasy and science fiction to explore God's truth in fantastic ways. He finds such story-theology connects with readers on both cognitive and emotional levels. Besides writing and programming, he enjoys Bible study, Hebrew, theology, church history, and doctrine.

https://frankluke.wordpress.com/

The Kappa

O nce, there was a little girl who had an excellent brain. Her brain was so good, that little Hanako could tell her brain to tell her body to jump or run or eat cookies, and that's just what her body would do!

The favorite thing Hanako could do was stand on one foot, draw up her other leg and arms, and bend over. As she balanced, Hanako pretended she was a white egret looking for tiny fishes and frogs to eat. She could stand like that for a long time. That's how good her brain and body were.

But there was one thing Hanako's brain was not very good at. It could not pay attention to words like "no" and "don't." So when Mama said things like, "Don't eat these sweet rice balls before supper," Hanako ate every single rice ball. She did not even leave one for her mother.

Hanako and her mama lived in a small village surrounded by pine trees on a mountain in Japan. A small river rushed over stones by their house. Where the river widened into a swampy place, white egrets probed the mud for frogs and salamanders or stood on one foot and slept. The water's happy laughter and the egrets' beauty called to Hanako every day. Her mama could not keep her home no matter how many times she said, "Don't go to the river. An evil spirit might steal you." There were small, mottled crabs to find under rocks, fingerling fish swimming hard against the current to watch, and cool breezes to tease Hanako's black hair.

One day, after a refreshing rain had washed the forest, Hanako strolled through the pine trees, headed toward the river. A tiny *mew* caught her attention. She left the path to poke through azaleas and ferns. The trees and azaleas sprinkled her with water.

Under the fifth fern, she found a tiny black bobtail kitten. Its blue eyes shone in the shade. Its fur stuck out in little wet spikes as it wobbled toward her and mewed again. The poor, thin kitten was wet and shivering. Hanako picked him up and cuddled him in her arms. Cold water soaked her sleeves. She ran back to her house.

Her mama scolded, "You're all wet. Did you fall in the river? I keep telling you it is too dangerous for you to go to the river alone. Don't go where I can't rescue you from evil spirits."

"Mama, look. I rescued a kitten who was all alone in the forest."

"Oh!" Mama said. "The poor little kitten. Let me get towels for both of you."

Once they were dry, Hanako tried to feed the kitten with milk from a spoon. She and the kitten got wet with milk, so Mama dried them off again.

Then all three of them rode a bus to a city with a pet store. They purchased a red collar with a golden bell, kitten milk, and a doll bottle to feed the starving kitten.

The store clerk said, "That is a handsome kitten."

Hanako said, "His name is Maneki!"

Her mama stroked the soft kitten. "You must be kind to the kitten so you will have good luck."

Hanako did not need the promise of good luck to be kind to Maneki. She knew that all kittens deserve to be treated kindly.

On the ride back home, Hanako rubbed her cheek against the most beautiful cat in the world.

Every day, Hanako stayed home to care for the kitten. She fed Maneki bits of solid food with chopsticks and pretended she could not see the lump he made when he hid under her blanket.

Maneki grew and grew. He played with Hanako and with every fly that flew into their home. He ate the flies, but he did not eat Hanako. Maneki followed her everywhere, except outside their home. Maybe he was afraid he would become wet and hungry if he went outside. Hanako had to carry Maneki if she wanted him with her outside, but he grew into a heavy cat.

One day, Hanako opened the front door, revealing a sweet day where the sun and clouds played tag, the river laughed loudly, and a gentle breeze cavorted through the pines. She stepped out and sat down to put on her shoes.

Maneki mewed and pulled on her sleeve.

"Stop that," Hanako said.

Mama called, "Where are you going, Hanako-chan?"

The cat still pulled on her sleeve. Hanako said, "Mama, I am going to the river to catch crabs and watch the egrets."

"Stay inside and play with Maneki," Mama said. "The river is a dangerous place for little girls."

"I will be safe." Hanako gently removed Maneki's claws from her sleeve.

He mewed and butted his head against her hand.

"You are too heavy to carry all the way to the river." Hanako gently shoved his head back inside, got up, and slid the door shut. Hearing the cat's pitiful cry, Hanako said, "I won't be gone long. Don't cry." She considered taking him, but again concluded he was too heavy.

Hanako ran through the bamboo grove and the pines to the river's rocky shore. She turned over stones, found crabs, and tossed them into the river.

An egret slowly stepped over on stilt legs to see what she was throwing into the water. Would it be something good to eat? Oh, yes, crabs are very good to eat. "Kuk-kuk-kuk," the egret said. The bird stepped closer.

Suddenly it flapped its great wings and flew away. One white feather spiraled down from the sky.

What had frightened the egret? Hanako watched the bird shrink smaller and smaller as it flew farther and farther away. She dropped the last crab she had caught hiding between two boulders.

A shadow slid along the nearest boulder.

Hanako spun and stared at the creature with a beak and shaggy black hair on its head. The hair hung like a hula skirt around the top of the head where a shallow dip, like a bowl, held muddy water. A tadpole wriggled in the water. A bumpy turtle shell covered the animal's back. Its two muddy-green legs had webbed toes. Its two arms had webbed fingers. The thing stunk like rotting weeds.

Hanako backed against the boulder, knowing that this thing standing as tall as her was dangerous. "What—what are you?" she stammered.

The thing cackled. "What I am is not important. What is important is what you are. You are a little girl. You are delicious."

"No!" Hanako picked up a stone and threw it at the thing. The projectile bounced off its hard belly.

The thing grabbed her arm. As strong as a hundred grown-ups, it jerked her toward the river.

"No! Don't drown me!" She kicked its knee.

The thing snarled. "Yes. You will be the most delicious girl I have ever eaten."

A black cat smashed into the thing. "Mine!" he hissed.

The thing let go of Hanako. "Oh! Maneki! I did not know. Oh! She is yours."

"Mine, Kappa. Don't touch what is mine." Maneki growled. He rose on his hind legs, balanced, and bowed toward the thing. Then, he sat back on his haunches.

"Oh, no!" The kappa wrung his hands. "No. Please."

The cat stared at him with shining eyes.

"Oh! Oh!" cried the kappa.

When someone bows to you, you must bow back, even if you were going to eat that someone.

The kappa turned his eyes to Hanako who bowed to the creature even deeper than the cat. "Oh!" The kappa bowed and the water sloshed out of the dip on his head. The tadpole wriggled down between the rocks. Gray, wrinkled stuff lay at the bottom of the dip. "Oh!" The kappa staggered and fell. His arms and legs flopped. He looked weaker than a kitten.

Maneki hunkered down like he was going to pounce. "If you don't go back to the river, your brain will dry out and you will die. Do you want to die, kappa?"

The kappa groveled. "No. Oh, no. Please let me go back to the river."

Maneki batted him on the beak once. "Go, and never touch my Hanako again or I will eat you!"

"Oh! Oh! Oh! Thank you, Maneki-san. Oh!" The kappa crawled into the river and sank into its depths.

Hanako dropped to her knees and hugged her beautiful cat. "Maneki-neko, how did you get here?"

"Your mother opened a window. Now she is crying because she is afraid to tell you she has lost me."

Hanako rubbed her cheek on his head. "It will be wonderful when Mama hears you can talk."

"No, I can't." The cat raised one paw and held it next to his ear. He mewed.

Hanako laughed and rose with Maneki in her arms. "You will never again be too heavy for me to carry." She kissed him and he purred.

As she carried her cat all the way home, her brain decided that perhaps the words "no" and "don't" might occasionally be worth heeding.

Lelia Rose Foreman raised and released five children while following her pediatric dentist husband around the world. So far everyone has survived.

www.leliaroseforeman.blogspot.com

Celebration

The city of Harath had become a place of shrouds. Black curtains hung in every window and black flags flew from every tower. There was no sound of music or merriment. Despite the late hour, there should have been revelers. Harath was known for producing the finest wines on Other Place, a fact the elves disputed every chance they got, miserable backstabbers that they were. No one cared about elf lies, and for good reason, as countless bottles of quality wine flowed from wineries established thousands of years ago. The residents of Harath were joyous and celebrated life, but not today.

Midnight came and went. Clouds blotted out the moon and stars as if they shared the city's mood. Few fires burned and no lanterns were lit. This meant no one noticed short figures clothed in black garments sneaking through the city streets. The stunted and smelly beings stood between two and four feet tall, and they left not an inch of skin uncovered. Awkward as their appearance might be, they were as silent as falling snow as they moved through the cobblestone streets.

The furtive people were careful in case they might run into dogs, burglars, or various scary beings of the night. That last category was less worrying than it sounded since the scary beings unionized last year. Still, there was a chance, however small, that they would be noticed. That wouldn't do. The smelly crowd used every trick they knew to avoid making the slightest sound. They kept to the back alleys and less traveled roads on their way to the castle.

Castle Sea Crest was a real castle, one of those fine old castles that remembered they were built for war and not just huge mansions. The walls were yards thick, the bricks made of granite, and the towers soared high above the prosperous city. There hadn't been a serious threat in generations, but the royal family kept Castle Sea Crest in good repair. After all, you never knew what the future held.

The black-clad figures stopped near the edge of the castle. Guards patrolled the outer walls every fifteen minutes, and even in such a time of woe they kept a strict schedule. Timing would be tricky.

Guards armed with spears and torches came near. The crowd edged back into the shadows and waited for them to pass. Instead the guards stopped, and one took a silver flask from his pocket. He took a sip and offered it to another guard. The man waved it off.

"These last few days food and drink taste like ashes in my mouth."

The first guard put the flask back and looked down. "Dark times, indeed."

"I fear worse ones are to come," the second guard said. He shuddered and looked at the castle before leading the other men away.

Once they were gone the crowd returned. They were silent as cats, in part because they'd gagged themselves before beginning this mission. Fifteen minutes more until the guards returned.

A window high up on the castle opened. The crowd below tensed, relaxing only when they saw more short figures in black wave to them. The group in the window lifted a large leather bag six feet long and two feet across. They slid it out the window and lowered it with ropes to the ground below. The waiting crowd took the large bag and carried it into the shadows.

One by one the figures above climbed to the ground using the same ropes they'd lowered the bag with. The last person threw the ropes down. Below him the crowd hung a rope net between the castle wall and a nearby house. One leap sent him fifty feet down where the net caught him. They gathered up the net and ropes before fleeing into the night.

They'd only gone a block when alarm bells rang from the castle. Piercing lights shone in windows, and the drawbridge came down with a thud to release dozens of knights on horseback. They raced through the city streets, screaming at the top of their lungs the whole time.

"To arms! To arms! Wake the citizenry and seal the city! The King's body has been stolen!"

One of the black-clad figures pulled off his gag. "So much for the mannequin."

"I really thought that would fool them until morning," another replied. "Maybe it shouldn't have been smiling."

"Hurry," a third whispered.

Harath's slumber ended as doors and windows flew open. Men and women ran outside to see what the noise was about. This slowed the knights from reaching the alleys where the black clad figures scurried with their heavy load. The delay wouldn't last long, and the black-clad crowd broke into a run.

They reached the city's outer wall and ducked into a small building. More people in black waited for them and opened a secret door hidden in the floor.

All of the short figures went inside with the large bag and their belongings. From there, they went through sewers and tunnels until they reached another door a mile from the city. They peeked outside in case the knights had already gotten this far, but the noise and light was still far off.

It took them the rest of the night to get through the vineyards and fields around the city to reach the safety of home. Home was a network of caves well away from farmland and human habitation. The rocky ground supported neither grapes nor wheat, so it lay empty.

Empty places are where goblins live.

Back in the safety of their cave, the goblins pulled off their disguises. Black cloaks and pants were replaced with regular leather and cotton clothes, and black soot was washed off from around their eyes. They set down the bag they'd brought so far and cheered as still more goblins poured into the cave. Their numbers grew until hundreds of goblins crowded around the bag. The air rippled as the collective craziness and stupidity of so many goblins close together began to warp space.

"You did it!" a goblin with a crooked staff cheered. He had green skin and blue hair, and wore heavy robes made from an old carpet.

"You doubted us, Estive?" one of the returning goblins teased. Now out of his disguise, he had pale skin and small eyes. Unruly brown hair covered his shoulders in greasy locks that stained his leather clothes.

"Doubt you? Brat, you and Oler broke into a castle in the capital city of a kingdom, and on a day when the humans are riled up like wasps when you hit their nest. You're lucky you're still breathing."

"Hmm," Oler muttered. Oler was hulking by goblin standards, with dense muscles and strong arms and legs. His leather clothes didn't quite fit, and his fair skin and brown hair were always dirty.

"Show us, show us!" goblins shouted.

Brat and Oler untied the bag and carefully took out King Justin Lawgiver, a sight to behold even now. His skin was wrinkled and his hair white, but there was a strength to him, a look of nobility. His clothes were fine linens dyed deep blue, with a sable cape and fur-lined boots. He still wore his signet ring and jeweled crown. The King smelled of lavender from the perfumed oils he'd been anointed with.

"Speech!" the goblins yelled. "Speech!"

Brat smiled and said, "We snuck in by—"

A goblin waved his arms. "Not you. Justin!"

Estive rolled his eyes and pushed his way to the front of the group. "None of that! You get things ready, and do a good job! It's not often we have a guest."

The goblins hurried off, one saying, "Wouldn't want to look bad in front of the King."

It took two hours of hard work, something few goblins bothered with even for a minute, but they made the cave presentable. Colorful streamers dyed with berry juice hung from the cave walls. Tables and chairs of dubious quality were brought out and dusted off. A large table was brought out for Justin Lawgiver to rest on since he was the guest of honor. Goblin cooks who'd been abducted and dragged here against their will were politely asked to prepare a banquet.

Musicians played horns and fiddles as goblins piled their plates high with heaping helpings of food. There was some concern that they'd offend Justin since goblins eat what humans couldn't stand the sight of. The fear proved baseless as the King was being a good sport about the matter. That wasn't surprising given that he was dead, but he'd been a good one even when he was alive. One goblin set a plate of food beside the King on the off chance he'd feel better and ask for a snack.

The celebration was in full swing with raucous music, copious food, and much laughter. It went on for hours and even the goblin cooks joined in. Once the music and gorging was done, the goblins gathered around Justin Lawgiver's body. They fell silent, but their expressions were not dour, nor were their tears. A few goblins gave the King a pat on the back and some encouraging words before they settled down.

Estive gathered up his ratty robes and struck his staff on the cave floor. Bang! The goblins turned their eager eyes toward him. Once he was sure he had the crowd's attention, he waved his staff over the cave and addressed the goblins. "Friends, allies, neighbors, people we tied up and dragged here, we come here together to bid a fond farewell to Justin Lawgiver, who through no fault of his own was King."

"Poor guy," a goblin said.

Not bothered by the interruption, Estive pointed his staff at their esteemed (and deceased) guest. "Justin, also known to us as Big J, J Master, and the Guy with the Crown, was an honest, hardworking man who gave his people a chance to make the best of themselves that they possibly could. I'll never understand how he lasted so long. Forty years a King and every day of it a struggle with other kings, merchant guilds, his nobles, and especially his family."

Brat shook his head. "Four sons and one throne. I do *not* like that math."

Getting a little annoyed, Estive said, "You'll get your turn. Justin fought the longest battle I ever knew to make sure his people never fought at all. He created alliances, brokered trade deals, soothed wounded egos and tried so blasted hard to keep everybody from killing each other. The job took years off his life, no question. If the world was fair he would have been born a potter or yam farmer.

"Instead he was surrounded by petty, vindictive, greedy, and otherwise not at all nice people. Any one of us would have run off in a heartbeat, but he stuck it out and made it work. My theory was he used magic or possibly blackmail, but I've been told by people who know such things that he didn't.

"And he was good to us!" Estive shouted. Goblins chorused their agreement as Estive said, "No more anti-goblin raids by the army. No more goblin hunting parties for the nobles. No more bounties on goblin heads. He put a stop to that here and in neighboring lands. They hated him for it, but he stood strong no matter how they yelled at him and threatened him."

Oler belched and scratched himself.

"That's why we had to do this. Poor Justin wasn't even cold and his family started fighting. 'I want to be King!' 'No, I want to be King!' They should have been giving him a proper send off after the good he did for them, and instead they brawled over who got his stuff. Greedy bums one and all." Estive banged his staff on the cave floor again. "The guy was dead, and they still weren't going to leave him alone! So, brothers, friends, hangers on, and idiots who wandered in, we have come together to bid a fond farewell to dear Justin Lawgiver, King to the Humans, and ensure his peaceful rest."

A goblin in the crowd waved to get Estive's attention. "You're sure he's not a goblin?"

"We've been over this," Brat said. "Several times."

"I mean, it makes more sense if he's always been one of us," the goblin continued. More goblins nodded, proof that the man/goblin debate still wasn't settled.

Estive lost his patience and threw a rock at the offending goblin, missing by inches. "He's twice as tall as you are and four times as heavy! And, I might add, he was born instead of falling out of a giant mushroom like we are!"

"I'm just saying," the other goblin persisted.

"Just say it somewhere else." Estive waved his staff at Brat for him to come over and take his place. "Before we bid goodnight to Justin, I'd like to ask the people who knew him best to say a few words."

Oler picked his ear and farted.

"It's Brat's turn first, Oler," Estive said. He stepped away from the body and let Brat speak.

Brat brushed his dirty hair aside and spoke to the goblin mob. "We were able to break into the castle by—"

Estive threw a rock at Brat and hit him in the shoulder. "Talk about the dead guy!"

"Okay, okay! Geez." Brat rubbed his shoulder and began again. "The first time I met Justin was twenty years ago. The boys and me had broken into his castle for some food. It wasn't hard when they just dump their potato peelings and coffee grounds in buckets where anyone could get them. Anyway, we were nearly out when Justin and his knights came by. Me and Oler hid up in the rafters and waited for them to leave when a rafter gave way and dumped me on the floor, and both my buckets landed on my head."

Brat laughed. "Hoo boy, was that embarrassing! The knights went for their swords, and I was about to run when Justin broke out laughing. He went down on his knees and then sat down so he didn't fall over. I'd seen him plenty of times before that, but that was the first time I saw him laugh. When he got his breath back, he told the knights to escort me outside the castle, and he let me keep my stuff. Then he said that from now on he'd have his cooks leave their kitchen scraps outside the walls where we can get them."

There was a pause as Brat looked at the King. "Most people won't do that for you. I mean, he couldn't eat the stuff, but he still could have kept it from us or burned it."

"We should have done more for him," a goblin said.

"After that I checked in on him every chance I got," Brat continued. "So many people shouted at him, demanding stuff. Most of the time they wanted gold, but his sons kept demanding his crown. I found him once when he was alone. He was watching little kids playing in the streets, and he had this big smile. I went over and said he should go play with them. He shook his head and said, 'There are things a King cannot do.' So I said, 'But you want to,' and he nodded."

"We tried," Estive said.

"We tried," Brat echoed. "I got him laughing a couple of times, and I made a few of his enemies look stupid. I can't take too much credit for the last part when they were already as dumb as toast. But it was a little bit of happy against a whole lot of sad. Today we're putting things right. Justin will be with friends from now on, and let those jerks argue without him. Oler, it's your turn."

Oler looked surprised. He tried to back away, but other goblins nudged him up to the King. Oler wasn't sure what to do. He'd seen funerals before. Most of the time people said profound things about the dead guy. Oler wasn't good at that. Other times they were polite and poetic. He *really* wasn't good at that.

"Go on," Brat urged him.

Oler looked at the King for a while as he tried to come up with honest words to say. He placed his right hand over Justin's stilled heart. "We will meet again."

Estive and Brat patted him on the back and let him join the other goblins. As one the goblins gathered around the King and lifted him up. They carried him to a small chamber in the cave network and placed him there with the streamers and a plate of food (just in case).

With the King safe in his tomb, Estive placed a folded piece of paper in Justin's hand. "A map, should you get lost on your final journey." He placed his staff across the King's chest, saying, "My staff, should the trip prove tiring." Finally he took two dice from Brat and slipped them into the King's pocket. "Loaded dice, because you're the unluckiest man I've met, and anything that tips the odds in your favor is good."

From there the goblins gathered rocks and wet clay. They carefully placed the rocks across the chamber's entrance, fitting them together so tightly it was hard to see between them. They mixed the clay with powdered stone from the caves until it took on the same color as the native rock. They pressed the clay between the rocks and over them like cement. Goblins heated the clay with fire until it became hard as stone. More goblins chiseled the clay to remove any imperfections. Normally goblins wouldn't go to so much effort, but there are things you'll only do for a friend.

When they were done, the entrance to the chamber was gone, covered so well it looked as if it was a solid wall and always had been.

Brat gave an approving smile. "Even I couldn't break into here. If the humans find our cave and searched it, they'd never find Justin Lawgiver."

"I hear tell you can't be a king without a crown," a goblin said.

Estive waved his hands. "Nonsense! William Bradshaw King of the Goblins doesn't have a crown, and he's the best King our people ever had."

"If it's true Justin needs a crown, then he should get to keep the one he has," Brat said. "I won't see him demoted for silly reasons like being dead."

Oler sneezed.

"Good point," Estive told him.

The goblin that brought up this topic said, "What I mean is, if Justin Lawgiver has his crown then his sons can't have it. That means none of them can be King."

Brat laughed at the news. "Couldn't happen to a nicer bunch."

Estive looked at the camouflaged tomb. He tapped it with his knuckles and smiled. "He's safe now. We did it."

"That we did." Brat smiled and looked at the others. With their solemn duty done, he said, "Let's go throw ducks at people."

Arthur Daigle was born and raised in the suburbs ofChicago, Illinois. He received a degree in biology from the University of Illinois Urbana-Champaign, which sounded like a good idea at the time. This led to work as a zoo intern at Brookfield Zoo, an assistant fisheries biologist at the Max McGraw Wildlife Foundation, and a research assistant at Morton Arboretum. Most recently he's been employed grading high school essay tests and as a garden associate (yeah, the job market is that bad). In addition to writing, Arthur is an avid gardener and amateur artist. Arthur is the author (no jokes, please, he's heard them all) of three books. These include *William Bradshaw King of the Goblins*, *William Bradshaw and a Faint Hope*, and *William Bradshaw and War Unending*. These books were almost inevitable given that the author has been a fan of science fiction and fantasy since he was old enough to walk. Major influences include the works of the puppeteer and filmmaker Jim Henson and the British artist Brian Froud. Expect more books in the Will Bradshaw series, as all attempts to stop Arthur from writing have failed.

https://www.facebook.com/arthur.daigle.52
https://www.goodreads.com/author/show/6523979.Arthur_Daigle/blog

The Nether Lands

The ultra-modern Markthal in Rotterdam might be the last place you'd look for ancient artifacts capable of stopping a demon. High-end designers sold in store fronts next to upscale second-hand stores give a unique feel to a unique town. I entered an antique shop that had been open since the beginning of the sixteenth century. Although when it had opened five hundred years ago it wasn't an antique shop, it was just a shop.

I'd never been here in person, having only done business with them online. They specialized in magical and spiritual items, and I use magical and spiritual items in my line of work. I'm a Hamal, which my father said meant guardian or protector in some ancient Akkadian dialect. I hadn't devoted myself to becoming fluent in the language. I'm not a scholar. I'm a brute and very happy with my brutish life.

Inside the store I browsed while a pale-skinned Nederlander fretted over which armoire to buy. The owner, Jos, kept his distance and interjected various pieces of information at critical junctures. He was smooth, making both pieces of furniture look appealing but subtly moving the man towards the more expensive of the two. It was also the less magical of the two. Everything in the shop hummed with magical energy. Most of the items had only absorbed the energy from more powerful artifacts. Yet even that residue could be harmful in a house of discordant energies. Jos clearly thought this man's house was one of those.

The issue was solved when the man's wife entered the shop, looked at the two price tags, and chose the more expensive of the two. She didn't seem to care what they looked like, only how much it was. Jos gave her a sheet on the history of the item complete with interesting talking points for parties, and she gave him a big smile. As they left I stepped up to the large man.

"I need something to banish a demon."

"Well, I think you have the wrong stor—" I handed him a card with a series of numbers and letters on it.

He nodded and punched my purchaser's code into an app on his smart phone and waited for confirmation. It wasn't a password but a complex algorithm that changed every time I wanted to make a purchase. I had to solve equations and answer questions to get the code and then it was only good for twenty-four hours. And since I was doing it in person there were additional questions to answer. He handed me the phone as the questions came up and stepped behind the counter.

He made a show of putting together a plate of cheeses and breads, but I knew there would be a security switch back there. When he threw it the store would go on lockdown and he would pull a weapon and kill me. That was, if I got the questions wrong. When you dealt with the things I was asking for you had to be prepared for evil to come knocking on your door. The last question was a language one, an Akkadian conjugation. I hated language questions.

"Sorry about this last one, going to take me a second. Had nightmares on the flight over and I'm tired." Sweat began to trickle down my spine, and I saw his hand slip under the counter.

I selected my answer and the screen turned green. The tension in Jos's shoulders eased, and he brought me the plate of food.

"Welcome to the store mister … Tariq Jones?"

"Grandma married a Jones."

"Ah, yes. It will be just a moment while I check our inventory."

I consumed half of the food while he was typing on the phone. I choked a little on the dry bread.

"Do you have something to drink?" I asked around the bread still in my mouth, little bits flying out into the air as I did so.

He sneered but grabbed me a cold beer from a mini-fridge behind the counter.

"What kind of demon are you hunting?"

I swallowed the beer and bread. "I don't know. One of our Readers had a vision of a demon in Rotterdam so they sent me out. That's all I have."

"If they had a vision of a demon, why don't you know what kind?"

"Our Readers aren't normally psychic in that way. They read information from the world, hence why we call them Readers. Newspapers, internet, books, anything written, and they use magic to find patterns and oddities. They gather data and intel and form solid conclusions about what is happening. But this vision…." I took another long swallow of the beer. "It wasn't a conclusion, just that there was a demon. So here I am." I killed the last of the beer and raised my eyebrow inquiring about another one. He handed me a fresh one while throwing the empty bottle in the recycle bin.

"I have a couple of options for you. First is a chastity belt worn by the illegitimate child of Charles the Fifth. He worked in an asylum with the demented and was said to have loved and cared for them with such compassion that the belt has become an anathema for any evil."

"Do I have to wear it for it to work?"

"No, just have it on you. It will add power to any banishment ritual."

"Okay, what else?"

"I have a badge worn by Lothair the First. It isn't all that powerful for banishing, but it can trap a demon's attention for hours, even days."

"Like they can't stop staring at it?"

"Um...."

"Why the hesitation?"

"Because it is in the shape...." He trailed off as a customer walked in and browsed the books near the front of the store. Leaning in close he said, "In the shape of things not mentionable in polite company."

"What?" I barked out a laugh making the customer look up. "That can't be real?"

Hunching over, Jos said in an angry whisper, "I assure you it is real. It is crude but it is what it is. The Emperor was said to have used the body of his lover as the fuel for the fire that cast it. She may or may not have been a nymph, and he was enthralled with her. He couldn't cast her face since it would shame his wife the Queen."

"You are just a collection of strange, my friend."

He straightened and beamed. "We strive to please."

The customer wandered on to another store.

"So just those two?"

He hesitated.

"What? What are you holding back?"

"I have one very special item that I hesitate to part with. It is ... unique."

"Aren't all these things unique? Isn't that why they do what they do?"

"Well, yes, but not like this. Those things are not unique items. Their heritage is unique. There are many badges and many chastity belts. But there is only one of these." He left me standing at the counter, pulled down the security gate, locked it into place, and then led me into the back. Setting a strong box on the table, he opened it to reveal a pistol that would send steampunk enthusiasts into convulsions of pleasure.

"This is the pistol given to the one and only Charlemagne by the Maestro Pensatore."

I squinted. "That can't be right." Once again, I wasn't a scholar but in my line of work you learn about old stuff. Demons like and hate old stuff. "Gun powder hadn't even been discovered in China at that time."

"Indeed it had not. And pistols didn't come around until the fourteenth century, five hundred years after this was made." He ran a hand over its polished gold, iron, silver, and wood surface. "Let alone another thousand before something this complex was made."

"So it's a fake."

"That was my thought, too. Eight generations ago one of my ancestors procured it for the family and has passed the story down for generations. But I knew better when the story was told to me. I brought in expert after expert; they all agreed it couldn't be as old as they said. It was laughable. An old woman who had been taken by a swindler." He looked at me trying to keep a solemn face on, but I could see the smile fighting to get free.

"Okay, I'll bite. But…."

"But one expert caught something that I had not. Every expert that examined the pistol agreed it had to be from the mid-to-late eighteenth century. But one expert saw something none of us had. It's an electrical weapon."

"What?"

He picked up the weapon and with care undid several clasps and lifted out the firing lever, and I saw there wasn't a gear or spring underneath but a long black rod. It sat centered in a dark hole, not touching the sides. As he pulled it out, the rod came near to the side of the hole and jumped to the right. It was a magnet.

Using a small flashlight, he lit up the hole that I could see was several rings covered in wire. It was a simple, yet effective electrical generator.

"So it has to be newer. From the late 1800s or something."

"Except my grandmother bought it in 1763. And I don't question that date because I have the records since then."

I'd seen enough impossible things to roll with it. "So what did you figure out?"

He nodded at my acceptance of the impossible. "It was all in the name of the gifter, Maestro Pensatore. Master Thinker. Do you know who else was named Master Thinker?"

"Nope." I didn't like guessing games.

"Archimedes. Do you know who he is?"

"I'm a brute, not an idiot."

He raised his hands in apology. "Well, Arch means master and medes means thinker."

"So, you're saying a dead Greek guy gave Charlemagne an electric pistol?"

"Yes, but no. He was not dead. Still may not be dead. I believe he was a Katask."

I whistled. "Now that I've heard of. Like the Demiurge or Zeus?"

"Yes. They are makers, or constructors. I brought in an Oracle to confirm my theory and learned two things. It was made by Archimedes and my ancestor was an otherworlder."

"Archimedes built this to hunt demons?"

"No, to kill something supernatural Charlemagne was having trouble with."

"What kind of supernatural?"

"Don't know."

"Then how do you know it will kill a demon?"

"Because my grandmother, my mom's mom, not the ancient one, killed a demon with it."

"How much?"

"Once again, I'm not sure I want to let this go. It's been in the family a long time."

"And it could have been wiping out demons that whole time. I guarantee my family will take care of it."

"A thought just occurred to me, why didn't you go to the guard for artifacts? They would have let a Hamal use them."

I glanced away. "The Primitus Guard and I aren't on the best of terms."

The earlier tension returned to his shoulders. "And why would that be?" His eyes shifted to the right where a weapon must be stored.

I held my hands up. "No worries. I'm Hamal. I'm just not in an Order."

His lip curled up in a snarl. "A bounty hunter." He pulled the pistol closer.

"No ... Well, at least not usually. My family has always been unbound. We take commissions from the Orders. We're specialists, heavies. Blood of Asherbanipal and all that."

"What do you mean not usually?" He still hadn't let go of the pistol strongbox.

"I mean if I run across a bounty in the course of my work, I'm not going to turn it down. But I don't go looking for them, and I don't accept contracts for them."

"And why doesn't the Guard like you?"

"Because I'm unbound. They think it means we have no code of honor. Which we do, it's just looser than the Orders'. That's why they hire us, because we can do things they can't." I sighed, "My people aren't like the Guard, Orders, and Emirs. We play it too loose sometimes. We aren't above making a quick buck. We take care of each other and do our best to keep innocents safe. We're a lot like your people. It's one of the reasons we like doing business with you rather than your competitors. Tradition is only worthwhile as long as it doesn't hold us back."

"Three million."

"Two million and you throw in the other two items."

"Two and a half and you get the chastity belt."

"Two and a quarter. Both items and your family can visit the pistol when they want."

"I need it up front."

"You have my purchaser's code."

He pulled out his phone and began to push buttons.

"I'm going to go grab some food real quick and then I'll be back."

Dad was going to be furious at me spending the money without authorization but once he saw the gun it would be worth it. Even if it didn't kill the demon, it was awesome.

Back in the shop Jos had everything packed up ready to go. "How are you going to find it?"

"Bounce spell. Gonna hit up Grote of Saint-Laurenskerk—I'm sure I didn't say that right—to power it."

"Old Church might be better than St. Lawrence."

"Naw, the violence gives me a better edge at finding a demon. A church that resisted the Nazis; that's where I'm going to get my biggest boost for a demon bounce back."

"That's your area, I won't argue. Good luck, my friend."

I grabbed a taxi and found the doors of the church unlocked. It was empty save for the few clergy up front standing in a loose circle having a conversation. Sitting on one of the plastic chairs, I waved off a priest, or whatever they're called, and bowed my head as in prayer. Pulling out an old piece of parchment from my inside pocket, I unfolded it and laid it on my lap. I spoke a few words in Akkadian and the strange cuneiform writing began to glow and pulse with magic until the image of the sun stood out in chromatic splendor on the page. It took on depth and substance as the pulse intensified.

Looking up, I confirmed that no one was looking and whispered a word of power to crack the corner of a stone tile. Using my knife I pried up the chipped piece and laid the parchment over the hole. I set the chip in the center of the sun, which was now producing enough heat to singe the hairs on the back of my hand. In an instant the sun reached out with flames made of cuneiform symbols and devoured the stone chip.

"Lamādu gallû addāniqa." Find demon please.

It wasn't eloquent but it got the job done. I really did hate languages. The sun pulsed and a hum began to build under the paper. I wasn't worried about the priests hearing it. The vibrations were contained to the magical spectrum. Soon the entire building shook with the power of the spell. The chip had connected it to the building allowing all the years of worship, power struggles, and violence to be co-opted for the moment.

I had to work hard to stay upright as the bone-shaking thrums sent their power out into the city around me. The spell worked like radar pushing the sound out into the unknown. Except only demons reflected sound back. As I waited for a return I closed my eyes and focused on receiving. The pingback wouldn't come as a sound but would form an image in my mind. No, image wasn't the right word. A map, knowledge of where to go. It was a magical thing and not easily explained in ordinary terms.

When it came, it hit like a freight train and I fell to my knees. I didn't have to fake the tears as the images of horror ripped through my brain. Words of hate and images that drove a mind beyond insanity rolled over me like waves. It was the taint of the demon, the slight touch of its twisted heart. If it hadn't been faded by distance it might have broken me right there.

I got back in the chair and looked up. It had only been seconds, the priests were still moving towards me, but it had felt like an hour of assaults. I wiped my tears and tried to wave them away but they kept coming.

"*Gaat het met je, vriend??*" the young priest said.

I didn't know what he said. "No, thanks."

He furrowed his brows. "Are you all right, my friend?" His words were crisp and measured.

Still reeling from the demon's touch, I thought for a moment he could see the taint on me. Had my face become demonic in the moment of torment? That was crazy. I'd done this before, seen it done before, it wasn't anything like that. This had been stronger than I was used to but I think that had to do with the church rather than the demon. There was a lot of power here, more than I expected.

"I'm fine. Dead wife. Sad." I wasn't speaking like a simpleton for his benefit, I just couldn't create complex thoughts right at this second.

"I pray with you." The priest began to kneel next to me.

"No, you don't nee—" A scream broke free of my throat before I knew it was coming.

A second demon's touch hit me, tearing deeper into my psyche than the first. I don't remember falling, but I could feel the cold stone under my cheek as rivers of fire laced through my soul. My eyes were open and I could see the frantic look on the priest's face, as if looking through binoculars. Behind him was a girl with half of her head shaved and the other half dyed a bright purple.

Where had she come from?

They weren't here and now with me, they were in a different world, a different place. I was in a realm of terror where human souls were tortured by monstrous beings that my mind couldn't contain.

And as the first had, it passed and I pushed myself up onto all fours. I could hear the priest rambling in the background but it was like my head was swaddled in cotton. Blood dripped to the floor from somewhere on my head. It wasn't much blood so it wasn't a threat.

Then I vomited as the third wave hit. I don't remember much after that, just pain and terror as a third demon chased me through the passages of my own mind. Memories and thoughts that had once been my personality now became my pursuers. The evil clawed at my insides as family and friends morphed into grotesque beings warped by the presence of the demon. They rent my flesh and pawed at my sanity trying to pull me down with them. Only my training in psychic attacks allowed me to keep moving, to stay alive.

When I woke there were three EMTs kneeling over me tending to my wounds. Behind them was a police officer holding his pistol out but not trained on me. Another officer was examining the antique pistol that had been in the bag at my side.

"Careful, that's a three million dollar antique," I croaked out pointing at the officer.

All five of the officials frowned at me. Either they didn't speak any English or not enough to understand what I had said. The girl with the purple hair translated for me.

The cop holding the pistol said, "I know what he said, I just don't understand why he's carrying it in a shopping bag." His English was better than mine.

"Didn't know I was—" I broke out in a coughing fit. "Sorry, didn't know I was going to buy it."

"You said your wife just died."

"Yes. She died from cancer. She had always wanted to come here and so I was sightseeing when I saw the pistol. She would have loved it. She would've redecorated our whole front room around it and it made me sad. The owner of the shop said I should come here to pray and seek solace."

"Do you often have seizures?"

"Is that what happened?"

"So, you've never had this happen before?"

"No." I had been stalling while I recovered my wits enough to stand. The EMTs tried to keep me down but I assured them I was fine. The bag still contained the chastity belt and badge. I picked it up and slid it onto my arm. Spreading all ten fingers I focused my thoughts on silence and stillness.

"*Naḥarbušu.*" I hated using my freeze spell on them.

I mean, I didn't hate freezing them. The spell had no ill effects other than a little confusion. Well, a lot of confusion when I disappeared in front of their eyes, but no physical effects. But it took a long time to prepare the spells ahead of time and bind them on the mind. I wouldn't have time to do it again before facing the demon.

Three demons, not one. That's why I couldn't spend time messing around with the cops. Three demons' essences had assaulted my mind. Except as I gathered up the pistol and strongbox I could quite shake the feeling that it wasn't three separate demons, but one demon in three places. That wasn't possible. A demon this small just didn't have that power. There are legends of people and creatures with bi-location powers but they're of iffy reliability at best. But demons were bound to the human who had summoned them. They couldn't split themselves and travel at will. And no human, no matter how great, could command a demon that would be capable of such a feat.

A demon that could be in three places at once wouldn't be hiding. It would be tearing a path of destruction through the world. A demon like that causes destruction on a Godzilla level. Nagasaki was the result of such a demon. A Japanese response to the attack on Hiroshima gone horribly wrong. No, this demon wasn't of that power level but still, the thought itched at my brain.

Outside I looked for a cab but there were none in sight. The spell would only last another three minutes so I had to be out of reach by then.

"I can take you where you need to go, Hamal," a voice said from behind.

I jumped and brought my hand around, power surging, ready to annihilate the threat. But it was only the woman with purple hair. Except it was the woman with purple hair. She should be as frozen as the rest of them but here she was standing in front of me.

Her golden skin radiated in the midday light as she stood, one hand on her hip. Her low slung jeans didn't quite meet the end of her T-shirt and I could see the taut muscles of her stomach. Her eyes were liquid black, the irises as dark as the pupils, and it felt like you could fall into them forever. They were so warm and comforting I wanted to live in them, dwell in them, be—

She looked away and I blinked. I had taken a step towards her without realizing it. I took in a deep breath to fill my lungs with air. Her eyes had been more important than breathing.

"Sorry about that," she said, her voice a little breathy as though we had just broken from a passionate kiss.

I spun the ring on my middle left finger around so I could touch the gem with my thumb. Using the magic bound permanently to it I looked at her with the Eyes of Truth. She looked as she did now, save that she had a red aura of magic around her, and instead of a heart in her chest she had a glowing ball of magma. She was a demon by definition, something born of hate, but there was no menace to her. Many demons, especially the old ones, who had been allowed to roam freely on Earth left the chains of evil behind. It didn't mean they were good, only they were as free as humans to choose to do right and wrong. With her skin, eyes, and red aura I knew what she was.

"You're a lilitu."

She smiled and there was real joy in it. "I'm glad to see they still teach about us."

"Will you give me your name?" It was a big question.

Names didn't have power like some claimed, you couldn't control something just by knowing their name. But names led to knowledge and knowledge was power.

"I will, but not right now. Your spell was impressive, for a human." She smiled again and I found it lifted my spirits. "But it will wear off soon. Let's go and then we can talk about who I am and why you were looking for demons."

I hesitated. I needed to leave but I needed to know she was safe, too. She hadn't been in the church before I had sent out the bounce spell.

"I am not her. I'm not Lilith. Can we go now?"

It didn't answer the question, but it did make me feel better. I waved for her to lead the way. With the Eyes of Truth still up I could see she wasn't lying. More than that, I could see she didn't want to be associated with Lilith and her insanity. Again, she might not be good but she wasn't all bad. I needed help, and she seemed willing to help. We got in her Mercedes and left the church behind.

I indicated for her to pull over to the curb after five minutes of driving in silence. Immortal beings were like that, always comfortable with the silences.

I stepped out of the car. "I need to make a phone call real quick, will you wait for me?"

"Do you want me to wait for you?"

I could feel the tug of her sensuality. "Yes. I need help right now, and you're what I have."

"Oohh, you flatter me."

"I didn't—"

"I'm kidding. I'll wait. It has been a long time since I have smelled the blood of an Assyrian king, and I'm not willing to give that up yet."

"That's … disturbing."

"I give you my word, I mean no harm."

Again the Eyes of Truth confirmed she wasn't lying. I don't know how a demon was promising aid and no harm without lying but there it was. I closed the door and stepped inside the small coffee shop. I ordered two coffees black and sat in a chair by the window to make my calls.

"Jos."

"It's Tariq. I need the name and number of that Oracle."

"I don't give my friends' information out so easily."

"I get that but there are three demons on the loose in your city. Or possibly one that can be in three places at once."

"That is impossible."

"I know. That's why I need more intel. They're strong and I got the impression they're just beginning their plans."

"I will have her call you."

"Fair enough. But do it as soon as possible. I don't want to face this thing at night."

"De mazzel."

"Thanks. I need all the luck I can get."

I dialed the next number.

"Tariq, what's up?"

"It's bad here, Dad. There are either three demons or one demon that can be in three places."

"How did it feel?" He was a Hamal so he knew the process.

"How it felt isn't how it could be."

"You need to learn to trust your instincts, son. They're better than you know."

"But how could it be in three places at once?"

"That is disturbing."

"I think I should wait till you can send backup."

"That might be a good plan."

"I have an Oracle that's going to call me. I'll let you know what she says."

"How did you get that hookup?"

"From the guy that sold me the three million dollar demon-killing pistol made by Archimedes." The patrons were giving me sideways glances.

"Okay… you spent three million dollars?"

"No, two and quarter but it's worth three. And really? That's what you got from that statement?"

The barista, or whatever they're called in the Netherlands, set the two coffees down on my table with the little disposable cups of cream and packets of sugar. I didn't know how ancient female Akkadian demons liked their coffee.

"I have to go, Dad. My lilitu chauffeur is waiting for me."

"Excuse me?"

"You heard me. Send backup."

I gathered all my goods together as someone licked the back of my ear.

I knocked the chair over standing up and bringing my fist up to throw a force punch spell. Nothing was near enough to have performed the act of personal space violation. I knew my eyes must be wild because the other guests slipped out the nearest door, even the emergency exit. Trying to regain my dignity, I put the phone in my pocket and headed outside. Juggling the coffees, I opened the door. I noticed the demon was wearing a different shirt as I slid in. The T-shirt had given way to a low-cut sequined blouse with thin straps. It was the same color as her hair and had no back to it save for a single tied string.

"You changed your shirt?"

She looked down in surprise. "Oh, I didn't mean to." The shirt morphed back into the worn cotton T-shirt from before.

"What do you mean you didn't mean to?"

"Well, I control my impulses for the most part, but your bloodline is like an aphrodisiac to me." She frowned as though that was a problem.

She hadn't started the car yet, and I considered getting out and finding my own way. But my phone rang and she pulled away from the curb.

"Tariq."

A musical voice replied, "Jos said you need my help finding some demons." It sounded like she was high.

"Yes, ma'am. Or possibly one demon that can be in three places at once."

"And you believe this demon to be a major threat?"

"I suspect. I don't know if that is the same thing as believe."

"Honesty. That is rare. But I believe you are correct and the situation is not good."

"No, ma'am." I wasn't sure if she was a new Oracle or one of the originals from ancient Greece but it was better not to take chances and be polite.

"Meet me at the New Ocean Paradise in thirty minutes."

"Yes, ma'am."

I looked at the other demon in my life right now. "The Oracle wants us to meet her at the New Ocean Paradise in thirty minutes."

"Really?"

"Yes, ma'am." No reason to show disrespect to her either.

"All right. It's only like fifteen minutes away."

"Can you tell me your name now?"

"Sari. Do you know it?"

I concentrated on what I had learned about lilitu. Lilith was the most well-known but there had been hundreds of them originally. The Catholic Church had killed many of them and at the present time we only knew of a dozen or so. Sari wasn't one of the names I remembered.

"I don't think so."

She gave me that heart-skipping smile again. "Good. Means I'm doing something right."

I looked straight forward to avoid staring at her slender neck. "What do you mean?"

"I mean, I've been trying to be a good girl for the last three hundred years or so. And if the Hamal don't teach about me, then I must be on the right track."

"You need someone else to tell you that?"

She bit her lip. "Well, yeah. You know what I am."

"A lilitu."

"I'm from the otherworld. I was closer to what you might call a dryad once. Beautiful. Inside and out. But my home was taken from me, and I let vengeance twist my heart. It twisted me until I became a demon. And I was banished to the underrealm. You know what that is?"

"Yeah, I just spent a few minutes in it back at the church."

"Ah, that explains the vomit." She swerved around a slow moving car. "Twenty-five thousand years ago a sad man called me forth to this world. He didn't want me to hurt anyone, he didn't want power; he only wanted someone to talk to. His wife and child had died and he was lonely. I spent the next sixty years as his friend and lover. Before he died, he unbound me and let me wander the world. I killed him as a result."

My hand inched towards the strongbox that held the pistol. She didn't miss the movement.

"When I think about it, I'm filled with such melancholy that I might wish for you to use that pistol on me."

"You have remorse over the killing?"

"I'm not sure if that is the correct word. Even now my emotions are not like your emotions. Do you know what happens to unbound demons?"

"They can do whatever they want."

She smiled, but it didn't have the same power to it. There was sadness in it now.

"Yes and no. I was corrupted by my birth as a demon. Right and wrong, good and evil, were not concepts I could readily understand. I didn't do evil. I was a good creature in my own mind. It took me fifteen hundred years to overcome that deficiency."

"But you said you've only been trying to be good for three hundred."

"Just because I learned the difference doesn't mean I wanted to change." She looked away so I couldn't read her face. "Or even could change. I had been what I had been for so long that I didn't see other paths. I didn't look for them."

"What changed?"

"That is... personal. But the important part is I did change. It took me a while. I spent three hundred years thinking I was being good only to find out I was destroying people's lives by my manipulations. So then, I started again, in good faith and with guidance, three hundred years ago."

"And now you're good?"

She pursed her lips to the side. They were luscious. "That is hard to say. My birth still distresses me. I think I have a good grip on good and evil, but still, it is only based on the perspective of others. There is no such connection made in my mind to actions I take. Only the guilt I have when I do it wrong."

"That sounds horrific. I'm sorry."

Her life changing smile was back again. "I've never had anyone apologize for the struggles of my life."

"Well, if you're trying to be good, I think you should have the benefit of the doubt."

She stopped the car in front of a floating combination Chinese restaurant and motel and got out, ending the conversation. Immortals are abrupt like that. I tried not to stare at the way her hips moved but there was magic there. Real magic made to entice me.

The smells of the Chinese market on the first floor of the boat pulled my eyes away. Mixed with the tang of the harbor, it was overwhelming to say the least. At the top of the gangplank I felt a hand touch my shoulder and spun to see who it was. There was no one even near.

"You okay?" Sari asked.

"Yeah, just thought …." I trailed off as I felt the slime on my shoulder.

"It knows you're looking for it, and it's trying to scare you off."

"I know. It's not been the first time I've been slimed." It was the first time it had happened without the demon being present, however.

We chose the lower buffet restaurant and waited for the Oracle to show up. We didn't have to worry about her finding us; she was an Oracle after all. We were on our first plate when an exotic olive-skinned woman with hair so black that it sucked in the light around it sat down. She didn't look at us because her eyes were the milky-white of the blind.

"You seek the demon yet dine with another?"

"She's helping me."

"You cannot trust her. She cannot trust herself."

"I have told him so."

"And have you asked him to end your life as you should?"

"I'm not sure I'm there yet."

The Oracle nodded her understanding. "I cannot help you find this demon. It is … hidden even from my sight."

It took me a few seconds to process what Sari had said and catch up to the Oracle's statement.

"What does that mean?" I asked.

"I do not know. But I am not omniscient, only powerful. It may be that something is hiding it from me. It may be that I just cannot see it."

"I'm sorry for making you come all the way out here."

"If that's all she had to say, she would have just called. She has more," Sari said with fried noodles hanging from her mouth. How did she make that look sexy?

"Indeed, I do. I may not be able to see the demon but I can see you. If you hunt the demon tonight I cannot see you in the world tomorrow."

"Like I die?"

"Like you are sent to the underrealm."

I swallowed hard. "That is a fate I would like to avoid."

Sari shuddered and sweat broke out on her forehead. "Yes, it is."

"Yes, you would. But if you wait until tomorrow night to begin the hunt you will fail."

"That doesn't leave much of a window."

"Such is the world."

"When *can* I hunt it?"

The Oracle stood, nodded to us, and left, that lovely immortal abruptness at its best. I stood to chase her but Sari stopped me.

"They have rules. They are forbidden from saying certain things that would change the future in drastic ways."

The Oracle turned around near the door and spoke across the crowd. She didn't raise her voice, but I heard her like she was speaking directly into my ear.

"You should stay here tonight. I stayed here once, and it was just the most charming experience." She smiled and wiggled her fingers goodbye.

Sari chuckled. "Clever."

"What?"

"This place has never been described as charming."

"So?"

"She can't tell you what to do so she told you something else to help. Staying here will get you closer to the goal."

"Really?"

"Really."

"Thank you."

"For what?"

"For helping me."

"Are you saying goodbye?"

"Well, yes. I mean, no. I mean, I thought you would be leaving."

"What made you think that?"

"Well, you offered to give me a ride, not fight demons with me."

"And that's all you want from me?" That urgent pull again. "You wouldn't like my help?"

"I honestly don't know how to answer that. You tell me you want to be good but that I can't trust you."

"But I can help you trust me."

"How?"

"Bind myself to your purpose."

I went very still. "You will what?"

She shrugged like she was talking about what TV show to watch. "It's not that big of a deal." She picked up a chunk of orange chicken with her chopsticks. "When your purpose is done, I'll be free again."

"But you're giving up your free will."

"To fight evil. I think it will help me on my road."

"What road?"

Even through her complexion I could see some color rise in her cheeks. "Never mind. I know you're a good guy and won't take advantage of me. Or at least, not in any way I wouldn't enjoy." She had good bedroom eyes.

"Well, we better go get some rooms."

"Rooms?"

"Rooms." I reaffirmed and her shoulders slumped a little. "If I have time, I'm going to bind some spells."

"Don't you need tokens, focuses, and ingredients for that?"

"Nope. Blood of Kings, remember? I have certain ones I can do without all that stuff. Things that are more complex require more stuff, of course, but these are just brute spells cause that's what I am, a brute."

"Pity I won't get to find out." She bit her lip and raised her eyebrows. And my blood pressure with them.

They had two adjoining rooms and I saw what Sari meant about not being charming. The rooms were clean but worn and the smell from the restaurants and market did not make it a relaxing atmosphere. But I had been in worse and this would serve us for the night.

Before binding my spells I drew a knife across Sari's left bicep and left thigh drawing blood that was leaving and going to the heart. I wasn't a theorist so I didn't know why it had to be like this, but I knew it worked. With a few words of binding, she knelt and swore herself to my purpose. I felt her power twitch at the edge of my perception. For as long as I hunted this demon, she was mine to command. She stood up and was closer than she should have been, the knowledge of what I was thinking clear in her eyes. She broke eye contact first because I don't think I would have been able to. I closed the door to her room as she healed the cuts.

I concentrated on adding a few more banishment spells and one more force spell to my arsenal. I wish I had time to prepare the freeze spell but I would need focuses or several days for that. I checked in with my dad, who assured me backup was on the way. I told him what the Oracle said, and he warned me not to mess around with this stuff. I told him I was taking her advice and not going hunting. I ignored his questions about Sari because I didn't know how to answer them.

I meditated, centering myself and removing the distractions that had cropped up in my mind. Mainly the sight of Sari's stomach every time she moved. Thoughts like that could be deadly. Not just because they could be a distraction at a crucial moment but because she was a demon. Getting into bed with a devil was never a good idea.

Deep in the reaches of my mind the feeling of being watched returned. I knew it wasn't my body being watched, but my psyche. I felt for the presence and found nothing. Still, every time I focused I felt like there was something to focus on. And every time I found nothing I could detect the residue of evil left over. Whatever was trying to find me was better at hiding than I was at forcing the issue. I had been working on the evil presence in my mind for hours when I felt the first spider legs of evil crawl across my neck.

I stood, looping the chastity belt around my chest like a bandolier. The… uh… business end was on my back and I was fervently hoping it had been washed at some point in the last six hundred years. Slipping the badge into my pocket, I loaded one round bullet into each of the stacked barrels of the pistol.

The doors opened between the rooms, and Sari stood in a tactical vest carrying two curved short swords. I stared at her, at the door, and then at her again. I had slid the safety chain into place, I was sure of it. She looked at the object of my interest and shrugged.

"I see you felt it, too," she said as she sat on my bed.

"Yep."

"We're going to go kill it now, right?"

"Nope."

"What? If we can feel it like that, it has to be on this floor, like one or two doors away." She paused. "I guess it could be directly under us, but I got the feeling it was in that direction." She pointed away from her room.

"Me too, but going after it is a little too close to hunting. And there is no way in... well, there is no way I'm going to the underrealm."

"What're we going to do then?"

"You're going to sit there looking like your beautiful self, and I'm going to open the door and stand behind it. When it comes through the door, drop to the ground, and I'll shoot it in the back."

"I'm bait?"

"Irresistible bait."

"Keep that up and I might just have to take advantage of you."

I felt that sensual pull again.

"Really, right now you're going to do that?"

"I was just teasing you. Open the door." Again with that mind-altering smile.

I slid in behind as I pulled the heavy door open and rested the pistol on the doorknob.

"You wouldn't think I was beautiful if you saw my true self, you know," she said as she leaned back in a casual pose.

"I did look at your true self with the Eyes of Truth. You look just the same." I was looking out the crack between the door and doorframe into the hall.

When she didn't say anything back I turned to look at her. She was still in her casual pose but there was a tension to her body. She stared at me with an intensity that made my skin crawl.

"What? Why are you looking at me like that?"

"Are you sure of what you just said?"

"Yeah."

"And you are of sufficient power to use the Eyes of Truth?"

"Yeah, I use them all the time."

"And all you saw was me in this form?"

"Well, I saw your power in a red aura, sex, violence, and a touch of healing. And I saw your demon heart rather than a human heart but those are metaphorical rather than literal."

"I have not returned to my true form in many years. If I did so now, would you be okay with it?"

"While we're waiting to fight some kind of super demon that can be in three places at once?"

"In my true form I will have more of my power available to me."

"Then by all means." Then I thought better of it. "It won't drive me insane, will it?"

She laughed. "No, I'm not that kind of demon."

She shimmered and her skin glowed more. Her eyes changed from liquid black to royal purple, the pupils taking on a diamond shape. Her hair lost its purple hue and became like rays of sunlight. And her bust decreased in size which seemed like a human thing. She could make any man fall for her with those eyes, but she was worried about how well-endowed she was? Besides those changes, she was exactly the same. No, she was more beautiful.

"This was what I had to be worried about? You look amazing. I guess it is a little worrying because I might be distracted at a crucial moment."

She frowned at me and rushed into the bathroom. There was a shrill giggle of glee and she came back out staring at her hand.

"It's gone."

"What's gon—" A woman's scream full of pain and terror tore through the motel. "Well, now it's a rescue, not a hunt." I flowed out the door. Sari was hot on my heels.

I had the pistol out, and I cranked the handle to charge it as we waved other guests back into their rooms. The next room was empty. Sari had done her locked door trick on it. The next door was blocked by magic that Sari couldn't get around. We went to the next room and opened it and found two children huddled in the corner crying.

Sari said squatted down to their level, "We're here to help. What's wrong?"

They couldn't speak through the tears but pointed at the doorway to the room that had been protected by magic. The adjoining rooms must have contained a family and they'd left the door ajar. I didn't hesitate and burst into the room, pistol ready to fire.

Blackness filled my vision and lungs. Not smoke, more like fog, but as black as the deepest points in space. My eyes were useless and my knee slammed into something hard and pointy. I spun my ring around and brought up the Eyes of Truth but still couldn't pierce the inky veil. I screamed in frustration, ready to fire into the darkness.

Sari sang out from my left, *"Ego Sum Fax,"* and light exploded out of her, pushing the darkness away.

The concussive wave of light pushed me back as it hit with physical force. I had no time to look at her as the new light revealed the squat, putrid form sitting on the woman in front of me.

Its claw-tipped feet were on both sides of her head and its bottom was crushing down on her chest preventing her from taking life-sustaining breaths. The foul head, dripping with ooze, hovered just above hers. Its lips were a whisper from hers as its grotesque tongue traced the outline of her plump mouth. The woman's eyes were open and staring into the demon's eyes but her pupils were big enough to wipe out any trace of irises.

It turned to look at us, and the woman whimpered in pain. It would have been a scream if her lungs weren't being crushed. It looked at me as I brought the pistol to bear on it. Its gaze shifted to Sari, and he became visibly excited at the sight of her. He didn't lunge at her, he flowed like smoke, claws stretched out to bury in her throat.

I body-checked him with my shoulder, using a force spell to increase my speed. I slammed him into the frame of the open doorway, revolted by the feel of the putrid skin. We rebounded, and I fell to the floor. He followed me down. Sari was moving towards us but she was going to be too late. And I didn't think she could take the demon anyway. She had been as transfixed by its eyes as the woman on the bed had.

Its hands were on my shoulders, pulling itself up my body. The wind had been knocked out of me. I couldn't get a word of power out. None of my spells would help me. Its eyes were closed as it hovered above my face, wanting to savor the first moment it took me over. Then its lids disappeared and behind them was a portal into the underrealm.

I felt myself being pulled in, dragged down into the depths where even demons went mad. My life was disappearing and there was nothing I could do about it. I moved my arms but they were in encased in wet sand, inching along. I got one arm around its waist and then I was in torment.

For a thousand years they did nothing but kill me with fire. Burning me alive, body preserved by some supernatural power until there was nothing but ash remaining. Then like some twisted form of the phoenix I was reborn to start it all again. Sometimes they used flames, sometimes lava, one particular tormentor loved liquid metal. Every second of it hurt like the first touch of heat. I never got used to it, never grew stronger from it.

After the first thousand years, they got creative. Deaths and tortures as varied as the stars of the sky. Contests were held to see whose victim could scream louder or cry longer. And the worst of it was that each regeneration brought a regeneration of hope. The physical pain was nothing compared to when they took your hope from you. When that broke its thunder would echo in your mind for days.

I don't know how many eons I had been there before they brought my little sister out to torture in front of me.

I don't know how many deaths and rebirths of the universe I watched her suffer before they gave me the choice of watching her suffer or letting her go if I tortured our mother. I know how many eons I killed my mother. I remember each slice, each burn, each act of violence against the angel of light that was my mother. My mind shattered into smaller and smaller pieces with each death. I was no longer human, only pain and anguish in bodily form.

The day the light broke through to my wretched existence… that was a special day. I'd never seen light its equal in all my endless lifetimes, piercing my faceless tormentors with power and beauty. Their twisted souls burned in the light. The underrealm began to shake as the light bored through the ground like water through air. With fury the sky shattered, and I was lifted up towards the light on a hand of beauty and grace.

I came through the hole in the sky the light had torn open, and I was in my body again, the demon on top of me. Its eyes were no longer locked on mine, but on the badge of Lothair I held in my hand. Sunlight streamed through the open window. Sari collapsed underneath it holding the curtain aside. Tears were pouring from her eyes as she stared into mine. The natural light seared into the flesh of the demon on top of me and it wriggled to escape.

I held tight but it wasn't as hard as it should have been. Its gaze was still fixed on the badge. Grunts and snuffles of pain issued from its deformed mouth. It screamed as I recited a banishment spell. Screams of my own paired with his and I could hear the children joining in on the chorus from the other room as well. The woman, roused from her nightmare by the sunlight as I had been, screamed at the scene around her as well. Sari whimpered as I fought. She had overcome the badge's siren call. She had saved my life.

The banishment spell, aided by the chastity belt's power slammed into the demon and bounced off with no effect. I stared wide-eyed as it began to recover from the effects of the sunlight.

With its stocky legs the demon pushed off of my stomach and leaped to the side. It stumbled, still not fully recovered. I lunged for the pistol still lying where I had dropped it, put it against the foul creature's demon heart. It tried to bat the barrel away but my finger on the trigger was quicker.

There was no flash of flame indicating the demon had been banished. There were no screams or curses hurled at me. There was only a slight blue light and the demon ceased to be. Not banished, ceased.

I shambled over to Sari as she retched and cried out in loud sobs. The woman was still cried, but it was quieter now that her children had joined her on the bed.

"You saved me."

"It made me think such terrible things. Things of such evil and I…." Sari touched her lips. "I enjoyed them."

"No, you didn't." She looked up at me. "It lied to you." I caressed her face. "It told you that you enjoyed them, but it lied."

"You weren't there, you—" I put a finger to her lips.

Whispering a spell of strength I lifted her as though she was a child. Normally, I could have lifted her without the spell but after fighting the demon all night I needed some extra oomph. Besides, the spell took the edge off the pain as well. I paused to utter another spell with the last of my strength. The family on the bed fell quiet as the vanishing spell removed the last several hours from their mind and put them in a deep, restful calm.

In the bathroom, I set Sari on the counter. I washed her face and brushed the hair out of her eyes. Looking deep into those bright purple eyes, I brought her sight into mine. It wasn't something I was good at, but I was determined right now. She swayed with the strange perspective, but I steadied her with hands on her hips. I stepped back and stared at her chest.

"Really?" she said harshly. "You want to do this now?"

I smiled. "I have the Eyes of Truth on. What do you not see?"

Her physical eyes squinted in concentration though they saw nothing. And then with astonishment her eyes went wide. She had seen what I saw the instant I had looked upon her after the nightmare. Her demon heart was gone.

She wasn't human, she was... whatever she had been before, but she wasn't a demon anymore. Didn't mean she was good. Her past would always haunt her, but she wouldn't be at risk of falling back into the evil ways so easily anymore. We hugged for a long time, a simple act of celebration and triumph.

Breaking the embrace, I said, "Do you have any idea what that thing was?"

"Yes. It was my... it used to be my brother. Back when I was a demon, I mean. It was a Bakhtak, nightmare demon."

"Are there more of them, or could it be in three places at once?"

"What you felt was not it being in three places, but its consciousness burrowed into its victims. It is gone for good, which is good because you were more susceptible to it than you should have been."

"Why do you say that?"

"Because it takes days for them to be able to bond with you enough to send you into nightmares like that."

"Why do you think it was so easy?"

She looked up exposing her long neck again. "Either he'd been working on you already or the bounce spell let him in more than you wanted."

"Probably that. I hadn't been prepared for the three hits."

"It's why the banishment spell didn't work either."

"What do you mean?"

"That spell was strong enough that I thought it was going to take me out. But it bounced off of him because when the Bakhtak goes into you, you go into it. The spell felt your presence and bounced."

"I don't ever want to deal with one of them again."

"I'm just glad it's over and you're safe."

"And because you're no longer a demon, you're no longer bound to my purpose."

"Your purpose is over anyway."

"Nope." I shuddered at the memories of the underrealm. I don't know if they were just a nightmare or I had actually been there, but it felt real enough that it didn't matter. "Still gotta find the snake who was controlling him."

"Then I am still bound to you."

"But you're not a demon. That kind of magic doesn't work on you anymore."

"Who said anything about magic?" Her eyebrow shot up.

"Well, then my lady, let's go hunting."

Born deep in the Ozarks, David Millican read and dreamt of the world outside. Traveling the country wherever work was found, like the hobo's of old he rode the rails, sleeping under the starry sky. After quenching his wanderlust the need for home returned. Now you can find him back in the forests of his birth shelling peas, shucking corn, and writing of worlds beyond this one.

Cave focuses primarily on Fantasy and Science Fiction but has been known to dabble in the realms of Mystery. He enjoys the exploration of moral quandaries through the lense of alternate realities. He also enjoys exploring other cultures and customs in his writing which leads to some interesting situations in his stories. Even more interesting search histories on his computer.

Talori and the Shark

On the outskirts of the underwater village of Coral Bay, a mermaid glanced up at the watery distortion of the sun. Talori enjoyed a morning swim before beginning her sister's lessons. She saw a shell cart pulled by a white hippocampus coming toward the house. A frown tugged at her lips. She replaced it with a smile and swam out to greet Mako, her father. "What a pleasant surprise," she said as he stopped the cart. "I didn't expect you for a few days."

Shadows under his eyes belied the weak smile he offered. "Is Delphalyn still asleep?"

"For now. I was going to wake her soon."

"Let her sleep. I have some bad news and I would rather discuss it with you first so we can determine what we should do from here."

"What happened?"

Mako didn't respond. Instead, he got out of the cart and pulled it to the small sea rock corral.

Talori helped put the cart away and fed Triton, the hippocampus her father used in his travels. She stroked the animal's long face and spoke quiet, soothing words. Her mother had once told her about horses, a sort of land hippocampus that humans rode as transportation. Talori couldn't imagine a hippocampus with four legs and a tail as silky as its mane. She was rather fond of Triton. His large green eyes were expressive and intelligent. He had a powerful body, and his neck crested with a flowing mane. Pearly fur gave way to iridescent white scales, dancing with rainbows of color as the light touched them. When she finished, she saw her father floating with his head low, one hand on their pillow-basalt-and-sea-rock home. She swam behind him and said gently, "Whatever has happened, I'm sure we can work it out. But first you need to tell me about it."

As Mako described the business deal he'd entered with the slippery merman, Prospero, Talori felt her heart sink. Searing, consuming anger filled her. There had been many times Mako disappointed her with his poor business decisions. But this was different. He had completely ruined them. The more he talked, the less sure she was that they could make something work out.

"And now, I have nothing," he finished. "He's coming tomorrow to take the house and the business." His voice broke. "He's even going to take you girls."

"What? How could you let this happen?" Her silver eyes flashed green with anger.

"Talori—"

"You promised me," she interrupted. "You promised you would never go into business with him."

"This isn't how I wanted things to happen. I was thinking only of you girls and giving you the life you deserve."

"We already had the life we deserved," she snapped. "You treat us like royalty, even though we're not. But now you've ruined everything!"

"Please forgive me, Talori," Mako whispered, not lifting his head to look at her. "What are we going to do? We've both heard what happens to the mermaids Prospero takes. I can't let him do that to you or Delphalyn."

Talori tried to cool her anger long enough to think logically. "Delphalyn just started her apprenticeship with Marina a few days ago. Marina has already said she's never had such a gifted apprentice before. Perhaps if we talk to Marina we can set it up to look like Delphalyn caused a damaging accident which would leave her in Marina's debt. As you have nothing to pay her with, Delphalyn would have to be Marina's slave until such a time as the debt was repaid. We will have to set up a false contract and make sure Marina has the same story we do, in case Prospero checks with her."

"What about you?"

"There's nothing to be done for me, Father," Talori said, looking out over the coral beds from which their town received its name. Their bright colors and small, cheerful fish mocked the pain she felt. "I have no skills to put toward an apprenticeship and I am far past the ideal age to marry. Even if I wasn't, no one here is interested in a plain mermaid like me."

"You're not plain, Talori. You are beautiful."

She allowed herself a small grin. "And you are biased. In any case, having Delphalyn suddenly unavailable will be suspicious enough. If we're both gone, Prospero is likely to discover your deception."

"You could swim away."

"I don't swim from my problems, Father. I face them. Attempting to swim away has already cost me one family member."

Mako put a firm hand on Talori's shoulder. "You are not at fault for your mother's death, Talori. You must stop blaming yourself."

She didn't answer. What her father told her did not change her feelings. She could never erase the memory or the guilt from her heart. If she hadn't tried to swim away from her mother that day, the shark prowling near their home would never have chased her. And her mother wouldn't have died trying to save her. She ignored the burning sensation in her eyes and turned to Mako. "I suggest we go speak to Marina immediately and then let Delphalyn know as gently as possible. She's going to be very upset."

"Before we do, I have something for you. I know it doesn't make everything better," he said handing her a small package wrapped in kelp. "But I thought of you when I saw this. The flower is a rose. They grow on land in human gardens. Perhaps, you can use it to think of me when...." Mako's voice caught and he didn't finish his statement.

As the kelp fell away from the exquisite comb, Talori gasped. Tiny seashells and pink pearls no bigger than pinheads swirled in the form of a flower Talori had never seen before. It was breathtaking. "Shouldn't you give this to Delphalyn?" she asked. "This comb's beauty would look far better with hers."

"I got Delphalyn a comb. This comb, and all its beauty, belongs to you. Someday, you will see that you are not as plain as you believe."

Talori doubted that. Everyone she knew considered her plain, at best, with her pale skin and silvery green scales. Hair the color of seafoam created an unruly halo of curls about her. A proper mermaid should have sleek waves and be brightly colored. Village gossips held her lack of beauty to be the fault of a human mother, though they'd never been able to prove it. Talori's family moved to Coral Bay after her mother died. Delphalyn was too young to remember much about their mother and neither Mako nor Talori spoke of her much. Talori knew her mother had been human before meeting her father, but she remembered her as being a beautiful mermaid. If Talori was ugly, it wasn't her mother's fault. She cleared her thoughts. "Let's go talk to Marina."

Prospero arrived promptly at Mako's shabby house the next morning. He sneered as he looked over the simple structure and the nearby gardens. There wasn't much value to be seen. But then he remembered the two mermaids waiting for him. They would more than make up for the lack of monetary value. He pushed through the door and saw Mako with a plain mermaid. "I thought you had two daughters."

"I do. But only one is still with me." Mako glanced at the mermaid before continuing, "You see, the younger made a terrible mistake during her apprenticeship while I was gone. As I did not have the money to pay for the damage, her mistress has claimed her as a servant."

Prospero narrowed his gaze. "How convenient."

"You are welcome to investigate the claim if you don't believe us," the mermaid said, her silvery gaze daring him to question her.

"Perhaps I will. And you are?"

"Talori."

"Ugly little guppy, aren't you?" he jeered. She didn't respond, nor did she seem at all bothered by the insult. "All right, Mako, say goodbye to your daughter and then get out." He waited outside the door where he could hear any conversation inside.

"I really am sorry, Talori. I should have listened to you."

"A little late to think of that now."

"There's still time. You can swim away, I won't stop you. Perhaps you could get to the surface, find a human to take you in…."

"We've already discussed this. There's no guarantee there's anyone up there, and I'm not a fast enough swimmer. Even if I could get away, what would you do? Prospero wouldn't let you get away with it."

Sensible, although ugly. Perhaps there is a use for her, Prospero thought. When she and Mako exited the house, Prospero turned to see them hug. He grabbed Talori's arm and began to pull her away. "You've said goodbye long enough." To his surprise, she yanked out of his grip. "Don't forget, twit, I own you now."

"No one owns me," she snapped. "I don't care what the law says. I will follow you to resolve this problem, but touch me again and you will regret it."

He was tempted to beat her then and there. But Talori had shown strength he hadn't expected. Better to leave her alone, for now. "Get in the cart." She did so without arguing. He clasped a rusty iron cuff around the base of her tail, the mark of a slave. Prospero turned to the now homeless merman, floating helplessly in front of the hut. "Goodbye, Mako. A pleasure doing business with you."

After several hours, they arrived in Aquapolis in a grand neighborhood. Unlike the simple structures of Coral Bay, these homes were built with the finest materials. Crushed seashells sparkled in the walls. Doors were gilded with gold and other fine metals. Upon arriving at his house, he took Talori around back where several servants waited to take care of the tired hippocampi and fine cart. "You'll sleep in there with the animals," Prospero sneered. "Until I find a better use for you, you will work, eat, and sleep in here. You will only come into the house if and when I call you."

Without waiting for a response, he swam down the lanes of Aquapolis. Wealthy mermaids smiled and twittered as he passed. Normally he would have paused to enjoy their company, but for now, he had business to attend to. Outside of town, he entered a large kelp forest. The first time he'd swum it had been unnerving, not that he would admit to that. He felt rather than saw the fish swimming nearby. Small sharks occasionally passed through the seaweed. The long blades of kelp swayed with the currents, brushing against his tail and body. The forest was dark and quiet. When he reached the end, a large dormant volcano rose before him. He knew the Shark dwelt within and swam to the entrance.

The guard frowned. "What are you doing here?"

"Now, Dune, is that any way to treat your cousin?"

"Answer the question, Prospero."

"I have business with the Shark. Let me in like a good boy."

Prospero found a trident in his face. "Watch yourself," Dune growled. "I can make you disappear, and then who would take your place as the ocean's biggest con artist?" For a tense moment, Prospero wondered if Dune would strike him. Then the trident lowered. "Go in."

Prospero flicked his tail and swam into the dark tunnel. Eerie blue lamps glowed along the cavern walls as strange fish danced in their light. The tunnel widened into a spacious room lit with opulent chandeliers. Shells of all shapes and colors decorated the walls. Fine glass mosaics depicted scenes from the arena and a particularly large one showed a great shark with a merman in his mouth and a trident in his belly.

"What do you want, Prospero?" The deep voice came from the shadows.

"I have something that may be of some value to you. I've recently come into possession of a mermaid I have no use for."

"How does one possess a mermaid?"

"Some merpeople just shouldn't be allowed into business, we'll leave it there."

"In other words, you conned some member of her family and now you're stuck with her. So what's wrong with this mermaid? Not stupid enough for you?"

Prospero scowled. "Her intelligence isn't the problem. Talori is ugly and has no skills or talents whatsoever. I have no place in my home for an ugly mermaid. I thought, given the current rumors, you might be interested in taking her off my hands."

He could hear the distaste in his host's voice. "What exactly do you think I could do with her?"

"There's talk that you're looking for a wife. I could make that search much easier for you."

"At what cost?"

"Oh? I hadn't really thought of that."

"Don't lie to me, Prospero," the Shark spat. "If you want me to even consider taking this mermaid, you'd best be truthful with me."

"Well, she may be ugly, but she seems healthy enough and bright. Didn't even try to swim away when I came to claim her. But I have run into a string of bad luck so, it will be a substantial amount." There was a pause and Prospero knew his host was weighing his options. "Of course, if you're not interested, I know a variety of establishments looking for new recruits. I'm sure I could—"

"I'll pay your price."

Talori's thoughts were jumbled as she followed Prospero's servant to the meeting place. She'd gone from a poor merchant's daughter to a slave overnight. The vast unfairness of her plight had burned deeper than the fear of what might happen when Prospero claimed her. She knew anything of value would be taken, so she'd hidden the rose comb under her curls. The way he looked at her made her shudder in revulsion. She wasn't at all upset when he'd called her ugly. Perhaps if she was too ugly, he wouldn't want her for his entertainment. And it was true. He hadn't wanted her. At his soonest convenience, he had sold her to the Shark. She shivered at the thought. Some rumors said the Shark was a retired pirate and others claimed he was a merman of the court, banished for his ugliness and cruelty. He was said to be ruthless and cunning and to have killed dozens of his enemies. What would he do with her? She wished again that she had insisted on going with her father on his trips. They could have started Delphalyn's apprenticeship early. She could have prevented all of this if she had only been there.

"We're here," the servant said as they stopped at a corner. "Sorry we're late, Dune."

"Quite all right. Are you Talori?" he asked, looking at her.

"Yes."

"Come, we are expected at the minister's for the wedding. You can go, Brine."

Talori gaped at him. "Wedding?"

"Didn't Prospero tell you? You are to be married to the Shark."

"Don't tell me that's his actual name."

"You might want to respect his desire for anonymity, considering your fate could have been much worse."

Talori didn't need to be reminded. "I suppose a slave shouldn't ask questions."

Dune bent and unclasped the iron cuff on Talori's tail. "You're not a slave anymore, Talori." He led the way through the neighborhoods of Aquapolis. Despite her heartache, Talori was fascinated by the sights. She'd always dreamed of going to the capital. Fabulous gardens filled with exotic plants and lit by algae-covered lamps gave splashes of color to the city. Pet dolphins and porpoises played in stone corrals. Colorful fish darted between plants and rocks. The streets were crowded with merpeople and carts drawn by hippocampi.

They stopped at a small sea rock house and Dune knocked on the door.

A grandfatherly merman opened it. "Ah, Dune, you're running a bit late, you know. And you," he continued turning to Talori, "are you a consenting party?"

Talori nodded. She didn't trust herself not to blurt out that she hadn't been given a choice.

"Mother, do hurry along. We still need a witness for this wedding."

"Don't rush me, Nereus." A plump mermaid came into the room, fingering a pearl necklace about her neck. "So this is the bride? She hardly looks ready for a wedding."

"I didn't know," Talori murmured.

The minister's wife smiled. "Oh, angelfish, don't you worry. I can help you."

"Lovey, we are on a schedule."

The mermaid turned to Nereus, her blue eyes suddenly flashing venomous green. "It is her wedding day and she deserves to feel like a princess, no matter what your silly schedule says."

"As you wish, Vivian."

Vivian smiled again and took Talori to another room. "I'm sorry, my dear. Mermen simply don't understand, do they?"

"I suppose not."

"Now such a frown will never do," Vivian said, pulling a brush through Talori's hair. When it caught, she asked, "Oh, what's this?"

Talori pulled the rose comb out of her hair. "All that's left from home. My father gave it to me before...." Her voice trailed away and tears burned her eyes.

"Oh my dear, don't cry. The Shark is not a villain, no matter what the rumors might say. Things will work out."

"I wish I believed that."

"You lean on my faith then, angelfish. What do you think of yourself?"

Talori looked in the mirror. In a short time, Vivian had pulled Talori's unruly curls into a stylish updo with the rose comb holding everything in place. A string of green pearls was draped through her hair, bringing out the color. "I look pretty."

"Of course, you do." Vivian placed a necklace of pearl and shell around Talori's neck. "Green pearls bring luck and fortune to a marriage. Have faith, Talori."

The wedding was very short, little more than a verbal agreement to swim through life together. The Shark never appeared. Instead, Dune stood in for him. Talori couldn't help the bitterness creeping into her heart. How could they swim together when her husband hadn't even bothered to show up for the wedding? Dune clasped a marriage cuff around her tail and though it was light, Talori felt pulled down by its weight more than the slave's cuff Prospero had used. As they left the minister's home, she wondered what would happen to her now.

"No, stop! Please!"

Talori gasped as she saw Mako swimming toward them.

"Who are you?" Dune demanded.

"I'm her father. Please, I beg you, I'll pay any price. I'll be slave to whoever owns her. Please just let me bring her home."

"The wedding is over. You're too late," Dune replied, his tone harsh.

"Wedding?"

"You heard me correctly." Dune's voice softened as he continued, "I'm sorry, sir. There is nothing you can do now. Go home."

Mako's face crumpled as Dune helped Talori into a luxurious cart pulled by four lavender hippocampi. Her heart ached as she turned. "Please, Dune. Let me say goodbye to him at least."

Dune nodded and Talori got out of the cart and swam to her father.

"I'm sorry," Mako cried. "I'm so sorry I wasn't fast enough."

Talori tried to sound brave. "It'll be all right. The Shark has married me. Prospero has no hold over me or you anymore."

Mako paled. "The Shark?"

"Talori," Dune called. "I'm sorry, but we do need to go."

She nodded and ignored the stinging in her eyes. "Take care of yourself and Delphalyn. We'll see each other again. I promise."

The Shark flicked his tail as he waited for his bride to appear. Bride. He ground his teeth. Why did he get himself into this mess? He knew the answer. The idea of Prospero selling some poor mermaid into a fate worse than an arranged marriage sickened him. And in all honesty, he was lonely. While he certainly hadn't started searching for a wife, he couldn't deny wanting someone in his life. When Prospero mentioned rumors, the Shark knew his mother was behind them. He growled in frustration. Hadn't that witch caused enough problems? He heard the sound of voices in the cavern entrance and swam to the dark corner he used the few times visitors came. He turned to see Dune lead an enchantingly beautiful mermaid into his home. This couldn't be the ugly mermaid Prospero had sold him. "Who are you?" he demanded.

"My name is Talori, sir. What should I call you?"

"The Shark suits me fine."

"No."

"No?"

Talori glared at the darkened part of the room he sat in. For a moment, he almost thought she could see him. "I will not call you the Shark. I am your wife and will call you by your name."

He considered for a moment. He could make something up. Then again, she had a point and that annoyed him. "And if I refuse?"

"I'll call you the Slug instead."

Feisty and beautiful, a lethal combination. "Rio."

Talori blinked. "What?"

"You asked and I've told you. My name is Rio."

She smirked. "Rio."

"Is that amusing?"

"Hardly seems like a sharkly name."

That they could agree on, though he wasn't about to admit it. "Believe it or not, it's true."

"So, Rio, are you going to come out of hiding?"

He sputtered for a moment. "I am not hiding."

"You wouldn't attend your own wedding and now you're sitting up in that dark corner. I realize I'm not the most beautiful mermaid in the ocean, but the least you could do is come down for a proper introduction."

For a long moment, Rio couldn't respond. Had she really just referred to herself as ugly? Perhaps he misunderstood her.

"Hello?"

"No one sees me, Talori. Not even you. I have many servants here and they will follow your orders as they would my own. I have secured a personal maid for you and she is waiting in your chambers. My butler will show you to the place. Tonight, you may take supper in your chambers as I'm sure you'd like time and space to think. Tomorrow I would appreciate it if you joined me in the dining hall for meals."

"Will I see you then?"

"No. I live in darkness and that is where I must stay. Welcome home, Talori." He paused, trying to think of the proper way to word his next comments. "I'm sure being sold into an arranged marriage is not what you ever wanted. But I do hope you'll find happiness here with me." He then left the room. He sought out the old lava flow which led to the surface. The sun was setting in a fiery display over the ocean. What had driven Prospero to say Talori was ugly? Skin the color of alabaster pitchers he'd found in shipwrecks and eyes like barracuda scales, beautiful and dangerous.

Rio looked out over the darkening ocean from his seat on the volcanic rocks. No one else knew about this little haven. As the moon rose above the distant waves, he tried to rein in his thoughts. He had to remain distant from Talori, no matter how tempting it might be to do otherwise. It would be safer for both of them, but especially for her.

The months crawled. There wasn't much for Talori to do around Rio's grand home. There were servants to do the chores. They lived close enough to a large sea market to make producing their own food unnecessary, so there were no gardens or animals for her to tend. She had never been particularly artistic, and even if she were Rio didn't need her artistic skills. In fact, the longer she stayed, the more certain she was that Rio didn't need her at all. It made her sad in a frustrating sort of way. As it was, Rio was attentive to her needs and listened at mealtimes when she spoke. He was always kind and frequently left gifts for her. But still she never saw him. They had their meals together, if one could call it that, and nothing else. Despite her best efforts to remain optimistic, she found herself homesick and wishing she had just one friend.

Rio seemed to notice as one evening he said, "You look upset, Talori. Is something troubling you?"

"Not exactly," she replied. "There hasn't been much for me to do here and I'm used to being more, well, useful."

Rio didn't respond for a moment. "Do you like it here?"

"Yes, you've been very kind and attentive. I just…." her voice trailed away. How could she explain her feelings to him?

"Come here, Talori."

Nervous anticipation filled her. She swam into the dark corner Rio stayed in. Before her eyes could adjust enough to see anything, she felt a piece of kelp go around her face, covering her eyes. "Hey!"

"I am sorry, Talori. But I can't risk you seeing me."

A charge went through her arm as Rio took her hand. It reminded her of the time an electric eel had gotten into the corral, except the tingling she felt now was pleasant. Her heart beat faster and her thoughts seemed to dissolve into bubbles. "Where are you taking me?"

"A secret place. I'll let you know how to find it again, but for now, you're just going to have to trust me. Do you think you can do that?"

What little brain power she retained from Rio's touch shouted *no*, but she heard her heart's soft answer. "Yes."

"Follow me." He squeezed her hand and together they swam. She stayed close enough to feel the powerful surge of his tail. They went through a narrow passage, and at times, Rio had to let go of her hand to lead the way. He continued to speak to her until the passage widened and he was able to take her hand once again. The water warmed as they continued, and the pressure lessened. Suddenly she felt her torso break free of the water entirely. Warmth bathed her skin. Her hand reached up to the blindfold. Could it be? A hand covered hers. "Not yet. I know you're anxious to see the surface, but allow me to go first."

"You're going to leave me here by myself?" she said, panicked.

"No, I'm just going to another part of the island. You'll still be able to talk to me, but…."

"I won't see you." She couldn't have kept the disappointment from her voice if she'd tried.

"It's safer for you this way." There was a pause. "You can take the blindfold off now."

With trembling hands, Talori pulled the seaweed from her face. The bright sunlight dazzled her and it was several moments before her eyes adjusted. She gasped as her eyes took in the beauty of the outside world. "This is incredible!" For a while she practiced breathing, surprised that it seemed so natural. Her lungs filled with air as the wind rushed down her nose. She took a deep breath, inhaling the salty scent of the ocean and the crisp freshness of the air. She giggled. "I can't believe I'm actually at the surface."

"I come here often," Rio said as Talori spun around in the water, her smile brighter than the sun itself. "It's a quiet place to think."

"What do you think about?" she asked, still taking in the sights around her.

"Everything. I think about my past, my future. Lately, I've been thinking frequently of you."

Talori stopped and turned in the direction of Rio's voice. "Me? Why would you think of a plain little mermaid like me?"

For what seemed forever he didn't answer her. Finally, he asked, "Why do you say that about yourself?"

She looked away, unwilling to let him see her face as she replied, "I know I'm not very pretty. Everyone at Coral Bay was quick to let me know. I'm too pale, too curly-headed and far too opinionated. That's why Prospero sold me to you, isn't it?"

"Prospero's opinion is the last you should base your beauty on. I've never seen anyone more beautiful than you."

Talori blushed and mumbled, "You must not see very many mermaids."

"More than you would think. I wish you could see yourself the way I see you."

Her heart swelled. Maybe they could build a normal relationship. "Will I ever get to see you?"

There was a pause. When he answered, Talori could hear his frown. "No, Talori, I don't think you will. It's complicated, but believe me when I say it is truly safer for both of us that you not see me."

"Why?"

"The story is too long to go into at the moment. If you keep watching the sky, the sun will set and then fill with millions of stars."

"Stars?"

"Just watch the sky."

They sat in silence for a long while. As stars began dancing in the sky, Talori watched in wonder. She'd never seen anything so breathtakingly lovely in her life. "I wish my father and sister could see this," she sighed.

"You miss them, don't you?"

"Very much."

Rio sighed. "I can't go with you to visit them. However, I can send you to Coral Bay for a few days if you'd like."

"You would do that for me?"

"It'll be a little while, I've got some business to take care of first."

"Business? So you're not a retired pirate?" She blushed as she realized what she'd said.

Rio laughed. "Is that what they're saying now? Funny how quickly people forget noble families when they stop being newsworthy."

"Noble?"

Ignoring her question, he continued, "No, I'm not retired and I'm not necessarily a pirate. Granted, most of my trading is done above surface with the humans who sail these waters and I can't be sure they're all honest. But I try to do business with good people and merpeople. Prospero is my one exception and that's a long story in and of itself. But, enough of that. If you'd like to visit home, I can arrange it."

"Oh, Rio, that would mean so much to me."

"Consider it done then."

Before she knew it, the blindfold was once again tied snugly around her face. She felt Rio's hands resting on her shoulders and she leaned against him. Talori closed her eyes and imagined things were different. That she could be with him without the blindfold. That he would trust her with whatever secret kept him hidden.

Rio sighed as though he sensed her thoughts. He kissed the top of her head, his breath warm on her scalp. "Let's go home."

In the weeks before she left, Talori tried to learn more about her mysterious husband. But it seemed there was little to learn. Eventually her curiosity gave way, and she reveled in the attention he paid her. Things she wished for in conversation became reality. While she never saw him, she saw tokens of his affection on a daily basis. She even stopped thinking of herself as the plain, little mermaid from Coral Bay. He came to see her off, staying in the shadows where she couldn't see him. As her maid put things in the carriage, Rio requested she not give his real name to anyone, not even her father. She agreed, though she still didn't understand the reasons. "I'll miss you," she said.

"Probably not as much as I'll miss you," he teased. "When you return, we'll go up to the surface again. Perhaps then I can give you some answers."

When she arrived in Coral Bay, Mako was overjoyed to see her. But he worked often and his time with her was short. He'd joined the business team selling whelks and abalone along the countryside Marina had told him about.

He was living in a small hut near Marina's home, but it was a temporary situation. He planned to marry Marina once he had more to offer than just his love. It thrilled Talori to see her father looking so happy and carefree. There was true promise for his future. When he explained how he had followed Prospero once he was sure the merman wouldn't see him and arrived too late to stop the wedding and bring her home, he begged her to forgive him.

"Perhaps, Father, this is meant to be."

"He treats you well, doesn't he?" Mako asked, worry showing in his eyes. "We can find a way to free you. I'll help you escape."

Talori took his hand. "Please don't worry about me. I have never been so happy in all my life. The Shark is good to me."

"You don't know his name either?" When she hesitated, Mako frowned. "Oh, I see. He must have his reasons, I suppose. I won't ask you anymore. I'm glad he treats you like a princess. It's all I ever wanted for you."

Delphalyn was less kind. Jealousy over Talori's new home and situation had changed her. She knew some of it wasn't Delphalyn's fault. Her sister had always been easily swayed by the opinions of others, and it seemed the village had filled in the missing details with rumors of their own, permanently tarnishing her reputation among them. But it hurt to have her sister treat her so poorly. "That marriage cuff looks like it was meant for a princess, not a poor merchant's daughter," she sniffed the morning Talori planned to return to Aquapolis.

"I suppose so. I don't think the Shark necessarily intended to marry a poor mermaid."

"What does he look like?" Delphalyn asked, curiosity momentarily overcoming her sour attitude. "Is he dreadfully ugly?"

Talori hesitated. "I don't know what he looks like. No one sees the Shark."

"What? Are you telling me you haven't even seen your husband? How do you know he's not a monster?"

"What you look like isn't what makes you a monster, Delphalyn. It's what's on the inside. I know his heart is good. He has treated me with as much love and respect that could be expected from an arranged marriage."

"I know how you must feel," Delphalyn said with feigned sympathy as she put an arm around Talori's shoulder, "but be honest with yourself. Why would he hide himself from you if he had no secrets?"

Talori pushed her away. "You don't understand the situation, Delphalyn."

"Do you?"

It was mid-afternoon when the carriage pulled up to the Shark's cavern home. Talori felt emotionally spent. The entire ride she'd agonized over her sister's words. While she knew she shouldn't take them to heart, the fact remained she hadn't seen the Shark. Rio could be the monster her sister claimed, for all she knew. She didn't want to believe it. He had to have a good reason to be so secretive. But what was it?

She went to her chambers and looked out the window. Her room looked over the capital city. Bioluminescent lamps glowed over the streets, while sunlight glimmered on the shell-encrusted buildings. The easy currents rippled through, causing kelp beds to sway. Flashing scales as fish swam past sparkled like the crushed seashells on the city buildings. Talori sighed and picked up a new book Rio must have left for her. Her mouth lifted in half a smile. She'd never had much reading material at home, usually old newsletters made from seaweed and lost dolphin ads scrawled on bits of sea rock or kelp. These books exuded quality. Thin pages from pressed kelp bound with smoothed fish skins. The ink never faded or smeared, which fascinated her the first few times she'd held one of her new books. Rio had told her about a merman who discovered the squid ink solution. Rio. Maybe he could help her sort through her muddled feelings. He might even take her to the surface again. After all, he had promised to do so before she left.

Talori searched the house and when Rio wasn't found, decided to go to the surface on her own. Perhaps she could find him there. If she did, maybe she could catch a glimpse of him and put her fears to rest. She turned with a resolute flick of her tail to the dining hall and swam through the hidden door into the extinct lava flow. Her heart thundered in her ears as she saw the tunnel for the first time. How had Rio ever had the courage to follow this to the end?

Strange creatures glowed around her, the only light in the pitch darkness. Something brushed past her and she swallowed a squeal. Slowly light filtered through the water and she could see the sun's distortion becoming clearer. She swam as quietly as she could, hoping Rio wouldn't hear her if he was sitting on the volcanic rocks. Talori saw the outline of a merman ahead of her as she came closer to the surface. She paused for a moment. Even through the water's distortion, she knew this was no monster. Determined not to alert him to her presence, Talori moved slowly. Her eyes widened as she broke the surface. The evening sun shone on skin as dark as hers was pale while his scales shimmered deep green and bronze. He was broad and muscular, his shaggy hair black with a hint of silver. "Rio?" she breathed.

He turned to her, and for a moment time stood still. Amber eyes flecked with green in a handsome face Talori could never have imagined. "Talori? No, get away from here! I told you never to see me."

"But, Rio—"

"GO!" he bellowed, his voice harsh and gravelly. Nothing like she normally heard. She watched in horror as he convulsed on the rocks. Slate gray replaced the green scales and the flukes of his tail hardened and elongated. Strange growls came from him. "Talori, go now!" he cried.

"What's happening?"

"For your life, go!" He looked at her, wild cruelty in his darkening eyes. "Please, go." The words came out as a menacing whisper.

Talori spun around to flee down the narrow tunnel. Behind her she could hear a monster thrashing about. She screamed as something grabbed at her fins. At one point she saw a side tunnel and turned into it. Pressing herself against the side and hardly daring to breathe, she watched as Rio passed by. Somehow in looking at him, she had caused him to become the monster his alias implied. Gray sharkskin replaced his colorful scales and appeared in patches over the rest of his body. While she hadn't seen much of his face as he swam past, she'd seen the teeth. Large, deadly shark's teeth brought flashbacks from the day her mother died. For a brief moment, she'd been married to a merman as handsome as he was kind. Now he was changed. Tears filled her eyes. "What will I do now?" She followed the new tunnel until she came out into the open ocean. A lone house, built from the shell of a giant clam, stood before her.

"I wondered when I would see you," a feminine voice said.

"Who's there?" Talori asked, trying to locate the speaker.

"A friend. You won't be able to see me, dear. Like the Shark, I value my anonymity."

"You know Rio?"

"Quite well. He is my son."

"What happened to him?"

"Just what I warned him would happen. He never did listen well."

"This is all my fault. What can I do?"

There was silence. An invisible hand took Talori's. When she squealed, the voice said, "Do not be alarmed. But if we are to discuss this, it would be best to do so inside." Talori followed her invisible hostess inside the clam shell. The water around her reeked of kelp and something she couldn't identify. Strange jars lined shelves along the walls. In the center of the home, a volcanic vent glowed. "You're a, a...."

"Witch?" the voice supplied. "Yes, the name fits. Now, in order to understand what happened, you need to accept two facts. First, not all things can be explained and second, I am a witch. Try to stay on my good side."

Talori's skin prickled. "Go on."

Bottles and jars floated through the water while ingredients were poured into a large abalone shell. "I suppose in the strictest sense of the word, what is happening to Rio is my fault. When he was a young man, I placed a curse on him. Accidentally, of course."

"How do you accidentally put a curse on someone?" Talori demanded.

"Would you share his fate?"

"If it meant we could be together, yes," she replied, surprised by her resolve.

"An interesting idea, could be amusing. But that's not why I brought you here. It truly was an accident. I suppose when you saw him, you did not see the scars."

Scars? Talori thought. Now that it had been mentioned, she did remember a thin stripe around Rio's torso.

"Let me help you. Our family was once quite important. The king is my cousin, believe it or not. And Rio, like many mermen of the court, often fought in the arena. A strong and agile merman like himself easily bested most of the poor creatures brought in. But one day everything changed. A great shark released into the arena quickly showed Rio what it meant to be outmatched."

Talori thought of the mosaic at home. The merman in the shark's mouth had been Rio? Why hadn't he ever told her?

"The beast would have killed Rio, and I had to act quickly. I summoned a spell, but in my haste I didn't phrase things properly, and instead of it hitting the shark and making it docile, it hit Rio. It was some time before I realized the extent of my mistake."

"Why didn't you try to undo it?"

"Frankly, at the time I didn't think it mattered. Others came into the arena and killed the shark, and I brought Rio here, sure I would soon bury my son. His injuries were extensive and the magic did not help. Sharkskin appeared over his scales. In some way, the curse merged him with the shark, but only partly so. And I didn't see him becoming more like a predator. In fact, the sharkskin began sloughing away as he healed. When it became clear Rio would recover, I turned myself invisible to cheat the spell's effects. Had we seen each other, the curse would have come to fruition with no way for me to save him."

"But I don't understand how you being invisible prevented that. Wouldn't it have made more sense to turn him invisible?"

Rio's mother laughed. "Magic doesn't work on logic, Talori. I can't even explain how I realized the curse's trigger would be someone making eye contact with him. To go back to my story, I continued to care for him. Naturally, he was furious when he learned what had happened. He forbade me from ever seeing him again. Made things very difficult for me, as news of my being a witch had me banished from the king's court. Anyway, he moved into the dead volcano and built the reputation of the Shark, distancing himself from his past and trying to prevent his future."

"This is all well and good, but how do I undo this? He's a monster now."

"Are you afraid of him?"

Talori hesitated only for a moment. "No."

"It does not take long to fall in love, does it?" Talori heard a chuckle, and then Rio's mother said, "This is going to require courage. You must go back to Rio's cavern. He is not fully a shark, nor will he be if you act quickly. Take this." A bottle was placed in Talori's hands. "You must follow these directions precisely. It will be dangerous."

"Whatever it takes, I'll do it."

"Do not interrupt. You will need Rio's strongest guards to help you bind him. Most of the spell is concentrated in the scars on Rio's body. Even in his transformed state, you will be able to see them. This ointment must be massaged in. It has magical properties and will neutralize the curse, though it will take time."

"Why would he need to be bound?"

"Have you ever touched sharkskin, Talori? There is a reason it is used for armor. It is tough and barbed. You will bleed. I don't think I need to explain to you what happens when a shark smells blood."

Talori shuddered. "No."

"Use the entire bottle."

"And you're sure this will undo the curse?" Talori asked.

"You don't believe me?"

"It just seems a little, I don't know, simple."

"Hmph. Humans tell stories in which all it takes is a kiss. Don't talk to me about simplicity. Besides, you're sure to change your mind when you get started. One last thing, Talori. This kind of thing only works when there is deep abiding love felt between the cursed and the rescuer. A once-in-a-lifetime kind of love. Had I tried, it would have killed him."

"Who could love him more than you? You're his mother."

"And a witch. Witches learned long ago to guard our hearts from love. Heartbreak is a dangerous thing, and loved ones can be used against you. It is better for us to be distant, some might even say cold. Be sure you know your heart before you get started. Now go, you have little time."

Dune and the other guards were waiting in the hall when Talori swam through the entrance. "Dune, I need your help."

"Where were you?"

"I met the Shark's mother and she's given me a solution."

"And you trust her? It's her fault he's like this."

"I know, but we have no other choice."

Dune frowned. "She's a witch."

"Do you have a better idea?" When he didn't respond she said, "I need you to come with me and bring someone else who is strong enough to hold him down."

"Very well." Dune motioned for one of the other guards to follow. He led the way to Rio's room. "Are you sure about this?" he asked.

"As sure as I can be."

"I hope it works." He reached for the doorknob, but Talori stopped him.

"I'll go in first. You come in after me." With her head high, she opened the door. Rio turned to her with a growl. His handsome face had been replaced by a grotesque hybrid of shark and man. "Rio?"

"What are you doing here?" he snarled. "Come to stare at the monster you've created?"

"No, I'm here to help you."

"Leave me be."

She swam closer, ignoring the instinctive desire to flee. "I can't leave, Rio. I'm your wife. I belong here with you."

He stopped pacing and looked at her. His eyes were dark and soulless. When he spoke, he almost sounded like himself. "Talori, there is nothing you can do. Leave me. I won't blame you."

"But you would, and I would never forgive myself." She moved until she floated directly in front of him, close enough to reach out and touch him. "I need you to trust me, Rio."

"You didn't trust me." The growl in his voice returned.

"I should have, and I'm sorry. Let me help you now and this can all be a bad memory. We could be a normal couple, explore the surface together without you hiding in the shadows. Let me bring you into the light." She placed a gentle hand on his cheek. "Please, Rio."

He bared his teeth and snapped, but Dune and the other guard pulled him down. "What is this?" he roared.

"I wouldn't have them do it if it wasn't necessary," Talori soothed. "Just relax." She poured a glob of ointment onto her hands. It warmed in them and seemed to glow in the dim light of the chamber. *Please, Poseidon, let this work,* she prayed. She then rubbed it down along the length of the scars.

Her hands burned, and Rio screamed in agony. "Are you trying to kill me?"

Talori paused. Had she been tricked? But when she glanced at the area she'd worked on, she saw a glimmer of green. She rubbed a little more, and a barbed piece of sharkskin fell away, revealing an emerald scale. Maybe it was working.

"Talori, what are we going to do?" Dune asked as Rio struggled to free himself. "I can let you escape."

"No. It's working! She said it might be slow, but look. I'm going to finish. Please, just keep him down." She poured another glob into her hand. The ointment burned, mingling with her blood as her hands scraped against the sharkskin. Rio's cries became more animal and desperate. He nearly escaped as the two guards turned him over. She bit back sobs as he bellowed in outrage. "Please, Rio, just a little while longer and this will all be over."

"It's over now." Rio freed an arm and flung the ointment bottle against the wall.

"No!" She swam over to the shattered pieces. Clumps of ointment clung to it and she cried in despair. Before she could think, she felt herself slammed against the wall.

"What did you think you were doing?" Rio demanded, his monstrous face a breath away from her.

She choked. "Rio, please, it was helping."

"It won't matter. You won't live to see another day," he growled, his jagged shark's teeth bared.

"No, Rio, please!"

He bellowed again as a trident pierced his shoulder.

"Go, Talori!" Dune shouted, pinning Rio to the wall.

"Dune, no! Don't kill him! Just hold him down." Talori picked up the shards of glass, wiping as much of the ointment as she could salvage on to her hands. "I hope this is enough." She worked it into the last bit of the scar tissue as Rio became more still. When she finished, she took strips of bandage and wrapped the wound on Rio's shoulder. Her husband continued to grow quieter as she worked until he finally stopped moving at all. "Release him, Dune."

"He's still a monster."

Her heart threatening to break within her, Talori said, "I know. But right now he isn't a threat. Release him."

Dune frowned but let go of Rio, who slumped to the floor.

"Help me get him to the bed and then you can go."

"Talori, this isn't a good idea. What if it's just an act?"

"Please, Dune," she begged. "I can't do it by myself."

The other guard and Dune lifted Rio's limp body and place him on the clam shell bed. The two left and Talori sat on the side of the bed next to Rio. Along the scar, his green and bronze scales glimmered under the gray sharkskin. Nothing else had changed. Rio lay with his eyes closed, not moving. His breathing slowed and sounded more labored as she waited for some change. Some sign that she'd done things right. "I'm sorry," Talori sobbed. "I followed the directions just as your mother said to. Please get better. I've already lost my mother. My sister resents me. I couldn't bear to lose you too. You've given me so much and I need you here. I don't understand why it stopped working."

This kind of thing only works when there is deep abiding love felt between the cursed and the rescuer.

Talori's heart shattered further as the words echoed in her memory. "Oh. Love was missing. I know I love you with all my heart, but...." She sighed. "I should have known you could never love an ugly mermaid like me. It was foolish of me to think I could save you. I'm sorry." Exhausted, Talori allowed

217

herself to slip from her seat to the stone floor. She hardly felt its cold surface. Pain like nothing she had ever felt radiated from her heart outward. She'd always thought it was an old fish tale that mermaids could die of a broken heart. Was that what was happening to her? The ocean pressure seemed to build around her, threatening to crush her with its weight. Her gills ached with the strain of breathing. Just as she was about to lose consciousness, a hand took hers.

"I wish you wouldn't say that about yourself, Talori. There is nothing ugly about you."

The pain eased and hope blossomed within her. "Rio?" She looked up to see him smiling down at her, looking as handsome as he had the first time she'd seen him.

His smile broadened, and he scooped her into his arms. "Come on, love. It wouldn't do for both of us to die of a broken heart. Bit melodramatic, don't you think?"

A weak laugh bubbled from her as he laid her gently on the bed. He wrapped her hands in bandages and then held her close. "Oh, Talori," he sighed. "My beautiful, wonderful Talori. What would I do without you?"

She leaned against him. "I don't want to imagine."

"Me neither. Are you feeling up to a swim to the surface? I can carry you if you're too weak."

Talori giggled. "After the ordeal you've been through, you're worried about *me* making it?"

He led her to the lava flow and together they swam up to the ocean's surface. Stars glittered across the sky as the moon glowed silver above the waves. Talori reveled in the sensation of being held in Rio's arms with no secrets between them. His voice flowed over her. "In case I haven't made it quite clear, I love you, Talori."

She turned to him, her silver eyes glowing with joy. "I love you too."

Rio pushed a stray wisp of hair behind Talori's ear. "Will you marry me?"

"We're already married, Rio. Or did you forget?" Talori teased.

"Believe me, I haven't forgotten," he replied, the low timbre of his voice sending shivers through her. "But you deserve better than a proxy wedding. I'm sure my mother would be willing to arrange all the details, if it's something you wanted. No doubt she's skulking around somewhere. We can invite your family to come. Marry me, Talori. Marry me in the light instead of the shadows."

Wrapping her arms around Rio's neck, she smiled. "Very well. I will marry you again. Whenever and wherever you want."

In the soft moonlight, the couple pledged their love to one another in a promise that would never end.

Jessica L. Elliott has been writing since she could hold a pencil. Her first book, Charming Academy, was published in 2011 and followed by fairy tale retellings and sweet romances. When not visiting unicorns and fairies in her imagination, Jessica lives in southwest Kansas with her family.

www.jessicalelliott.com
www.facebook.com/JessicaLElliottAuthor

Reviving the Sword

Alastriona glanced up at the sun over the clearing where they'd spent the night. It was well past time to get on the road. Her heart filled with anticipation—maybe today would be the day. The centaur tossed her bag over her shoulder. The red markings on her back glowed in the late morning light. Wisps of her red tail flowed in the gentle breeze as she bent over and grabbed *Kingdom Defender*.

"The sword fits you." Arnhyder, Alastriona's traveling companion, stretched his back legs. "The jewel matches your eyes. When you picked it up, it seemed to come to life."

Alastriona stared at the gryphon. "Really?"

Arnhyder blinked his solemn, dark eyes and ruffled his feathers. "Why would I lie to you?"

She shrugged, a delicate action for a centaur. "No one's ever said that before."

Watching Arnhyder extend his wings and take off, Alastriona strapped the sword behind her back and settled into a traveling gallop. Had the sword begun to come alive? Would what she had longed for and searched for over mountains, through plains, and even endured wetlands for finally happen? A memory blossomed of the glowing emerald stone in the hilt of the sword as her father ran a cleaning cloth over the blade.

"Alas." Papa used his pet name for Alastriona. "One day, *Kingdom Defender* will be yours. She will empower you with courage and foresight."

Alastriona reached her small hand toward the blade. Her father moved the sword from her reach.

"No, Alas. *Never* touch its blade. The oils in your skin will ruin the ripples of color. That is why I clean it every evening."

Alastriona admired the dark blade that shimmered with a rainbow of hues. Her eyes landed back on the glowing, green gem at its hilt.

"How, Papa? How will I bring *Kingdom Defender* to life?"

"You'll figure it out, Alas. When it's time, the sword will speak to you."

The memory faded. Alastriona laid her hand reverently on the hilt at her shoulder and sighed. Thirty-five rings had formed in the trees of the forest since her uncle had placed the sword in her hands. The stone still remained dull and no power filled the centaur.

They covered many miles despite their late start. As the sun set, Alastriona sat near the fire and watched the rotating spit holding her fish. Arnhyder had eaten his fill already. She preferred to cook her meat.

"Where's home for you, Arnhyder?"

"In the mountains."

She nodded. "Do you miss it?"

The gryphon offered his strange shrug. "Family's still there, but it was time for me to stretch my wings and explore."

The fire popped, releasing a cedar scent.

"What about you?" Arnhyder asked.

Alastriona remembered home: the fire, the forest, and the other centaurs, father, uncle, and the fun they had together. She shook her head.

"I don't have a home."

Arnhyder's eye sparkled in the firelight. His brow seemed to arch.

"My family was slain. I was the only survivor. There's nothing left for me there. I run to avoid the memories. Okay?" Her words were harsh, but she didn't care. The pain still raked across her soul like claws across bare skin.

"I'm sorry," Arnhyder said.

The next day the terrain gradually changed from flatlands, to rolling hills, to sparsely populated woods. By the time Alastriona was ready for the midday meal, Arnhyder had moved on ahead. Alastriona was wondering how she would get his attention, when he returned and landed beside her.

"We've found some company," he said. "It appears that a group of humans have an elf surrounded. Shall we even the odds?"

His voice held a hint of excitement. Alastriona wondered if it had anything to do with the anticipation of a fight.

"Humans have never been friends." The memories of human offenses marched through her mind like a parade of migrating geese. She drew *Kingdom Defender*.

Arnhyder nodded and took off with Alastriona right behind him. She galloped through the woods until she saw the glade ahead of her, then slowed so her hooves wouldn't echo through the ground and give her away.

Leaving the last tree behind her, she took in the scene. Five humans surrounded a single female elf. Three more humans lay on the ground unmoving. Alastriona grinned. The elf had made her attackers pay. As she watched, a sixth man climbed the rock the elf kept at her back so no one would attack her from behind. Just as the man moved to jump onto his enemy, Arnhyder swooped down and grabbed him. As the gryphon's talons sank in, the man shrieked, alerting the others to their presence.

"Gryphon!" one man called.

The two women closest to Alastriona replaced their blades with bows and arrows. Before the first could let loose her shaft, *Kingdom Defender* silenced her. Alastriona distracted the other's aim when she came crashing down on her.

She turned as she felt hands upon her back. A red-bearded man with wild green eyes clung to her waist. Her sword's length prevented her from using it against him. His hands clawed at her as his feet gained footage around her girth. Before long he would be securely mounted on her back with her hair in his hands to steer her. She reared, trying to unseat the man. As she came down, she heard his cry. Spinning around, she felt him slip from her back. She rose to bring her hooves to bear, only to see the blood oozing from him. Alastriona crashed back down and spun to attack the next person.

"Easy, girl," Arnhyder said. "They're all gone. Our friend here just saved your hide."

The elf was slender with dark skin and short brown hair; she didn't look like any elf Alastriona had seen. The elf's brown, almond-shaped eyes looked up at the centaur. The intensity of battle fury still burned in them.

Alastriona smiled. "Thank you."

The elf bowed, displaying formality and tradition.

"The pleasure was mine. I have never had the privilege of seeing a gryphon and a centaur in battle."

"It looked like you could use some help," Arnhyder said. "I always say, 'live for the adventure.'"

"If you want adventure, then stay with me. It seems to follow me around, but here, I am forgetting my manners." Again, she bowed. "Sagishi Erufu at your service."

"Arnhyder Greif at yours." The gryphon inclined his head to the ground.

"Alastriona Álago." The centaur shifted her arm to rest at her waist and bent over it, providing her family name in the traditional response the elf required.

As she straightened, she tossed her red hair over her shoulders and bent down to wipe her blade clean on the grass. The sun caught the lines of the folded metal and turned them into glistening rainbows.

"That is an amazing sword." Sagishi's eyes roamed over *Kingdom Defender* as only one who admires swords would. "It seems to have a mind of its own. While you were wielding it in battle, it almost glowed."

Alastriona gazed deep into the elf's brown eyes. Sagishi's eyebrow rose and disappeared behind the hair that framed her face.

"Did I offend you?" the elf asked.

Alastriona stood and repositioned her sword into its scabbard.

"No. It's just that both of you have now implied that my sword has some kind of hidden life. I haven't sensed anything of the sort with *Kingdom Defender.*"

Sagishi shrugged. "I'm simply stating what I saw. Is it of elven make? I seem to recall seeing a similar sword in action once, long ago."

Alastriona shook her head. "I don't know. It's possible, I suppose. It has been in my family for generations, passed on from father to son." She paused and placed a hand on the hilt.

"Yet, you are not a son." Sagishi stated the obvious, her tone neutral.

"No." Bitterness choked the word. "My father did not have a son. His life was cut off too soon."

Alastriona looked to the grass and allowed her hair to hide the tears that glistened in her eyes.

"And yet, your father has a daughter to be proud of. A warrior in all senses of the word. You rescued me."

"You're a fine centaur. You do the Álago family proud," Arnhyder agreed.

Alastriona smiled. Leave it to the gryphon to cheer her up.

"You must be hungry and need a rest after that battle. My camp is back behind those rocks over there. I have food and mead," Sagishi said.

"Honey mead of the elves?" Arnhyder's eyes brightened with excitement.

"None other." Sagishi moved to lead the way.

Alastriona caught a shift in the elf's eyes, but Arnhyder was already in conversation with Sagishi as if they had known each other all their lives. As Alastriona followed, she considered the elf's words. Was *Kingdom Defender* of elven make? She tried to search her memory for any hint of its origin, but nothing came to mind. A stray memory tickled at the back of her mind, but no amount of trying would bring it forward. Unease settled over her.

During their meal of dried fish, fresh berries, and mead, Alastriona tried to set aside her feelings. The food satisfied her hunger, and the mead quenched her thirst. It also seemed to loosen Arnhyder's tongue.

"Sagishi, where are you from?"

The elf repositioned her weight on the box where she sat and raised her dainty face to look at him. "I'm from far away. I have wandered from home for many years. A catastrophe took my home and family. Ever since, I have not called any place home."

"I'm sorry." Arnhyder took a bite of fish.

Alastriona didn't think she heard the same compassion in his tone as when he had said those words to her. She tried to push the feeling aside. After all, Sagishi had the same experience she had.

"I left home for adventure." The gryphon glanced up. "Look where it has gotten me—two pretty girls."

Sagishi rolled her eyes. "I've seen far too many years to be called a young woman."

Alastriona squinted. She saw many harrowing experiences in the elf's eyes.

"How old are you?" She placed her hand over her mouth as she realized she had spoken her thought aloud.

Sagishi laughed, a light tinkling sound like a babbling brook. "I'm two-hundred-fifty years old. Young enough to travel the world, and old enough to know there's more to life than traveling." A wistfulness filled her voice.

Alastriona was almost sad she had asked. Arnhyder, on the other hand, plowed straight ahead.

"What's wrong with traveling? You can go where you like with no one to tell you what to do!"

Again Sagishi laughed, but Alastriona sensed that the laughter covered up a deep longing or sadness. The centaur understood that feeling all too well.

"Arnhyder, how would you feel about traveling if the home you loved was destroyed—utterly and beyond any hope of rebuilding?" Bitterness now colored the elf's voice, turning it hard and cold. "Not only the place, but all the people, gone in one day. People who should have lived at least three of your lifespans, cut off in their prime. And it all could have been stopped. If they would've been warned...."

A bird sang its song far above them. Alastriona wanted to silence it. Sagishi's words had opened her own wounds. *Warned*, she thought. *There had been no warning for Papa, Uncle, or the others. Who would have warned us?*

The elf stood. "I am sorry. I let the mead do my talking. There are still several more shadow lengths before the sun goes down. Enough time to move through these human-infested areas."

Arnhyder repositioned his back feet. "Alastriona, what would you say to traveling with her? She promised adventure, and I think the greater our number, the safer we'll all be."

Alastriona looked at her traveling partner. Would another person make that much difference? She shrugged.

"If you don't mind, I don't."

"Then it's settled. Will you allow us to join you, Sagishi?"

The elf paused in gathering her things. She bowed. "I'd be honored to have such fine warriors accompany me."

The rest of the day passed without any problems. They skirted the human habitats and avoided the few hunting parties and farms they saw. Arnhyder's normal, easygoing temperament put both the elf and the centaur at ease. Nightfall found them on the edge of a plain. The sunset filled the sky, reflected in the grasses blowing in the slight wind.

"Nothing ahead as far as I can see." Arnhyder landed beside Alastriona. "The plain is just that—plain."

Sagishi groaned. "Please, don't start again with your terrible puns."

Alastriona hid a smile. Arnhyder had regaled them all afternoon with his humor. She really didn't mind. It made the passage of time easier, but Sagishi had tired of it quickly.

"We'll camp over there." The elf pointed to a grove of trees off to the east. "I'll set up my tent. Arnhyder, go find us some food for the night. Alastriona, go get firewood."

"Yes, Your Majesty." Arnhyder dipped his head in a mock bow.

Sagishi's eyes turned dark, and she scowled at him. "If you were anything but a gryphon, you would feel the wrath of an elf."

Arnhyder cocked his head and opened his beak. "Remember, I live for adventure. Come try." No malice filled his voice.

"Enough, you two." Alastriona stepped between them. "Arnhyder, please don't antagonize her. I'll go search for some wood." She set her pack on the ground, repositioned *Kingdom Defender*, and walked off, leaving the two still squabbling.

The grove wound back into the depression between two hills, creating a wedge. Alastriona wondered if it would be better to camp here, where they had their backs to a wall, or out where Sagishi had chosen, where they could see someone approaching. Alastriona shrugged. She was in a group now. She could rely on her companions and their past experiences.

Grass grew thick between the trees, carpeting the ground. Alastriona longed to lie down and let the cool blades soothe her travel weariness. Instead, she shook her head and continued to look for firewood. Strangely, none lay on the ground. She wandered farther into the grove of trees. They towered above her, hinting of age and wisdom.

Wisdom. A sigh escaped her. *Will I ever unlock the wisdom and foresight held within my sword? Or has it been lost forever?*

A breeze whispered through the branches above her head. She looked up and blinked as the greens and yellows of the oaks above her disappeared. In their place fire rained down from the sky, great rocks burning as they fell. No longer was she in the grove. She was in the forest of her childhood. Flames engulfed the forest. Panic ensued. Other centaurs older, taller than her ran ahead of her.

"Alas," her father called, "run for the lake."

She galloped, but couldn't seem to go as fast as the others. Looking down, she saw an image of herself as a young girl. Not comprehending, but feeling the heat from the conflagration, she ran as fast as her little legs would go. Blood pounded in her ears while flames sprang up around her. Her back began to burn. The pain pushed her ever faster. At last, the cooling water lapped at her hooves and made its way up to her waist. The burning on her back ceased.

Looking around, she found her family. They huddled together and watched their home burn.

Alastriona blinked. The night sky blazed with stars. Gazing around, she saw the grove behind her. The ground sloped upward. *How did I get here?* She spread her fingers, running them through the cool green grass. Turning around, she headed back down the hill. She puzzled over the strangeness of what had happened. She had never sleepwalked; this dream was different. It was more of a memory than a dream.

When she arrived back at the grove, extreme exhaustion overtook her. She unsheathed *Kingdom Defender*. A soft glow filled the path, grass, and leaves with a green hue. Alastriona traveled back toward her companions.

"Alastriona!" Arnhyder called. "Come have dinner. Aren't you hungry?"

Alastriona blinked. The gryphon and elf sat around a fire.

Sagishi stood and motioned to the centaur. "Alastriona. Come, what took you so long? I went ahead and found some wood for our fire."

Standing with the comforting warmth of her sword in her hand, Alastriona stared around her. How much time had passed?

Sagishi walked toward her.

"Alastriona? Come to your senses. What is wrong with you?"

"I don't know. I went to find wood. Where did you get the wood?"

Sagishi pointed off to the edge of the grove. Even in the light of the slivered moon, Alastriona could see the sticks and windfall lying around. She shook her head to clear it. No words came to her. She repositioned her sword into the scabbard and noticed that the green hue that had filled the path in front of her had shifted to come from behind her.

"What did you do to your sword?" Arnhyder landed beside Sagishi. "Are you okay?"

Alastriona walked forward. "I'm hungry. Did you get some fish, Arnhyder?"

She noticed the looks Sagishi and Arnhyder gave each other, but ignored them. She had no answers for what had happened, nor for why the gem in her sword suddenly glowed a brilliant green.

Alastriona ate her meal in silence. Even Arnhyder understood her need for meditation, for he only whispered occasionally to Sagishi. The elf sent sidelong glances at the centaur, but didn't comment. After filling her stomach, Alastriona began to explain what she could.

"So, you're saying that you felt wisdom radiating from the grove, and the next instant you were in some dreamlike memory from your childhood, and then you found yourself beyond the grove with no recollection of how you arrived?" The disbelief was strong in Sagishi's voice.

"You felt tired both times you entered the grove, correct?" Arnhyder scratched his shoulder with a hind leg.

Alastriona nodded. "Extremely."

Arnhyder stood. "Well, let's go investigate."

"Investigate?" Alastriona stared in wonder at her friend. She knew he was reckless, but this was even too much for him.

"Come on." Sagishi walked past them both, letting her hand pull at Alastriona's arm as she went. "We're not going to figure this out by sitting here. Oh, and bring the sword," she said almost as an afterthought.

Rising to her feet, Alastriona grabbed *Kingdom Defender* and followed the others. As soon as she reached the edge of the trees, she felt the call. A deep longing to curl up under the trees and listen to their stories filled her being. The weight of the sword in her hand suddenly seemed too much and pulled the point of the blade toward the ground. Her feet slowed until she stood still. The voices of her companions drifted to her as if on a summer breeze.

Alastriona breathed deeply. The scent of mulching leaves and mint filled her nostrils. The place radiated with a faint green tint. Without thinking, she felt her hands pull the sword from its scabbard. She gazed transfixed as the rippled hues danced in the green light.

As she watched, the ripples began to move, softly at first and then more rapidly. The rhythmic movement brought a peace to her heart she had not known since she'd seen her family for the last time. Her breathing slowed, and she settled to the ground, her eyes still fixed on the blade.

Alastriona's vision blurred. With sure movements, she used her free hand to wipe at her eyes. When her hand fell away, she saw a plain before her. Humans formed a line of warriors. She looked to either side of her and found Sagishi on her left and Arnhyder on her right. Beyond them other elves, centaurs, and even gryphons stood ready to fight.

The soft glow of rippling green hues came back into focus. *What had that been?* It wasn't any memory Alastriona had ever had before. *Could it have been a foretelling?* With bewilderment she watched as a single tear landed on the blade resting in her arms. A rainbow of colors gleamed from its edges. With care, she shifted the cloth between her arm and the blade and used it to rub away the stain. A hand on her shoulder caused her to look up into almond eyes set in a heart-shaped face.

"Place the blade into the ground, Alastriona," said Sagishi.

Alastriona looked to Arnhyder.

He nodded. "Elves know more about magic and swords."

Alastriona nodded. He had a point. With care, she touched the tip of the blade to the grass. As if she was replacing the sword into its scabbard, she pushed it into the ground. A sigh filled the air encompassing her. She knew it didn't come from her. Instinctively, she inserted the blade in the ground up to its handguard.

"Would you look at *that*!" Arnhyder moved closer to her. "The grass is twining around the hilt! The color...."

Alastriona felt Sagishi's grip tighten on her shoulder. The centaur didn't blame the elf; instead, she leaned forward to watch, never letting her fingers leave the hilt. The soft grass wound its way like a caress around her hands until it reached the pommel and the stone. The green light shone brighter. Alastriona squinted, but never looked away from her sword.

"*Kenyoku majikku.*"

The words sighed through the leaves above them. Alastriona felt Sagishi's surprise radiate through the hand on her shoulder, her sharp inhalation of breath disturbing the silence.

"*Erufú kenyoku soshté majikku.*"

Alastriona's eyes never left her hands or the gem in the pommel that pulsed with the words.

"*Koka difénda-a káta-na na ohu kudesahu yokeim kéntau-rosu kudeho yúki.*"

As the last words faded into the breeze rustling the leaves above them, a light so bright that Alastriona had to close her eyes burst from the gem. When she opened her eyes again, darkness surrounded her.

Arnhyder's voice sounded loud in her ears. "I could live a thousand lives and never see anything like this! What *was* that?"

A soft chuckle which built into a joyous laughter came from Sagishi. Alastriona blinked and looked upward. Stars outlined the elf's head.

"That, Arnhyder," Sagishi said when she regained her composure. "That was the magic of the elves!" Awe filled her voice. "I never expected to hear or see it ever again."

"How can it be?" Alastriona's voice seemed small and harsh compared to the soft whisper of the magic.

"This place must be an ancient elven village. I can feel the presence of many wise ancestors." Longing filled Sagishi's voice.

Arnhyder surprised Alastriona with his words. "We will leave you to wander the grove tonight. Come, Alastriona. I'd like to take a look at your sword in better light, if you don't mind."

Alastriona looked back down to the sword. Through the dim green light, she could see that the grass was no longer crawling up her hands, but waving gently in the breeze. With a nod, she began to pull *Kingdom Defender* out of the ground. The blade slid free without a sound or even a feel of scraping rocks. Alastriona shook her head. After all that had happened that night, it shouldn't have surprised her, but it did. Once the blade was free, Alastriona glanced along its length to make sure nothing had harmed it. Satisfied, she replaced it in its scabbard. Once the sword rested in its customary place on her back, she stood. Addressing the trees, she bowed low.

"Alastriona Álago thanks you from the bottom of her heart for bringing the power back into my sword, *Kingdom Defender*, and giving the foresight to me. If I can ever repay the debt, I will."

"My debt will be difficult to repay, young centaur."

The same voice she had heard on the wind whispered, only this time in a language she could understand.

"Your blade will tell you what I require. Be aware, it will come one day, when you least expect it."

Alastriona bowed again, her right hand resting at her heart, her left held at her waist.

"I will listen and try to honor you, most noble of elves."

"We know. That is why we healed your sword. The healing of your mind will require your own magic."

"My mind?" Confusion clouded Alastriona's thoughts.

"Yes, your mind. Young centaur, you have been hurt and hold bitterness tightly to your being. As long as you carry this weight, you will not be able to use your sword as it was meant to be used."

The wind picked up, and Alastriona shivered. She turned to see Arnhyder's wide dark eyes gazing at her.

The sunrise cast purplish-pink hues across the land, coloring the fog around the grove. Alastriona gave one last glance at the strange trees and turned. As she did, she noticed Sagishi. The elf's shoulders sagged; her eyes were clouded with an undecipherable feeling. Alastriona walked over to her new friend.

"I didn't have the opportunity to thank you last night for what you did."

Sagishi waved away the compliment. "Do not thank me. I have none of the elven magic left in me. Thank them." She gestured to the trees.

"I have, and I have accepted the debt they laid upon me."

Sagishi's dark eyes pierced to Alastriona's soul. "They spoke to you, too?"

The centaur nodded. A sparrow chirped in the bushes. Sagishi turned away. Alastriona frowned. Had she said something wrong? For a moment, she had seen into the elf's soul, but as suddenly as the sun going behind a cloud, it had left.

"Leave her be." Arnhyder strode up beside Alastriona. "Much weighs on her heart. She'll come around. In the meantime, let's go. You never know what adventure awaits us."

A smile creased Alastriona's face. "No we don't, Arnhyder, and you live for adventure."

"That I do." The gryphon lifted into the air.

Shaking her hair behind her shoulders, Alastriona readjusted her pack. The weight of *Kingdom Defender* was a comfort. She wondered how the sword would speak to her, but she didn't doubt the voice that had spoken the night before. One day, she would repay the debt. Until then, she would protect Sagishi; that she knew. With a contented sigh, she lengthened her stride into a gallop to catch up with Arnhyder and the elf.

Even as a young girl, Kandi J Wyatt, had a knack for words. She loved to read them, even if it was on a shampoo bottle! By high school Kandi had learned to put words together on paper to create stories for those she loved. Nowadays, she writes for her kids, whether that's her own five or the hundreds of students she's been lucky to teach. When Kandi's not spinning words to create stories, she's using them to teach students about Spanish, life, and leadership. Her books include the Dragon Courage series, a middle grade to young adult fantasy, as well as *The One Who Sees Me*, a Christian historical fiction. You can find out more about her at kandijwyatt.com.

http://kandijwyatt.com

Mothers' Night Out

"Thank you so much for covering Alaina's shift tonight," Josie told me when I stepped into her infant classroom at 6:45.

"No problem," I told her. "When I clocked out at five, I got some dinner and a couple snacks for later." I held up my hands to show her my grocery bag and my fast food leftovers.

A flicker of a frown passed over Josie's face. I checked my attitude, because I knew she was a health nut. Whatever. She was forty-four, the same age as my mom, and looked every bit of it. All that kale and avoidance of gluten wasn't doing her any big favors. "What's left over from your dinner?" she asked.

"Half a hamburger."

She frowned a little more this time and told me, "You'll have to finish that now before the families arrive, but you can put your drinks in the little fridge over there by the sink." Okay, maybe she wasn't judging my choice of food after all. She just didn't want me eating in front of the kids. I went to throw the hamburger in the trash. "No!" Josie said sharply, stopping me. "I prefer you just eat it, if you don't mind."

"I'm really not hungry," I told her, reaching for the handle to the trash cabinet.

She put her hand on the cabinet to block me. "I'm afraid I must insist that you finish it. So it won't leave a smell."

Fine. I took the hamburger out and ate it in three big bites right in front of her.

"Thank you," she said, not even fazed by my rudeness. She actually looked a little grateful, if that made any sense at all.

After I put up my snacks, I asked, "When did we start opening in the evenings? Is it a special event?"

I'd only been working at New Tradition Day Care since June when I graduated from high school. The place was open normally from 7:30am to 5:30pm. It was a really nice, high quality center, with its own parking lot and ringed by beautiful spruce trees that separated it from a large park. They charged a ton for tuition—not that my measly paycheck reflected any of it.

Josie didn't stand around while she talked, she kept busy taking all the cotton sheets off the crib mattresses and tossing them to me, then replacing them with waterproof plastic sheets. "Actually, Mallory, this is a regular thing," she answered. "We keep it pretty hush hush. We wouldn't want all the parents to know we have a Mother's Night Out program or we'd be overrun." She tossed another sheet to me. "Alaina usually helps me, but she just *had* to go see KISS in concert. She said it only happens once in a blue moon, and she couldn't miss it."

Done with the cribs, she got out a couple big plastic bins and gathered all the soft toys into them. Into the bins went the dolls, stuffed animals and even some of the plastic toys like the blocks that could be squeezed. I helped her once I began to understand that she was only leaving out hard plastic toys, the kind that can't be destroyed. "Alaina said I'd only have to work until 11:00," I double-checked. "Is she really coming back to work after a concert like that? I wouldn't."

"She understands her responsibility," Josie said, putting the bins in a closet where the babies couldn't get to them.

"I can stay all night if you need me to," I said. "Then she won't have to rush."

Josie paused and looked me right in the eyes. "I'd prefer you to leave as planned." Then she smiled. "Besides, I think you're scheduled to open tomorrow morning for regular care."

"We could just switch schedules. I feel bad about ruining her good time. Why don't you call her?"

"No."

That answer sounded final. I knew the tone well from my mom. I didn't push it any further.

Headlights came in through the front windows of the room, and Josie quickly pulled the blinds all the way down to block them out. "The parents are arriving. Before they come in, there's something you should know. These aren't babies that go to this day care regularly. We're going to have nine of them. There are two sets of twins and one set of triplets in this group. The youngest is an only child and only nine weeks old. The oldest baby is Ms. Dierdre's son. He's eleven months and the third born of a triplet group, but his brothers don't need to come here anymore."

Ms. Dierdre was our Center Director. "I didn't even know she had kids," I confessed. Josie just shrugged and didn't offer any more information because the first mom was entering the classroom.

She was introduced to me as Shelley Gray as she pushed her two babies into the room in a two-seat stroller. She wore yoga pants and a tank top like she was headed for the gym instead of a job. The woman was lean and fit, I noticed. Though her babies, two boys, appeared to be about six months old, she didn't look like she had recently given birth. There wasn't a hint of leftover pregnancy fat left on her. Mrs. Gray was sweet as could be and seemed delighted that her babies would have a place to stay for the night. She never stopped smiling for a second, thanked us a hundred times, and only had a moment of worry cross her eyes when Josie introduced me and explained that Alaina was going to be late.

"Oh, well, I'm sure you have it all worked out, like usual," Mrs. Gray said. She winked at me. "You'll learn a lot from Ms. Josie. Everyone in town says she's the 'Baby Whisperer' because she knows everything there is about taking care of babies."

Josie gave an *aw shucks* look that made me laugh out loud. A diaper bag was passed over, and I took it to the counter to put the bottles in the refrigerator. I noticed there were only two. "Um, Mrs. Gray?" I said, trying to catch her before she left. "There aren't enough bottles for the whole night."

Mrs. Gray looked uncertainly at Ms. Josie, who said, "Two is all they'll need. They're going to bed at eight."

"O—kay," I said, but I let them know in my tone that I thought it was stupid not to have a back-up. Some *baby whisperer*. Everyone knows babies wake up hungry in the middle of the night.

Within the next twenty minutes all the moms had shown up with their kiddos. While they weren't all in work-out attire, they all were amazingly healthy looking. All of them had sleek, long hair, strong arms and long legs.

The other thing they had in common was the desire to give their kids unusual names. Mrs. Diedre's son was Maccon. The two girl twins that were nine months old were Susi and Timber. The triplets were Lowell, Canagan, and Channon. Channon was a boy, mind you, and Canagan was the girl. Weird. Mrs. Gray's twin boys had more normal names. She was kind enough to name them Channing and Colin. The tiniest baby was Felan, a little girl.

Once again, I was kind of glad the babies would all be asleep early, because I didn't want to have to say those names over and over again all night long.

Ms. Dierdre was the last mom to arrive. She came in a little harried at 6:30 and apologized for being late. She went to plop little Maccon down on the floor, but he refused to bend his body to sit. So, she made sure he was steady in standing position and let go. Maccon smiled giddily, took two steps and fell to his bottom.

"He's walking now," Ms. Dierdre told us. "Just a couple steps, but he'll be good at it within the next week or so if he's anything like his brothers."

Josie took the diaper bag from Ms. Dierdre and asked, "So, this will be his last overnight visit then?"

Ms. Diedre beamed with pride. "I think so. It's about time. His brothers learned to walk at ten months. He's been slow. I'd keep an eye out on him tonight, though. He's liable to try to jump out of the crib."

"*Jump* out?" I said. I'd babysat a lot of babies over the past four years, and I'd seen babies climb out of cribs but never jump.

Ms. Diedre just patted me on the shoulder and said, "You'll be gone before then, so you won't need to concern yourself about it. Ms. Josie knows what to do."

Maccon was a cute boy with pretty hair that was blond at the roots and dark at the tips. His mom had dark hair with a cool streak of blond close to the front that ran from where she parted it to where her hair was cut just below her shoulder. I once asked a co-worker if she dyed it like that, but I was told it was natural and she'd had that streak of blond her whole life.

Ms. Dierdre followed Josie over to the counter and spoke quietly while I sat on the floor and played with the babies. I heard her say, "There isn't any worry about Alaina getting here in time, is there?"

"No. She knows the schedule."

"Okay," Mrs. Dierdre said warily. "Because, you know I can't control what will happen if she's late."

Wow, I thought. Alaina must have some problem with tardiness. It sounded like if she were late one more time she'd get fired.

"She'll be here," Josie said with confidence.

Ms. Dierdre seemed to accept that and smiled. She walked over and kissed her baby on the head. Maccon reached up her arms for a hug, and she pulled him up to her again. He kissed her cheek and then opened his mouth. "Ow, Maccon! No!" Ms. Dierdre shouted and put her baby back on the floor a little roughly. "No biting." She put her hand to her face but not fast enough for me to see that her son had broken the skin. I'd have to remember that kid had some sharp teeth. On the floor, Maccon grinned, and I noticed he hadn't grown his front two teeth yet. So far he only had two fang teeth on the top.

I followed Mrs. Dierdre to the door of the classroom, "Um, Ms. Dierdre, Alaina didn't say how much I get paid for this tonight. Is it the same rate as during the day?"

"Oh no," Ms. Dierdre said. "This is special. You get twenty-five an hour."

"No kidding. Really?"

"Yes." She winked at me. "It'll be easy money. The babies will all be asleep in an hour."

That was kind of funny, actually, since I didn't even earn half of that per hour during the daytime hours and had to work very hard with the hyper little devils. I kind of wanted to text my mom and tell her what I was being paid. She said I'd never get paid more than minimum wage if I didn't go to college.

I did the math in my head and then said to my boss, "Hey, I'd be happy to work all night, so Alaina doesn't have to rush here after the concert. Do you want us to call her?"

Ms. Dierdre's lip seemed to snarl at the suggestion. She looked past me to Josie. "Alaina better be here on time. You make sure she understands that."

Geez. I guess Ms. Dierdre let me know what she thought of me, didn't she? What was so awesome about Alaina anyway? I'd been in the classroom with her before, and she didn't do anything super special with the kids. In fact, sometimes I thought she was kind of lazy and just sat in the rocking chairs holding sleeping babies so she wouldn't have to help do anything. I bit my lip on my thoughts as I watched Ms. Dierdre leave the room.

Josie didn't say a word to me about the way Ms. Dierdre behaved toward me or the fact that I had just tried to go over her head and get my boss to approve me staying all night when Josie told me I couldn't. Once Ms. Dierdre was gone, Josie put me straight to work. We had nine babies who all need to have bottles, baby food and clean diapers before being rocked to sleep. She knew the kids well and told me that we needed to start with the youngest first.

It was kind of amazing to watch her work. At times she seemed like she sprouted extra limbs, because she could do so many things at once. She could balance a bottle-fed baby on her knee while spoon-feeding a baby in a high chair, all while keeping a little one from crying by bouncing them in a bouncy seat with her foot. I needed a few directions, but I think I was keeping up with the pace she needed. When I started the diaper changes, she told me to leave the babies wearing just a diaper. No pajamas. I thought that was a strange request, but I guessed between that and the plastic sheets she was trying to avoid the mess of babies who leaked out of their diapers at night.

I had Susi and Timber in the high chairs eating some kind of homemade, pureed beef stew when I noticed that both of those baby girls only had their top fang teeth too. How weird that three babies in the same class grew their fangs before their front teeth. "Is that unusual?" I asked Josie. She shrugged like it wasn't a big deal to her.

"I see that all the time," she said.

Now I was curious, and I began to check the other babies. The triplets were only growing their bottom teeth, because they were still only about five months old. Channing and Colin, however, had some growing nubs just under their upper gums. Incisors.

At 7:30 Josie dimmed the lights to the play area a little bit, giving the room a nice soft glow. The crib area, which was three-quarters blocked off by a glass partition, was mostly dark, with just enough light coming in through the windows to make everything visible. When the lights were on in that area, it was just too bright for sleeping. Josie played soft piano lullaby music on her iPod and ran it through a speaker in the crib room.

There were two rocking chairs in the room. While the bigger kids played on the floor, we each took a baby in our arms, wrapped it up in a blanket and rocked it to sleep. I'd seen babies nap in the swing and in bouncy seats during the daytime, but Josie insisted that every baby sleep in a crib at night. When I put the first baby, little Felan, in her crib, Josie stepped up beside me and carefully took the blanket off the baby and out of the crib. I thought the baby looked so exposed lying there mostly naked on a white plastic bed sheet with no soft blanket to cuddle with. Josie was insistent about this too, and she snatched the blankets off all the babies I put down in the cribs.

Maccon gave me the hardest time, being the oldest. He was kind of heavy, pushing twenty-five pounds, and he kicked and hollered a lot. Josie had to take him from me and did some kind of magic on him. Within seconds, she had him calmed down and sucking his pacifier for all its worth. She put him in his crib, took his blanket and then took his pacifier.

"Can he sleep without that?" I asked.

"It's safer for him this way," she said. "So he won't choke."

"Choke on a pacifier?"

Josie said nothing about that. She turned her back to me and reached into his bed again. I walked away, because she was clearly not interested in telling me why she was being so peculiar. All I could think was that she had a really strong fear of Sudden Infant Death Syndrome and didn't want to take any chances.

I got out one of my sodas and popped it open. The dim lights, soft looping music, warm baby bodies and rocking had practically worked me into a coma. It was only 8:30, and I needed all the caffeine I could put into my body to stay awake for the next two and a half hours. Josie emerged from the crib area and smiled.

"Are all the puppies sleeping?" I asked her.

A weird look crossed her face. "What did you call them?"

"Oh, sorry," I said. "I have a habit of calling crawling babies puppies."

She snickered. "That's actually really funny," she said. Then she started laughing harder and had to cover her mouth so she wouldn't be too loud.

I couldn't help but laugh a little too, but I was laughing at her and not my nickname for babies. "It's not that funny."

"No," she said with a snort. "It is. You have no idea." Then she waved her hand and calm herself. "You did great, Mallory. They should all sleep for a while. They usually do."

"What do we do now?"

"You're welcome to read a book or check your emails. You just need to stay awake and look in on the sleepers every fifteen minutes or so."

I didn't have a book, so I watched some music videos and checked a bunch of websites out on my phone while we passed the time. After rinsing out all the bottles and cleaning the toys with bleach-water, Josie settled down to read a romance novel. My eyelids began to droop and my phone jerked in my hand. Staying awake was proving to be difficult.

I heard a big BAM from the crib area, followed by an eerie silence. Three seconds later a baby's scream jerked me to full attention. Josie bounded to her feet and bolted to the crib area. I couldn't believe how fast she moved for a lady her age. I'm twenty-five years younger than her, and I was barely out of my seat before the baby was in her arms. I peeked around the glass partition to see Josie hugging little Timber tightly and whispering "Sh, sh, sh, it's okay, sweetie" over and over again.

"Is she okay?" I asked as quietly as I could, kind of amazed that none of the other babies had woken up. Josie carried Timber out to the play area and bounced her gently as she walked.

"She fell out of her crib," Josie said. "I didn't know she'd learned to pull up to stand yet, and I haven't lowered her mattress." She pulled the baby away from her chest, and I could see the big knot on her forehead.

"You want me to fill out an accident report and call her mom?" I asked Josie. That's what we did during the daytime when a kid got hurt.

Josie shook her head. "No. We can't call the moms. They don't have phones with them."

"What?" I'd never heard of that before. What mother leaves her kid at a day care, overnight no less, without being able to be reached in case of emergency?

"The moms are ... doing something where they can't be reached." She kissed Timber's boo-boo and then sat down with her and a blanket and started rocking her all over again. "Timber will be okay. It's just a bump. Mom can't do anything about it anyway."

"What if there's a fire or something? What if there's an intruder? I don't know if I'm comfortable being here without being able to call the moms if something happens."

Josie frowned at me sharply. "You only have to be here another half hour," she snapped. "Then you won't have to worry about it."

"Sorry," I said, probably with a little too much attitude. Josie didn't say anything to me, even after she put Timber back in her crib.

"Won't she fall out again?" I asked after a few minutes. "Do you want me to lower the base?"

"We can't do it right now," she said. "It'll make too much noise."

"But—"

"Let *me* worry about it, Mallory."

Josie was done with me. I was done with her too. She sounded like my mom. Twenty-five bucks an hour or not, I was ready to go. I started putting my stuff together with my purse.

The classroom phone rang. Josie dashed to it and turned down the volume on the ringer before she answered. After a moment she asked in a tone that got me a little concerned, "What do mean you won't get here in time?"

It had to be Alaina. Apparently, the concert ran long, and the traffic getting away from the arena was ridiculous. She hoped she'd be here by 11:30, but it would be close.

"You may as well not come."

"It's only half an hour late," I said. "Isn't it better that she's here than worry about her being a little late? I mean, is Ms. Dierdre really going to fire her for that?"

Josie ignored me. "You don't understand, Alaina. It's not just you getting in here in time. I've got to get Mallory out."

"Yeah," I agreed. "I'm ready to go home."

"Okay," Josie sighed, still talking to Alaina and not acknowledging me. "Just be safe and keep an eye on the time. If it gets too late, turn around and go home. Mallory will have to stick it out."

"Wait. What?"

Josie hung up the phone and looked back at me. "You offered, didn't you?"

"Yeah, but...."

"Think. You could take home three hundred dollars for the whole night."

Okay, that was worth suffering through some sleep deprivation and Josie's unintentional impressions of my mom.

Josie paced back and forth, pulling back the blinds once and a while to glance out to the dark parking lot. Honestly? I was pretty offended. I thought I had done a pretty decent job helping her get all these babies fed and to bed on time. That was a pretty mad rush, and it went smoothly. Why was she acting like me staying the whole night with her was going to be the worst thing that ever happened?

At 11:40, Josie sat down on the toy shelf next to me. "Look," she said seriously, "I don't think Alaina's coming, and there are a few things you need to know."

"Okay," I said. I pretended to be interested, because, honestly, how hard could it be to watch a group of sleeping babies?

"Right after midnight all the babies are going to wake up."

I knew it! I knew she was insane to think they would sleep through the night.

"They will all wake up at once, and they are going to be loud and very hungry. One of the moms usually drops off something for them to eat by our back door."

I looked over at the windowed door that led to the fenced-in playground. Was a mom delivering some fresh pumped breast milk or something? That was different.

"They will all eat in their cribs. Don't try to take the ... babies ... out of their cribs."

"Okay," I said. I wondered how little Felan at three months old was going to hold a bottle by herself in her crib, but I figured Josie knew what she was talking about.

"And don't let them bite you," Josie added. "That's really important."

"I'll do my best," I said with a smile. She didn't smile back, and I let mine fade. Josie was weirdly intense, and it creeped me out just a little bit. I followed Josie to the diaper changing area where she pushed the regular latex glove box aside and pulled out two pairs of thick rubber gloves out from under the counter, the kind you might use in some science experiment with acid or something. She plopped them down on the changing pad.

"You'll need these," she said.

"Am I going to clean the toilets or something?"

Josie didn't say no, and I rolled my eyes.

"Look, Mallory," Josie said, grabbing me by my shoulders. "I'm not joking around here. What's about to happen is not going to be like anything you've done before."

"I've babysat overnight for people before," I told her. "I can handle it. Although I still don't get what the big deal is about Alaina coming late and me leaving. You guys act like there's a crazy killer that comes out after midnight."

"There is."

I'll admit my heart hitched a second, but I brushed it away. Surely Josie was pulling my leg. The phone rang, and I actually put out my arm to block Josie so I could get to it first. It was Alaina.

"Hey, I'm turning into the parking lot now," she said. "Can one of you be at the front door to open it for me? I'm going to run."

"Yeah, I can open it," I said.

"Is that Alaina?" Josie asked. We saw the beams from her car headlights coming toward the window. "Tell her to turn around and leave. Now!"

"She's going to run in," I said.

"She won't make it."

"If I grab my keys, I'll run out while she runs in."

"No!" Alaina's voice shouted it over the phone at the same time as Josie shouted it my ears. I heard a baby whimper in one of the cribs. Then another.

"They're waking up," Josie said. "We're out of time. Tell Alaina to stay in her car and get out of here."

"Alaina?" I spoke into the phone.

"Go to the front door. Fast!"

I ran out of the classroom and down the hallway to the front door of the building with Josie screaming after me to stop. I had my hand on the deadbolt, and I could see the back end of Alaina's car. She had parked in in the handicap spot right in front of the building. I turned the lock to open. Alaina came running up.

Then, and it happened so fast, she looked to the right and screamed. Something huge jumped past the front door in a streak of gray. And Alaina was gone.

"Oh no!" I screamed. "Oh no, oh no! Alaina?" I began to open the door, when Josie ran up behind me and shut it tight. She shoved my hands away from the lock and twisted it closed. I barely registered that Josie had just left the infant room unattended. "Did you see that, Josie? Alaina? What just happened?"

"I need you in the room," Josie said, dragging me away from the front door.

"I've got to go out there and see if Alaina's okay," I said. "I heard we had coyotes in the neighborhood. Last month Miss Stephanie found a dead cat carcass on the playground. Maybe it was a...."

"Come on, Mallory," Josie said, tugging at me with all her strength down the hall. "We need to do this quickly."

"I need to call 911 or something."

"No you don't. You need to help me with the babies."

I heard them before we got to the classroom door. All nine of them were awake, all screaming and wailing. It was the most awful noise I'd ever heard. Baby panic mixed with some growling. I'd heard Josie joke about babies sounding like pterodactyls when they cry, but this was like a swarm of them. Josie opened the classroom door and the noise doubled, so loud I cupped my hands to my ears. She grabbed the rubber gloves and shoved them into my chest for me to put on. I watched her pull on her gloves and clench her hands. Her expression had a fierceness that frightened me.

"How do we calm them down?" I asked.

"We're going to feed them."

I stepped into the crib area to find all the cribs rocking back and forth violently. The babies were screaming, their eyes huge and their mouths open so wide. They sounded like they were in pain. Even tiny Felan was pitching the biggest fit I'd ever seen.

"Should I start picking them up and rocking them again?" I asked, starting to reach for Felan.

"No!" Josie shouted and batted my hands away. "Don't touch them."

Then there was a succession of cracking sounds that sound like an army stomping over a field of skeletons. The cries changed pitch, going from that familiar "wah wah!" to something long and eerie. More like a wail.

Or a howl.

I stood in the center of the crib room with the cribs in a rectangle around me and gaped as the legs of the babies grew and twisted. Then their arms lengthened, and their tiny fingers grew claws. Those sweet chubby faces contorted while hair sprouted all over their bald little heads. In horror I watched nine sweet babies turn into animals.

Wolf cubs.

"What's happening?" I spoke in a whisper, all the voice I could muster as I watched the puppies writhe around on their mattresses.

Once they finished their transformation, their cries calmed down. They barked and sniffed. I stepped closer to one of the cribs and watched what used to be baby Channon walk around in a circle and then make himself cozy in the corner of his crib. I leaned toward him, and he looked up and me and growled, baring all his teeth. He had more than just a couple canines now. I backed up, and behind me another wolf jumped up, its front paws on the top of the drop side. It barked and growled at me. I screamed and flung around. It was—used to be—baby Maccon. A dog leash that strapped him to the crib prevented him from leaping at my head.

"You put a leash on him when you tucked him in?" I asked Josie.

She nodded. "Good thing too. I also put one on Timber, just to be sure. The others shouldn't be able to jump out. They aren't pulling up yet."

"You knew this would happen," I said.

"Yes. It happens every month."

She led me out of the crib area.

"So the mothers are also...."

"Yes. And they are territorial and have a strong maternal instinct, which means they don't stray too far from this building at night. They hunt in the surrounding park, and one is always right outside."

I went over to the window and looked behind the shade out to the darkness. "Alaina?"

"She knew better," Josie said. Her tone of voice sounded hard, but I could see the tear streaks on her face.

"What happens now?" I asked.

"One of the mothers will drop some food by the back door in a few minutes, something they've hunted. We'll feed it to the young, and then they should settle back down and sleep out the night."

"Should?"

"They usually do."

"You're very calm about this."

SLAM! Something got thrown against the glass panes of the back door. I shrieked and Josie gasped. It was good to know something rattled her. "It's just the food," she told me, taking my hands and looking me square in the eyes. "Just some fresh meat. Usually cats or rabbits."

"That was a loud noise for cats or rabbits," I said.

Then we heard a moan come from near the back door. Josie let go of my hands, and we both rushed to the door where we found Alaina pressing her face against a bloody pane, her hands splayed out to both sides of her head, and her hair tangled in knots.

"Oh, my sweet Lord!" Josie shouted. She opened the door, and Alaina's upper body collapsed inside. I dragged her all the way in, and Josie shut the door as fast as she could. I looked out the glass panes and swore I saw two eyes glowing from under the plastic slide in the corner of our play yard.

"Is she dead?" I asked, as I let go of Alaina on the colorful mats the covered the floor. Blood was smeared all over her skin. Her brand new concert t-shirt was ripped to shreds, and her shoes were missing. Below her mini-skirt, dozens of deep scratches covered her legs from ankle to thigh.

Alaina moaned again, answering my question. Josie rolled Alaina onto her side to check the girl's back and neck. After looking carefully at every part of her, she said, "Let's get her cleaned up."

We both grabbed some washcloths and wet them in the sink. A couple minutes later we got most of the blood off of her, and found that she had been bitten several times as well as scratched. The deepest punctures were just below her rib cage, where the wolf probably held her to carry her to our door. I applied pressure to those bites because they were still bleeding.

"What does this mean?" I'd seen a movie or two about werewolves. I knew in the stories that werewolf bites were bad things. By the look on Josie's face, I had to guess that all those stories weren't far off the mark.

The baby wolves began howling again from their cribs. Maccon kept trying to jump, but his leash held him in place. The noise of his crib banging against the wall was driving me crazy. "What do they want?"

"They want to eat, Mallory," Josie said, her patience gone. "The mothers are supposed to bring food. They usually bring us the first hunt of the night. It should have been here by now." She took the blood-soaked washcloth from my hands and got me a fresh one. "Alaina was a distraction, I think. They'll get the food to us in a few minutes."

Fifteen minutes passed, and no food arrived at the back door. The wailing from the cubs was so loud it made my brain rattle inside my head. "Why aren't they coming?" I cried.

"I don't know."

I pulled the wash cloth away from Alaina's mid-section. It was soaked through as well. A thought came to me. I dared to say it out loud. "You don't think *Alaina* was the first hunt of the night? You don't think they mean for us to feed *her* to the baby wolves?"

"Of course not," Josie said. "They know Alaina. They wouldn't do that…."

"Did they know her when they attacked her? Clearly not, or they would have let her get to the door."

Josie took the washcloth from me. Her hands were trembling. She moved slowly to the trash can and reached for another washcloth. The stack of them tumbled down on her. I jumped up and grabbed a couple and went back to Alaina's side.

"I don't think I can save her," I said. "We need to call an ambulance."

"We can't," Josie said. "There's no way the EMTs could get into the building. There's no way for them to get her out."

The blood stopped pumping out of the bites on Alaina's shoulder, and I heard a long exhale come out of her mouth. I knew she was gone. In the crib room, the baby wolves were going crazy. They could smell the blood. Timber and Maccon were both jumping so hard, their cribs were nearly tipping over.

"Josie," I said, putting my hands on the older woman's shoulders. "We're going to have to do something."

She nodded and stood up. I took Alaina's arms, and she grabbed her feet. Together we dragged the body across the room, past the opening to the crib area where the cubs sniffed and growled at us. Josie opened the supply closet door. I let go of Alaina's arms to pull out some of the extra bouncy seats and mats that were stuffed in there, and then we put Alaina on the floor inside the closet, scrunching her knees up to her chest so that she would fit. Josie closed the door.

"I'll see if we have anything in the kitchen they can eat." She walked out of the baby room and closed the door behind her. I watched her go down the hall to the kitchen while the wolf cubs howled behind, too acutely aware that the dead body of my co-worker was just on the other side of the closet door. I felt trapped. I couldn't run anywhere, because I couldn't get out of the building. I couldn't leave the babies, even if they were wolves. What if something happened to one of them? Would I be held responsible? How did werewolf mothers react when their babies got hurt at day care? I thought of Alaina's body and began to shiver uncontrollably. There was no way out of this night.

A couple minutes later Josie reappeared, carrying a bowl of meatballs in barbecue sauce and a bag of sandwich meat. "This was all the meat I could find." It was probably going to be part of the lunch served to the older kids the next day. "Don't reach too far into the cribs," she instructed. "You need to toss the food in there and get your hand back as fast as possible. Do you understand?" I nodded.

We divvied up the food and headed for the cribs. Josie took one side of the room, while I got the other. I tossed some food at baby Channon, and he snapped the deli meat right out the air. His food was gone before I even got to the second baby. Timber jumped up to the rail of the crib, yanking hard on her leash. I tossed the food behind her onto the mattress. She turned around and gobbled it up.

"This isn't going to be near enough food," I said.

"I know," Josie answered. "It's going to have to do, though."

"Isn't there some kind of symbol we can stick up in the window that will help the wolves know that we need some more food?"

"Wolves can't read."

Then she shrieked and cussed, followed by a quick stream of, "Oh no, oh no, oh no…."

"Are you okay?" I asked, throwing the last handful of my food into a crib and turning to her.

"No!" she shouted. She spun around and pulled the glove off her right hand. Puncture wounds went deep into her forearm, and blood streamed down her arm. I looked past her to see blood dripping from the fang teeth of Maccon. He kept lurching toward her for more. I grabbed Josie by the other arm and yanked her away before Maccon managed to move the crib close enough to get hold of her shoulder.

"Damn it!" Then there was another stream of cussing. Who knew that the lead teacher of the infant room, a woman known for soothing any crying baby to sleep in seconds, could have so many foul words in her vocabulary?

"Let me help you clean that up," I said, leading her to the sink. I helped her rinse the wounds off and got out some bandages from the first aid kit. Once she was looking better and some color had returned to her face, I asked, "What does this mean, Josie? Are you going to be okay?"

She bit her lip to calm herself before saying, "I'm sure you've seen a werewolf movie or two, or maybe read a book about them, right?" I nodded. "Well, there is something that's pretty consistent with all their stories."

"If you get bit by a werewolf, you turn into a werewolf."

"That's right," she said.

"But these are just babies. Doesn't that make a difference? It wasn't a full grown wolf, so…"

Josie shook her head. "Even if it did work like that, which it doesn't, Maccon is almost a year old and standing. He'll be walking in days. In wolf terms, he's full grown."

Some of the wolves in the crib room began to settle down now that they had eaten something. The younger ones seemed satisfied for the moment. I could still hear Maccon growling and tearing at his mattress.

"Will it happen tonight?" I asked.

"No," she said. "Probably tomorrow night." She held her arm close to her chest and raised her eyes to the ceiling in an attempt not to cry. "I've been so careful all this time."

"How long have you been doing this werewolf daycare?"

"About nine months," she said. "In a pack, the males do the hunting while the females stay with their cubs until they're old enough to join their fathers. Diedre and her sisters are modern, independent women, though, and they wanted to do things differently. They all held off having babies for a long time so that they could have their careers and enjoy the hunt themselves. It was Diedre's idea, since she ran a day care, to have the infant cubs cared for on full moons by someone she trusted. When her sisters agreed that they would help pay for it, they all allowed themselves to get pregnant. I've been taking care of the cubs since Dierdre's children were six weeks old."

"So all of the moms I met are Ms. Dierdre's sisters?"

"Yes," Josie said.

"Have you had any accidents here before?" I asked.

"No. Alaina and I have been taking care of everything without incident until tonight."

"So, I'm just bad luck," I said.

Josie sighed. "It's not you. It was bound to happen eventually."

A huge crash sounded from the crib area. The wolves started howling again, so it took a second before I realized that I could hear the scramble of paws on the linoleum floor. Maccon rounded the corner from the crib room and came running right toward us, the chewed up leash trailing behind him.

"Get up on the changing table!" I screamed at Josie. Using her good arm, she launched herself up to the table and got her foot up just before Maccon took a bite out of her sneaker. I climbed upon the counter next to the sink. There were cabinets that stuck out from the wall above the counter, so I couldn't get back from the edge, and I stood like I was perched on the window ledge of a building, with my toes half an inch over the counter. Maccon wasn't as interested in me, because he could smell the blood on Josie and the changing table was shorter. He jumped all around the table, trying to get high enough.

I reached over to the cabinet where we keep the baby crackers and puff snacks. I opened it carefully, took out a container and popped the lid. "I'm going to throw these on the floor," I said to Josie. "Then you run for the door and get out of the room."

"I'm not leaving you here by yourself," she said. "How will you get away?"

"I don't know," I said. "But he's going to kill you." I threw the food. The noise caught Maccon's attention and he ran toward the sound. He began gobbling up the munchies on the floor. I knew it wouldn't take long and I readied another package to throw before he finished. Josie lowered herself as silently as she could on the far side of the changing table. The door to the hallway seemed a thousand miles away, and I didn't know if this non-meat snack would keep the cub's attention once she started toward it.

She took a step, but the play mat under her feet squeaked. Maccon raised his head at the sound. I shook the container in my hand, but he didn't care about that noise. His senses were better than that, and he knew his prey had moved. He waited. Frozen in place, Josie reached out with her arm toward the changing table as if she would climb back onto it in slow motion. The edge of her bandage caught on the vinyl changing mat and made the slightest whisper of a sound as she tugged it free. It was enough of a sound to send Maccon running.

Josie didn't have time to climb or jump. Instead, she lunged for the back door which was only two feet to the left of her. She opened it and leapt up onto the toy shelf to the far side of it. Maccon rushed right out the door and she slammed it shut behind him, locking him outside.

"What did I just do?"

"You saved our lives," I said.

"I sent a baby out into the night unprotected. He could get lost."

"He's not really a baby right now," I reminded her. "Plus, at least one of the moms is out there. She'll help him."

"He'll wake up in the morning a naked, helpless baby. I have to get him."

Josie had lost her mind, I could tell. I jumped down from the counter and ran to her, but it was too late. She had already opened the door. Maccon bounded in and leapt at Josie. She fell backward with the baby wolf on top of her. He clawed at her chest and opened his mouth to take a chunk out of her face. I threw the food container at the wolf and it bounced off the top of his head. I got closer and sprayed bleach water at the dog to distract it, and that worked for a half second. I knew I was running out of options. He opened his jaws again and Josie screamed.

A giant wolf burst through the still open back door. She bit into the scruff of the cub's neck and pulled it away from Josie. With the baby wolf struggling in its jaws, the mama wolf looked up at me, revealing a stripe of white hair from her eyebrow to between her ears, and growled. She backed out of the door.

I pushed the door shut as fast as I could and knelt over Josie. She had passed out. Her chest was bleeding badly. I grabbed some cloth bibs and what was left of the wash cloths and patted her until she stopped bleeding. I didn't want to put her in the closet with Alaina's dead body, so I pulled her out of the classroom and laid her down in the hallway. I tucked a couple receiving blankets under her head and put another one over her chest and then left her out there.

The noise and the smell of the blood had the baby wolves riled up again. Even little Felan was barking and whining in her crib. Timber struggled against her leash and kept turning round to bite at it. I knew it was just a matter of time before she gnawed through hers too.

I went back to the sink area and cleared everything off the counter. I got up on the counter and lay down so that I fit my body against the wall in the thin space between the counter and the cabinets. In this position I was about half a foot from the edge of the counter, and I thought even if Timber got free of the crib, she couldn't get to me in this position.

It was well after two in the morning now. I wanted to call my mom and tell her I loved her. I wanted to tell her that I was sorry about being such a jerk all through high school and not working harder toward my grades. I wanted to tell her she was right about me never succeeding at anything because I probably wouldn't live through the night. I didn't though. My phone was on the far side of the room.

Out in the hallway, Josie woke up. She sat up and looked through the window. I gestured for her to stay out there and pointed toward the cribs. I couldn't see the babies from where I was nestled, but she could. By her horrified expression, I guessed that Timber had chewed through the leash. Josie nodded and stayed in the hall, lying back down on the blankets.

A few minutes later Timber's crib crashed over, and the cub was loose and sniffing around the room. She pawed at the door to the closet for a long time, clearly smelling the bloody corpse of Alaina inside. I stayed as still as I could, and my arms and legs tingled from the effort. Timber came into the changing table area and discovered the remainder of the munchies on the ground and gobbled them up and licked the blood from Alaina and Josie off the mats. She sniffed the air and went toward the back door, maybe catching a whiff of the mama wolf's musky odor. Then Timber began to pull toys out of the shelves and shake them around, clearly looking for something else to eat. I watched the wolf for thirty-five minutes before she finally walked around in a circle six times and then plopped down on one of the play mats. She put her muzzle down on her front paws and closed her eyes.

I realized then that the whole room was quiet. All of the cubs had finally dozed off.

I tried to stay awake, but I'd been so tense with fear for so long that the second I let the fear go I fell asleep without even realizing it.

Josie woke me up by lifting my arm from where it dangled off the counter and placing it by my face. I was mortified that I had fallen asleep and very grateful to still have my hand.

"What's happening?" I asked.

"Sunrise," she told me. She had raised the shades a bit, and I could see the golden glow beginning in the sky. Over on the play mat, the naked baby form of Timber slept soundly. I got down and stretched out my body. Carefully, I picked up the baby and put her back in her crib. All of the other babies were naked and asleep in their cribs, looking like innocent cherubs.

"Come on," Josie said. "The moms will be here soon to pick up the children, and we have a lot of cleaning to do before the center opens for business."

I could feel myself gaping at her. "We're really going to open today? Like nothing happened? There's a dead body in the closet."

But Josie put a finger to her mouth to shush me, nodding at the sleeping babies around us. "It'll be handled." She pulled me away from the babies, her grip tight on my arm. "Let's get started."

I scrubbed the remaining blood off the floor from where Maccon attacked Jose while she began cleaning up the food that had spilled on the floor in the crib area. The babies began to stir. She had me diaper them and put them in clean clothes while she threw away the plastic crib sheets and scrubbed the mattresses and sides with bleach water.

Ms. Dierdre came in the door right about 6:00 am wearing a jogging outfit. Holding her hand for support, Maccon toddled in beside her, dressed, his curly hair bouncing around his ears and just above the superhero bandages on the back of his neck. She wasn't smiling, but she didn't exactly look pissed off either.

"I'm sorry about putting Maccon outside," Josie began to say. Ms. Dierdre put up a hand to stop her.

"It was the only thing you could do," she said. She rubbed his head. "He's safe, and it was time for him anyway. I shouldn't have brought him here at all last night." She had him sit down with some toys in the play area—just a normal ten-month-old trying to figure out a ring stacker.

I croaked, "Um, we should tell you...."

"Where is she?" Ms. Dierdre asked.

"The closet," Josie answered.

Ms. Dierdre opened the closet, and Alaina's hand flopped out. My boss didn't react much, like seeing dead bodies wasn't a new thing for her. Very carefully, and with more strength than I would have imagined a woman of her size, she picked up Alaina's body and carried her out of the room. A moment later I saw her putting the body in the trunk of her car outside. Josie was already cleaning the blood out of the closet.

"Where is she taking Alaina?" I asked.

"I don't know," Josie said, not meeting my eyes. "I don't think I want to."

The other moms pulled into the lot as Ms. Dierdre closed the trunk. I watched them talk with each other outside. Seeing them as a group, it was obvious from their mannerisms and features that they were all related. When they came inside, there were all kinds of sweet greetings and gratitude. Mrs. Gray brought us some donuts and coffee. I told Timber's mother about her pulling up to stand and escaping from the crib. She looked nervously at Ms. Dierdre, who shook her head slowly. Timber wouldn't be coming to werewolf day care again either.

Finally, all the moms and babies were gone except for Ms. Dierdre, who turned to Josie. "Now, show me that arm you've been tucking behind your back."

Sheepishly, she pulled her arm out to view. It was very swollen and red around the bite mark. I couldn't believe Josie had hidden that so well. I would have been crying.

Ms. Dierdre held the arm very tenderly and looked into Josie's eyes. "I'm so sorry. You'll need to come with me now. I'll help you get through this."

Finally, Josie let out one little sob and then bravely said, "All right."

Ms. Dierdre led Josie to the classroom door. I followed them.

"Um, Ms. Dierdre?" I asked. "Do you mind if I call in sick today? I'm so tired."

Honestly, I was pretty sure I was about to quit, but I'd start with being polite.

"Of course, Mallory," she answered with a sweet smile that didn't at all suggest that this kind-hearted woman who ran a day care could possibly be a blood-thirsty werewolf by night. "Rest up. 'Cause I'm going to need you again tonight."

"Tonight?"

"Full moons last three nights," she said softly and then winked. "You're my new lead teacher for the infant room. I'll find you a good assistant."

It felt like I just stood there and gawked at them for twenty minutes before I asked, "How much does it pay?"

"Fifty per hour good enough?"

And Mom thought I'd never get a good paying job without a degree.

"I'll be here."

D. G. Driver is an author of YA contemporary fantasy. Her award-winning Juniper Sawfeather Novels series about a teen environmental activist who discovers mythical creatures includes the books *Cry of the Sea* and *Whisper of the Woods*. The third book, *Echo of the Cliffs*, will be released in 2017. She also has a sweet romantic ghost story, *Passing Notes*, available and stories in several anthologies including one about a pirate queen teaming up with a dragon in *A Tall Ship, A Star*, and *Plunder* and a fairy tale about true love and a quest to keep it in *Tomato Slices*. Excerpts from all her books and stories are on her website. Please visit and sign up for her mailing list. When she's not writing she is, in fact, teaching babies in a day care or singing in a community theater musical.

www.dgdriver.com

The Mage and the Spotted Wyvern

A chill traveled up Drezzyk's neck. He shivered, pushing his auburn hair out of his eyes before glancing around the thick forest. Drezzyk hadn't fully learned how to use his magic, except for a few accidental spells, but he had a strong feeling in his gut that something was off.

"Master, something doesn't feel right," Drezzyk said.

"What is it?" Kelvnar asked with a composed expression.

"My neck has chills."

Kelvnar smiled. "That could be just nervousness. You have much to learn about magic."

Leaves crunched behind them. Drezzyk stopped abruptly, turning around. Nothing besides forest surrounded them.

"What is it?" Kelvnar asked.

"I heard something," Drezzyk said.

Kelvnar sighed as he straightened his long yellow robes. "You're just nervous after leaving Taelisph. They aren't coming after you, boy. I'm sorry I had to leave you there, but the magic was being stubborn in you, and the only way I could get it out, was to force it. Do not fear; it should come easier now. It's like a wagon, at first the wheels are stiff when they're new, but the more you ride, the easier the wheels turn."

"Master, it's not that." Drezzyk paused. "I'm sure something is there."

"Something really has you rattled hasn't it, boy?"

The frog in Drezzyk's pocket stirred. He opened the pocket to retrieve his friend, but the frog hopped away into the bushes.

"Freckles!" Drezzyk called.

"You and that bloody frog." Kelvnar chortled through his nose.

Drezzyk dropped to the ground, crawling toward the azalea bush in search of his red frog. More leaves crunched from behind. He spun his head around to find more than twenty large reptilian creatures standing on two legs approaching them. Drezzyk quickly stood, hitting his head on a tree branch hanging above him. He cursed under his breath and rubbed his head.

"Master," Drezzyk whispered, "are those dragons?"

"No, they are descendants of dragons. They are called draeyks, but they are dangerous."

Drezzyk gulped as he noticed his master tying his long, curly, white hair behind his back. He only did that when expecting a fight.

"Good morning," Kelvnar began, "what can we do for you?"

"Coome withh uss," one of the creatures hissed.

"I believe I'll have to decline. Any business you have with us, you may discuss here."

"Noo, coome orr diee."

"Very well," Kelvnar said.

He lifted his zylek, the wooden staff glowing gold, and pointed it toward the creature. Gold swirls of energy glided through the air, seizing the draeyk. It snarled in response, unable to move.

"Killl themm," the creature said.

Kelvnar turned to his apprentice. "Now is the time for magic."

Drezzyk stood, dumbfounded, unsure of what to do. He raised his hands, but his mind froze. He had studied spells, but with the exception of his time in Taelisph, he'd been unable to use magic.

Kelvnar worked fast, spinning his zylek to shoot gold spheres of light at the creatures, knocking them backward. He defeated six of them with his magic before the rest reached him. The wizard repositioned his zylek, using it like a quarterstaff to block their sharp claws. He held them well, but his footing slipped on a rock.

"Drezzyk," he called. "Help!"

The apprentice's hands tingled, but otherwise, no magic formed for him. He shivered as he backed away. Two of the creatures shifted from Kelvnar and rushed at him. His hands trembled as he aimed them at his foes. He jerked his hands forward, desperation tugging at his mind. One of the draeyks halted, frozen in a blue aura. Drezzyk stood open-mouthed while he raised his arms skyward then slammed them back down, willing his magic to follow his lead. The creature's body followed the motion of Drezzyk's arms, first floating into the sky—shrieking all the while, before slamming into the ground. The second draeyk paused, glancing back to its companion before tackling Drezzyk.

The impact of the creature knocked his breath out. He rolled on the ground, dodging swipes from claws as he moved from left to right. Drezzyk reached to where a rock lay on the dirt, just out of his grasp. He squeezed his eyes closed, willing the rock to come to him. When he opened his eyes, the rock rolled into his hand. He clutched the rock, gritted his teeth, and smashed it against the creature's reptilian snout. The draeyk shrieked as it rolled off of him. Drezzyk stood, continuing to beat the creature's skull with the rock. It glowed blue in his hands, embedding itself with power, as he continued to drive the rock down, over and over. His eyes glowed blue, then his entire body followed, while he continued to smash the draeyk's skull repeatedly. The creature stopped moving, but he didn't cease hitting it.

Drezzyk finally exhaled and tossed the rock to the ground. He glanced around, but found nothing. Ten draeyks lay dead where his master had fought them, but all the others had vanished. He glanced at the two he had defeated, and back to the ten his master had fought. *Where are the rest of them?* He searched the area, finding only the strange footprints of the creatures with three claw marks webbed at the tip and one claw mark to the side.

"Drat," Drezzyk said.

He put his hand on his pocket, remembering his missing friend.

"Oh, please, Freckles. You have to be here somewhere. I can't do this *alone.*"

Ribbit.

Drezzyk's neck tingled as he twisted his head from the left to the right frantically, searching for his friend. *Please be all right, Freckles.*

Ribbit.

Dashing forward, he moved rubble aside. His face burst into a wide grin when he spotted his friend, diving to retrieve the red frog.

"Freckles." A loud rush of air escaped his lungs.

Drezzyk petted his frog gently, inspecting him for injury.

"You had me worried, Freckles. I thought for sure something had happened to you."

Ribbit.

"I'm glad you're safe."

Ribbit.

"Do you think we should go after Master?"

Ribbit.

"I was afraid you'd say that."

Ribbit.

"You're right. I don't know how far we'd get without him."

He tucked the frog into his shirt pocket before finding his pack on the ground. Grabbing it, he began following the draeyk footprints. He wondered what the creatures wanted his master for.

They followed the tracks for several hours before Drezzyk decided to take a break. He sat on a log to catch his breath. Drezzyk let Freckles out of his pocket, and the frog promptly stuck out his tongue to grab flies. Thunder rolled in the sky a few minutes before rain sprinkled. Drezzyk let his head fall back, grateful for nature's water. He opened his leather costrel as he focused his power, directing the rain to funnel into the small leather pouch. Even if he couldn't always focus his magical ability to fight, he had learned a few useful skills. The light rain quickly turned to a tempest. Dark clouds rumbled with thunder and sharp cracks of lightning electrified the sky. Drezzyk grabbed his meager belongings and his trusty frog before rushing into the thick forest where fat raindrops pummeled his skin.

Drezzyk noticed a small cavern to the north. He ran to it, smiling until he lost his footing and slipped on a wet stone, tumbling to the ground. White-hot pain shot through his ankle. He gritted his teeth as he tied a piece of his robe around it. A few wet branches lay outside of the cavern. He slid himself over to grab them. Drezzyk broke the branches into pieces, moving them into a tepee in the center of the cavern. Concentrating on the branches, he held his hands toward them, wishing for warmth. His clothes were soaked through, and he shivered from the cold. The branches smoked, but no fire erupted. He closed his eyes, tensing his hands in front of him. They shook three times before he opened his eyes. A blue fire glowed on the now dry branches. Smiling, he rubbed his hands together in front of the fire.

He removed Freckles from his pocket and the frog hopped near the fire. Opening his pack, he removed a small black book entitled *Spellweaving for Beginners*. He'd been studying it for years, but magic still only came sporadically to him. It had been one of the things which frustrated his master, Kelvnar, more than anything. He read again about how important it was to use his emotions to fuel his magic and concentrate on a clear objective. Showing his emotions and concentrating, two things he'd never been very good at. However, he pressed on, knowing he'd need to use magic to free his master. He couldn't let his incompetence seal his master's fate.

Drezzyk held his hand in front of his face, palm up, to stare at it.

"Fire," he whispered, trying to focus his emotions.

He focused on his hand, picturing the element he wanted, and trying to feel the emotion which went with it—anger. Drezzyk had never been an angry person. He growled as he tried to create the element.

"Firay. Fier. Flame. Flachè," he said. A small spark formed in his palm, but disappeared.

He sighed. "Flaming frog hairs. I just can't do it."

Ribbit.

He glanced to Freckles. "What?"

Ribbit.

Freckles opened his mouth, his tongue flashing into the air with a flame escaping it. Drezzyk watched in awe. The red flame, two inches in length and one inch thick, shot through the back of the cavern, illuminating the rocky walls. It continued through the darkness for several long seconds before disappearing. Drezzyk raised an eyebrow, wondering how deep the hollow went.

"Freckles … you can make fire?"

Ribbit.

"I'll be a tickled frog belly. Even my frog can make fire better than me."

Ribbit.

"Okay, Freckles. I'll try again."

Drezzyk took a deep breath, glaring first at Freckles, then at his open palm. Knowing Freckles could create a better flame infuriated him. When his eyes squinted hard enough for him to barely see, a blue flame appeared in his palm. His eyes widened as he stared at it. A broad grin spread across his face. The flame began to fade. He frowned and glared at the flame once more, pushing more anger into it. The flame glowed brighter.

"Wow!" he exclaimed, shaking his hand in front of him.

The flame shot forward through the air and into the darkness. The cavern grew even brighter than with Freckles's flame. Drezzyk watched in fascination as the flame disappeared into the endless abyss.

He smiled, looking at his hand. "I did it."

A low rumble echoed through the cavern. He glanced into the darkness. A growl preceded the rumble of approaching footsteps. Drezzyk stood abruptly, and then took a step backward.

Out of the darkness, there appeared a creature with blue scales and black spots, standing on two legs with two massive wings protruding from its body. It was reptilian, like the draeyks, but this thing was larger and had wings. The creature expelled a blue fog toward him. Drezzyk grabbed one of the burning branches and held it in defense. His fire froze, encased in ice, as was the rest of the branch. Drezzyk swiftly dropped the branch before stumbling from the cavern.

The rain poured over him as he came out of the cave. He kept his eyes on the entrance, backing away as fast as he could. He shivered from his rain-soaked clothes. The creature stepped to the opening and stared at him. Drezzyk struggled to remember his lessons on creatures of the land. At first, he thought it was a dragon, but he knew that was wrong. Dragons were larger with four legs. This creature only had two legs.

He gasped, "A wyvern…."

It roared into the storm—silencing the thunder surrounding them.

Drezzyk felt his pocket, noticing Freckles's absence. He searched frantically and spotted the frog resting at the wyvern's feet. He looked up at the creature, shivering.

"Freckles, hop!"

Ribbit.

Drezzyk's eyes widened. The wyvern tilted its head before glancing to the ground. Its head arched downward until it rested inches from Freckles. The wyvern sniffed hard, nearly pulling Freckles from the ground.

Ribbit.

Bemusedly, the wyvern tilted its head the other way, staring at Freckles.

Its mouth opened as a haze of blue frost escaped it.

"No!" Drezzyk screamed.

Freckles hopped away before turning to the creature with opened mouth to spit out fire. The red flame hit the wyvern's jaw. A deep growl escaped the creature's mouth.

Drezzyk ran back toward the cavern, his hands glowing blue. He pointed at the frog and the wyvern. Magic stormed from his fingertips in waves. The wyvern and the frog froze, immobilized by Drezzyk's power. Drezzyk gaped, astonished he had used the spell successfully.

"That is enough," Drezzyk said. "We are not here to fight. All we want to do is stay out of the rain."

Sorry. A voice echoed inside of Drezzyk's head, sounding like an iron gate being dragged over concrete.

"What?" Drezzyk asked. "Who said that?"

I did not mean to offend.

Drezzyk stared at the wyvern, eyes transfixed.

"You can talk?" he asked.

You can as well.

"Well, of course humans can talk. Humans can barely shut up, especially inside a pub. But you're a wyvern."

Yes.

"Okay...." Drezzyk brushed a hand through his hair.

Can you release I?

"Will you be good?"

Yes. Your friend intrigues I. Your power intrigues I. Respect is earned.

Drezzyk scrunched his eyebrows. Raising his shoulders, he let his power fade. Nodding to him, the wyvern sat by the fire, licking its arms. Drezzyk returned to the cavern to sit next to Freckles. He scooted closer to the fire, trying to warm himself from the rain outside.

"How many wyverns are there?"

I do not know. I have lived here three hundred years in peace by I self.

"Doesn't that get lonely?" Drezzyk asked. "I don't know what I would do on my own. I am glad to have Freckles with me."

Sometimes. But it is peaceful as well.

Drezzyk rubbed his hands together by the fire. An idea sprang to him and he furrowed his brow.

"Do you ever think about getting out? Seeing what the world looks like now?"

I do not understand. The world surely looks the same. Humans fighting each other everywhere, and nature growing. Or, have such things changed? His head lolled forward, staring intently at Drezzyk.

"No ... I suppose not. Still, it is more exciting out there than sitting in a dark cave all the time." It took every bit of his willpower for Drezzyk to not draw backward.

Exciting? I suppose. However, I do not enjoy excitement. I enjoy peace. Tell me, human, is there peace out there as well?

"Some." Drezzyk sighed.

Tell me, human, why do you want I to leave? The wyvern began to lick his paw nonchalantly.

Drezzyk inhaled. "I need help. My master has been captured by draeyks. I need to free him, but I do not know if I am strong enough."

It stopped and stared at the apprentice, its green eyes almost bulging from its head. *You want I to help you?*

Drezzyk nodded.

What do I receive in return? It squinted at the young magician.

"Honor?" Drezzyk asked. The wyvern at this moment reminded him of a snake poised to strike.

A rumbling growl repeated from the wyvern for several minutes. Drezzyk dropped his head and exhaled.

Honor means nothing for I. What can you offer me that I cannot achieve myself?

"Adventure?" Drezzyk paused. "I know you like peace, but peace is not allowed in my life. I am to be a mage. My life is to be an adventure. I want to help people. To save people. I want to end wars, to end conflicts. I don't want the hate between humans. I don't want the draeyks to hurt and kidnap humans anymore. All I want is peace, but the difference is, I have the courage to go out into the world and try and change it, while you hide in a cavern away from it. I am not strong, like you. I will die trying to achieve my goal, yet you will live because you choose to hide. I want your help; I do not want to die. We both want peace, we both don't want war. But the only way I can see for us to truly accomplish that for this world, is by helping each other."

The wyvern's head tilted. *You speak well … for a human. You are right, I am a coward. Enlighten I human, why should I not freeze you into a slab of ice and shatter you into a million pieces for saying such words to I?*

"Because Freckles and I intrigue you?" Drezzyk trembled. "What have you to lose? If you choose to come back, you can. But give me a chance to prove to you this world is worth saving."

You want an alliance? Fine. I will give you thirty suns to change my mind that what we do makes a difference.

Drezzyk smiled. "Deal."

When do we leave?

"Morning."

Good. One more night of rest.

"What is your name?"

Kelvermore. And yours?

"Drezzyk. Good night, Kelvermore."

Good night, human Drezzyk.

Drezzyk opened one eye as a chill breeze brushed across his face into the cavern. He yawned before standing to walk outside. The wyvern, Kelvermore, stood on his two legs while stretching wings into the brisk morning sun. Drezzyk smiled at the magnificent beast. The night before, he had known Kelvermore to be beautiful, but now that he saw the creature glistening in the sunrise, he fell speechless. The wyvern's blue scales sparkled beyond any diamond.

"You are beautiful," Drezzyk whispered.

Kelvermore turned around, tilting his head as he inspected the young mage.

Strange words. I assume they are a compliment.

"Yes, they are," Drezzyk said.

Then, I accept them. Are we ready to go?

"Yes." Drezzyk held his pack high.

Then he strolled past the wyvern, patting his pocket to double check for Freckles.

Where are you going?

Drezzyk spun around, his left eyebrow raising. "I'm going to search for the draeyks who took my master."

Wouldn't it be easier to ride my back?

"Are you sure?" Drezzyk asked, his eyes bulging.

It should be fine, as long as you hold on tight.

Drezzyk gulped. Kelvermore stepped toward him, lowering his head. Drezzyk stared at the wyvern's neck for several long seconds before inhaling and climbing atop.

"Do you know where to go?" Drezzyk asked.

Kelvermore tilted his head. *Draeyks are small lizards. They are easy to find. They smell bad.*

Before Drezzyk could utter another word, Kelvermore spread his wings and leapt into the air. Wind immediately caught underneath the animal's wingspan and he flapped them furiously. Drezzyk held on tighter, sweat beading down his face. His eyes drifted to the ground. He watched as the ground moved farther and farther away. His entire body trembled in such fear that he had to close his eyes.

After Kelvermore stabilized, Drezzyk opened his eyes to notice the trees a half a league below them. Kelvermore's wings stretched out, but he only had to flap them every few minutes, choosing to glide on the wind. Once Drezzyk stopped shivering, he could appreciate the beauty of the forest below.

Kelvermore's head tilted down and the beast dove to the ground. Drezzyk's grip tightened as the wyvern descended into a small clearing in the forest. Kelvermore's legs hit the ground hard, shaking the entire creature and Drezzyk on his back, causing his head to spin. He hopped off the creature as bolts of white-hot pain shot through his legs. Drezzyk gritted his teeth as he touched the inside of his legs, pain searing all the way through his body. The wyvern's scales had cut through his breeches and into his skin.

"Look at what you did! You've torn my breeches, and bloodied my legs!"

Now is not the time.

Drezzyk glanced up, noticing he stood in a draeyk camp. At least forty of the creatures crowded around them, each snarling viciously. Drezzyk faltered, his eyes shifting left and right as he inspected his surroundings. He grabbed Freckles from his pocket and gently set the frog on his shoulder.

"Freckles," he whispered, "I need you now more than ever. Show them that fire you created. We can defeat them."

Ribbit?

"Well, we can try."

We can defeat them, Kelvermore said.

Drezzyk gulped. "Set my master free, and I will leave you unharmed."

The draeyks surrounding him tilted their heads before the first one snarled and leapt at him. Drezzyk was caught by surprise. He cupped his hand over Freckles on his shoulder as he dropped to the ground to roll forward. His hands turned blue as he stood. Anger surged through him, making the magic flow freely through his body. His anger boiled for these creatures taking his master, and for them threatening him, Freckles, and Kelvermore. He glanced to his right, spotting a long branch nearby. Concentrating, he closed his eyes. When his eyes opened, the glowing branch flew toward him. He caught it in his hands before stepping forward to smack the first creature in the jaw. Next to him, he saw Kelvermore slashing at creatures, one after the other, breaking the bones of the draeyks.

Drezzyk smiled. He held the branch like a quarterstaff. He fought fiercely as Freckles spat fire from his shoulder. The frog aimed for their eyes, blinding many of the creatures. Sweat poured over Drezzyk's brow while he fought, but he didn't feel fatigue. His makeshift quarterstaff held strong, powered by the magic surging through him. Soon, all around him, the drayeks fell. He turned, seeing one sneaking from behind Kelvermore. Drezzyk channeled his power into the branch before throwing it into the air. The tip of the branch sharpened as it flew in the air to penetrate the neck of the last draeyk.

As the creature shrieked, Kelvermore spun around to find the creature at his feet. *Thank you.*

Drezzyk smiled. "Anytime."

A low rumble distracted him. He spun around to find twenty more draeyks charging them. Drezzyk's eyebrows raised as he stared at his weaponless hands.

"Freckled frog feet," he cursed.

Kelvermore flapped his wings and roared. A blue fog escaped his mouth, traveling slower than a turtle race.

Drezzyk watched with fascination as the fog froze all twenty of the draeyks to blocks of ice. He let his mouth fall agape.

Ribbit.

"Wow is right, Freckles." He turned to the wyvern. "Why didn't you do that before?"

Where would be the fun in that?

Drezzyk smiled. "So you are having fun?"

No comment.

Drezzyk chortled.

Where is your friend?

Drezzyk shook his head before peering around the camp.

"Master?" Drezzyk asked.

He searched the camp until he found a small wooden cage. Inside his master sat, hands bound, and snoring. Drezzyk smiled as it brought to mind the time his master snored through the worst thunderstorm of the year. It came as little surprise that he had slept through a rescue attempt and related brawl! Without proper use of his hands, or especially a zylek to guide his magic, his master was left defenseless. If he channeled his magic without a zylek, it wouldn't have control as it came out, and would likely kill everything in a league radius, including himself. Drezzyk didn't need a zylek. He wasn't a wizard; he was a mage. Wizards had magic inside of themselves which they released, while mages used elements in the air around them as energy. Drezzyk knew he'd never be as powerful as his master, and training as a mage was much more difficult than if he'd been a wizard, but he wouldn't trade it for the world.

He focused on the particles in the air, channeling them through himself, and out his hands, but the bars did nothing.

He sighed. "Drat." He looked to the wyvern. "Kelvermore, help."

The wyvern stepped next to Drezzyk. His claw swiped at the bars, tearing them apart.

His master, Kelvnar, opened his eyes.

"My boy, you found me," Kelvnar said.

The young apprentice knelt to untie his bonds and noticed they glowed a faint red. Had they also been magical restraints?

Together, they staggered out of the cage to survey the carnage surrounding them. Kelvnar glanced to Drezzyk, eyebrows raised.

"You did all this?" Kelvnar asked.

Drezzyk grinned. "I had help."

Kelvermore roared into the sky behind Drezzyk.

His master's eyes bulged. "You befriended a wyvern?"

Drezzyk's cheeks turned red. "It seemed the right thing to do."

"You are stronger and wiser than I would have believed." His master inspected the creature. "You are beautiful."

Thank you. Kelvermore radiated to both of them.

"Ah, he has mind speech, too."

"Yes," Drezzyk said. "Master Kelvnar, this is Kelvermore." Drezzyk paused, his head tilting. "My, this may get confusing."

Kelvnar smiled. "Indeed, it may."

Ribbit.

Drezzyk glanced to his shoulder, seeing Freckles watching him curiously. He looked back to his master. "Master, you'll never believe it. Freckles can create fire."

Kelvnar's eyebrows furrowed. "Come now, do not jest. Now you must be seeing things."

"No, honest." He glanced to Freckles. "Come on, Freckles. Make fire."

Ribbit.

"Freckles!"

Kelvnar laughed. "Come, it seems you need some rest. Your mind has wandered to the impossible. And you are behind on your lessons."

Drezzyk glared at Freckles. "This is not over, Freckles." He turned back to Kelvnar. "I can create fire, too."

"Can you now?" Kelvnar raised a brow.

Drezzyk grinned sheepishly before concentrating on his hand. Nothing happened. He frowned. Still nothing happened. He gritted his teeth, but not even a puff of smoke rose from his palm.

"Snapping frog tongues," Drezzyk growled. "I swear I did create fire."

His master laughed, clasping him on the shoulder. "I believe you, my dear boy."

"Why were those creatures after you, master?"

"They thought I had something, or knew where it was."

"What?" Drezzyk asked.

"A magical stone."

Drezzyk's eyebrows rose. He exhaled softly, used to his master's cryptic answers. "What does it do?"

"Cures the incurable."

"Do you know where it is?"

"No … I do not. But it seems someone wants it badly." Kelvnar adjusted his robes.

"What do we do now?"

"We leave. You have much more to learn, and many more years before you are ready."

"Ready for what, master?"

"You will know … when it is time."

Where are we going? Kelvermore tilted his head.

Kelvnar raised his eyebrows. "Wherever the road takes us."

Craig A. Price Jr. is the author of *The Crimson Claymore*, an epic fantasy adventure novel that has garnered millions of reads, was featured in fantasy, had more than 17,000 votes, and more than 1,000 comments/reviews on the social networking platform for readers and writers, Wattpad.

http://www.CraigAPrice.com

The Very Last Dragon

Once upon a time in a faraway kingdom, Sir Manly Strongarm decided to rid the land of every last dragon. "After all," he told his war horse, Leonidas, "even though no one has seen a dragon in recent years, there could still be one lurking, waiting to menace young, beautiful maidens and, more importantly, sheep."

For as long as Sir Manly could remember, he had dreamed of becoming a dragon slayer like his renowned father, who had died during the kingdom's second-to-last civil war. Strangely, his father could single-handedly kill a dragon, but fell to the swords of men. That war happened during Sir Manly's infancy and had grown into legend, reinforced daily by the battered red shield with its gold, strong-arm emblem which hung in the king's great hall.

So without the king's knowledge or permission, Sir Manly took up his own red and gold shield, patted his father's dragon-killing sword in its sheath upon his belt, and mounted Leonidas.

"Come on, Leo. 'Tis time we set out to do something besides training and eating and training some more. Something heroic."

Leonidas snorted and shook his mane. The horse liked eating, after all. And training was not so bad either, especially when he and Sir Manly could gallop at full speed at the quintain. It was even more satisfying when Sir Manly's lance missed the target and the weighted balance knocked the knight out of the saddle.

"This way," said the knight, jerking on the reins. "We must take the northern road. Dragons will most likely be hiding in the mountains beyond the River Gorse."

Since Leonidas almost always did what his knight commanded, the horse plodded north on the road leading to the distant Highlands.

The journey took several days. Sir Manly felt no great urgency to meet his destiny. Instead, he savored the fair weather of early summer. If night fell as he and Leo neared a town, they stayed at an inn, but most nights they camped beside a stream. While Sir Manly sat beneath the trees, watching the winking lights of fireflies and listening to the singing frogs, Leonidas ate his fill of wild grasses.

On the seventh day, the road began to wind upward into the foothills. Now, whenever Sir Manly saw peasants working alongside the road, he urged Leonidas to a smart trot and made a show of catching the peasants' attention.

Several times a day, this was the exchange:

Sir Manly: "Greetings, peasants. Have you had any trouble with dragons in these parts?"

Peasant: "Beggin' yer pardon, Sir Knight, but there be no dragons in our 'shire."

Undaunted, Sir Manly urged Leonidas to prance away with the horse arching his neck to show off his flowing mane.

After three more days of following winding roads by day and sleeping beneath the stars at night, peasants became more and more difficult to find. The rising hills grew desolate and wind-swept. Sir Manly began to think seriously about turning back, even though it went against his sense of honor to admit defeat.

His sigh became a gasp when a maiden with long yellow hair, wearing a patched green dress dashed into the road under Leonidas's nose. The horse whinnied and reared, nearly dislodging Sir Manly.

"Young lady," Sir Manly said, "have you no more sense than to step in front of a moving horse?" He brushed at some dust on his red and gold surcoat.

The peasant girl had fallen to the dirt, covering her head to protect it. At Sir Manly's words, she looked up. "You're a knight! You can help me!"

"Of course, I can help you." Sir Manly straightened in the saddle. "What seems to be the problem?"

Leonidas snorted and stamped a front hoof, but the maiden did not appear to notice. She rose gracefully. Sir Manly thought she might be comely, if she washed the dirt off her face and hands and bare feet. And if she changed into a dress that wasn't patched and two sizes too big. And, of course, if she brushed that tangled golden hair.

"Well, sir," she said, "a dragon has been stealing my sheep."

"A dragon?" Sir Manly's pulse quickened. At last he would begin to live up to his father's illustrious name! At last, his own name would be engraved on the marble dragon statue in the castle courtyard. He could see it now: Sir Manly Strongarm, Dragon Slayer.

"Yes, Sir Knight, a dragon." The maiden's voice interrupted Sir Manly's reverie. "Last night the beast took our best milk ewe, and the flock is fast disappearing. I can't go to my father and tell him because he is ill and would

266

die of a broken heart at the news." She sniffled and wiped at her eyes.

"How many of your sheep has the dragon taken?" Sir Manly asked.

The girl studied her dirty fingers for a moment and held up four on each hand. "This many."

"Eight, eh?" Sir Manly frowned. "By now the beast will have developed a taste for mutton."

"I can't afford to lose any more sheep." Now, the girl appeared ready to burst into tears. "Please, can you help me?"

Sir Manly hated to see anyone cry. His personal code of honor would compel him to offer his handkerchief, and invariably the weeping person would blow his or her nose, soiling the cloth. Then, of course, he would insist the person keep his handkerchief. He'd lost many of them over the years in this manner.

"I am a knight," he said in his most confident voice, hoping to ward off the maiden's tears and rescue his favorite handkerchief. "Point me in the direction the dragon was last seen, and I'm off to save the rest of your sheep."

"But I haven't actually seen the dragon, Sir Knight, though I've found claw marks." The girl pulled something from her belt pouch. "And this." She handed the object to Sir Manly. "Careful. The edges are sharp."

Sir Manly gasped. A dragon scale! Glinting greenish-gold in the sunlight, it fit in the palm of his glove.

"I have an idea where the dragon might be living," the girl continued. "There are many caves at the edge of our holding, and a few of them are big enough for a dragon."

Sir Manly tore his gaze from the dragon scale to peer at the girl. "Have you a name, lass?"

She dropped a little curtsy. "Golda Drake. Only daughter of Wort." Her lips curled into a smile. "He calls me Goldie."

The knight tried to speak, but the words caught in his throat, and he had to clear it. "Wort Drake? THE Wort Drake?"

Goldie's face brightened. "Have you heard of my father?"

Sir Manly snorted. "Good heavens, girl, your father's deeds are legend in the South. Thank goodness our new king doesn't hold grudges, like the former king did, or I might be compelled to arrest your father."

"Arrest him?" She planted her hands on her hips and looked as if she might impale the knight with the daggers in her glowing eyes.

Sir Manly held up a gloved hand. "Not to worry, gentle maiden. The current king has pardoned your father of all charges, real and imagined. The Lion of the North may live out his days in peace."

"Lion of the North?" The maid's face twisted with annoyance. "Why wouldn't they call him the Dragon of the North?"

"I didn't give the name to your father," Sir Manly said with a shrug. "I was only a babe in arms during the second-to-last civil war and a castle page during the last civil war."

Goldie still regarded Sir Manly with suspicion. "So what are you going to do about the dragon?"

"Dragon. Oh, yes!" He returned the dragon scale to her. "Bless me, but I'll have to go after it. Just point the way to the caves."

The maiden shook her head, and her tangled hair fell over her shoulder. "It's too difficult to explain. I'll have to show you."

Leonidas tossed his mane with a snort. Sir Manly hesitated. While he thought about how to tactfully dissuade her, Goldie got a running start and pulled herself up behind Sir Manly.

He turned his head. "That's no mean feat, my girl."

Goldie shrugged and gripped the back of the saddle. "My father taught me to fear nothing."

Sir Manly sniffed, and his nostrils flared. Was that sulfur? "Pardon me," he said, twitching his nose, "but do you eat a lot of eggs?"

"No. Why?"

"Never mind." Sir Manly faced forward and nudged Leonidas. The horse locked his legs and bowed his head. "Leo! Forward!"

With a grumbling neigh, Leonidas began to walk. As they headed into the fields, Sir Manly wondered if there was more to this daughter of Wort Drake than he wanted to know.

Sir Manly gave Leonidas free rein, and the horse picked his way through the rocks, avoiding the many gopher holes pock-marking the area. After they'd crossed the fields, Goldie pointed out a game trail leading to an even rockier area. Soon, they worked their way down a path cut into the side of a cliff. Sir Manly had never been so thankful that Leonidas was sure-footed. Whenever the knight glanced down the sheer drop-off, his stomach lurched.

At last, they reached the bottom of a canyon. Goldie poked Sir Manly and pointed up at the rocky cliff. Several dark holes looked like promising dragon caves.

"Well, my girl, this is where we part company. I shall find your sheep thief and slay the beast."

"I don't think so, Sir Knight." Goldie slid down from the horse's tall back. "You may yet need my help."

Leonidas nodded his head.

"What can you do, lass?" Sir Manly stared at the girl in confusion. "You have no armor, no shield, and no weapons. The dragon would tear you to pieces." He should be able to locate and slay a dragon. After all, they were too large to easily hide for long. But the maid did have knowledge of this terrain and might prove truly helpful, even if she was a bit ... odd.

When Goldie smiled, she met Sir Manly's gaze with the most piercing eyes he'd ever seen. They were an unusual shade of gold, and the pupils were not quite round. Sir Manly blinked away the sweat that dripped into his eyes. Surely he was seeing things in this heat. He shook off a feeling of dread and dismounted.

Once he felt steady on his feet, Sir Manly stared up at the caves and decided the largest would be the most likely place to find a dragon. He took a step toward it.

"Where do you think you're going, Sir Knight?" Goldie balled her fists on her hips.

Sir Manly huffed in exasperation. "I believe the beast must be in this largest cave."

"And, of course," she said with a smirk, "you being the bold knight plan to clomp around the cave in your noisy armor and slay him while he sleeps? The dragon will hear you coming and burn you alive before you catch a glimpse of him in the dark."

Sir Manly frowned. How could he admit he hadn't actually thought that far ahead? Instead, he asked, "What do you suggest, young lady?"

Goldie scanned the sky. "Dusk will come soon. Dragons sleep in the day and hunt at night. If we wait here until then, the dragon should emerge from the cave. You can catch him by surprise."

Sir Manly was not able to keep the annoyance out of his voice. "Just how do you know so much about dragons?"

The maiden turned to face him. "All of my sheep were stolen in the night. And aren't dragons like very large, scaly bats? Bats sleep in the day and hunt at night." When she grinned, Sir Manly blinked. Was the heat affecting his eyes again? For a moment, her teeth appeared sharp.

No matter, Sir Manly couldn't refute her logic. "Very well," he conceded with grudging respect. "We shall wait here until dusk."

While they waited, Leonidas cropped grass nearby. Goldie picked a lapful of daisies and proceeded to make a chain with them.

Fighting drowsiness, Sir Manly decided he'd best walk around in order to stay alert, as well as use up some of his nervous energy. Shortly he would battle a dragon. At last he would prove his valor!

He pushed himself off the ground and paced back and forth. When the shadows lengthened, Sir Manly walked over to Leonidas as quietly as he could. Grasping the trailing reins, he led the horse to the other side of a boulder, out of sight of the cave. Then he took his strong arm shield off the horse's saddle and headed back to Goldie.

She was nowhere to be found.

"Aggravating little wench," he mumbled. After all her bluster and bravado, she had run away.

Just as well, he told himself. He needed no distractions when he met the dragon.

Placing his feet carefully to make as little sound as possible, Sir Manly crept toward the cave. He hid himself behind a rock near the entrance, slid his sword from the scabbard, and waited.

As the sun's glow faded behind the hills, Sir Manly heard something moving deep inside the cave. Instead of coming closer to the entrance, however, the sounds morphed into a metallic clanging. Surely the dragon's scales wouldn't make *that* noise?

"What on earth is going on?" He stood and peered into the cave. A glow shone from around a distant bend. It bobbed up and down, as if someone were moving about.

Sir Manly entered the cave and followed the light. He stepped on something which made a loud *crunch*. When he looked down, a pile of bones and a sheep's skull lay nearby.

Clutching his sword tighter, Sir Manly kept going. There were more bones, and now he could see the glitter of coins and jewels in bigger, neater piles than the bones. A dragon's hoard! Sir Manly had always wondered if the legends were true. But why did dragons collect such things? They never went to market. They didn't tithe on Sundays. And they didn't pay taxes to the king. What use had a dragon for such valuable treasures?

The clanging became louder, and the light moved just ahead.

Sir Manly flattened himself against the wall of the cave. He held his breath and peered around the corner.

Goldie was cooking a meal over an open fire. She banged a metal spoon against the side of an iron pot and then stirred the bubbling contents. A lantern sat on a shelf of rock in the wall.

Breathing a sigh of relief, Sir Manly sheathed his sword. "What in blazes are you doing, young lady?" He strode toward the girl.

Goldie rose gracefully and smiled her toothy smile. "Making something to eat. Aren't you hungry?"

"But where's the dragon?" Sir Manly frowned. "This *is* a dragon's cave, is it not?"

Before he could blink, Goldie shimmered by the flickering flame of her lantern. She transformed, growing taller and heavier. Her arms and legs grew scaly, and her nails lengthened into long, razor-sharp claws. A forked tail and bat-like wings sprang from her body, and her head and neck elongated, snake-like.

Sir Manly's feet were rooted to the ground. His fingers fumbled for the sword, but he couldn't seem to grasp the hilt. His mouth went dry and sweat beaded on his forehead. He braced himself for death by dragon flame or teeth or claw. The beast opened its mouth....

And the dragon laughed, an unnerving sound which echoed through the cave. Sir Manly stared at the huge open mouth, filled with sharp teeth. Was he being toyed with like a cat plays with a mouse before eating it?

Then an old man stepped into the light. Though advanced in years, muscles corded his bare arms. He crossed those arms across a barrel chest and stood proud, confident, like a man to be reckoned with.

"You be from the king?" he asked in a gravelly voice.

"I am Sir Manly Strongarm, and yes, I serve the king." He glanced back at the dragon, who wore Goldie's smile. It looked even creepier on her dragon face than it had on her human one.

"You were sent tae arrest me?" the old man continued.

"No!" Sir Manly held up his gloved hands. "The king did not send me at all. I was just, um, bored and decided to look for dragons." He removed his helmet and clutched it under one arm.

"Looks like ye found one, didn't ye?" The old man smiled almost as unpleasantly as the dragon.

"You must be Wort Drake." Sir Manly coughed to cover his embarrassment, for his voice cracked on the name.

"Aye." Drake's bushy white brows came together in a frown. "What of it?"

"You need to know that the former king is dead, and his son who now reigns has already pardoned you." Sir Manly wiped the sweat from his eyes.

Drake looked up at the dragon, who nodded. "Well," he said, "if that be the case, then I suppose we'll have tae let ye go."

Sir Manly moaned in relief, but Drake was not finished.

"I dinna know what tales are bein' told in the South about the civil wars, but know now that the North has ne'er seen eye-tae-eye with the South as it pertains tae the survival o' the noble dragons." He glared at Sir Manly. "Just don't ye be tellin' any of yer fellow knights about the very last dragon, or she'll hunt ye down, tear out yer heart, and eat it."

The dragon leaned forward until her snout nearly touched Sir Manly's face. He stopped breathing when he smelled the sulfur on her hot breath. It was difficult to remember what the maid Goldie had looked like.

Sir Manly took a step backward. "Dragon? Did someone mention a dragon? Never saw one in my life."

The knight blinked when the dragon's scales sparkled in the firelight. The long neck twisted inward while the tail snaked around, growing smaller. Finally, the folded wings melted into the human form of what Sir Manly had once thought a comely maiden. He rubbed his eyes and stared at her.

Goldie glided closer and smiled at Sir Manly. She reached up and twined her long fingers in his sweaty hair. "You find me attractive, don't you?"

With a squeal of alarm, Sir Manly pulled away from Goldie and shoved his helmet upon his head.

Drake guffawed, and the dragon laughed as well. "Then begone with ye, dragon slayer!"

Sir Manly turned and ran past the dragon's hoard and the sheep bones. It was full dark now. At the cave's entrance, the knight tripped over a rock, slid down a sharp drop, and landed painfully on one knee. He limped over to Leonidas, pulled himself into the saddle, and urged the horse away.

As they ascended the steep trail, Sir Manly risked a glance back. A shape, as of a large bat, flew high into the sky, dark against the glow of the rising moon.

"Well, Leo," he said with a sigh. "If she is the very last dragon, we were born too late to be dragon slayers."

Leonidas snorted and tossed his head. He placed one sure hoof ahead of the other until they were well away from the caves. It was back to the castle, back to training and eating at last.

And even now in that country, on a cloudless night, you might catch a glimpse of what appears to be an over-sized bat. If you do, it would be prudent not to investigate too closely.

Katy Huth Jones grew up in a family where creative juices overflowed and made puddles to splash in. When not writing epic fantasy with dragons or talking birds, Katy plays piccolo and flute in a regional symphony. She lives with her husband Keith in the beautiful Texas Hill Country. Their two sons, whom she homeschooled, have flown the nest and live creative lives of their own.

http://katyhuthjones.blogspot.com/

The Adventures of Zero:
The Quest for Wormsroot

"Come on, Zero! Not afraid, are you?" shouted Ryn.

Our ball was stuck high in a tree. The tree was broad and could probably support my weight, but the ball was so high up that it was hard to see. How had it got to that height?

I'd had the ball in my hands, safe and sound, and was about to throw it back to the older boys when a bird swooped down and stole it. The creature soared into the air and wedged the ball into the crook of a tree, then swooped around and around, laughing at me.

"Oh, forget it; he's too scared!" said someone else.

"Maybe he wants to run home and get his brother's help!" jeered another boy.

I shook my head to clear the daydream and approached the tree. "Fine!" Of course, no bird had taken it. Dung-headed Ryn had kicked it up there when another boy had bet him he couldn't kick it over the tree. Since I was the smallest and weakest of the group, it was decided that I'd go up. As always, they hadn't asked my opinion of this decision, since that was of no interest to anyone.

The lowest branches were an easy leap. As I pulled myself up the tree, I saw a small mammal higher up. It was gray, with a big, bushy tail. It seemed to dance its way up the tree, daring me to follow, and I gave chase. I was determined not to let it get away from me. I might be smaller than the other kids, but I could surely beat this rodent!

It quickly lost me, and in my pursuit, I'd lost track of the ball. I couldn't even do that much right.

"I can't see the ball! Where is it?" I called out.

"The other side of the tree from you, and a bit higher!" was the reply from below. It sounded very far away.

I dared not look down while working my way around the tree to the other side. Sure enough, there was the ball, just out of reach. With a sigh, I climbed up a few more branches. As I reached for the ball, a loud crack resounded through the air.

This was not good. I risked a look downward, realizing the ground was too far away to jump; much too far.

CRACK!

With a second crack, the tree began to tilt.

CRACK!

With a final crack, it began to fall. The ground started rushing towards me, and I knew I was in trouble. As fast as I could, I scrambled around the tree to the side farthest from the upcoming ground. It was at a steep angle, enough to get my feet under me as I rode it down.

Just as the tree was about to hit the ground, I leaped from it, pushing hard with my legs, soaring clear and landing in a perfect dive roll to come up on my feet. The kids all cheered, and for a moment, I felt like a king.

At least, that's what I meant to do and what should have happened. I did jump and attempt to roll, but the landing involved bouncing, sliding, and scraping rather than any kind of graceful maneuver. Nor was there any cheering, just cries of alarm.

"Zero!" someone called as my friends came rushing over.

"Are you all right?" asked Ryn. He was about my age but at least a hand's breadth taller, if not two. Everyone was taller than me, the runt, the adopted son of a blacksmith.

"Yeah," I lied. I felt woozy, and my leg screamed with pain when I tried to stand up.

"You don't look it," he said. I was sure there was genuine concern in his voice; at least, I wanted to believe that and decided it was true.

I shook my head to clear it, but that just made things worse and the ground rushed up to meet me. Why did it do that?

"We'd better take him to the healer," said a female voice, probably Rose; she was the logical one. I couldn't make my eyes focus to be sure. There was a persistent ringing in my ears, too, so it was hard to guess who was speaking.

"I'll be fine," I said and winced as I heard the slur in my words. I tried to stand up, but the world wouldn't stay steady, and I fell again. This time, someone caught me.

"I'll carry him. Run ahead and tell the healer we're coming," someone said in a deep voice which I couldn't place.

"Hang in there, Zero," a soft voice added.

The world was moving around me in a strange way and was far too bright. I couldn't focus my thoughts, and my stomach felt ready to rebel.

"Where am I?" I couldn't remember how I had gotten to wherever I was.

It was too bright to tell, and my mind felt sluggish. Had I just woken up? When was breakfast?

"Easy now, we're almost there," said the owner of the deep voice. Was it my father?

"Dad? Mom? I can't see!" My voice wasn't working right. I couldn't even understand my own words, so how would anyone else?

"Lay him down over there," came a familiar voice. "What happened?"

"He was climbing a tree, and it fell. He jumped clear, but I think he hit his head."

"Go and fetch his parents, and the rest of you get out. I need room to work," said the owner of the voice, who sounded older. I felt I knew him, but it was hard to think through the fog in my head.

Time passed, or seemed to. Everything went dark for a while, then the light in the room slowly returned. My mind cleared, and the room settled around me.

I was in the healer's hut.

As my mind cleared, memory flowed back. I must have been hurt when the tree fell, and Ryn had carried me here.

I started to sit up, then someone called, "Not yet, son."

"Yes, sir," I replied and lay back down.

My head hurt, and most of my body was sore, but it was bearable now. The healer must have worked his magic on me again. Was this the tenth time he'd had to treat me or the eleventh? Well, at least I was keeping him in practice.

"Now, how did you end up here this time?" asked Healer Tanyl.

"Our ball was in a tree, and I climbed up to fetch it, but the tree came down when I reached the top."

"Well, at least this time your story matches your friends'," he grumbled.

I could hear him banging around the shop but couldn't see him. He was probably cleaning up after working on me. I knew much of what he did, but I had yet to discover how he worked his magic. He always sent me away when he used it on others, and I'd never been in any condition to pay attention when he'd used it on me.

"I've used most of my remaining wormsroot on you," he said.

"I'll get you some more," I offered.

"No need," he said, moving away to work elsewhere.

Even with the healer's magic, it was a full week before I could move about without getting dizzy. Ryn and the others had lots of fun with that, once they knew I was going to be okay. Ryn and Rose had rushed to my side when I was hurt, though, and that showed they did care about me.

My father was a blacksmith, and my older brothers helped him in the forge but not me. I was the runt of the family; too small, too weak and too late. Most days I was ignored, but sometimes I was sent on errands too trivial for the others. Today was one of the days when I had no jobs to do, so I headed for the healer's hut.

"Did you fall again?" Healer Tanyl asked as I entered. He was bending over, using a mortar and pestle to grind up a reagent. By the scent, I was sure it was fronseweed. The bittersweet smell filled the room and reminded me of the many days I had sat and watched him when I was younger. He never paid me much heed, no one did, but I had studied him. For over a decade I had studied everything he did, everything he read, and everything he said. I was as ready as I would ever be.

"No, I just wanted to see if I could help you," I responded.

He stopped what he was doing and looked up at me. "How can you help?"

"You're grinding fronseweed. It's a root found in the marsh where the drier land meets the mud. The flower is yellow with a white pistil. It's used in mixtures to dull the senses."

His eyes widened. He lifted a jar from the table and said, "And this?"

"Buckwart, found in tropical regions growing on the shaded side of trees. It's used to sweeten drinks and often to make medicine taste better."

He repeated the exercise a dozen times, then stopped and asked, "How do you know all this?"

"I've been studying you for years," I told him. It was more than that. I had taken careful note of all the reagents that he used on a regular basis, and memorized all the facts I could find about them. My mom had even gotten me a copy of one of the books I'd seen Healer Tanyl using for reference. I had studied that book for several years in preparation for this day.

"Why?"

I sighed. I'd been right: he'd never noticed me. So much for that dream. "I was hoping that one day you would ask me to be your apprentice."

He shook his head and returned to his grinding, working in silence for a while. Then, just as I had decided to give up and go home, he gestured to the cabinet where he kept the reagents he used regularly. "Organize that for me."

I walked over to the cabinet, which was in a terrible state. Most of the jars were open, none were labeled, and many were stacked so hazardously that I was afraid even to breathe near them.

I almost asked him what had happened in here, since it wasn't like him to be so careless, but thought better of it. Unsure where to start, I took everything out of the cabinet and organized it on a nearby table. Seeing a rag, I wiped down the shelves and then put the jars back in, grouped first by how they were used and then alphabetically by name.

As I finished he came over and looked at my handiwork. "Huh. You do know a lot about these reagents."

"You're a bit low on sulfur, wormsroot, and mandrake," I noted.

"The caravan will be in town tomorrow, and I can buy more," he said, rubbing his chin. "Do you really want to be my apprentice?"

"Yes."

"Huh." He eyed the cabinet and looked back at me. "What do you get if you take the dust of black pearl and firestone and mix with a sulfur suspension?"

"A very stinky explosion," I said.

"Huh."

He looked back over at the cabinet. "You're serious about this, aren't you?"

"Very much so," I replied.

"Huh."

He was quiet for a time and then looked at me. "There's more than head knowledge to this."

"Teach me, then," I said.

"Do you know where to find wormsroot?"

I nodded. "It only grows in Timiren's Valley. It must be harvested by the full moon or it will lose its potency."

He pulled down another jar from the cabinet. "And this?"

I looked at it and almost snapped off the answer, but something held me back. I rocked it back and forth in my hand, watching the grains pass over each other. It looked right and smelled right, but there was something wrong.

"Stumped?" he asked.

"No, it's wormsroot, but there's something wrong with it."

"And that is?" His voice held a note of surprise. I wasn't sure if that was good or bad.

"I'm not sure. It looks and smells right, but there's something the matter with it."

He took the jar and replaced the top. "It was harvested under the new moon and is therefore worthless."

"Then why do you have it?" I asked.

"It's safe to consume but tastes foul, so makes a good placebo," he said with a grin. He grew serious again. "But you could tell. How?"

"I don't know."

"So you're finally at a loss for an answer?"

"I guess so."

"Huh."

He searched another cabinet and came out with a scroll, which he spread out on the table. It was a chart of the cycles of the moon for the rest of the year.

"This cost me a week's earnings, so be careful with it. I want you to make an exact copy. Be careful to get everything right."

I could read, but I was doubtful about my ability to perform this task. I hadn't written very much in my life; the need hadn't arisen. I wanted this position as his apprentice, however. It was that or a life as a useless runt in a house of blacksmiths.

I took a deep breath and then another. I had to focus on this task. No looking out the window or watching clouds; I needed to concentrate.

Looking around, I found a table where I could sit with my back to the window with nothing of interest in front of me and slowly began to copy the chart. As I made each stroke of a symbol or number, I compared it to the original. The room darkened around me, but I didn't stop. It was painfully slow, and my wrist and back ached, but I kept on writing.

As it started to become too dark to work, I felt a hand on my shoulder. I looked up at the healer.

"The sun is about to set; you had better go home," he said.

I had copied about half the chart. "I'll come back tomorrow to finish this."

"Tomorrow I'll be out. I need to buy sulfur and mandrake, as you noticed."

"And wormsroot," I added.

"No, the caravan that will be here tomorrow doesn't sell that. I'll have to send someone to the city for it."

That would triple the price of the expensive root. "I'll get you some."

His eyebrows lifted. "Really?"

I took an empty container from the counter. "I'll fill this and trade it for an apprenticeship."

"Do you have any idea how much that is worth?" he asked.

I nodded. "I've studied the price sheets. This much wormsroot would cover my apprenticeship at the normal rate."

"Huh." He leaned over and looked at the work I was doing. "This is very good work."

"Thank you."

"If you can raise the money, either by that jar of wormsroot or other means, I'll give you an apprenticeship."

"Thank you!" I yelled and ran for home. I was sure I heard a "Huh," as I left.

The next morning, I went looking for my father before sunrise. He was talking with my mom about their plans for the day. When he noticed my presence and greeted me, I said, "Dad, I have to leave for a few days."

"Oh? Where are you going?" he asked.

"I'm running an errand for Healer Tanyl," I said.

"And why are you doing this for him?" he asked.

"Because he's going to make me his apprentice," I said with a huge grin.

"Healer Tanyl is taking you on an apprentice?" he said with amazement. "Why, I bet every kid in town has tried to get that position. How did you manage it?"

"Healer Tanyl must have noticed how brilliant he is," said my mom proudly.

"I haven't definitely got the job yet, but this errand will clinch it," I said.

He nodded thoughtfully and said, "That makes sense. Take the crossbow and some provisions with you. Opportunities like this don't come often. Take whatever you need to secure that apprenticeship."

"Thank you!" I said and ran off to pack.

As I left, I heard my mom say, "What are you doing? He's too young to go off alone like that."

"He will remain too young until he does. You have to let him become a man," responded my father.

It was a common argument between them. She was always trying to keep me safe, and he was always trying to make a man out of me. I sighed, knowing that they each loved me in their own way.

I didn't wait for the rest of the conversation, since I knew if I did my mom would stop me and insist that I take along my older brothers. It would be more a case of them taking me on this errand, and that would not prove my ability to Healer Tanyl. Mom meant well, but my father was right; I needed to do this myself.

I took the crossbow, some bolts, some clothes, and all the provisions I could stuff into my sack. If things went well, it should only take a few days to hike out to the valley and get the wormsroot, then a few more days to hike back. Still, it would be good to have company for the hike.

I shouldered my pack and walked to where Ryn lived with his sister Rose. I wasn't sure if I had any real friends, but they were the closest I had.

They lived in an orphanage near the town's outskirts, the same orphanage where my parents had found me. I was too young to remember that day, but my mom often spoke of it. Since we didn't know my real birthday, we celebrated that day instead. In a way, it was my birthday. It was the day I had gained a family, and the best day of my life.

Ryn and Rose were not so fortunate. They had entered the orphanage as older children, and they seemed to rebel at any attempts to place them in homes. The story they told everyone was that their parents were famous warriors who had been killed in a battle, but no one really believed them. Most likely they'd just been abandoned, like most of the kids in the orphanage. The hero story was cool, though, so everyone played along with it.

What *was* true was that they knew how to live in the woods. Several times over the years, they had left the orphanage and traveled into the wilds. They'd been gone for weeks at a time and then suddenly came back. They didn't talk about what they'd done, and after a while people stopped asking.

It would be cool to be a famous warrior. *I could see myself racing up a hill, holding a sword over my head and approaching the enemy. I screamed out a battle cry and charged. My men struggled to keep up, and that was good. I would take the brunt of the enemy's first volley.*

Stumbling into a tree shattered my daydream. Thankfully, this time no one was around to see. With a sigh, I kicked some stones and pressed on towards the orphanage.

I found Ryn and Rose behind the building, throwing rocks at a grizzled old tree. The tree had been struck by lightning at least three times and was quite dead, but it refused to fall over. The blackened husk was at least three times my own height, and if any balls got stuck in it, they could stay there. That was for sure.

Rose and Ryn were pretty much my opposite in every way. They were tall, with broad shoulders and fair hair. Rose always wore hers in a ponytail, while Ryn kept his roughly cut at about shoulder-length. They both had fair skin and green eyes. They usually wore clothing made from random pieces of torn leather they had found, and were almost always together.

"Hey!" I greeted them as I approached.

"Zero! Good to see you finally remembered how to walk," commented Ryn.

"What's the sack for? Going somewhere?" asked Rose.

"Yes, and I was hoping you'd come with me," I said.

"Where to?" asked Ryn.

"Into the wilds. I need to collect some roots for Healer Tanyl," I said.

"It looks as if you expect to be gone for a while," commented Rose.

"At least a few days, perhaps a week," I said.

"Sounds good to me. Let's go," said Ryn.

"Beats sitting around here," agreed Rose.

"Definitely," I replied and we started walking towards the wilds.

As soon as we were out of sight of the town, Ryn stopped. "We need to pick up our stuff first," he said. "Stay here; it'll just take a few minutes."

Rose and Ryn ran off, and I quickly lost sight of them. I had assumed they were going to pick up things from the orphanage, but they went off in a completely different direction.

The sun had risen another finger's breadth before they returned. When they'd left me they had been wearing scrap leather, but they came back in studded leather armor with massive hammers slung on their backs. At their waists, various bags were attached to their belts, including a pair of canteens each. The equipment appeared to be in very good condition. I knew enough from my father's forge to recognize high-quality weapons when I saw them.

Ryn was also carrying a staff in one hand, which he tossed to me. "Take this. I'll teach you to use it as we go."

I didn't know what to say, so I thanked them, and we headed down the trail.

After we'd walked for a while, I finally asked, "Where did you get all this?"

"Our parents left it for us. We keep it hidden out here where thieves won't find it," said Ryn.

"With all this gear, though, why are you living in an orphanage?" I asked.

Ryn shrugged. "Have to live somewhere, and it's as good a place as any."

Rose smacked him in the back of the head, and said, "That's where our parents left us years ago when they went on an important mission. They promised they would be back." She paused to take a deep breath, and I saw that her eyes were moist. "At first we stayed in the hope that they'd come back for us, but now it's kind of become our home."

I wasn't sure what to say to that, but I *was* sure that this was part of their real story. The uneasy silence continued until Ryn began his normal banter.

The two of them filled the walk with their constant joking until Ryn commented, "It'll be dark soon. We need to find a place to camp."

I looked around and shrugged. "Does it have to be anywhere special?"

He blinked at me, then looked over at Rose and back to me. "Have you never been out here before?"

"Sure, lots of times, just never overnight."

"You really do need us," said Ryn. He looked around for a moment and said, "Head towards that clump of trees. We can make camp there."

Once we reached the trees, they got to work building a fire and explaining to me about the necessity of setting watches. Ryn started to teach me the staff while Rose set traps: for breakfast, she claimed.

After it grew too dark to practice, we gathered around the fire. Ryn asked, "Where exactly are we going?"

"I have to get some wormsroot for Healer Tanyl." I rooted in my pack and pulled out the container. "Enough to fill this."

"Why not just buy some? We can take you to the city where I'm sure a dozen shops stock that stuff," commented Rose.

"This is very expensive. I could work for a year and not earn enough to fill this container."

"So we collect it, then. Okay, where?" asked Ryn.

"It has to be harvested under the full moon, and grows in only one place around here," I told them.

"When is the next full moon?" asked Rose.

"Two days from now," I said.

"And where are we going?" asked Ryn.

"Timiren's Valley." It was too dark to see but that seemed to get a reaction from them.

"Are you serious?" asked Ryn.

"No, he's just pulling your leg," said Rose.

"I am serious," I said.

"But do you know what's in that valley?" asked Ryn.

"Wormsroot," I replied.

"That's not all," said Rose in a hushed voice. "The cat people live there."

"Cat people?" I queried.

"Werecats," said Ryn.

"So?" I asked.

"So I hope you like being ripped to shreds and eaten raw!" said Ryn.

"Do you know what werecats are?" asked Rose.

I shrugged. "Well, based on the name, I guess they're people who turn into cats during the full moon."

"According to legend, when great warriors fall in combat, if they have pleased the god of the forest they can choose to come back as werecats: humans with the ability to take on the form, speed and strength of a jaguar."

"Come on, you don't actually believe that?" I asked. I had heard the legend. The cat people were said to be vicious hunters who lay in wait for hapless travelers to enter their territory and then sprang out and ate them. It sounded like a story invented to make kids too scared to wander off, and I had never believed it.

"Think about it, Zero. All the strength and power of a jaguar, and the intelligence of a man," said Ryn.

"Oh, they're real. Very much so," said Rose.

"Look, I just have to gather enough wormsroot to fill this container and get it back to Healer Tanyl."

"Why?" asked Ryn.

"Because if I do, he's agreed to take me on as his apprentice," I said.

"*You?*" gasped Ryn.

"Healer Zero; there's almost a musical sound to it," said Rose.

"Yes, me. Please don't back out now; I need to do this," I pleaded.

"How deep into the valley do we need to go?" asked Ryn.

"Not very far. Wormsroot's quite abundant in there. I'm not sure why it's so expensive."

"Probably because most people who try to harvest it end up as dinner for the cat people," said Ryn.

"How much will that container be worth when it's full?" asked Rose.

"It will cover my entire apprenticeship," I told her.

She whistled.

"The entire thing?" asked Ryn in astonishment.

I nodded. "Please, this is my big chance!"

They looked at each other, and Ryn shrugged. "If we wait as long as possible to get close and stay on the edges, we should be able to gather some roots and get out unnoticed—I hope."

We arrived at the valley a day early, so Ryn spent that time trying to teach me how to defend myself with the staff. His idea of teaching involved telling me what to do, then laughing and making jokes whenever I got it wrong.

When the sun was directly overhead, we scouted out the edge of the valley. It was eerily quiet as we pushed through bushes looking for a suitable area to find wormsroot. It would grow where the ground was moist and exposed to direct moonlight.

"Is this it?" whispered Rose.

She was standing near the edge of a mossy area, partially shaded by the nearby trees. I carefully made my way there, making sure I didn't step on any wormsroot.

"You said it would resemble lots of little worms just under the surface, and that's what this looks like," said Rose.

"Wow!" I gasped. She was standing at the edge of a large patch of wormsroot. There was more growing in this patch than I had ever seen, even in pictures; more than enough to fill Healer Tanyl's container. "Yes, this is perfect."

"Let's go back to camp and rest. We'll come back when the moon is high enough in the sky to give us light," said Ryn.

He led the way back out of the valley and up over a hill. Behind the hill, we made camp and returned to staff practice for a while.

As night approached, Ryn said, "You should get some sleep. We might have to run all night after picking the wormsroot."

"You're still talking about the 'cat people' legend?" I shook my head in disbelief.

"It isn't just a legend. Look, I'm serious. The cat people are real, and you'd better be ready for them. I think that patch might be close enough for us to pick the root and get away before they notice us, but you'd better be ready to move fast."

His tone was more serious than I'd ever heard before. Something about this valley really concerned him; the cat people myth, or maybe something else.

I shrugged and climbed into my bedroll. "Wake me when it's my turn to keep watch."

I was tired enough from working with the staff but not ready for sleep. I lay back and studied the sky. It was easy to find patterns and shapes in the stars, and soon I was watching great battles between heroes and monsters.

After what seemed like a few seconds of daydreaming, Ryn was shaking me and the moon had moved from the horizon to directly overhead.

"What?" I muttered.

"It's time to gather your worms," he said.

"Wormsroot," I corrected him, grumbling. I pulled myself out of the bedroll and tried to wake up as I packed my things.

Rose brought me a canteen and some dried meat. "Here, drink now and eat as we go."

She left to see to her packing, which gave me a moment to move around and try to clear my mind. Images of the war in the stars were still bouncing around my head. When I'd fallen asleep, they had followed me into my dreams.

I gasped as I tripped over a rock near the edge of the camp. Winded, I pushed myself up onto my knees, my head cleared by the fall. As I placed my hand on the ground to push myself upright, I had to stifle another gasp.

Before me lay a paw print, just like any left by the various cats around town except for one major difference: these prints were bigger than my hand. The cat that left them must have been massive.

Was this real? It couldn't be. No cat is that big. Ryn must have put it here to scare me. Well, I wouldn't let him have that satisfaction. I would act as if I hadn't even seen it.

"Are you all right?" he asked.

I stood up the rest of the way. "Sure. Are we ready to go?"

He nodded, and we headed off. When we reached the mossy area where the wormsroot grew, I handed each of them a bag. "Put as many as you can in the bag. We can sort them out tomorrow in the daylight."

They nodded and got to work, all business tonight. There was no joking, no mock fighting, just rapid gathering of roots. Something really *was* bothering them and this worried me, so I also worked as fast as I could.

A low rumbling growl from the woods caused the blood in my veins to freeze. Ryn and Rose stood up slowly, dropping their collection bags and drawing their hammers. They were like mirror images, dropping into a fighting stance with their backs angled towards each other. They held their massive hammers in front of them, just above the shoulder, ready to strike.

I looked past them to the source of the growl. At the edge of the woods stood three huge jaguars, their black fur glistening in the moonlight and their bright yellow eyes boring through me.

I lifted my crossbow and released the safety catch. I would only get one shot. Hopefully, Ryn and Rose could take one jaguar each. My mind was unnaturally clear as the danger of the moment washed over me.

"Take the bags and run," said Ryn.

He and Rose moved past the bags and towards the great cats.

I snatched up the bags, tied them shut and attached them to my belt while the standoff continued between the two humans and the three cats.

Once the bags were secure I took aim again with the crossbow, backing up slowly so that I'd have time to shoot when the cats charged. They would be fast and accurate.

"Run," hissed Rose.

I knew running was pointless. A jaguar would catch me before I'd taken five strides.

The decision was taken from me as all three cats leaped as one, each towards a different human. My crossbow was already on target, which was just as well because otherwise I'd never have released the shot in time. The bolt struck the jaguar under its right shoulder, and it cried out in pain. I dove to the side to get out of its flight path.

Despite being in pain and wounded, when it hit the ground, it seemed to fold in on itself and launched off at a new angle right towards me. I tried to get out of the way but this time the cat caught me, knocking me to the ground. Stars danced in my vision as the beast bit my shoulder.

Searching for anything I could use, in a panic, my hand chanced on a rock. I smashed it as hard as I could into the side of the cat's head, over and over, until it released me.

I tried to scramble away, but the powerful paws pressing into my chest ensured I couldn't move. The cat roared, and I was sure it was going to bite me again, but a golden colored streak slammed into the side of it, sending it tumbling away.

As I tried to get to my feet, dizziness swept over me. I felt very cold. I couldn't feel my left arm anymore, and that meant the wound was serious.

The battle raged around me, and I knew I had to get clear. I scanned the clearing and saw not only three black jaguars but two massive lions, one male and one female.

The lions stayed between me and the jaguars. They worked as a team, just as the three others did against them. They seemed far more intelligent than I would have thought possible for an animal.

The jaguars tried several charges, but broke off as the lions turned to meet them. Each time they seemed ready to fight, the jaguars backed off. It was as if they were reluctant to hurt the lions, but that didn't make sense. The lions didn't counter-attack, they just paced back and forth between me and the jaguars.

Rose and Ryn were nowhere to be seen, which puzzled me. I knew they would never have left me there alone; for all their ribbing, they were always there for me when I was hurt or in trouble.

The male lion stood his ground, but the lioness paced over to me. Her bright green eyes were somehow familiar. Before I could make the connection, she knelt down for me to get on her back.

She was large enough to carry me, so I moved slowly towards her and climbed on. Then she stood up and started running. I held on as long as I could with only one arm, but at some point I fell off and then there was only darkness.

When I came to, the sun was a full hand's breadth above the horizon, and Ryn was standing watch. Rose was nowhere in sight.

"Ugh," I groaned and tried to sit up.

"Easy," said Ryn.

He came over and helped me to sit and then drink some water. As he did, I noticed his brilliant green eyes. It couldn't be—could it?

"Where's Rose?" I asked.

"She'll be back soon. Eat and drink. You need to rest after last night," he said.

My shoulder decided this would be a good time to remind me of my injury. It felt as if it were on fire. I cried out in pain, and my eyes watered. I forced myself to take some deep breaths.

"Shoulder?" he asked.

I nodded.

"We cleaned it as best we could, but we don't have anything for the pain. We need to get you to Healer Tanyl."

"I'll be fine. Do we have the wormsroot?" I asked through gritted teeth. Healer Tanyl's magic would take care of the injury; I just had to endure it until then.

"Over there, waiting for you."

Gritting my teeth against the pain, I worked my way over to the bags. With my good hand, I began sorting through what we'd collected. I was surprised at the quantity we had gathered.

I tossed out everything that wasn't wormsroot, and then sorted the usable roots from the unusable ones. As I was working, Rose returned and came over to me.

She sat down opposite me, and her vivid green eyes met mine.

"Sorry I couldn't hold on for longer," I said, taking a chance that I was right about what had happened last night.

She sighed. "How's the shoulder?"

"Feels like it's on fire, so it's probably infected," I said.

She nodded.

"So you two are cat people?" I said, wanting to know more.

She smiled and nodded. "The jaguar clan rules this valley. We come from the lion clan. Our people are nomads; we wander the lands in family groups while these jaguars, unlike their natural brethren, are fiercely territorial and loyal to their jamboree."

"I really thought you were joking, you know, just teasing me," I said. My mind spun, trying to make sense of what she'd told me.

"Sorry about that," said Ryn as he joined us. "I had hoped we might be able to gather your root and get out without being seen. Then you could have gone on believing that the cat people were a myth, and our secret would be safe."

"You can trust me, but why does it have to be kept secret?" I asked.

"Because if anyone finds out, we'll be hunted down and killed," he replied.

"Humans destroy what they don't understand," said Rose grimly.

"Are the jaguars still out there?" I asked, looking towards the treeline.

"There's a whole clan in the valley, but none of them followed us," said Rose.

"Hey, I wanted to say how impressed I am with you," said Ryn.

"Not today, please," I responded.

"No, I'm serious. You did a good job on that jaguar while you were pinned down. She won't soon forget you, that's for sure!"

I met his gaze and waited for the punchline, but none came. "Let me guess: they all survived?"

Ryn nodded. "Werecats are notoriously hard to kill, and all cat people heal fast. I'm sure they're all sitting around somewhere, eating a meal together and cursing you."

I sighed. "I don't know whether to be happy that I didn't kill anyone or scared that they're alive to come after me."

"They won't come after you. As I said, they're fiercely territorial. To pursue you would mean leaving their land, and they haven't done that since your grandparents' time. If you return to the valley, they'll attack again; otherwise, you're safe."

"Did we get enough wormswood?" asked Rose.

I looked over the haul. "About twice as much as I need."

"Great!" she said.

I split it in half. "Here, take this to the city and sell it. Healer Tanyl deals with a merchant named Franz. Franz will give you a fair price if he thinks Healer Tanyl sent you."

"You're sure you want to do this?" asked Rose.

"Based on what you said, that's worth a lot of money," said Ryn.

"Yes. Take it. The two of you will never have to live in the orphanage again. I'll use the remainder to pay for my treatment and cover my apprenticeship."

"That works out well, since they'll be kicking us out in a few months anyway," said Ryn.

"Why?" I queried.

"They seem to think we're too old to go on living there and that we should find a respectable job or something," grumbled Ryn.

It took a couple of days to make the trip back to town. We didn't discuss the cat people again, but I caught Rose gesturing towards my arm once or twice while talking in low tones with her brother.

When we finally reached Healer Tanyl's house, Ryn said, "We're off to sell the roots."

"You're still planning to come back, aren't you?" I asked.

"Of course. We'll sell the roots, party a little, and then come back to the orphanage. We'll check on you when we get back," he said. Ryn knocked on the healer's door and the two of them ran off.

Healer Tanyl came out, took one look at the filthy bandage on my shoulder, and frowned deeply. "What is it this time?"

"An animal in the woods," I replied.

"Well, get in here, then," he said.

When we were inside, I handed him the container of wormsroot. "As promised."

He took the container and examined it. "Huh." Putting it down, he said, "Let's see what you've done to yourself this time."

He pulled off the bandages, which didn't hurt as much as I'd expected, and poured clean water across my shoulder to remove the dried blood and dirt.

For the first time, I turned to examine it myself. The wound was nothing like I had expected; instead of deep tears from the jaguar's teeth, there were only a few small puncture wounds.

"Oh," I said. The puncture wounds suggested that the cat had just been trying to hold me, not rip my shoulder to shreds. But why would it do that? And why had it hurt so much, when there was no sign of infection?

"You went to the valley and harvested this root."

"Yes," I said.

"This is the bite of a jaguar."

"Yes."

He met my eyes. "It will heal by itself in a few more days. You'll just have to live with it until then."

"Are you sure?" I asked.

"You are in no danger from that wound. In a few days, you won't even be able to tell you've been bitten."

He got out clean bandages and covered the wound again. Afterwards, he sat in silence for a while, and I stayed quiet, too, thinking. It seemed odd that he should bandage up such a minor wound.

He sighed. "It would be best if you didn't tell anyone how you got that wound."

"Why not?" I asked.

"People are superstitious, and it will cause you even more grief." He sighed again, then smiled gently at me. "You completed your part of the agreement, so from sunrise tomorrow you will be my apprentice."

The pain in my arm seemed to recede, beaten back by the joy I took in that simple statement. I was no longer a worthless runt. I had found purpose and meaning.

"I will send word to your family. From now on, you will live here in my hut. A healer must be ready to serve at any time, and to do that you must be here. It's best not to show your face till that bite mark is completely gone."

I had done it! I resisted the urge to scream and shout, but my joy must have been apparent because Healer Tanyl's face lit up with a big smile in response.

Healer Zero, I said in my mind. Rose was right. It was musical, and the best song I had ever heard.

Vincent, father, and husband of nearly two decades, holds degrees in both Math and Computer Science. In addition, he has published an astronomy journal, numerous articles, poetry and other works. He got his start in writing fiction as a small child, losing himself in the worlds he dreamed up in order to escape the doldrums of normal life. Now, using his formal education and extensive career experience, he excels in creating fictional worlds of depth and rich fantasy, while maintaining a foundation of reality based on science and technology.

Website: http://www.vincenttrigili.com

Ishka's Garden

Eilean Ren
Capital of Fae Realm
Royal Home

Beneath the alabaster arches over my narrow windows, something flutters against my curtains, interrupting my reading. I squint toward the sound as I rub my earpoints. They're sore from concentration. I've spent my half-day studying the techniques recorded in the leather-bound journal of a master arborist.

A tree in my garden needs pruning before the Moontide Festival. The tree that I've come to think of as *Seesha's Tree*. My little friend will be so pleased with her new home. Fesh designed it well and picked the perfect branch. The two of them favor my Mergone and not many Fae can say a pair of the winged creatures live nearby.

Surrounded by elaborate furnishings and bare walls, I've kept the drapes drawn against the white light from our orb. Unlike many of the other worlds Arún has visited, we do not have a sun-star here, but we have captured a chemical reaction in a sphere situated at the tip of the tower that stands in the center of our capital. The reaction is much smaller, but it brightens the city and keeps us warm.

Dark and quiet better suits the melancholy that haunts me today, preferring self-pity over action. Action is for heroes.

There's more scratching at the silks.

"Who's there?" I call. No one answers, but it sounds like a bird trapped in a net. Helpless creatures always pull me from my cloistering, even when my family cannot. When I hear a *bzzzt* followed by the soft tinkling of bells, I know what's found me.

I cross the polished floor. Veins of sparkling gems crisscross the expanse, broken by white woven throw rugs that my mother had cleaned last week. It was a less-than-covert attempt to force me from my rooms. It worked for a time. Though, reading on Arún's balcony probably wasn't the ousting my mother had in mind.

When I throw back the fabrics, light pours in and a green Hum-Fairy hovers at my eye-level with crossed arms and mouth twisted with frustration. She's round and curvy, but still only as big as my palm. Her wings are obscured by her movement as she zips one way and then another, a glowing blur in motion.

"Oh, Seesha, I'm glad you're home," I say and lift my hand to her. I've been favored with a long-time friendship of Hum-Fairies. They're gentle creatures, always traveling, but elusive in the realms.

She settles on my fingertips, stepping down into my palm, the tops of her wings stretch out above and behind her like the ornate fins of a fishdancer, and the bottoms pool in soft, feathery puddles on my skin. She's covered in luminescent plumage, something between a Skybird and a fairy; sentient, but not Fae. She folds her arms again and taps her foot on the fleshy part of my hand, just below my thumb.

"Were you resting? Have you found someone to be the night to your moon?" she asks, her ever-changing mood already shifting from irritated to concerned to elated. Despite her lack of vocal cords, and though her short beak doesn't move, I can hear her voice as easily as if she'd spoken in my ear. Every Fae can communicate with a Hum-Fairy, but time and practice makes telepathic communication with Hum-Fairies effortless. She's been my friend for years, and she knows how my disposition turns. "Have you lost color since I've been gone?"

"There is no one. This has not changed," I say. "And I was reading. The Mergone needs pruning. My memory needed refreshing on technique." She doesn't know about Arún or she wouldn't begin as though nothing has changed. "And I'm as pale as I've always been, from my milk skin to my colorless eyes to my snowy hair."

"My home is still here?" Her statement is part question.

"Fesh has been waiting for you." I beam at her, dancing on my toes, happy she's returned from the human realm. Fesh will be so pleased. He won't just be overjoyed; he'll get bright orange and spin loops in the air. "He asked me to help him build something for you. He said you would be back soon."

Seesha strokes her chin. "We spent our sleeping dreams together. He can always tell when I'm ready to return. The same as I can with him." She leaps into the air, her eyes twinkling. "I'll meet you there." She's thinking of Fesh and seeing him. He always brings a languid smile to her face. Wanderlust tickles her feet. Lately, she's been in New York at Arún's request.

"See you both in a bit," I say.

"We must find you a mate, Ishka. It isn't good to be alone," she says. And then, with a zip, she races away toward her mate. The sound of tiny wind chimes trails after her. I sense her until she's too far away. Proximity affects the telepathic connection.

I tie my slippers slowly. Seesha's going to love the surprise Fesh planned and I want to see it, but giving Seesha alone time with Fesh is probably the less-selfish choice. I don't bother with a formal veil since I won't see dignitaries or politicians in this part of the palace. Not anymore. Not since I made my position clear.

I open the door, surprising a maid as she hurries from one place to another. Her eyes widen when she sees my bare face. Or it maybe she's startled that I've not met an untimely demise as the rumors proclaim. "Princess," she says, dropping a nervous curtsy. "May I assist you?"

"No, I'll find my own way." I turn, not willing to endure the censure or the pity.

I am a princess that will never be queen. A blighted daughter that will never become a mother.

Down the hall, I stop long enough to study a tapestry depicting Arún saving a small village in another realm, riding his winged steed to triumph. My brother was always the hero.

He'd say, "Enjoy this peace," with his pale sideways grin. Then he'd kiss my cheek, fashion a geode portal, and return to wait for his mate to arrive in New York. It wasn't until he left home to stay in a foreign land that he appreciated our city.

After his marriage, he brought his wife to meet us. She delighted me, captivating me with her sometimes sardonic humor and unintentional disregard for our ways. She was a starburst in my shadows, unlike any other I've known.

Two corridors and many thoughts later, I find myself at the door to my brother's unoccupied apartment rather than standing at the gate to my private topiary.

Arún loved to be the hero and look what it earned him: a self-sacrificing death. Now Arún is gone, and the dead cannot grant permission. I let myself into his rooms without hesitation.

From the balcony off his living quarters, I study the beautiful city formed from ancient stone by my ancestors. Circles of color illuminate the streets as Fae use magic in their daily life. Each Fae possesses a shade of magic unique to them, and a rainbow of spheres dance in the light from the spire at the center of the acropolis.

The trees on the promenade below are orange, yellow, red, and Arún's favorite shade of green. The scented breeze whispers of the blooms of the bell-vines growing inside my walled garden. Moisture rises up from the ground to water all our living things. Cisterns never run dry, and fountains sparkle, draped in diamond-water cascades.

Arún's mate did not weep as she escorted his body through our streets, but I heard her cry echo my own even as I found comfort between the fountains with the Hum-Fairies that choose to live near the ancient Mergone.

Leaf clippings from the thick-trunked Mergone branch fall around my bare feet. Our lightstay lamps are made from cultivated Mergone wood. The sap doesn't evaporate after cutting and holds magic longer than anything else. One spell can light a home all night. The Mergone are carefully cultivated here.

I'm pruning with magic-made shears, knitting molecules and cells back together, healing the tree even as I take from it. I wiggle my toes in the soft grasses and hum a tune the musicians played while I ate mid-day meal. A zephyr stirs the dress I wear.

Royalty employs the best seamstresses, skilled in magically animating prints. And this dress is one of my favorites, giving me hope in the possibility of a happiness beyond. The fabric spins with moving reproductions of galaxies from across the realms.

We're at the center of the circle-shaped space, enclosed by castle walls and surrounded by a manicured garden, at the center of a sun shape formed from mountain stone. The ancient hardwood is the crown of my garden, surrounded by a lush green carpet and blooms of all shapes and colors.

Seesha zooms by my head and then settles on my shoulder, moving in quick little jerks as she studies our surroundings. "Don't trim our branch. It's perfect."

"Mmmm," I agree, moving past the wide and gnarled limb where Fesh asked me to hang their little tree house. Seesha had always dreamed of living in the majestic tree. Just outside their tiny home, we put a glassed-in swing. When either of them sits in it, the globe glows as bright as a lightstay spell lamp. "I haven't seen Fesh this morning," I say.

"He's gone to fetch my mother from across the city," Seesha answers. "She was offered a home by a musician when she paused to hear a melody." My little friend darts from my shoulder to her gently swaying swing.

I envy Seesha's freedom. All over our kingdom, when a Fae sees a Hum-Fairy, they are welcomed, invited in, provided a home, but have the opportunity to refuse or move at any time. They are a good omen. But their lives are their own, their presence counted a blessing, no matter how short their stay. Capturing a Hum-Fairy, removing their free choice, is an offense punishable by exile.

A noise in the bushes pulls me from my peaceful reverie, and I stare across the lawn to the large-tailed bird shape that Arún commissioned after a bird he saw in Central Park. It was his way of sharing his travels with me. I lower my hands and the shears disappear. Dark eyes stare out at me from beneath the lifted foliage wing. A shimmer wraps around the tall, masculine figure. I take a step forward, blinking to clear my vision, but he's gone.

"Did you see that?" Seesha says and then she zips by my head, zooming toward the shrub.

"Did you see it, too?" I jog after her, curious what creature has been caught in the greenery.

"Something's here," she calls behind her as she darts into the foliage.

She gasps. And then something closes. Like a box snapped shut.

A muscular man wrapped in robes, his face hidden behind a wrap of linen, bursts out and bolts across the promenade to the thick bell-vines that grow up and over the highest wall. At the base of the bulwark, he glances over his shoulder at me. Moments stretch into something longer, as he stares at me and I stare at him.

Be the night to my moon. I shake my head to banish the errant thought.

When he looks away, I tug at my skirts, lifting the hems as I go. This dress isn't made for running. In his hand, a glass box swings at the end of a chain. He hooks the metal loop to a spot on his belt. Inside the cube, Seesha presses her tiny hands against her prison.

"Ishka...." she begins, but she's so far that her words are too faint to make out.

"Stop," I cry, waving my arm wildly. "You can't take her. She's made her home here. They will exile you." But I'm too far to catch him. I've never heard of a Fae kidnapping a Hum-Fairy. It's unthinkable. I summon magic, but I'm out of practice with attack spells. My hands tingle with the surge of energy they hold. The only formulas I can call to mind are my shears and a cloudburst.

With one hand I send a fluffy cloud to weep on his head, hoping desperately that the moisture will make the creepers slick. With the other, I send the shears toward the vines above him. But the snipping is too late and his hands must be more calloused than mine. And then he's over the other side and into the city.

He didn't slip. He didn't fall. He's escaped, and now I can't sense Seesha's thoughts.

When I reach the bottom of the barrier, I hesitate and press my ear to the thick stone. Footsteps are running away, but Seesha makes no sound.

My heartbeat thunders in my ears, like galloping pasture hounds. I'm not made to be a hero. I bite my bottom lip. Seesha needs my help, but my veil is in my room. I haven't been out of the castle in years. I refuse. And I haven't gone unveiled about the city since I was a little girl.

Reasons, I have plenty.

And then I think of Fesh, home soon with Seesha's mother, and how badly I missed her while she had been gone. They will miss her, and she is my friend.

I grasp the gnarled branch, ignoring the bite of rounded barbs in my tender skin, hauling myself up the twisted vines, avoiding the snipped ones. The wall is as wide as my arm is long, and I climb atop to stare over the city, trying to catch sight of the kidnapper. I can see the dark hood on the man receding into the distance, amid wandering shoppers and pedestrians in the food row.

And then I look at the street below. It's a long ways down, but I don't have much time. The young bell-vine doesn't cover the exterior of the wall yet. So I grab the nearest tendril, hoping it's strong enough to bear my weight so I can jump to the ground outside. It's a tough plant, but I've never tried to swing on one before.

I turn my back to the street, blow three short breaths, and begin the descent. Halfway down the wall, I run out of length. Now I have no choice but to drop.

I open my hands, becoming weightless, falling through the air, giddy with a thrill I haven't felt since the blight burned away my wings.

And then I land in a puddle of reality as my ankles roll and the balls of my feet meet the street. Pain shoots up my legs, reminding me I'm not who I once was. Thank goodness. I gasp as I pitch forward, flailing, and a nearby woman rushes to assist, dark hair loose and flowing. She catches me before I fall forward to the pavement.

"Are you all right, Miss?" she says.

I tuck my hair behind my ear, and it is her turn to gasp. She nearly drops me when she curtsies. "Princess," she whispers, studying my face.

Yeasty, spicy smells waft out of the bakery on the corner, and her emerald-eyed scrutiny makes me uncomfortable while I regain my balance. "What?" I bark at her, gathering my star-field skirts and prepare to run.

She startles. "Oh, nothing. I just thought you were scarred." She lifts a hand to my jaw as if to smooth her hand along it. I scowl at her, processing her words, but say nothing. "You're lovely. You shouldn't hide," she breathes, and then her eyes widen when she realizes what she's said. She drops her hand and curtsies again before she trots away.

Without time to correct or ponder, I bolt after the criminal, praying I haven't lost him.

He leads me through the market and beyond, ducking between stalls and vendors. The streets empty of people and the buildings grow shorter as we go. This far from the orb, the shadows are larger, seeping out of the corners and alleys until I have to weave between them. While I know they can't hurt me, I avoid them. The blight caught me in the shade.

I shiver, wrapping my arms around my middle. Crime doesn't happen here, but I study the windows for angry faces and sneaky eyes.

The roads feel smaller, a too-tight coat, but I've seen the Architect's plans. All thoroughfares in the city are the same, running in straight lines, organized and logical. This is an optical illusion, an emotional mirage.

The kidnapper slips into a doorway, and I sag against the stoop of a blackstone house. A door squeaks behind me, the wood grinding against the floor as the door is pulled open. I leap forward, but spin quickly, hand held up.

"Who's there?" an elderly voice groans. I can't see the face, but no more movement is made. This Fae means me no harm.

"Oh, I beg your pardon," I say, and then I slip three stoops down.

I press my ear to the roughhewn door he entered. The stranger hasn't come out, so that means I go in. Seesha's life may depend upon it, and I cannot bear the thought of losing her. Arún would save her.

"Everyone should try heroics at least once in their life," he'd say, and shove me forward.

Today will be my once.

With my toes on the threshold, I summon magic, holding it in my hands, rocking back and forth. I have a grafting spell at the ready. I'll use it to … tie something together. Or graft an apple tree to a peach. Maybe I can horticulture the kidnapper into submission.

I grimace and swallow. This isn't the best hex for actively going into battle, but I can't think. I'm not skilled at this, but I'm the only chance Seesha has.

I kick the door, but the opening isn't dramatic and my bare feet aren't protected. The door swings open slowly, and pain explodes in my toes, radiating up my calf. I whimper and stumble in, sputtering threats, trying to see through the rush of tears.

Blinking rapidly, I lean on the square table in the middle of the room and something crinkles under my hand. As my eyes clear, I realize that I'm leaning on a workbench and it's covered in scraps of parchment. Under my fingers, I see a hasty scrawl that reads, "Hello, Princess. Thank you for coming." Seesha's prison rests at the corner, the top thrown open.

I scowl at the note. There's something strange about that note, as though the writer knew I would be here. Then that means….

He knew I was following him the whole time.

Holding still, I glance around the room from beneath my lashes. A blaze burns in the fireplace. Lightstay lamps illuminate the room. Though the spells aren't strong, the light is still there. I wish it was brighter.

They all brighten. Someone is reading my mind without permission.

But, rather than creating a mental block, I continue the study of my surroundings, allowing the probing. I don't want to scare them away or inspire an attack. I have nothing to hide.

There's a noise across the room, and my eyes are drawn to a low bed along one wall. A small someone is tucked beneath a tattered cover, and I'm drawn to the bedside. In a trance, I walk slowly toward the bed until I can study the figure tucked beneath the sheets and cover. My mouth falls open and my jaw slacks.

An ashen-skinned little girl rests in the bed. Dark veins in her cheeks mar her features like black webs. Her ear tips quiver with each breath she drags in. She has the blight.

There's a squeak behind me and a tinkling close to my ear. In a burst of neon, Seesha dives over my shoulder to the child on the bed, hovering over her face.

"Seesha," I gasp, waving to her, gesturing for her to follow me. "You're free."

"Ishka," she says, but doesn't act surprised or turn toward me.

I frown at her dismissal. She had been kidnapped, and I am here to save her.

"Should we go?" I ask, pointing toward the door.

"Later," she says. "Be still."

Her command catches me off-guard. I'm not used to being bossed around by anyone, much less one so slight. She should be terrified of being trapped again.

"First, I want to…." Her words trail away.

And then I see a shadow out of the corner of my eye. The now-unmasked kidnapper is upon us, standing nearby. He doesn't advance. Now is our chance.

"He's here, Seesha. Let's go." I turn toward the door, leaping forward as though I'm being chased. Her response stops me short.

"No," she says, settling on the chest of the frail Fae, smoothing her hands over the cheeks. "Merrick, meet Ishka," she says and the man bows to me. "Your healers can heal this," she says.

"Merrick?" I hiss.

"Yes, he's a nice fellow. Your healers can heal this," she repeats.

I throw up my hands. I've come to save the Hum-Fairy who's busy worrying after her captors. "Maybe," I growl, begrudging the admission.

"No, they can," she says. "We will do this." And she shakes all over, filling the air with bell sounds.

The child's eyelids flutter, rasping only one word. "Merrick?"

The kidnapper rushes forward, but stops when he bumps into me. He presses a scrap of paper into my palm before he kneels at the bedside.

"You brought her?" The little girl breathes the words like a prayer and joy radiates off her.

His face splits in a smile that rivals the sphere, and again my jaw slackens. His teeth, his eyes, he sparkles with mirth. I'm struck by the kindness in his face. He's said nothing, only beamed at all of us.

Something crinkles in my hand, and I glance down at the paper. In a harsh scrawl, I read, "I cannot speak; I was born without a tongue. Forgive my impertinence. My sister, Mol, has always wanted to see a Hum-Fairy. I was worried the blight would take her before she could. I am not practiced at communicating with Hum-Fairies. I will accept my punishment." A rush of tears floods my eyes. Merrick was his sister's hero, too, and I see Arún sitting at my bedside while the blight burned through my insides.

I turn to my friend as she does loops in the air, to the delight of the child. "Seesha?"

My friend stops her acrobatics long enough to telepath. "He explained it to me as we ran. I tried to relay the message, but I couldn't reach you, you were too far behind. I am here of my own free will." Seesha sprinkles starflakes over Mol, and tiny fingers reach for the falling light. "Now Merrick cannot be justly exiled," she says with a nod. And then she beams at us both. I hear the next words as a whisper in my mind. "Night to your moon."

I plop into the lone chair at the roughhewn table, watching the three play, as ideas takes hold. Today might still be a day for saving.

I smile at the politician as he travels through the Great Hall. His eyes widen at the sight of me. I'm not so dead as they all think. I glance sideways at Merrick and the little one beyond.

Mol is dancing between the mid-day musicians. Her face shows almost no trace of the blight. Her insides are like mine now, but today she plays, chasing after Seesha and Fesh. She begged the seamstresses for a dress like mine. My mother obliged. Merrick stayed by her bedside as the healers fought back death, conversing all the while with me on paper.

Tonight, I didn't pull away when he reached for my hand. I squeezed his fingers when hope tiptoed through my heart. Merrick is so different than Arún, but they're both heroes through-and-through. And maybe they're rubbing off on me.

Bokerah Brumley is a speculative fiction writer making stuff up on a trampoline in West Texas. When she's not playing with the quirky characters in her head, she's addicted to Twitter pitch events, writing contests, and social media, in general. With two urban fantasy novella releases scheduled for 2016, Bokerah has too much planned for this year, but is happily doing it anyway. She lives on ten permaculture acres with five home-educated children and one husband. In her imaginary spare time, she also serves as the blue-haired President of the Cisco Writers Club.

Her work can be found in *Havok Magazine* (July issue), *Southern Writers Magazine* (Summer 2016 issue), *The Clarion Call, VOL. 2: Echoes of Liberty, The Stars at My Door* (April Moon Books), and several more upcoming anthologies.

She was awarded First Place in the FenCon Short Story Contest, Third Place in the *Southern Writers Magazine* Short Story Contest, and Fifth Place in the Children's/Young Adult category for the 85th Annual Writer's Digest Writing Competition. More recently, she was selected as a 2016 Pitch Slam! finalist and a Fic Fest 2017 Middle Grade Mentor.

http://www.bokerah.com/

Absolutely True Facts about the Pacific Tree Octopus

"This is going to be the worst weekend ever," Liesel's big brother Henry moaned, banging his head against the car window.

Liesel looked up from her notepad and blinked at him. "The worst? Why?"

The trees rushed past them, tall and green, a constant wall of woodsiness. It looked like the pictures in a fairy tale book, and Liesel fully expected to pass the Big Bad Wolf or the Three Bears' cottage at any moment.

"First things first, Mom took away all my electronics. She said her cellphone may not even work out here." Henry rolled his eyes. He was twelve, four years older than Liesel, and Mom said "so plugged in it's a wonder his fingers don't spark."

Liesel shrugged at this. She didn't even own a tablet or a phone yet, though she did sometimes like to watch animal videos and fun facts on YouTube and Nat Geo.

"Secondly, it rains like two hundred inches a year in the Olympic Peninsula. By the time we get home, we'll probably have webbed feet."

Liesel gaped. Two hundred inches? She didn't even think she was that tall ... though that was hard math ... *twelve goes into two hundred* ... yeah, she was definitely not that tall. "All at once?" she whispered.

Henry snorted. "Yeah, sure, all at once. We'll wake up one morning, and we'll be under sixteen feet of water."

Liesel turned red. "Well, it *could* happen." She leaned back to catch sight of the blue sky winking through the treetops. "It's sunny now."

"*Now.*"

"The forecast calls for fair weather," Mom said from the front seat.

"Give it a chance, Hen."

"Thirdly," Henry dropped his voice low, eyeing the back of Mom's head. "There's absolutely nothing to do here. No rides. No pool. Just trees, trees, trees."

Liesel held up her notepad. "I think it'll be fun. I made a list of all the animals I want to see. I went online and found out what kinds live here and how common they are. I want to see an American black bear and a bobcat and maybe a cougar, though those can be dangerous … but if not a cougar then maybe a Pacific tree octopus…."

"A Pacific tree what?" Henry looked at her if she had sprouted those webbed feet right in front of him.

"The Pacific tree octopus." Liesel turned a page in her animal notebook and held out the picture she'd printed off the internet. "They're awesome. I read all about them on this website. They're possibly the smartest animal in this area. They can swing from tree to tree with their eight legs and grow up to six feet in diameter. Their tentacles allow for extreme man-u-al dex-ter-i-ty." She sounded out the big words. "Their only known predators are bald eagles, ravens, and Sasquatch."

Henry doubled over laughing.

"Stop it." She scowled at him. "What's so funny?"

"You … you … you are!" His face pinched up like a prune and his whole body shook. "Tree octopus? Even for a little kid, you're so gullible."

"What's gullible?" Liesel whispered. She was beginning to get the feeling that she'd said or done something horribly stupid, and that was not a feeling she liked in the slightest.

"You'll never know. It's not in the dictionary."

Liesel crossed her arms. "Well, if it isn't in the dictionary, it isn't a real word."

In spite of the strength of this argument, Henry laughed harder.

"Stop it!" she shouted.

"Kids, quiet!" Dad said. "Gullible is in the dictionary, Liesel. Henry's being facetious."

Great, another big word.

"Facetious means 'saying something that isn't true to be funny,'" Mom explained.

"So lying," Liesel mumbled. She stuck her tongue out at Henry.

"Your sister isn't gullible," Mom continued. "She's just young. Liesel, gullible means easily tricked or lied to. What Henry should have said is that website was a hoax. There's no such thing as a tree dwelling octopus."

Liesel hung her head. "Being gullible wouldn't be such a big deal if people didn't lie so much."

Especially big brothers.

Liesel stuffed her notepad into her backpack and pulled out her Rubik's

Cube. It had been a stocking stuffer that Christmas, and six months later, she was no closer to solving it. Still, she liked turning it and watching the little colored squares click around.

"You're never gonna solve that thing," Henry said.

"Let's be quiet and listen to some music," Dad said. "We're almost to the cabin."

A few minutes later the gentle, steady swish of the tires over the pavement turned into the crinkly crunch of driving over gravel. The feathery branches of the conifer trees swiped at the car like reaching hands. Liesel put down her cube and squinted into the greenery. Was that a bear? Nope, a stump. What about ... no ... another stump.

They pulled up in front of a tiny cabin with a green tin roof. Dad and Mom began to pull sleeping bags and coolers out of the back.

"No internet, no electricity, no indoor plumbing." Dad snickered. "You kids are in for a rude awakening."

Liesel wandered towards the edge of the parking area. The gravel had a slick, black sheen, and the whole world smelt fresh and damp. Moss dripped from tumbled down trees. Birds sang a consistent piping noise. A muddy path curved into the foliage before disappearing in a particularly thick grouping of pines. It was perfect. Even if there weren't tree octopuses, there were bound to be bears or foxes or squirrels....

Something shook the branches of a nearby tree. Liesel grinned and stood on her tiptoes for a better look.

Her first wild animal. Probably just a bird or a squirrel, but still, a real live animal. Some fir needles shifted, and something slick and shiny peeked through. Black eyes glinted. Liesel's breath left her. She opened and shut her mouth, wanting to shout for Mom and Dad, but nothing came out. The creature extended a long tentacle.

"Mom! Dad! Look!" Liesel's voice escaped, much shriekier than she had intended.

The limbs of the tree shook and the fir needles closed around the creature. Then the tree behind it shook, then the next, all in a row, too fast to quite follow ... and it was gone.

Mom came running and grabbed her about the shoulders, Dad and Henry right behind.

"Liesel, baby, are you all right?" Mom's face had that "mom" look that usually foretold a trip to the emergency room or a long, probing "talk."

"I saw ... I saw...." Liesel's mouth clamped shut when Henry raised a mocking eyebrow. They wouldn't believe her. She was gullible, and tree octopuses didn't exist.... Still, that thing had looked an awful lot like a tree octopus.

"What did you see? A Sasquatch?" Henry smirked at her.

Liesel's chest tightened.

"Henry, stop teasing her," Dad ordered, but he had a smile at his face. He thought it was pretty funny too, Liesel could tell. She was a silly little girl who had believed in tree octopuses.

But tree octopuses were real. They were, and she was going to prove it.

That night Liesel couldn't sleep. She lay in bed, staring out the window at the clouds drifting across the face of the moon and imagining they were the reaching arms of an octopus. When Dad's snores and Mom's whispered breathing rang out from across the cabin, she wriggled out of her sleeping bag and fished a flashlight and her notepad from her backpack.

She turned to the page of notes she'd made on tree octopuses. Each animal got a page, with a printed out picture, and a list of facts that might help her spot them, like whether they were diurnal or nocturnal, where they lived, what they ate. She'd almost torn out the page on the tree octopuses when Henry had laughed at her. Now she was so glad she hadn't. A smile crept across her face at the thought of those reaching arms and shining black eyes. Henry would sure feel stupid when she caught one.

An octopus is extremely flexible. The only hard part of their body is their bony beak. Because of this, they can slip through any opening that their beak can fit through.

They hatch in water but soon climb onto land. They return to the water only to mate.

They eat small birds, insects, and sometimes rob nests for eggs.

Liesel tapped the end of the flashlight against her teeth. They had eggs in the cooler. They were for breakfast tomorrow, but Mom wouldn't miss one or two. Liesel could set a trap. She went over and opened the first cooler. The carton of eggs lay on top. Glancing around to make sure her family was still sleeping, she slipped out a pale white egg.

Now what?

She couldn't go poking around the forest at night, could she? It was cold … and dark … and there might be bears. Did bears like eggs too? Liesel shuddered. She'd wanted to see a bear, but not all by herself in the middle of the pitch black woods. Still, how to get the egg to the octopus?

A scraping noise made her jump. She whirled about and shone her flashlight at the nearest window. Tree branches moved against the glass. An idea tickled her mind, and she smiled.

She pulled her sleeping bag over so she could rest her back against the table facing the window. Then she opened the window ever so slightly—if an octopus could fit through small spaces, a crack would be enough—and set the egg on the sill. With that accomplished, she flipped off the flashlight so the octopus wouldn't see her.

Cold air trickled into the cabin. She pulled the sleeping bag closer around her neck. Her eyes felt heavy. No worries. The octopus would show any moment. It'd see the egg shimmering in the moonbeams and come for it. Then she'd see it. She'd see it, jump up, and slam the window shut, and it would be hers ... any moment now. Any ... moment....

"Wake up, sleepy head. What are you doing over here?"

Liesel jolted awake at Mom's voice. She struggled out of the sleeping bag and rushed to the window. It was shut, but white flecks were sprinkled over the sill like confetti.

"Darn it."

It had come. It had come, and she'd missed it.

"Huh," Dad said from over the camp stove. "I thought this was a fresh pack of eggs. We're one short."

"That's odd," Mom said.

Liesel gulped down her breakfast.

"What's your hurry?" Henry asked, looking up from his half-finished eggs and toast.

She shrugged. "I want to spot some animals today."

He smirked at her. "What animals are you looking for? Bigfoot? The Loch Ness Monster? Oh, I know! Santa Claus."

"Santa isn't an animal." She scowled at him.

"Ha! Liesel still believes in Santa."

"I do not." Liesel kicked him under the table. No, Liesel believed in tree octopuses and today she was going to prove she was right.

"Well, Mom and I need to set up the fire pit and gather some kindling if we're going to have a bonfire tonight," Dad said. "I'm looking forward to s'mores."

"Yum, s'mores." Mom smiled. "You guys want to help?"

"I think I'd rather stay in the cabin and read," Henry said.

"Oh dang, we're out of jam." Dad scraped the last bit onto his toast.

"Can I have the jar?" Liesel asked. It might come in useful for her traps.

"Sure, if you want it."

"What about you, Liesel?" Mom asked. "You coming with us?"

Liesel bit her bottom lip. Too many people might scare off the octopus. "Can I go for a walk on my own? I want to go someplace quiet to draw and wait for animals."

Mom and Dad exchanged a look. Dad shrugged.

"Well," Mom said. "There is a nature path that loops around the cabin. It's only about a quarter mile, but if you stay on the path, it's perfectly safe. Why don't you go with her, Henry? You can read while she watches birds."

Liesel's nose wrinkled. She didn't want Henry anywhere near her octopus, not until she caught it at least.

"Do I have to?" Henry moaned.

Mom gave him "the look."

Henry groaned and slammed down his fork.

Fifteen minutes later, Liesel followed her brother as he stomped down the path into the woods. With all the noise he was making he'd scare off every tree octopus in the forest. Thankfully, only a few minutes into their walk, there was a bridge over a small creek with a wooden bench in the middle. Henry plopped down on this and pulled a comic book out of his backpack.

"Look, go chase your birds. Just ... you know ... stay on the path or whatever." With that he stuck his nose in the pages of *Super Dude Squad*.

Liesel grinned. She wouldn't go too far from the path. Just a little bit.

She crossed the bridge and pushed through the fir trees until she found a clearing. Taking the jar from her backpack, she paused. What would she use for bait? Mom had used up all the eggs that morning. The octopuses also ate birds and bugs, however. Maybe she could catch some of those and put them in the jar.

Poking around under rotting logs produced a few nasty looking beetles. She caught one by the thorax and dropped it, squirming, into the jar. She'd rinsed most of the jelly off after breakfast. The beetle tried to climb up the slick sides only to slip back down. It landed helplessly on its back, rocking back and forth and twitching its legs. She placed the jar on the other side of the clearing in the shade of a stooping fir tree.

Now to wait.

Liesel sat with her back against a broad tree. The bark poked into her back at first, but she shifted until her fleece jacket cushioned her shoulder blades. The woods smelled like a mix between moist earth and Christmas trees. In the distance, the creek burbled, and every so often a bird called out.

She scanned the trees, looking for some sign of movement. Occasionally a branch would shake, but a moment later a bird would launch into the air, rather than an octopus swinging among the boughs.

How long until Mom and Dad or Henry came looking for her? She wished she had a watch or a phone ... something to tell time. Were tree octopuses even diurnal? She couldn't remember if she'd written that down. Her notepad was safely in her backpack, along with some granola bars and her Rubik's Cube.

Liesel took the notepad out and turned to the correct page. Nothing about diurnal vs nocturnal, though she had written down their scientific name of *Octopus Paxarbolis*. Like she'd ever need to know that.

They're extremely intelligent and curious.

Clever enough to steal the egg and shut the window behind them. Sneaky octopuses.

She took out the Rubik's Cube and started to mess with it, first turning it one way, then the other. Every twist made it worse, though. Maybe Henry was right. Maybe she'd never solve this thing.

Twist, turn, look up to check on the jar, twist turn again. Soon she had all but two of the squares on one side yellow. Her heart thumped. Could she get it this time? Where were those last two yellow squares? Ah, there was one! She turned the cube to get that new yellow square into place, and knocked two other yellow squares onto the blue side.

"Ugh!" She quickly tried to undo the damage, but somehow ended up with a green square smack in the middle of the yellow ones. How had that happened? "Stupid puzzle!" She tossed it across the clearing. It clanked against the jar before landing softly in the moss.

Liesel drew a deep breath in through her nose and counted to ten like her mom had taught her. Silly thing to get frustrated at. It wasn't like Henry was here, making fun of her ... but he would've made fun of her if he had been there, and that on its own was a frustrating thought.

Why couldn't, just once, she know something Henry didn't? Why did he always have to be right? Well, he wasn't right about the stupid octopus. She just couldn't prove it.

Liesel crossed the clearing and reclaimed the Rubik's Cube. She'd put it away for later. After all, if she solved it, it would be over, and it might be a while until the octopus showed up.

She turned and froze. There, sliding its tentacles into her backpack, was a small, brown tentacled beast, with shiny skin and black, glinting eyes.

"Octopus!" she gasped.

The creature pulled Liesel's granola bar out of the backpack. The foil wrapper crinkled as its agile tentacles tugged at it. With a rip, the wrapper revealed its golden contents. The octopus broke off a square and pulled it in towards its chomping beak.

It was smaller than she'd expected, perhaps the size of a dinner plate, though the arms going this way and that made it hard to judge.

The octopus munched quietly, its dark eyes never leaving Liesel.

How was she going to get that thing in a jam jar? Even if octopuses could squeeze into tight spaces, those arms seemed to be everywhere at once. There was no way she could just stuff it in the jar.

Still grasping half a granola bar, the octopus extended a tentacle. It waved the bar at her. Liesel blinked. Was it trying to share?

After a moment's hesitation, she reached for the granola bar. The octopus released it into her hand. A trace of slime clung to the wrapper, but Liesel forced herself to take a bite anyway. It didn't seem polite to refuse. Her teeth crunched into the sweet and salty mix of nuts and oats. She couldn't taste any octopus.

"Thanks," she said.

The octopus didn't give her much to go on. It didn't have a visible mouth. No smiles or frowns. Just two soulful eyes and a mess of wriggling arms. Still, something deep inside her told her it was *friendly*.

She sat cross-legged and held out her hand. The octopus grasped the ground with its tentacles then drew itself forward. Soon its thin arms brushed against Liesel's knee.

"Did you want more?" she asked.

The octopus's suckers gripped her wrist. It pried at her fingers which still held the Rubik's Cube.

"This?" She raised her eyebrows. "You like *this*?"

She loosened her grasp, and the octopus took the cube from her. It manipulated it between two tentacles.

"You can't eat it. It'll make you sick." Liesel tried to take it back, but the octopus pulled it away.

The octopus twisted the squares of the Rubik's Cube this way and that. Liesel stared, fascinated by the creature's apparent fascination.

"When they said 'manual dexterity' they weren't kidding."

She wished she had a camera. If she shouted, would Henry come? Or would it spook the octopus? She kind of wanted her parents to see it too … and other people. People everywhere. Could finding a tree octopus make her famous? Would she get to be on TV?

Fishing all the way to the bottom of her backpack, she found another granola bar. At the crinkle of the wrapper, the octopus put down the Rubik's Cube.

"You want this?" Liesel smiled. She broke the bar into three pieces and ate one. The second she held out to her eight-legged visitor. The octopus snatched it. Liesel plunked the third piece into the jar.

The octopus's beak clicked as it devoured the snack. Its tentacles tapped at the jar.

Please go in, octopus. Please go in.

The octopus stuck the tips of two tentacles into the jar and felt around the bottom for the granola bar. It couldn't quite reach.

Liesel held her breath, conscious of the jar's lid in her pocket. She slipped her hand over the lid.

The octopus tilted forward, up over the lip of the jar, then pooled at the bottom like a liquid. A couple of arms overlapped the edge of the container like fronds of a hanging house plant. Liesel swept in, pushed all the legs into the jar, and clamped the lid on.

She picked up the jar, her chest heaving. The octopus took up most of the space. It turned this way and that. Liesel was glad she'd already put air holes in the lid. If she took the lid off, the octopus would certainly wriggle out and run for the trees.

"I've got to show Henry!"

She started through the underbrush, back towards the path.

Click, click, click.

She glanced down. The octopus tapped against the glass.

"Don't worry. It won't be long. I just need to show you to my family … and take some pictures … and maybe call the TV people … but after that you can go home. I promise." She pushed through the trees onto the path.

Click, click, click.

"Just be patient."

Metal rasped against glass, and the jar lid moved beneath her hand. She quickly tightened it back in place. It rotated again, the octopus wedging its body against the inside of the lid.

"Stop it! I told you. It'll be quick … no more than a day or two."

Click, click, click.

The stupid thing wouldn't stop. Screwing the lid on good and tight, she stuck the jar into her backpack and zipped it shut.

There. Now she could have some peace.

When she came to the bench, it was empty. She huffed in annoyance. So much for Henry looking out for her. She sped up, determined to get to the camp and show her brother and parents her triumphant discovery.

Raised voices echoed through the bracken.

"I can't believe you left her alone. She's only eight!" Mom said.

"I didn't think she'd be stupid enough to leave the path," Henry whined.

"You shouldn't have left her."

Liesel snickered. Henry deserved a good talking to. Maybe Mom would take away his stupid comic books. But wait … she had left the path when she wasn't supposed to. What if she was the one in trouble? Better lie low and see what the mood was.

Diving off the path, Liesel listened. Mom, Dad, and Henry tramped by, feet from her but unable to see her through the dense underbrush.

"Liesel, baby, can you hear me?" Mom called. She sounded worried. Feeling guilty, Liesel considered standing up and showing herself.

"Beth, she's been gone less than twenty minutes, and you know how she is. She probably just sat down somewhere to draw pictures in her little notebook." Dad laughed. "Who knows? Maybe she ran into a tree octopus."

"Yeah, a tree octopus," Henry snickered.

Liesel scowled, suddenly not feeling guilty at all. They were still making fun of her. Well, she'd show them. She had the proof.

"Imagine if she *did* find one, though. Do you know how crazy scientists would go over something like that? Not just a new species, but a tree octopus?" Dad said. "They'd be crawling all over these woods looking for more. People would line up for days to see them in aquariums and zoos. The amazing arboreal cephalopod." He laughed again.

Liesel hesitated. Would they really put her octopus in an aquarium? In a small glass tank? A tank … like a jar. The octopus didn't seem very happy in a jar. It probably wouldn't like an aquarium tank either.

Her family's footsteps faded down the path. She needed the octopus. If she let it go, no one would ever know she was right. Maybe she could show her parents and they'd let it go free afterwards? But would they really? Her parents loved her, but she was only eight. They were always doing things "for her own good." What if they decided the aquarium was for the octopus's own good?

Her backpack shook slightly. She slipped it from her shoulders and unzipped the top. The octopus sat on top of the now open jar. It waved at her, holding her Rubik's Cube tightly in its tentacles.

She let out a hot breath. "Look, you have to understand. If I don't show them, they'll never believe me. It's awful not to be believed, to be wrong all the time. Well, this time I'm not wrong, and I need someone to know about it!"

The octopus's suckers tightened around her fingers, leaving little red circles in her skin. A bird cried out.

"Oh, darn it." Liesel picked up the octopus. It felt slimy but surprisingly light. She held it up to the nearest tree. "Okay, you can go, but ... oh darn it. Just go before I change my mind."

The octopus grasped a branch and swung up into the boughs.

"Hey, Liesel!" Twigs snapped, and Henry emerged from the trees. "I thought I heard you. Didn't you hear Mom shouting?"

She shrugged.

"What are you doing out here anyway?" He squinted at her. "Who were you talking too?"

"Nobody. Mom's not too worried, is she?"

"A little bit. You know moms. I knew you were probably okay. You aren't dumb enough to get lost out here."

Liesel's mouth dropped open. From Henry that was high praise.

"Come on. Let's go find them before Mom starts tearing up trees." As he turned back to the path, something hit the ground behind them with a clunk. "What was that?"

They both looked. There, beneath the tree, lay Liesel's Rubik's Cube, completely solved.

"Did you ...? How did you ...?" Henry stooped down and picked it up. He glanced from it to her then back again. "You really did it?"

Liesel hesitated. She glanced up at the tree. A tentacle emerged from the fir needles and waved at her.

She grinned. "Oh, Henry," she said, snatching the cube from his hands. "Don't be so gullible."

An author of eclectic fantasy work ranging from Young Adult Steampunk to Dragon themed Fantasy Romance, H. L. Burke roams the world looking for adventure. Her location changes often, but home always consists of her US Marine husband, two Super-Hero-Princess daughters, a sneaky German Shepherd, and her cat, Bruce Wayne. Oh, and a pet dragon or two.

website: www.hlburkeauthor.com

Find more stories from these authors and others at
www.fellowshipoffantasy.com.

Made in the USA
Lexington, KY
30 December 2017